ABOUT THE AUTHOR

MIRA JACOB is the founder of Pete's Reading
Series in Brooklyn and has a MFA from the New
School for Social Research. She lives in Brooklyn
with her husband, film-maker Jed Rothstein, and
their son. This is her first novel.

www.mirajacob.com

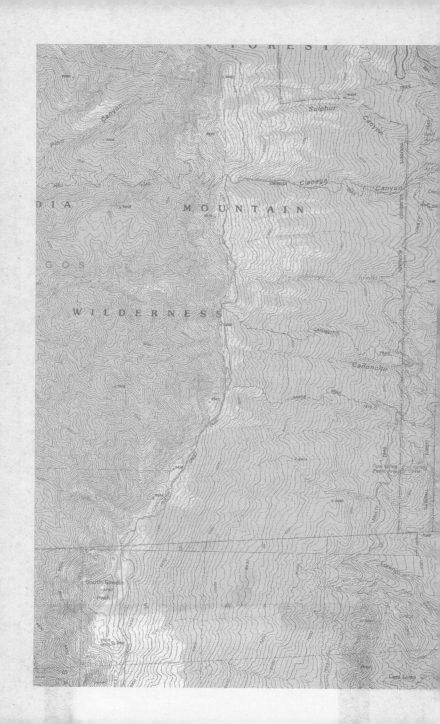

THE
SLEEPWALKER'S
GUIDE TO
DANCING

MIRA JACOB

B L O O M S B U R Y
LONDON · NEW DELHI · NEW YORK · SYDNEY

Bloomsbury Paperbacks
An imprint of Bloomsbury Publishing Plc

50 Bedford Square
London
WC1B 3DP
UK

1385 Broadway
New York
NY 10018
USA

www.bloomsbury.com

BLOOMSBURY and the Diana logo are trademarks of Bloomsbury Publishing Plc

First published in Great Britain 2014
This paperback edition first published in 2015

British Library Cataloguing-in-Publication Data
A catalogue record for this book is available from the British Library.

ISBN: HB: 978-1-4088-4114-3
TPB: 978-1-4088-4115-0
PB: 978-1-4088-4117-4
ePub: 978-1-4088-4116-7

2 4 6 8 10 9 7 5 3 1

Typeset by Hewer Text UK Ltd, Edinburgh
Printed and bound in Great Britain by CPI Group (UK) Ltd, Croydon CR0 4YY

To find out more about our authors and books visit www.bloomsbury.com.
Here you will find extracts, author interviews, details of forthcoming events
and the option to sign up for our newsletters.

For my father, Philip Jacob (1939–2006)

THE SLEEPWALKER'S GUIDE TO DANCING

PROLOGUE: A CHOSEN MADNESS

SEATTLE, JUNE 1998

It was a fever, a hot rage of words. For three nights in a row Thomas Eapen sat on the porch, one side of a furious conversation rolling over his tongue to spill out the window screen. The neighbors heard him; his wife, Kamala, could not sleep. Prince Philip, their aging and arthritic Labrador, had taken to pacing the hallway and whining. Kamala told her daughter all of this over the phone one early June evening, her voice as smooth as a newscaster's.

"I am thinking he's on his way out," Kamala concluded, and Amina pictured her father at the edge of the desert, waiting for a bus.

"Really?"

"Who knows. My judgment is impairing. I haven't slept since Saturday."

"You're kidding."

"Not kidding," sniffed Kamala, whose ability to sleep through anything that her insomniac husband could cook up (raccoon hunts, ditch fires, tractor mishaps) had long been a point of pride. Amina dropped her keys onto the kitchen counter.

"You are just now home from work?" Kamala asked.

"Yes." Amina placed her mail and camera next to the keys. The answering machine blinked anxiously at her. She turned her back to it. "Three nights? Seriously?"

"How's work?"

"Busy. Everyone in Seattle is getting married in the next month."

"You're not."

Amina ignored her. "What do you mean talking? Talking about what?"

"Telling stories."

"What kind of stories?"

"What kind of anything? Fits and nuts and now this man with his idiot yak-yak all the time!" Kamala said. "I told him his tongue would fall out and rot like a vegetable, and still he wouldn't shut up."

"You always say that."

"No I don't."

"Ma."

"But this is different, *koche*," Kamala sighed. Night noises snaked through the phone line, pressing New Mexico right up to Amina's ear—the hushed applause of the wind rolling through the cotton-woods, the hollow scritch of crickets echoing against the mesas, the click of the gate latch in the garden. Amina shut her eyes and felt herself in the darkening yard with the tickle of the wild grass at the back of her knees.

"You out in the garden?" she asked her mother.

"Mmm-hmm. You in the rain?"

"I'm in the kitchen." Amina checked the linoleum under her boots. Its yellow edges spoke of a former life, one in which the Crown Hill Apartments had been envisioned as good starters for middle-income families, replete with real marble fireplaces and sunny-day kitchen floors. Now they were a thin piss color, pocked with air bubbles that snapped when stepped on.

"How's the weather?" Kamala asked.

"It's raining a little."

"Nobody knows why you stay there."

"You get used to it."

"That's not a good reason to stay somewhere. No wonder that dirty man shot himself—all that time without sun and this devil woman tearing her pantyhoses."

"Kurt Cobain was a junkie, Ma."

"Because he needed more sun!"

Amina sighed. Had she known that leaving her copy of *Rolling Stone* in the bathroom on her last visit would make Kamala a self-proclaimed expert on all things Seattle ("The grunges! The Starbucks! The start-ups!"), she might have been more careful, but then, it served a good-enough purpose, this disdain her mother held for Amina's choice of residence. For one, it cut down on her visits. ("I never get warm here!" Kamala made a point of saying the few times she did come, rubbing her hands together and looking around suspiciously. Once, she told the very nice barista at Amina's local coffee shop that he smelled funny from "too much damp.")

"Did I tell you the mint is coming like one forest?" her mother asked now, her voice brightening. "Bigger than last year!"

"That's great." Amina opened her refrigerator. A collection of take-out boxes slumped together like old men in bad weather. She shut it.

"I made chutney and had the Ramakrishnas and the Kurians over last night, and they loved it! Bala wanted the recipe, of course."

"What did you leave out?"

"Nothing. Cayenne and cilantro."

Cooking was a talent of her mother's that Amina often thought of as evolutionary, a way for Kamala to survive herself with friendships intact. Like plumage that expanded to rainbow an otherwise unremarkable bird, Kamala's ability to transform raw ingredients into sumptuous meals brought her the kind of love her personality on its own might have repelled.

"So, what did they think about Dad?"

"What about Dad?"

"The talking or whatever."

"I didn't tell them! Don't be stupid!"

"It's a secret?" Amina marveled. "You're not telling the family?"

A secret between the Ramakrishnas, the Kurians, and the Eapens only happened once every five years or so, and usually came out within months anyway, the keepers assuring the kept-from that it was nothing personal, just family business, the kept-from uttering comforting words about being *family in this country anyway* even though no blood relation existed among them.

"No secret!" Kamala said a bit too emphatically. She tucked her voice a few notches lower. "No big deals. Let's not bother anyone about it, okay?"

"Well, did anyone else think he was acting funny?"

"He isn't acting funny."

"I thought you said—"

"No, not like that. He's going to work and all; he's fine with everyone else. All the nurses in the OR still follow him around like gaggling geese. It's just late at night."

It would have to be late. Thomas did his best to stay at the hospital until sundown, and his insomnia often kept him up between midnight and 6 A.M. Those were the hours he would sit on the porch and tinker some unfathomable object—a cricket gun, a pet petter—into life.

"He's probably just talking to the dog, Ma. He does that all the time."

"No he's not."

"How do you know?"

"I just told you! The dog is stuck inside whining! And besides, I heard him."

"And?"

"He was talking to Ammachy."

Amina stopped moving. Her grandmother had been dead for almost twenty years. "You mean praying to her?"

The sharp rip of weeds being yanked from the dirt came across the phone line with a small grunt. "No, I don't. I mean talking. Telling stories."

"Stories?"

Kamala huffed. *Rip, rip, grunt.*

"Ma!"

"Just stupid stories! How you won that photography award in the tenth grade! How I begged the man at the Hickory Farms to order some ginger pickle in 1982 and then that nuts goes and orders candied ginger!"

"Right in front of you? You were standing right there?"

"I listened from the laundry room."

To live in the Eapens' house was to acknowledge the sharpness of invisible borders, the separations that had divided it like two countries since 1983. It had been years since Amina had seen her mother wade into the yellow light of her father's porch, and as far as she knew, Thomas had never once crossed the gate into Kamala's garden.

"And you're sure it was Ammachy?"

Kamala hesitated for a moment. "He could see her."

Amina straightened. "What are you talking about?"

"He told her to go sit somewhere else."

"*What?*"

"Yes. And then I think he maybe saw . . ." Kamala's voice trailed off into silence, the world of grief that lived invisibly between all the Eapens revealing itself like a face waiting behind the curtains.

"Who?" Amina's voice pinched in her throat. "Who else did he see?"

"I don't know." Her mother sounded far away.

Silence.

"Mom," Amina said, worried now, "is he depressed?"

"Don't be dumb!" Kamala huffed. A flurry of activity released over the phone line in what sounded like something heavy being dragged. "No one is *depressed*. I'm just telling you is all, like that. I'm sure you're right, it's fine. It's nothing."

"But if he thinks he's seeing—"

"Okay! Talk to you later."

"No! Wait!"

"What?"

"Well, is Dad around? Can I talk to him?"

"He's at the hospital. Big case. Some young mother hit her head on the bottom of a pool two days ago and hasn't woken up." The Eapens had never spared their daughter the details of her father's work, so even at five years of age Amina heard things like *Her medulla has a ski pole lodged into it* or *His wife shot him in the face, but he should live.*

"Are you sure he should be working right now?" Amina had gone into surgery with her father once, in second grade. She remembered the sharp, bitter smell of the operating room, the glint of her father's eyes over his face mask, the way the floor rushed up to greet her when his scalpel ran a red seam down the back of his first patient's head. She had spent the rest of the day eating candy at the nurses' station.

"He's *fine*," Kamala said. "It's not like that. You're not listening."

"I am listening! You just told me he's delusional, and I'm asking—"

"I DID NOT SAY HE IS DELUSIONAL. I SAID HE WAS TALK-ING TO HIS MOTHER."

"Who is dead," Amina said gently.

"Obvious."

"And that's not delusional?"

"There are *choices,* Amina! Choices we make as human beings on this planet Earth. If someone decides to let the devil in, then of course they will see demons everywhere they look. This is not *delusional.* This is *weakness.*"

"You can't really think that." It was a wish more than a statement of fact, as Amina was well aware that Kamala, with her Jesus, religious radio shows, and ability to misquote the Bible at random, could and did believe anything she wanted to.

"I am just reporting the facts," her mother said.

"Right. Okay. Listen, I've got to get going."

"You just came home! Where are you going?"

"Out."

"Now? With who?"

"Dimple."

"*Dimple,*" her mother repeated, like a curse. According to Kamala, Dimple Kurian had been afflicted with low morality since the day her parents gave her *that ridiculous name for giggly Gujarati starlets.* According to Dimple, Kamala had *a Jesus complex where her heart should be.* "Is she still opening relationships?"

"Open relationships, they're called—never mind. Yes."

"So she can be with one boy then another, all in one week."

"Dating."

"*Chi!* Dirty thing. No wonder they had to send her to reform school! You run around with everyone and then cry 'Oh no, he thinks I'm a whore, he thinks I'm a whore,' when he thinks you're a whore."

"When have you seen Dimple cry about anything?"

"I've seen it in the movies. *Henry Meets Sally.*"

"*When Harry Met Sally* . . . ?"

"Yes! This stupid girl is with too many men and crying about 'Nobody loves me,' and then she goes with that poor boy and expects him to love her!"

"That's what you think *When Harry Met Sally* . . . is about?"

"And then what is he supposed to do? Commit with her?"

"He *does* commit to her, Ma. That's how the movie ends."

"Not afterward! Afterward, he leaves her." Her mother's conviction that movies continue in some private offscreen world had always been as baffling as it was irrefutable. Whole plots had found themselves victims to Kamala's reimagining, happy endings derailed, tragedies righted. "And anyway, *someone* should tell Dimple to call home. How can her parents know she is okay if she doesn't call?"

"Because I see her every day and I would tell them if she wasn't."

"Inconsiderate so-and-so. Bala gets so worried about her, you know."

"Tell Bala Auntie she's fine. And I'll call Dad tomorrow."

There was a round silence on the other end of the line. Had she hung up?

"Ma?"

"Don't call."

"What?"

"It's not something for on the phone."

Amina blinked at her cabinets in disbelief. "So, what, I've got to wait until I fly home to talk to him?"

"Oh," Kamala said, voice rich with feigned surprise. "Sure, if you think it's best."

"What?"

"When can you come?"

"You want . . . I should . . . wait, really?" Amina looked in a panic at the kitchen wall, where a bright list of to-dos for the Beale wedding hung like an accusation. "It's June."

"It's some big thing? So don't come."

"It's just a bad time. It's my busiest time."

"Yes, I understand. It's just your father."

"Oh, stop. I mean, if you really need me to come out, then of course I'll come, but . . ." Amina pressed her fingers to her eyelids. Leaving work in the high season? Insane.

Her mother took a deep breath. "Yes. That would very nice, if you could manage it."

Amina pulled the receiver away from her ear, staring at it. She had never heard a sentence sound less like it could have come from Kamala's mouth, but there it was, her mother's attempt at accommodation as discordant as the hidden message in a record played backward. *Something is wrong. Something is really wrong.*

"I'll get a ticket out next week," Amina found herself saying. She paused hopefully, waiting for a *Never mind,* a *Don't bother.* Instead she heard a long, strained grunt and the satisfying chorus of roots popping up from the ground. The muffled *thwack* of palms against pants beat through the phone line, and Amina saw her mother as she would be in that moment—standing in the garden, tiny puffs of cottonwood dander floating around her dark hair like dusk fairies.

"Okay, then," Kamala said. "Come home."

BOOK 1

WHAT HAPPENS IN INDIA
DOES NOT STAY IN INDIA

SALEM, INDIA, 1979

CHAPTER 1

"Traitors! Cowards! Good-for-nothings!" Ammachy had yelled in 1979, finishing the conversation that would finish her relationship with her son, as Thomas would only come back to India to bury her.

But what a calamity! An abomination! Divorced from the mother and the motherland in one fell swoop? Who could have seen such a thing coming? Certainly not Amina, who by age eleven was well versed enough in tragedy (she had seen *The Champ* and *Kramer vs. Kramer*) to understand that it came with tinkling music and bad weather.

And what was there to fear from the sunlight that dappled the Salem train station the morning of their arrival, making everything—the packed luggage and the red-shirted coolies and even the beggars—seem sweet and full of promise? Nothing, Amina thought, stepping down onto the platform and into the funk of other people's armpits. Plump arms sheathed in sari blouses brushed her cheeks, chai-wallahs shouted into car windows, and a coolie reached impatiently for bags she was not carrying. Somewhere above the din she heard someone calling her father's name.

"Over there, Dad," Akhil said, pointing at something Amina couldn't see, and Thomas gripped her by the shoulders and propelled her forward.

"Babu!" He clapped an old man on the back. "Good to see you!"

Wrapped in a bulky dhobi and skinny as ever, Babu smiled a toothless smile, his resemblance to a malnourished baby belying his ability to toss large objects onto his head and carry them through crowds, as he did with all four of the family suitcases. Outside the station, Preetham, the driver, loaded the freshly polished Ambassador, while beggars surrounded them, pointing to the children's sneakers and then to their own hungry mouths, as if their appetites could be satisfied by Nikes.

"Ami, come!" Kamala called, opening the car door, and once everyone else had taken their places (Preetham and Thomas in the front seat, Akhil, Kamala, and Amina in the back, Babu standing proudly on the back fender), they began the four-block ride home.

Unlike the rest of the family, Thomas's parents had long ago left Kerala for the drier plains of Tamil Nadu. Settling in a large house at the edge of town, Ammachy and Appachen had opened a combined clinic (she was an ophthalmologist; he was an ENT), and before his sudden death by heart attack at the age of forty-five, they saw 70 percent of the heads in Salem.

"A golden time," Ammachy would spit at anyone within distance, going on to list everything since that had disappointed her. Top of her list: her eldest son choosing to marry "the darkie" and move to America when she had arranged for him to marry Kamala's much lighter cousin and live in Madras; her youngest son becoming a dentist producing "the no-brains" instead of becoming a doctor and producing another doctor; the many movie theaters and hospitals that had since sprung up around the house, penetrating it with noise and smells.

"Bloody Christ," Thomas breathed as they turned onto Tamarind Road, and Amina followed his gaze. "You can't even see the house anymore!"

This was true. It was also true that what could be seen, or rather, what could not be ignored, was the Wall, Ammachy's solution to the changing world around her. Built of plaster and broken bottles, the Wall grew crooked and taller and more yellowed with every visit, until it resembled nothing as much as a set of monster's dentures fallen from some other world and forgotten on the dusty side of the thoroughfare.

"It's not so bad," Kamala said unconvincingly.

"It's creepy," Akhil said.

"New gate!" Preetham beeped the horn, and the family fell silent as the gate swung open from the inside, pulling the car and its contents down the driveway.

The house, for its part, had not changed at all, its two stories painted pink and yellow and slanting in the heat like a melting birthday cake. A small crowd had gathered in front of it, and Amina watched them through the window—Sunil Uncle, dark and paunchy; his wife, the wheatish and wimpy Divya Auntie; their son, Itty, head weaving from side to side like a skinny Stevie Wonder; Mary-the-Cook, the cook; and two new servant girls. Christmas lights and tinsel twinkled in the pomegranate trees.

"Mikhil! Mittack!" Itty gurgled as the car pulled in, arm hooking frantically into the air. He had grown as tall as Sunil since their last visit, and Amina waved back, full of dread. *Mittack* was her name, according to Itty, and *excitability* was the condition that made him bite her on occasion, according to the family. Amina fingered the faint half-moon on her forearm, sinking a little in her seat.

"Hullohullohullo!" Sunil shouted as the car parked. "Welcome, welcome!"

"Hey, Sunil." Thomas opened the door, taking long strides across the lawn to shake hands. "Good to see you."

This was a lie, of course, as neither of the brothers was ever particularly glad to see the other, but it was the only way to properly start a visit.

Sunil fixed a blazing smile on Kamala. "Lovely as a rose, my dear!" He bestowed cologney kisses on her cheek and then Amina's before turning and clutching his heart. "And who is this ruddy tiger? My God, Akhil? Is that you? Blossoming into a king of the jungle, are we?"

"I guess," Akhil sighed.

Suddenly, two hands wrapped around Amina's neck and squeezed hard, crushing her larynx. She pulled frantically at them, dimly aware of her mother patting Divya's arm in greeting, of the hot breath in her ear.

"Mittack!" Itty let go, patting her head.

"Jesus!" Amina gasped, tears in her eyes. "Mom!"

"Itty." Kamala smiled. She wrapped her arms around the boy, who grunted and buried his face in her neck.

"Hello." Divya stood in front of Amina, slight, pockmarked, and branded with the expression of someone expecting the worst. "How was the train?"

"It was nice." Amina loved the overnight train from Madras. She loved the call of the chai-wallahs at every stop, the smell of different dinners cooking in the towns they passed. "We got egg sandwiches."

Divya nodded. "You're feeling sick now?"

"No."

"Sick!" A voice snapped from behind Divya. "Already? Which one?"

Beneath the heat and the house and the blinking lights, Ammachy sat in her wicker chair on the verandah, sweating rings into a sea-foam-green sari blouse. The two years that had passed since their last visit had done nothing to soften her face. Long white whiskers grew out of her chin, and her spine, hunched by decades of complaint, left her head floating some inches above her lap.

"Hello, Amma." Thomas's fingers were firm on Amina and Akhil's necks as he marched them up the few stairs to where she sat. "Good to see you."

Ammachy pointed to the roll of flesh that pressed at the hem of Akhil's polo shirt. "*Thuddya.* What kind of girlish hips are you growing?"

"Hi, Ammachy." Akhil leaned in to kiss her cheek.

She turned to Amina with a wince. "Ach. I sent some Fair and Lovely, no? Didn't use it?"

"She's fine, Amma," Thomas said, but as Amina bent to kiss her, Ammachy snatched her face, pinning it between curled fingers.

"You will have to be very clever if you are never going to be pretty. Are you very clever?"

Amina stared at her grandmother, unsure of what to say. She had never thought of herself as particularly clever. She had never thought of herself as particularly bad-looking either, though it was obvious enough now from the faint repulsion that rippled through the hairs on Ammachy's lip.

"Amina won the all-city spelling bee," Kamala announced, pushing Amina's head forward so that her lips landed openly against Ammachy's cheek. She had just enough time to be surprised by the taste of menthol and roses, and then she was pulled into the too-dark house and down the hallway, past Sunil and Divya and Itty and Ammachy's rooms, to a dining room set with tea.

"So train was crowded? Nothing to eat? She's so happy to see you." Divya motioned for Kamala and the kids to sit and pushed a plate of orange sweets at them. "She's been talking of nothing else for a month."

"Itty," Sunil boomed, dragging a lumpy suitcase in behind him. "Your uncle is insisting we see what presents he has brought. Shall we take a look?"

"Hullo?" Itty nodded vigorously. "Look? Look?"

"It's nothing, really." Thomas took a seat next to Amina.

"Small-small things," Kamala added.

Ammachy limped in with a scowl. "What is all this nonsense?"

It was: two pairs of Levi's, one bottle of Johnnie Walker Red, three bags of nuts (almonds, cashews, pistachios), a pair of Reeboks with Velcro closures, a larger pair of hiking boots, two bottles of perfume (Anaïs Anaïs, Chloé), four cassette tapes (the Beatles, the Rolling Stones, Kenny Rogers, Exile), two jars of Avon scented skin lotion (in Topaze and Unspoken), several pairs of white tube socks, talcum powder, and a candy-cane-shaped tube filled with marshmallow, root beer float, and peppermint flavored lip balms.

"It's too much." Sunil tried to hand back the cassette tapes. "Really, we don't need."

"What need?" Thomas smiled, watching Divya sink her finger into the jar of Avon cream. "It's nice to have is all. What do you think, Itty? You like the Velcro?"

Crouched in a Spider-Man pose on the floor, Itty lunged slowly from side to side, mesmerized by the sight of his poufy white feet.

"You'll spoil him." Sunil reached for the scotch bottle, holding it up to the light and studying the label. "Shall we try a bit of this?"

"After dinner," Thomas said, and Sunil poured two fingers into his empty teacup, sniffing it.

"The Velcro is big thing in the States now," Kamala explained to everyone with a knowing look. "Easy peasy, instead of having to tie the shoes."

Ammachy snorted. "Who else besides this no-brains won't know to tie shoes?"

"Vel cow!" Itty shouted with unfortunate timing, fastening and unfastening his Reeboks until Ammachy smacked him with a powdered palm. She sniffed at all three flavors of lip balm and licked the tip of one before pushing them into Divya's pile.

"So, you people had a good trip in the airplane?" Ammachy asked.

Thomas nodded. "Good enough."

"How did you come?"

"San Francisco–Honolulu–Taiwan–Singapore."

Ammachy grunted. "Singapore Airlines?"

"Yes."

"Those girls are pretty, no?" She refilled Kamala's cup, saying, "Nice complexions."

"Try the hiking boots, Sunil." Thomas pointed to them with his chin. "The heel itself has shock absorbers!"

"Later. I have some work I should be attending to."

"Oh, yes, this one with his *people's practice*." Ammachy rolled her eyes. "You would think he was actually saving lives instead of teeth."

"Teeth are lives, Amma," Sunil said, glowering. "People need to eat to live."

"So, who all do you want to see?" she asked Thomas.

"I don't know. I haven't thought about it yet."

"Yes, well, your old classmate Yohan Varghese was asking about you the other day. I told you the wife died, no? Not that she was any real help, stupid thing, but two sons to raise on his own! Ach. And we should see Saramma Kochamma of course, just for one afternoon meal. And Dr. Abraham wants to talk to you. He's putting together that rehabilitative center, the one I told you about? Might be a nice thing to see." This last news was delivered with such practiced indifference that even Amina felt embarrassed.

Thomas reached for a jalebi. He offered the plate to Amina, who shook her head.

"Anyway, he needs someone in head injuries, so I told him you would ring." Ammachy poured milk into her own tea and stirred. "Maybe tomorrow?"

"It's not really my field." Thomas took a bite. "They would only ever need the occasional surgery."

"Well, no one asked you to become a brain surgeon," Ammachy snapped.

"No," Thomas said, chewing carefully, "they didn't."

Akhil reached for a jalebi, and Ammachy swatted his hand away.

"It's just an option." Ammachy scraped something from the oil-cloth. "But then I suppose Kamala likes it there? All of this women's-libbing and bra burning?"

"What?" Kamala sat up a little taller in her chair.

"I'm sure it's why she was so excited to go in the first place. Always wanting more and more of freedoms, is it?"

"Who burns the bras?" Kamala asked indignantly.

"How should I know?" Ammachy glared. "You're the one who chooses to live in there. Godforsaken place."

"*I'm* the one?"

"Who else? If you wanted to come home, Thomas would come. Men only go as far as the wife allows."

"Is that so?" Kamala leaned across the table. "Well, that's very interesting, isn't it, Thomas?"

"Amma, please. We've only just arrived."

"What's foreskin?" Amina asked. Everyone looked at her.

"God's foreskin place?" Amina repeated, and Akhil kicked her shin under the table. "Ouch!"

"What is this child saying?" Ammachy's face was rigid.

"Time for naps!" Kamala pointed toward the stairs. "Go. You are overtired."

"But it's the middle of the day!" Akhil protested. "We just got here."

"Jet lags! You'll be cranky tomorrow if you don't get some rest. Go!" Kamala stood up and ushered them to the base of the stairs, Itty hot on her heels. "Itty, you stay with us, okay? Your cousins need to sleep."

"Hullo? Cricket?" Itty asked, and Kamala shook her head.

"Not now. They need to sleep. You stay with me."

"Good job," Akhil growled as they left the table and dragged themselves upstairs. "Now we're going to sit up there in the heat forever."

"What's God's—" Amina asked.

"*Forsaken,* dope. It means abandoned."

"Oh." It was getting hotter with every step. Amina's legs felt curiously heavy, as if they were already taking a nap. "God abandoned America?"

"Probably." Akhil opened the door to the bedroom they shared and flipped the fan onto high, sending a small cloud of mosquitoes in all directions. "Ammachy thinks so."

"Does Dad think so?"

"No, stupid. Dad likes it. That's what they were fighting about."

"They were fighting?"

"What did you think that was? What do you think it is every time we're here? Ammachy wants Dad to move back. Dad doesn't want to move back. Ammachy gets mad at Mom about it. Classic immigrant dysfunction, duh."

"Yeah, I know, *duh,*" Amina said, annoyed that she didn't. Akhil was such a know-it-all when it came to India, like he was some big expert just because he was three years older than her and he'd been born there instead of in the States, like she had. She lifted the mosquito netting at the edge of one of the twin beds and climbed under. "But Mom wants to move back, too."

"So?" Akhil fell back onto the bed next to hers.

"So why does Ammachy get mad at her?"

Akhil thought it over for a minute, then shrugged. "Because she doesn't want to get mad at Dad."

"Oh." Amina's head sank into the pillow. "Do you want to move back?"

"No! India sucks."

Amina was relieved. This much even she knew. She shut her eyes, surprised by how quickly the blackness of sleep rose up to greet her, swift and persuasive as candor.

"She's half grandmother, half wolf, you know," Akhil whispered a few seconds later, and already half dreaming, she took it to be truth in the way unfathomable things can be. She had seen the cool lupine glow in her grandmother's eyes, her arthritic hands curled into paws. In the days that followed, her hand would instinctively cover her throat whenever Ammachy looked directly at her.

Where was everybody? The deep blue of evening shadowed Akhil's empty bed as Amina opened her eyes. She rose, letting the pressure in her head settle before shoving her feet into her chappals and walking across the hallway to her parents' room.

"Mom?"

Inside, Kamala shoved clothes into a dark dresser. She glanced up as Amina walked in. "Oh, good. You need to wake up so you can go to sleep on time."

"Where is everyone?"

"Daddy and Sunil and all have gone to see the neighbors."

"Where's Akhil?"

"In the kitchen."

Amina blinked against the dry air, feeling vaguely sick. "My head hurts."

Instantly Kamala was next to her, with a hand on her forehead. "You drank some water?"

"No." The water in Salem tasted like hot nickels. Amina tried to use it only when brushing her teeth.

"Go downstairs and get some right now."

Amina groaned.

"No! None of this Miss Needed an Enema Last Time."

"*Mom.*"

"You want it again? Four days no pooping?"

"Fine! Fine! Going!"

The sun had already set behind the Wall as Amina shuffled through the shadowed yard, toward the kitchen. The taller of the servant girls smacked a coconut against the cement, staring at her as she walked by. Amina waved and then pretended she hadn't when the girl did not wave back.

"Fingers out of the ghee, or I will chop them off!" Mary-the-Cook was shouting as Amina entered the kitchen. "How many times do I tell you this? Ah! The little one is awake now! What is it, *koche*? You want some bread and sugar?"

"Mom says I need water."

"Good, good." Black as a tire and perpetually struggling under the weight of her pillow-sized breasts, Mary-the-Cook was the exact same age as Ammachy, a fact that had been made incredible by the way time had expanded her body in the exact places it had contracted Ammachy's. The result was a face smoothed of any wrinkles, a body that moved like a jogging meatball. "Waterwaterwater. All week I have been making the water for you people! You remember last time, nah? Four days and still you couldn't—"

"I know, I know." Amina took the cup Mary-the-Cook offered. "What's for dinner?"

"Biryani." The cook nodded triumphantly to a bloody chicken carcass resting on the counter. "And maybe a little bit of this fool if he keeps talking such nonsense."

"It's not nonsense," Akhil said. "Anyway, how do you know? It's not like you were at tea with us."

"At tea? *At tea?* I have myself been working at this house since this boy's father was six years old only, and he thinks I have to be *at tea* to know what goes on?"

"I'm just saying Ammachy was pissed at him *again*. It's like she can't even look at him."

"*Pist?*"

"Angry. It means angry."

"Nobody is angry! Too much of love is all! All these years Amma works and works to send Thomas to school, and then he goes and marries your dusky mother and studies in America and what? Nothing!" For reasons unclear to anyone, Mary-the-Cook had always been Ammachy's strongest ally, regularly citing Ammachy's teaching her English as evidence of a kindness that no one else had seen. "Like every other so-and-so from here to Bombay, this boy runs off and works and works and does not come home! What is she supposed to do?"

"She could move to the States," Akhil said.

"Don't be an idiot! What move? She's too old." Mary frowned. "Besides, it's the children's duty, everyone knows. And she is getting old! What if something happens?"

"She's got Sunil Uncle."

Mary-the-Cook snorted. "That one is a miserable good-for-nothing. It's a miracle she lets him live here at all! Shouting at everybody, sleepwalking like some baby elephant, always unhappy!"

"Wait, what?" Akhil's eyes widened.

"Sunil Uncle sleepwalks?" Amina had only ever seen Scooby-Doo sleepwalk. She didn't know real people could do it.

Mary-the-Cook frowned. "Not important. Akhil, hand me an onion."

"Where does he go?" Amina imagined Sunil Uncle in the kitchen, making himself a six-foot-long hoagie.

"Akhil! Onion!"

Akhil reached into the basket behind him. "Seriously? All the time? Like, every night?"

"Doesn't matter," Mary-the-Cook said. "I am only saying that Thomas should be coming home. If he waits any longer, it will be too late."

"Have you tried to wake him up?" Akhil asked. "Because that's dangerous, you know. He could attack."

"Waking him? What fool would try to wake him? We are too busy trying to keep our own selves safe from harm."

"He hurts you?"

"Not me, *things*. He hurts things only."

"What things?"

"Things he himself has bought! The china for Amma's sixtieth birthday. That television set—you remember? Smashed like one cheap toy. The dentistry chair with its three reclining positions *and* the overhanging lamp."

Akhil's eyes narrowed. "How do you know he's sleepwalking?"

"What fool will break things he himself has saved up so long to buy? He's not Thomas, he can't be breaking and buying new all the time. And you should see how he cries over it the next day!"

"Wow." Akhil looked impressed. "Psycho."

"Psycho," Mary-the-Cook agreed, shearing the ends off the onion with a rusty blade.

"Well," Akhil said after a pause. "Dad always says Sunil Uncle didn't want to live here or be a dentist, that Ammachy forced him when he didn't get into medical school. Maybe he's doing it to—"

"Are you even listening?" Mary-the-Cook asked. "He's not *doing* anything, he's sleeping!"

"I mean subconsciously, duh." Akhil rolled his eyes.

"*Sub?*"

"You know, like what he wishes he could do while he was awake but can't."

"And what exactly is that?" Ammachy's voice, sharp as a blade, pierced through the darkened doorway. She materialized an instant later, curled like a shrimp, her eyes fixed furiously on Mary-the-Cook.

"Oh, hi, Ammachy." Akhil smiled bravely. "We were just—"

"I thought I told you to stay out of the kitchen." Her teeth glinted in the bad light.

"We just came for water. OW!" Akhil yelped as his grandmother grabbed a handful of his chub.

"If I catch you in here again, I will beat you with a stick. Understand?"

What wasn't there to understand? Amina made hastily for the door, Akhil coming up behind her. He pushed her out, and they both skittered across the darkened yard, careening around a pile of coconuts and through the pomegranate trees before running up the verandah steps. Only when they were safely at the top did they dare look back at the kitchen, where Ammachy shouted a storm of Tamil at Mary-the-Cook, who minced the onion with shamed gusto.

"Jesus!" Akhil glowered. "What was she . . . *spying*? She spies on us now?"

"She spied on us last time, too, remember?" Amina reminded him. "She spies on everyone, all the time. Anyway, you shouldn't have said that about Sunil Uncle."

"Why not? Everyone knows he's been unhappy for, like, *years*. Even Dad says he should have gotten out of Salem a long time ago, when he had the chance." Akhil rubbed his waist where he had been pinched. "So the truth hurts! Fuck her!"

"Fuck her!" Itty shouted from behind them, and Amina screamed. Her cousin's white sneakers glowed as he unfolded himself from behind Ammachy's chair. He looked at them expectantly. "Cricket?"

"It's too dark," Akhil said, and Itty's face sank. It seemed to Amina that her cousin waited the entire two years between their visits peering anxiously at the gate with ball in hand.

"We'll play tomorrow," Amina promised, and Itty nodded miserably.

"Hullo? Roof?" he tried, a close second in favorite activities.

"Nah," Akhil said.

"I'll go with you," Amina said.

Minutes later the two of them stepped off the upstairs verandah to the tiny ledge, climbing the ladder that would take them up to the roof. There, with the last burn of the sunset on the horizon and smoke from dinnertime fires growing, Amina could finally see over the Wall. The thoroughfare was clogged with its usual stagnating life, sluggish buses and cars honking in steady lines while rickshaws and bikes ran around them like beetles. The beggar children from the morning had scattered across the street, approaching any vehicle that slowed down long enough for them to get a hand through the window. Amina breathed in deep, sucking down the smell of gasoline and cooking onions, of cow dung and sewage and sweat, and Itty hummed to himself. Amina watched him watching Salem until it was too dark to see much of anything, and held the hand he offered to lead her back down into the safety of her bedroom.

———

Dinner that night was extravagant and tough. Burned by a chastened Mary-the-Cook, it was eaten joylessly while the adults discussed Indira Gandhi's state of emergency ("a colossal mistake," according to Thomas), and something called the Janata Party, which Amina thought sounded like something that might involve pajamas and cake.

"You watch," Ammachy said, pulling a thin chicken bone out from between her teeth and setting it on the edge of her plate. "These people are the same as every other political group. They talk and talk of change, and then they will do their best to bring the country crashing to its knees."

"Nonsense." Thomas helped himself to more rice. "We survived the British. You really think we can't handle ourselves?"

Sunil snorted from the far end of the table, where he had settled with pink eyes and a slur.

"Not the same, Thomas," Ammachy said. "An enemy from outside is easier to manage than chaos from within. And now there are so many of factions growing! Anti-Muslim, anti-Christian, anti-everyone!"

"Ah no!" Kamala clucked.

"T. C. Roy himself said there was a mob in Madras." Divya tried to shovel a handful of rice into Itty's moving mouth. "He couldn't even get out of the car for fear of his life!"

"Seriously?" Akhil looked worried.

"*Pah*—Roy's a hysterical." Thomas waved a dismissive hand. "You watch, things will even out again. It's a pendulum, no? Things swing one way, then the other, but India herself always thrives."

"Well, s'all very easy to say when you're gone, isn't it?" Sunil mashed rice between his fingers.

Thomas puffed up a little. "So I'm not allowed to have an opinion, is it?"

"I'm just saying, it's easy to look back with rosey-posey glasses when you live on the other side of the earth itself, nah? But those of us that live here, we have to deal with realities, you see. So it's quite different for us."

"Obviously. I wasn't saying India was an easy place to live, I just—"

"Well, it's not a *hard* place to live," Sunil interrupted indignantly.

"We've got all the modern amenities you do now. Refrigeration. Television. Movies and *whatnot*. Take a look around you, nah, brother? Things have changed."

"Who needs water?" Kamala asked.

"It was a simple statement, Sunil." Thomas moved small piles of food around his plate. "I was just saying that India has survived some three thousand years of change; she will survive a few more."

"She will *sssssurvive!*" Sunil crowed, raising fists into the air. "Did everyone hear it? The good doctor says we'll live! Thank God himself!"

And what would happen now? In the bulging silence that followed, Amina watched as veins pulsed and rose on Thomas's forehead and Sunil leaned forward.

"You're a drunk," Thomas said.

"You're an ass," Sunil shot back.

"Enough!" Ammachy smacked her hand on the dining table. "My God, grown men acting like small boys! Can't the first night pass without you ruining it?"

The cloud that descended on the table was potent enough for even Amina to realize that the first night had been ruined already. She looked from her grandmother to Divya to Kamala to Akhil, each face more uncomfortable than the last with the exception of Itty, who was peeking gleefully under the tablecloth at his just-remembered shoes.

"Don't get yourself so bothered, Amma," Thomas said at last, breaking his gaze from Sunil's. "We're just talking is all, right, brother?"

At the end of the table, Sunil sat with his eyes closed, his finger raised into the air as though taking the temperature. He pointed it at Thomas and pulled an invisible trigger before opening his eyes again. Then he lifted his glass and downed the last inch of gold.

"Right," he said.

CHAPTER 2

The sun rose flat and hard the next morning.

Hot. She was already getting hot. How could this be winter? Amina tried to imagine the New Mexico she had just left, the stars sprayed over the black sky, the December air turning her breath into white puffs, and found she could not. India was too much to imagine anything else.

In the cracked bathroom mirror, her black hair stood up from her head, while her nose was pocked with tiny red mosquito bites. It exaggerated the overall effect of her face (long, thin, too beaky to ever be considered beautiful), making her, she worried, as ugly as her grandmother predicted. She backed up, hoping against all odds that something had happened to make her boobs grow in overnight. It had not. Stepping into the tiled basin behind her, she reached into the pink plastic bucket and ladled a cup of lukewarm water over her head.

When she descended the stairs ten minutes later, she found Ammachy, Divya, and her parents hunched over a spicy breakfast. She

looked in vain for Mary-the-Cook, who might slip her a piece of cin-
namon toast, but the servant girls were there in her place, and neither
looked particularly helpful.

"Hello, monkeysoup!" Thomas smiled and pointed to the chair
next to him. *Sit.* "You sleep okay?"

Amina nodded. "Where's Akhil?"

"Outside playing cricket with Itty."

"They're not eating?"

"They ate already."

"Oh." The soupy smell of sambar made her stomach turn a little.
"Can I go, too? I'm not really even hungry."

"No." Ammachy placed three round idlis on her plate. "Eat."

"I can't eat that much."

"Start."

Amina picked up an idli, scowling. India sucked.

"So Preetham will take us and kids to zoo in the afternoon," Kamala said. "And should we take a rickshaw back? Thomas, what do you
think? Or you and Sunil can drop us and then go to the bank together?"

"Sure." Thomas took a sip of coffee. "Whatever works."

"Actually, Thomas and I are going to Dr. Abraham's office at
eleven," Ammachy announced. "So we will need Preetham."

"What?" Thomas's eyebrows rose with surprise.

"He's arranged for us to have a small tour of the facilities. Afterward we'll go to his house for lunch."

"But we can't." Thomas struggled to keep his face calm. "I told
Sunil I would go to the bank with him today and get the papers."

"Where's Sunil Uncle, anyway?" Amina asked.

"Chutney or sambar?" Kamala motioned for her plate.

"Sugar."

Ammachy ladled enough sambar to float a legion of idlis across
Amina's plate, saying to Thomas, "Sunil will not be out of bed until
twelve itself, if we are so lucky. You and he can go after."

"Twelve? In the afternoon?" Amina asked.

"Less talking, more eating," Kamala urged.

Thomas glared at Ammachy. "I already told you—"

"It's *arranged*, Thomas. I *myself* arranged it. Now, please don't make some fuss."

Sunil Uncle must have gone sleepwalking again! Amina was sure of it. Why else would he be in bed until twelve in the afternoon? She imagined him ambling through the yard in the middle of the night, arms stretched in front of him, feet wandering idly over roots and grass.

"How did everyone sleep?" she asked, looking hopefully at the adults around the table. No one would look back at her, not even Kamala.

Ammachy swiped her forefinger across a dot of sambar on the table. "It's just a tour, Thomas, nothing more. You can decide for yourself if it's something you want to pursue after that."

Thomas's nostrils flared. He said quietly, "We're not going. I told you I didn't want to meet with him, I don't want to meet with him. That's it."

Ammachy raised her eyes from the oilcloth, eyelids half-mast in a way that might have been mistaken for boredom if not for the drilling gaze underneath them. She shrugged. "Fine. I will cancel."

"Amma, you can't just—"

"I said I would cancel."

Thomas, body angled forward for the full impact of a fight, wavered in his chair. He opened his mouth to say something, then closed it.

"Thank you," he said.

"Don't thank me," Ammachy said icily. "I'm doing you no favors."

"Okay, Ami!" Kamala said a little too cheerfully. "You ready to go to the zoo?"

Amina nodded, pushing her mostly full plate to her mother and waiting for one of the adults to protest over how little she had eaten. No one did.

"They can grow to be sixty feet! And they kill elephants in one bite! And they growl like dogs!" Amina told her father at tea that afternoon, while her mother and brother slept upstairs. "And when they get mad, like really mad? They can puff out their hood and it's bigger than an umbrella. Like, you or I could stand under it in a rainstorm and not even get wet."

"Wow, really?" Thomas looked impressed.

Ammachy set a small dish of mixture on the table with a clack.

"And . . ." Amina racked her brain for the details Akhil would have wanted to tell. "It was a female! A girl cobra! But it's still called a king. I think. And it had built a nest even though there was no mate and no eggs!"

"Stop shouting." Ammachy winced, sitting down. "Did you comb your hair at all this morning? Why are you looking so grubby all the time?"

"*And,*" Amina said, ignoring her grandmother, "it almost got free and attacked us."

"Goodness! What did you do?"

"Don't encourage her, Thomas." Ammachy frowned. "Such spoiling I've never seen."

"Akhil and I stayed calm, but Itty pulled out, like, half his hair." Amina looked down the hall to the door of Itty's room. "Where is he, anyway?"

"Gone to the bank with Sunil." Ammachy brushed her fingers over the tablecloth, which had been changed from oilcloth to lace since the morning. "They will be back after they leave the papers."

"What papers?"

"The papers for the house," Thomas said. "I signed it over to Sunil."

"Oh." Amina nodded, confused.

"My father left a portion of the house to both of us," Thomas explained. "I gave my part to Sunil."

Amina looked up at the high dining room ceiling, the peeled paint around the base of the chandelier. "This house was yours?"

"It's still both of theirs," Ammachy muttered.

"It's Sunil's," Thomas said firmly. "He's the one who lives here and keeps it up. The papers were just a formality."

"Doesn't matter. You can sign whatever you want to, but this will always be your home."

Thomas shushed her and Amina felt strangely disappointed. She hadn't known that any of the house belonged to her father. She wondered now which part did. The upstairs rooms? The roof? The doorbell rang before she could ask.

"Aha!" Ammachy pushed herself to shaky legs.

"I'll get it, Amma."

"No, no." Ammachy waved Thomas down. "You sit."

But Thomas was already walking out of the dining room. Ammachy followed at a gasping pace behind.

"Thomas . . . I said . . ."

Amina, sensing something much more exciting than tea, followed. She stood in the middle of hall as Thomas threw open the door, letting in the flat haze of late-afternoon sunlight cut by a tall silhouette.

"Hello?" a voice inquired.

"Hello?"

"Goodness, Thomas, is that you?"

The figure stepped into the hallway, no less magnificent for its sudden definition. With light-coffee skin and a short buzz of white hair, the man standing in the doorway hardly looked like he could have emerged from the same Salem that Amina had ridden through just hours before, his white linen pants and pink shirt crisp as cut apples.

"Dr. Abraham," Thomas said, backing up quickly. "How nice to see you, sir! I wasn't expecting you."

"Chandy." Ammachy beamed. "So nice of you to be able to meet us! I hope it wasn't too much of a bother?"

"No botheration at all!" Dr. Abraham exclaimed, walking through the doorway and into the foyer. He nodded agreeably at the walls. "Glad to come."

Amina tugged on her father's hand. "Who is it?"

"Will you have a bit of tea with us, Doctor?" Thomas asked, oblivious to her. "We were just starting."

"That would be lovely, thank you." The man turned to Ammachy. "Miriamma, you're looking well. We miss you round the hospital, you know."

"Oh, *pah*." Ammachy looked pleased.

"And how is Sunil doing these days?"

"Fine, fine." Ammachy led the way to the dining room, where Amina saw that someone—Mary-the-Cook?—had sneaked in, placing an array of sweets and savories on the table, along with a fresh pot of tea and clean dishes. "Dentistry will always be needed, as you know."

"Though less so since the Brits left." Dr. Abraham waited for the laugh, and Ammachy supplied it, pouring a cup of tea.

"Sugar?"

"Yes, please. I can never get enough of sweetening." Dr. Abraham ladled four spoonfuls into his cup, stirred, and took a sip. "So, Thomas, what brings you back?"

Thomas nodded as though this was the first of many questions in an oral exam. "Just a family visit, sir. My wife hasn't seen her sisters in too long, and of course, we want the children to know the family."

"Ah, yes! The children." Dr. Abraham looked down at Amina, who stared back, mute. "And who is this?"

"This is my only granddaughter, Amina." Ammachy poured tea into her own cup. "She's eleven years old, and top of her class back at home. Champion of spelling itself."

"Really?" Dr. Abraham took a sip of tea. "And what next? Are you going to be a surgeon like Daddy?"

"I'm going to be a vet for puppies and kittens only," Amina said.

"I see," Dr. Abraham appeared unfazed. "And how are you finding India?"

"It's good. It's hot. Today we saw a cobra and—"

"You've met Thomas's son, Akhil?" Ammachy passed the doctor a bowl of plantain chips.

"Yes, yes, I believe I did on Thomas's first trip back. How old was the boy then? Six!"

"Four. He's fourteen now," Thomas said.

"And he is back in the States?"

"No sir, he's just upstairs with his mother napping. Sorry not to have him down to meet you, but I didn't—"

"Nothing doing! No problem at all. It's a big change for the children, no? But they recover quickly, I find. I think they know it's home, yes? Physiologically speaking, of course. What's the expression?" He paused, and Amina wondered if he was really waiting for an answer or just asking himself more questions out loud. "Ah, yes, they know it in their bones! Don't you think, Amina?"

He looked at her expectantly, and Amina nodded because it seemed better than not nodding.

"And how have you been, sir?" Thomas passed a tray of neon sweets. "Are you still splitting your time between here and teaching at Vellore?"

"No teaching at the moment. Everything has taken a bit of a backseat to getting this rehabilitative center into tip-top shape." Dr. Abraham set two plump balls of ladoo down on his plate as though they were baby chicks. "I would feel sadly if I didn't think the work was vitally important, of course, but what an opportunity . . . your mother has told you a bit of what we're doing?"

"A bit, yes."

Dr. Abraham nodded encouragingly.

"It sounds very interesting," Thomas offered.

"I'm so glad you think so!" Dr. Abraham smiled. "Of course it's not a neurosurgical wing, as I'm sure you're aware, but we are putting together a first-rate facility for trauma and recovery."

"Yes." Thomas looked vaguely panicked. "What a nice project for you all."

"You remember M. K. Subramanian from your class? He is in the process of interviewing the physical and cognitive therapists, while I am recruiting doctors from round the country. And what a stroke of luck that you are here at the right time! When your mother called, I could hardly believe it. Perhaps you'd like to meet with him tomorrow?"

Thomas smiled, clearly pained. "Well, now, you see—"

"Perfect! Tomorrow is perfect." Ammachy placed a pakoda on the doctor's plate. "We were planning on going to the hospital anyway in the late afternoon; we could stop and meet you both then itself."

"Fantastic. I would love to show you the facilities, and have you meet a few of the staff." Dr. Abraham tucked his napkin into his shirt collar. "Doesn't this look delicious!"

He busied himself with spooning a generous amount of chutney onto the pakodas, so he did not notice how Thomas dropped his head between his hands, how he rubbed his knuckles against the side of his head as if ironing out knots.

"Are these from Sanjay's?" The doctor raised a ladoo to his lips. "I do love their sweets, you know."

"I remember." Ammachy smiled. "I bought them especially."

"You needn't have gone through the trouble—"

"No trouble, no trouble at all."

A mewl escaped from somewhere deep in Thomas's throat, stopping the others as it turned into a full-throated groan. The doctor's eyebrows went up and Ammachy's back went rigid as Thomas pushed his chair back from the table.

"Dr. Abraham, sir, would you mind very much if we went for a walk in the yard?"

"Now?"

"Eat first, then talk!" Ammachy pushed a tin of mixture at the doctor.

"I'm terribly sorry." Thomas looked slightly ill. "If you wouldn't mind?"

"Oh. No." Dr. Abraham looked ruefully at his plate. "Of course not."

Thomas rose, revealing a damp *U* where the sweat had soaked through the back of his shirt, and walked straight out of the room. Dr. Abraham took the napkin from his collar and carefully folded it, nodding to Ammachy. Her mouth fell in a hard line as he followed Thomas into the garden.

And what were the men saying, under the shadow of the leaves? Amina watched them through the heavily slatted window, heads ducked to the onslaught of the white sun, arms tucked neatly over chests. They stared at the plants in front of them with such concentration that they might have been discussing fertilization or watering schedules. Dr. Abraham nodded once, curtly, and then again, a little more heavily. Arms were uncrossed, hands clasped. The men walked toward the front of the house with slow steps, where the whinny of the gate latch and the roar of traffic soon gave way to silence. Amina waited for her father to come back and finish his tea. Minutes passed.

"Where did Dad go?" she finally asked.

Ammachy, who appeared to be studying the tablecloth very hard, did not answer. Amina was about to ask again when a tear ran down her grandmother's cheek, as fast and unexpected as a live lizard. Amina panicked. Should she say something? Hug her? Both seemed equally impossible. Still, when another tear followed the first, Amina found herself holding her grandmother's hand. It was thin and pale and cool as marble, the skin almost moist with softness. Ammachy took it back as Kamala entered the room.

"Oof." Kamala yawned, sitting heavily in a chair and pouring herself a cup of tea. She stirred in sugar drowsily, finally glancing up at the full plates and empty seats. "Where did everyone go?"

Ammachy pursed her lips, as if to spit.

"Uncle and Itty went to the bank," Amina explained.

Kamala blew on her tea. "And your father?"

"Dad went out with Dr. Abraham."

"Really?" Kamala's eyes flew to Ammachy. "When?"

Even not looking directly at her, Amina sensed how her grandmother seemed to ignite suddenly, a palpable flame ready to damage anything it could. She was silent for so long that Amina thought maybe she hadn't heard Kamala's question. Then she leaned across the table.

"Fat like one angel," she spat. "Thomas was born so strong and fat, I knew he would become something. Engineer, head of the Indian National Army, best brain surgeon in all of America. He could have married anyone! Such dowries we were offered!"

Kamala looked at her stonily. "You should have taken them."

"It was not my decision." Ammachy stood up and cleared the men's plates so that they clanged and jostled and threatened to break between her hands. She turned her back on the table, marching toward the kitchen with stiff shoulders. "It was not my decision at all."

———

But where had her father gone? Now missing for more than six hours, Thomas had sent the house into tumult in his absence. Ammachy wandered from room to room, fighting with anyone who crossed her path. Sunil, having crossed her path twice already, found a bottle of toddy and was devouring it in the rarely visited parlor. Divya had tucked herself in a corner of the verandah. Itty ran circles on the roof. Kamala, Akhil, and Amina sat on the upstairs bed, playing their fourth game of Chinese checkers.

"Your move, Mom," Akhil said.

"Yes." Kamala glanced down at her watch and inched a blue marble toward a yellow triangle.

"What time is it?" Amina asked.

"Nine-thirty."

Akhil did an elaborate series of jumps, sliding one more marble into configuration.

Amina sighed. "I don't want to play anymore."

"That's just because I'm winning," Akhil countered.

"You win every game!"

"So don't play." Kamala rubbed her own forehead, smoothing out the lines that had settled into it.

"But there's nothing else to do!"

"Enough of whining! Go see what Itty is up to!"

But Amina didn't want to see Itty any more than she wanted to see the Chinese checkerboard, or the inside of her parents' sweltering bedroom, or Akhil gloating for the millionth time in a row. She pushed off the bed, heading instead to the stifling, fanless stairway, and lay down at the top of steps, letting the marble's momentary coolness slide into her. A whole muffled world rumbled under her ear, clicks and groans of the house, the *shup-shupp*ing of someone's slippers, slow, whale-like moans that she imagined coming from the depths of a huge, cool ocean. Her hip bones dug into the floor, and she heard something else. Singing. Was someone singing? Amina lifted her head off the floor.

"*. . . fingers in my hair, that sly come-hither stare . . .*"

Music! It was coming from below. Amina peeked over the stair-well. She crept down a few steps, and then a few more, until she was able to see into the parlor.

"*Witchcraft . . . ,*" the record sang, and Sunil along with it, his eyes shut, his face shining. A record spun in neat circles on the turntable, and next to it, her uncle followed, arms cupping the air in front of him, knees bouncing.

Amina stared in dismay as Sunil pivoted from one foot to the other, his hips cutting the air in deft strokes. It was like watching a muskrat slip into the Rio Grande, all of its clumsiness turned to in-stinctual grace. His meaty upper half arced, dipping near to the floor, then back up.

"*I know it's strictly taboo . . .*"

The lightness in his face was something Amina had never seen before. He was, she realized for the first time, a handsome man. Not movie-star handsome like Buck Rogers, not even tall and sharp-jawed like Thomas, but appealing all the same. He took one quick step back and twirled to the right, his hand guiding an invisible partner.

"Sunil!"

Both Sunil and Amina jumped as Ammachy appeared in the doorway, arms folded tightly over her chest, sniffing at the room. Amina turned and ran up a few stairs, so she wasn't sure what hap-pened next, whether her grandmother actually sent the needle skid-ding across the record or if Sunil had done it himself, but the quiet that followed hummed with potential disaster.

"This again," Ammachy said.

Shuffling. The sound of liquid being poured. A glass slammed on a table.

"You've had enough already, Sunil. Go to bed."

Silence. Amina leaned forward. They were switching rapidly be-tween English and Malayalam, which always just sounded like *argada-argada-argada* to her, until her grandmother demanded, "And where exactly is your brother?"

"I already told you, I don't know."

"So? You can't be bothered to look for him?"

A sigh, a snort. "Please, Amma."

"He's your *brother!*" Ammachy snarled.

"Argada-argada."

"What is that supposed to mean?"

Sunil loosed another sigh, but this one was forced, feigned boredom hiding anger. "It means that Thomas is Thomas and he will go where he wants when he wants. You of all people should know that."

"Oh, stop it with that. No one is interested in your babbling."

"Surprise!"

"Idiot! You're drunk. *Argada-argada-argada.*"

"I couldn't agree more."

Amina slid her feet over the edge of one stair, then another. She peeked around the wall to find her uncle slumped into a living room chair, all trace of music and movement sucked from him. Ammachy hovered over the chair, the bright green silk of her sari glowing.

"How dare you do this?" she hissed.

"What now?" Sunil shut his eyes, leaning his head back on the chair.

"Feeling sorry for yourself again. Today of all days!"

"I don't know what—"

"The house! You finally got him to give it to you."

There was a moment while this sank in, Sunil's bid for detachment redirecting. He sat up. "You think . . . you think signing over the house was *my* idea?"

"All the time he is giving you things, feeling sorry for you! *Poor Sunil didn't get the same opportunities, poor Sunil doesn't have enough!* And now you've taken the house!"

"He *gave* it to me."

"Because he is always taking care of you."

"Because he *wanted me to take it from him.*" Sunil rose from the couch. "You think he wants to live here?"

"He doesn't know what he wants yet!"

"He doesn't . . . You *believe* that, Amma? That Thomas has been gone these ten years because he doesn't know what he wants?" Sunil laughed, but underneath there was tightness in his voice. "You think he wants to *sit* and *rot* every day in this place instead of running off to America and sending checks?"

"He sends the money for you!"

"He sends it for *himself,* Amma! He sends it so he doesn't have to come. My God, you *must* know that by now."

If she did know it, Ammachy gave no sign, choosing instead to wrap the end of her sari tightly around her shoulders. "Go to bed!"

"You think Thomas would ever give me something he actually *wanted*?" Sunil shouted as she walked into the hallway, and Amina covered her ears, suddenly understanding that she had heard too much. She felt for the step behind her with one foot, then the other, hoping illogically that if she walked all the way to her parents' room backward, she would unremember the entire conversation. The knob was cool against her palm as she twisted it and shuffled into the bedroom.

"What's wrong with you?"

Amina turned around to find her mother frowning at her.

"Nothing." Amina sat on the bed.

"You're feeling sick?"

"No."

"Did you make BM today?"

"Yes!"

Akhil rolled his eyes. "Sure you did, poo bag."

"Akhil," Kamala snapped. "Enough. Your move."

"Helloooo, Mom, anyone home? I *won* already."

"Fine, so do something with yourself."

"Like what? Make Amina poo?"

Amina rushed at him, digging deep into his belly with her nails so that he shrieked, knocking over the game and the marbles, which spilled across the bed, providing an unlikely torture device as he slammed her on her back. He twisted his head to spit on her, and Amina grabbed an ear, pulling as hard as she could.

"AMINAKHIL! STOP THIS BUSINESS AT ONCE!" Kamala pushed between them, sharp hands collaring their necks. She forced them apart.

"Jerkface!"

"Diaper!"

Amina kicked at him again, and her mother squeezed her throat. "Ow!"

"My God," Thomas said from the doorway. "What is all that about?"

The family turned to him, panting, and Thomas walked into the room, a sweet and funky cloud of toddy on him. He smiled his lopsided smile, and no one knew what to say.

"You missed dinner," Kamala finally said.

"I know, I know. Sorry."

"Where were you?"

"Out."

"Out where? Doing what?"

"Well . . ." Thomas looked at them, as if considering something. "Making plans, actually."

"What plans?"

"Well . . ." He looked from Akhil to Amina to Kamala and back again. "Okay, listen. I have some big news."

"You do?" Kamala's hands dropped, and her voice was soft with excitement.

"We're going on a trip!"

"What?"

"To the beach! Sundar Mukherjee's wife is a travel agent, and she booked us rooms at the Royal Crown Suites in Kovalam!"

"What's Kovalam?" Akhil asked.

"Rooms?" Kamala's face darkened. "What for?"

"Kovalam is the beach on the peninsula," Thomas told Akhil. "It's very nice."

"But we don't have time, Thomas! My sisters will be—" Kamala began.

"We'll get to Lila's on time. We'll just leave here a little early."

"Early?" Kamala asked. "How early?"

"Tomorrow midday."

"*What?*"

"We need to rest, *koche*. A real vacation."

"Vacation?" Kamala's voice dropped an octave, like she was saying *drug binge* or *spending spree.* "Thomas, what are you talking about?"

"A break! A little peace and quiet! You know, a chance for us to just relax."

"I'm relaxed!" Kamala protested, looking anything but.

"No you're not. And how could you be with my mother nagging you all the time?" Thomas raised his hands into the air. "Impossible! She's made it impossible. It's not fair to you or the children. No wonder everyone is fighting!"

"A beach like Hawaii?" Akhil asked. "Does the hotel have TV?"

"Yes, I believe it does."

"Does it have a swimming pool?" Amina asked.

"It has a very nice pool," Thomas informed her. "I believe there's even a bar in the middle, where you can swim up and order a fizzy drink."

Amina gulped, dizzy with possibility.

"*Thomas,*" Kamala said sharply. "We can't just go."

"Why not?"

"You know why not!" She raised her eyebrow at the bedroom door, as though it were Ammachy herself. "Have you told her?"

"Don't worry about that! I will explain tomorrow. I'm sure she'll understand."

"Tomorrow? Understand? Have you lost your minds? Besides, what will the neighbors think? Everyone will talk!"

"Who cares what the neighbors think?" Thomas scoffed.

"*Everyone cares what the neighbors think!*"

"Kamala," Thomas sighed, rubbing his neck. "It's not such a big deal. We'll be leaving a few days early to go to the coast, that's all. Don't make it into a federal case, okay?"

Kamala got off the bed and opened the bedroom door. She looked at the children. "Out."

"What? No, Mom, this is a family *discussion,* right? We're entitled to—" Akhil started.

"OUT."

Akhil and Amina scooted off the bed as quickly as the marbles and bedsheets would allow, walking straight across the hall into their own room. They waited exactly five seconds after Kamala shut the door to slide out onto the verandah, where they could watch their parents but remain hidden in the dark.

"—can't. It's just not done," Kamala was saying.

Thomas opened his mouth to protest, but she cut him off with the flat of her hand.

"Bad enough the son leaves for America, then he comes home and stays for all of *three days only*?"

Thomas sniffed. "Don't let's start with all that."

"I am not starting anything! You yourself started this business!"

"Enough, Kam. I am warning you."

"You don't warn me when I'm warning you!"

"She *lied* to me!"

"So what, now you want to run away? All because Dr. Abraham came?"

"She told him I wanted a job!"

"And you told her you would come back after studies! So? You are two liars! So what?" Kamala spun toward the window and Amina ducked, but her mother wasn't looking at her. She was scooping up loose marbles and placing them in the game box.

"I did not *lie*, Kamala. It's not as though I planned this."

"No, of course not, His Holiness of Sainthood and Angels! You would never do such a thing!" Kamala shoved the top onto the game box. "You just studied the one branch in all of medicine that would be difficult to practice here and were shocked to death to learn that you *could not practice it here*!"

Thomas's mouth hung open. He blinked several times before answering. "You *saw* me, Kamala. I asked at Vellore. I checked in Madras. I even looked in Delhi, for the love of God!"

"Yes, you said."

"And what? You think I'm lying to you now?"

"No," Kamala said, uncertainty creeping onto her face.

"The technology is not here yet! What do you want? You want me to work some miserable job just so we can be here?"

"I am just saying—"

"Answer me! Is that what you want? How about if I become a dentist? We can live right here, upstairs."

"That's not what I—and anyway, what's so bad? So you don't do the surgery! You are still a doctor! We could still have a good life."

Amina had not known, until that very moment, that her father could look so bloodless, the color draining from his face until it looked like an angry husk. "What is so wrong with your life, Kamala?"

"We are not talking about me!"

"What is it that you long for? What opportunity have you not been given?"

Kamala fumed at the floor. "Nobody is talking about that."

"Is it the house? It's not big enough? You don't like your car?"

"Don't be a silly."

"You want to come back here, is that it? After all these years, after everything we have built for ourselves there, after all that I have tried to give you, you want to uproot the kids from their entire lives and just move back here?"

Kamala's lips clamped shut.

"What can you have here that you can't at home?" Thomas took a step forward. "Really, tell me! You sit here like some pained mermaid longing for her sea, but what is it, really, that you don't have back in the States? Your sisters who live in all different towns here anyway? Your independence? Enough help around the house? Someone to—"

"*Myself*," Kamala said.

Thomas swayed a little bit, as if slapped.

"Myself," Kamala said again, her eyes filling with tears she wiped away hastily, and Thomas's arms dropped in their sockets. They did not look at each other then, but at the floor. A moment later Thomas turned and left the room, shoes heavy on the steps. Amina leaned over the verandah's edge a few seconds later, watching him cross the yard, heading back to the gate. Akhil tugged her arm.

C'mon, he mouthed.

The lock screeched open again, letting Thomas back out to the street, and Kamala sat on the bed. Something round and hard moved

from Amina's throat to her gut, making it difficult to breathe. Akhil
frowned at her.

"Let's go, stupid," he hissed, and she turned and followed him back
inside, glad to have somewhere to go.

What was it that woke her? Late that night, Amina found herself
awake, blinking into the dark. Scraping footsteps. The settling of
weight. She stared at the fan cutting the air above her for several seconds before rising out of bed. The verandah was empty, but the tar on
the roof was still warm from the day's sun as Amina took the path
back up to the top. The high, warbling songs of newfound Tamilian
love rose from the movie theater down the street, along with smoke
from the beggars' fires and the bidi Thomas smoked, his back slumped
into a yellow chair, beer between his feet. He glanced over his shoulder
as she approached.

"Hi, Dad."

"Ami." He looked neither surprised nor unhappy to see her, and
though the night was too hot and she was a little too big for it, she
climbed into his lap, shoving her forehead against his jaw.

"You should be asleep," he told her, his breath burning her eyes.

"You should be asleep," she said, and he grunted.

"Are you having a good time?"

"Sure," she lied. "Are you?"

He nodded once, heavily. He sighed and she sighed with him, feeling his belly rise and fall at her back, his heart thumping behind hers.

"She's never satisfied," he said.

Kamala? Ammachy? Amina was scared to ask.

"Where did you go?" she asked instead.

He shrugged.

"Are we still going to the beach?"

His stubble scratched her forehead as he nodded.

Amina closed her eyes. The pool. Tomorrow she would be crawling through the clear turquoise while light dappled the walls around
her. Until her ears hurt. Until her fingers pruned. Maybe there would

even be a slide, one of those long ones that curled like a giant's tongue and spat you into the cool water.

"How is your brother?"

Why was he asking her? Amina opened her eyes to the muggy dark. "Mean."

Thomas laughed.

"No, it's true, Dad! He's worse here than at home."

"That's because it's hard for him here."

"It's hard for me, too!"

"Not the same way, *koche*. He was born here. He remembers more."

This seemed like one of those things that her father had wrong, like the time he said that being famous would be terrible. Why would it be harder to be somewhere you remember *more*? What about when you didn't remember anything if you'd ever even known it in the first place and everyone was always exchanging dark looks over it like you were blind or dumb or didn't understand what scorn looked like?

"That boy is going to be something else," Thomas said suddenly, wistfully, like he was seeing the end of some movie she couldn't. "He's difficult now, but one day he'll grow into himself, and then you watch. He'll shine brighter than the rest of us combined."

Amina's heart puckered with jealousy. She wanted to remind her father about how sometimes Akhil spoke so fast that you couldn't even understand him, and even when you could understand him, he didn't always make sense, but just then something crashed below them in the yard.

"What was that?" She jumped up, ran and looked over the edge of the roof, seeing a flicker of white. Now came a deep thud, followed by a string of curses and a growl.

"Shit." Thomas frowned at her side.

Down below, weaving like a ghost through a forest, Sunil wandered through the yard in his white mundu. He took a few steps forward and then turned back, bending over something. He dragged it toward the wall.

"Shit," Thomas said.

Amina blinked in the dark, trying to focus. What was he dragging? It was heavy, apparently. And dark. A chill shot through her. A body? Was it *Ammachy*? Sunil reached the gate and tried lifting whatever it was up and over. It dropped on his foot.

"AAAARGH!"

"Sunil, please!" And here was Divya Auntie, running across the yard now in her nightie. "Stop this nonsense and put it all back! You'll wake the whole house."

What on earth was he doing? Amina watched as her uncle bent over, tugging at something.

"Sunil—"

"GET AWAY FROM ME!" Sunil roared, stumbling backward so that Amina could finally see what he had been dragging.

"Is that our suitcase?" She looked at her father.

"Shit," Thomas said.

"BLOODY BULLSHIT ARTIST!" Sunil hit the lock on the suitcase so that it popped open.

"Dad, what is he doing?"

"*Shit.*"

The first item to fly over the gate was a hiking boot. The other soon followed, hitting the ground directly in front of the group of beggar children. One of them scrambled to pick it up, and another shrieked as a cassette landed in their midst. There were rustlings, and Amina watched a small shadow run to the gate, pointing to it. The rest of the children followed, staring up in wonder. At that moment, Sunil chose to get rid of the tube socks. One by one, the white balls flew into the night, and on the other side of the gate, children bobbed and weaved, snatching them before they landed.

"Sunil, stop!" Divya cried, tugging at his arm. He smacked her away.

Three more cassette tapes followed, and these caused a bit of a scuffle until one of the pairs of Levi's flew over and a full-on war began. Someone thumped someone. Someone else screamed. One of the jars of Avon cream shattered on the ground, but the next was caught, resulting in cheers. The candy cane filled with lip balms sailed into waiting hands. There was a small pause, and then Sunil raised Itty's tennis shoes above his head.

"No, no, Sunil!" Divya screamed, running at him. *"Nonononono!"*

But it was too late, the shoes were flying through the air and over the gate, twin satellites spinning into orbit and caught by swift hands. Divya scrambled for the lock, throwing her whole body against it until the gate clicked open. She shoved through it and stopped. The children watched her. She was breathing hard. She took a step forward, hands out, and they backed up. Amina watched as her aunt said something, reaching toward the children, and they scattered, running in all directions across the street, shoes and creams and cassette tapes tucked tightly under arms as they disappeared.

Amina was shaking. She did not realize this until her father put two hands on either side of her shoulders, pulling her toward him and clamping her still. Her face pressed into his ribs, and her mouth chattered.

"D-d-d—"

"It's okay," her father said, but she could hear the forced calm in his tone.

"W-we have to get Itty's shoes back! Or get him another p-p-pair! He's going to go crazy without them!"

"Okay," he said. "It's going to be okay."

Why was he picking her up? Amina hadn't been carried by her father in years, but there he was, scooping her up and crushing her, forcing her head down on his shoulder like she was some small, small child. Amina reared back, wanting to scream at him or scratch his face, and instead found herself crying harder.

"It's okay," her father whispered, rubbing her back as if she didn't know better.

They were packed. How this had happened was a mystery to Amina, who, along with Akhil, had been woken, fed a breakfast of toast and tea, and then led to the driveway by a terse Kamala. The sun was rising fast, spreading muggy air over them like carpet. Mary-the-Cook and the servant girls dutifully ran whisk brooms over the yard, sneaking looks their way but saying nothing as Itty howled and clutched his bare feet on the lawn.

"Itty, *koche, pavum,*" Divya said in a soothing voice. Her hair charged out of her bun in a haphazard corona; her eyes were red-rimmed.

Itty had been, as Amina predicted, inconsolable when his first shrieks rang across the pink morning. For the last two hours he moved from wracking sobs to soft whimpers and back as steadily as a commuter train on a loop.

Akhil walked over to him, tentatively patting his shoulder. "You want to go play cricket for a minute? We're not leaving yet."

Itty shook his head miserably, a gob of snot landing on his shirt. Divya sighed but forced a smile on her face when Amina looked at her, and it was this as much as anything else that sent Amina's stomach sliding into a greasy shame.

Bad. They were doing something bad. What, exactly, she wasn't sure, because no single element—the packed bags, the eating upstairs, the sweating outside now—seemed like a horrible act in itself, and yet somehow it had turned them against the Salem house, landing them up in the driveway like pillagers escaping with a country's pride. Outside the Wall, the morning traffic rose in a steady stream, honks and shouts multiplying on one another.

"Does Ammachy know we're leaving?" Akhil asked.

"Yes, of course," Kamala said.

"Then where is she?"

"She isn't feeling well this morning."

Akhil looked skeptically at his mother. "Are we even going to say goodbye?"

"Of course!" She bristled. "Who doesn't say goodbye?"

"Okay!" Thomas called, walking down the steps with two bags. "Almost done here!"

"Thomas, please." Divya clutched her pink sari tightly around her. "All year she has waited for you and the children to come. What will the neighbors think, all the commotion and sudden leaving?"

"Oh, pah." Thomas shrugged, shoving Akhil's backpack into the trunk. "Don't worry about that, it's no big—"

"And the party?"

"What party?"

"She was going to have a party for you and the children on Friday."

Thomas looked momentarily thrown. "She didn't tell me."

"It was a surprise."

Amina watched her father take this in. "Then I will tell her I am sorry."

Divya shook her head, walking into the house, and Itty wailed anew, the high-pitched whinnying. Akhil patted his head gingerly, and Amina crossed the lawn and crouched next to him.

"Hey," she said in the same soothing voice that all the parents were using, and it seemed like the right thing to do until Itty looked up at her and she had nothing more to say.

"Vel-cow," he whispered, panicked, tremulous.

"I know," she said, and he shuddered, ducking his head.

The hurrying sound of footsteps came from inside the house, followed by Divya and a much-worse-for-the-wear-looking Sunil.

"Ho! Thomas, what's this?" He was hastily tying a lungi around his plump waist as he walked. "Divya says you're leaving?"

Thomas nodded curtly, not looking him in the face.

"I thought you were staying until Saturday."

"We're going now," Thomas said, looking coolly toward the Wall. "We need to be somewhere more comfortable."

"Comfort . . . you . . . have you told Mummy?" Sunil managed at last, his face running from indignant to alarmed.

"I have."

Sunil walked a few paces toward the car and turned around. "You can't even manage a few more days?"

"Nights, actually."

The blood rushing to Sunil's face darkened it like a shadow, and Amina scooted closer to Itty and her brother, unsure if there would be another explosion. Instead her uncle swallowed, saying quietly, "Thomas, *bah*. That is no reason to leave."

"Oh, it's quite enough—"

"No, I mean"—Sunil cleared his throat—"you don't want to see me? Fine. I will go. But you stay."

"I can't."

"Can't?" Sunil snorted in disbelief. "What *can't*? Who *can't*?"

There was a long silence while Thomas struggled to come up with an answer.

"We can't," Kamala said, startling Amina and Akhil. "The children are sick with the heat, and I told Thomas to book one room at the beach."

This was a lie and they all knew it, but invoking the children had done the neat work of making the rest of the conversation impossible, and Sunil looked away, beaten.

"Just tell the neighbors the kids aren't used to the weather," Kamala continued. "They'll understand. Weak American constitution and all."

Amina could not look at anyone, not Sunil, not Divya, and definitely not Itty. She felt her mother's hands on her shoulders, propelling her forward, through the yard and up the verandah steps, down the hallway, past the living room and dining room and all the other bedrooms, to the one that smelled of camphor and roses and something else sweet and rotting, like a caramel roll left under the bed. The shadow of a fan cut across the pale blue wall, and in the bed, Ammachy was hunched under her sheets, her long hair loose from its customary braid, her eyes fixed on the pillow next to her.

"The kids would like to say goodbye," Thomas said, and if she heard him, it did not change her position. Akhil was the first to go to her, leaning quickly over to kiss her cheek and then standing back. Amina did the same, running back to the bedroom doorway when she was done.

"Amma." Thomas kneeled next to his mother.

Kamala joined him and had barely leaned forward when Ammachy's hand shot out of the covers, snapping across her cheek hard. For a few seconds there was a terrible soundlessness, the round shock that left Kamala clutching her face. Then she put down her hand, exposing a red welt, and everyone began yelling.

"Ma!" Amina cried.

"You bitch!" Akhil exploded, lunging at Ammachy. "You fucking bitch!"

"Akhil!" Thomas caught him with quick arms.

"What? It's true! Mom is so nice to her all the time, and why? So she can hear about how she's too dark to matter? So she can get *hit*?"

"Calm down."

"And you! The only thing Ammachy ever does is make you feel like shit! She doesn't deserve you!" Akhil's voice broke. "She doesn't deserve any of us!"

Thomas tightened his forearms across Akhil's chest and then began to whisper sternly, tenderly. *It's okay,* Amina saw more than heard; *you're okay, we're okay,* until the whites of Akhil's eyes stopped slashing furiously around the room, until he stopped struggling and just stood there, panting heavily, looking like he was going to cry.

"I need you to take your mother to the car. Can you do that for me?" Thomas asked, and Akhil bent to put his arm around Kamala, who was already rising on jittering legs. They left the room together. Thomas waited until their footsteps grew soft before turning back to Ammachy.

"You," he said, his voice murderously low, and Amina crouched against the wall as he began to pace. "What is *wrong* with you? Hitting! My God! Is there any shred of sanity left in this house?"

Ammachy glared at him.

"You think the kids will want to come back after this, Amma? You think any of us will want to—"

"Out!" Ammachy screamed. "Go if you are going!"

"You don't even enjoy it when we're here! Has that occurred to you? You're so busy thinking of how it *should be* that you can't even appreciate—"

"Cowards!" Ammachy roared. "Traitors! Good-for-nothings!"

Thomas's voice rose in a rapid, angry swirl of Malayalam, pushing Amina out the bedroom door and down the hall. The last words her father said to his mother were in a language that she didn't understand, and didn't want to. He was still yelling as she shot out the front door.

"What happened?" Divya cried, and Kamala, already ducking into the car with Akhil, said nothing. The servant girls stared openmouthed, Babu paced, and Preetham pretended to polish the steering wheel. Mary-the-Cook spat something on the ground, hands on hips, but even she took a few paces back as Thomas came barreling out of the house a few seconds later, his eyes wild and dark.

"Goodbye," he said, nodding curtly to his brother.

"Thomas, please!" Sunil said, but Thomas was already behind Amina, pushing her toward the car door. She scrambled into the backseat with her mother and brother as Babu unlatched the heavy steel gate to the main road and waved the car through.

"Are you okay?" Thomas reached for Kamala's face, but she leaned as far away from him as possible, her eyes turned to the road.

"Coward! You're as bad as she is!" Sunil shouted at Thomas through the window. He ran after the car, banging the flat of his palm on the trunk. "You wait. Your own children will leave you and never come back!"

And then they were out, on the other side of the Wall and rolling back down the dusty road, past the beggar children, down to the train station, where the Kanyakumari Express would take them to Kovalam Beach. For three whole days, they would stay in a resort built for rich Europeans. Akhil and Amina would eat pizza and French fries and begin to fight again without the fear of their grandmother to unite them. Kamala and Thomas would exchange pleasantries and logistics, a palpable coldness taking root between them. But it was Sunil's parting words that had done the most damage, and more than once Amina turned to find her father staring at her and her brother as though they had become unfamiliar to him already. Four years later, when Akhil died, she knew her uncle's words were ringing in his head much louder than any consolations the minister offered.

BOOK 2

THE FALLING MAN

SEATTLE, 1998

CHAPTER 1

"I've got to go home Monday to see my folks," Amina said, sliding into the wooden booth across from her cousin. Even early, it was crowded for a Thursday. She dipped her head to the cool pint Dimple had waiting, and swallowed.

"I've been here twenty minutes."

"I'm sorry. I was talking to my mom."

Dimple stared coolly at her. "You just went to see your parents last month."

"Three months ago. And by the way, Bala Auntie wants you to call."

"Oh for God's sake, Amina." Her cousin shook her head, glossy curls bouncing with candlelight. She plucked two cigarettes from the pack on the table and lit them, handing one over. "What now? You need to steam the rugs? Turn the compost?"

The last time Amina had gone home, Kamala had sent her to the roof to clean the leaves out of the rain gutters and for two days straight refused to pass on the phone, telling Dimple only, "She's on the roof and not coming down."

"No, it's not that. Something is wrong."

"Something is always wrong with your mother. What about you? What about that vacation you said you'd take?"

Amina looked around, avoiding her own reflection in the mirror behind her cousin. She hated seeing her own face right next to Dimple's—all beak and long chin and awnings for eyebrows, where Dimple's was a crisp, pert heart.

"Why is it so crowded in here?"

"Because the fucking Internet assholes have found the place and raised the price of everything. What happened to Bali?"

"Something is wrong with my dad." Amina took a short drag of the cigarette as concern darkened Dimple's face. Of all the parents, it was Thomas—who had defended her worst high school escapades and protested strenuously against her eleventh-grade exile to reform school—whom Dimple loved best.

"What do you mean? Like, sick? How come my parents haven't called?"

"No one knows yet."

"It's a secret?" Dimple's eyes widened.

"Of course not."

"What kind of sick?"

"There's just some . . . I don't know. He's incoherent or something. My mother says he's talking all night."

"Talking?"

"Telling stories."

Amina's cousin rolled her eyes, her face slackening. "For the last hundred years, yes. What's the fly-home emergency?"

"My mom thinks something is wrong." Amina swiped a stripe of condensation off her pint. "Anyway, I just want to go check in."

"What does your dad have to say about it?"

"My mom doesn't want me talking to him about it over the phone."

"So he hasn't told you anything is wrong."

"Yes, but that isn't the—"

"And when did you last talk to him?"

"Last week."

"And did he seem normal?"

Amina shrugged. "I mean, it's my dad."

Dimple squinted as she exhaled. "It's a trap."

"Oh, come on."

"It's a way for Kamala to get you back home. Where she can get you married." She pointed at Amina with her cigarette. "Before your uterus dries up."

"Oh, Dimple, stop. She hasn't brought up anyone in over a year."

"Proof!"

"No, this isn't that."

"Why not? Because the idea of your mother making some stupid plan without your permission is unthinkable?"

Amina took a sip of beer so she wouldn't have to answer. Kamala had set her up with various Syrian Christian men (or, as she called them, "Potentials") a total of twelve times. Eleven without Amina's permission.

"Because she wouldn't try the same bullshit over and over until it worked?"

Amina cleared her throat. "This isn't that, I swear. And anyway, there aren't even any good Suriani boys left, remember? She's given up."

"There were never any good Suriani boys. We're a failed culture."

It was one of Dimple's favorite theories, how thousands of years of obsession with a Christian God in a subcontinent of more dynamic religions had petrified the Syrian Christian community, turning them into what she alternately called "the stalest community on earth" or "India's WASPs." Amina braced for a full-on rant, but instead Dimple just blew a sharp plume of smoke from the corner of her mouth.

"I know what you're saying," Amina conceded. "But this is too low, even for my mother. She would never pretend that Dad was sick."

Dimple reached across the table to cup Amina's jaw and leaned in so close that Amina could smell her familiar, flowery perfume over the smoke in the bar. "Fool," she whispered, not unkindly.

Amina leaned back. The war over her soul and future had raged between Kamala and Dimple for too many years for her to take it personally. The bar was filling up, crammed with baggy pants, fleece jackets, messenger bags, and sneakers. Dimple scanned the room unhappily.

"Do you think it's really going to last?" she asked. It was the question that came up every time the cousins went out lately, her tone alternating between sarcastic and despondent. No one had been more discouraged by the rise of the Internet than Dimple, whose complaints ranged from having her neighborhood gentrified to having the gallery she ran compromised by what she described in fundamentalist tones as "the corruption of the quality image in the digital age."

Less vocal, if not actually less pessimistic, Amina was equally worried about the Internet, if only for the fact that it put her on the outside of something she feared might be generationally altering, like the civil rights movement or Woodstock. As "kids" just a few years younger than she flooded the city, scooping up armloads of vintage furniture and spreading through the neighborhoods on scooters, she clutched her trusty Leica, feeling like she was holding on to a wagon wheel in the face of the Industrial Revolution.

"I hate them," Dimple said before Amina could respond. "I hate what they do, I hate that they make more money than I ever will. Did I tell you someone suggested that part of the gallery be 'webcast'? What does that even mean?"

The cousins watched as a grinning guy in a baseball hat waved a twenty at the bartender.

"So how are things with Damon?" Amina asked.

"Over."

"I thought it was going well."

"He moved back in with his ex."

"Are you serious?"

"It's fine," Dimple said with a shrug. "Honestly, it saved me the trouble of having to get involved."

Five months older than Amina and therefore "well into age thirty," Dimple had been quietly moving through Seattle's supply of eligible men with a carnivorousness that occasionally scared Amina. It wasn't the number of men her cousin saw that unnerved her (truth be told, Amina had probably slept with more men, more often) but rather the impatience with which Dimple went through them, bringing them to meet Amina at bars and tuning out when they spoke, frowning like she'd ordered the wrong thing from a menu.

While some might interpret this as indifference, Amina knew the opposite to be true. Never mind how many relationships Dimple opened or ended with a shrug; the one thing she really wanted—and had always wanted, even in high school, when she turned scaring boys away into a kind of performance art—was someone worth sticking around for. At this point, the only thing more humiliating than having another relationship fail would be for Amina to openly acknowledge it.

"How about you?" her cousin asked. "Have you managed to have a conversation with anyone you're sleeping with?"

Amina took another sip of beer. "Why start now?"

An old Van Halen song pumped through the speakers, and half the guys at the bar threw up rocker fingers. The cousins sighed.

"Let's go," Amina said.

It was raining lightly as they left the bar, the soft, ceaseless, rhythmic kind of rain that is Seattle's lullaby. They stood out on the wet street while Dimple shook three cigarettes out of the pack, pressing them into Amina's hand.

"Thanks."

"Oh God!" Dimple clapped her hand to her chest. "I almost forgot! I told Sajeev we'd go out with him Saturday night."

Amina groaned.

"I had to, Ami. He's called twice since he moved here, and we keep putting him off. My parents are driving me nuts with all the messages they've been leaving." She switched into her mother's husky Indo-British whisper, and pursed her face into a perfect Bala Auntie. *"Dimple dahling, please do take the fine young man out. Mary Roy is calling all the time only. Everyone is wanting to know how he is."*

That their dislike of Sajeev Roy was hardly fair didn't stop the cousins from dreading him. When they were in kindergarten, it was his vulnerability that marked him, his constant thrashing at the hands of American boys, his eagerness to be part of their tight huddle. The girls had been relieved when his family moved to Wyoming, although

their own mothers' all-too-vocal admiration for his later successes
(MIT undergrad, a degree in engineering) still rendered him unap-
pealing.

"Can't you just go for both of us? I'm really going to be beat."

Dimple stared at her.

"Fine," Amina said with a scowl. "But I'm working until at least
ten, so it will have to be afterward."

"Yeah, fine, whatever. You sure you don't want a ride home?"

"Nah." They had reached Dimple's old blue Chevy van, moldering
in the parking lot like a wet elephant. Dimple opened the front door
and climbed in. She looked ridiculously small in it, like a child playing
grown-up. Even with her seat forward as far as it would go, her legs
were barely long enough to reach the brakes and clutch.

"Call your mother," Amina said when her cousin rolled the window down, and Dimple nodded even though they both knew she
wouldn't.

CHAPTER 2

"Thanks for meeting with me," Amina said, walking into Jane's office the next day. Jane swiveled around in her chair, perfectly pressed into her black suit, her red pageboy swinging. She pointed to the phone cupped to her head and then to the chair across from her. Amina sat.

"Yes, but it was a bar mitzvah. How do you miss the hora?" she asked irritably. Amina turned her attention to the floor-to-ceiling view of the Puget Sound to keep herself from getting unnerved. It was easy enough to do in Jane's office, the proportions of which (endless white walls, floor-to-ceiling windows) always made her feel like a gnat suspended in a glass jar.

The person on the other end of the phone was still talking when Jane hung up with a clatter. She frowned, repositioning herself in her seat. "I didn't realize we had a meeting scheduled."

"I'm having a family emergency and need to go home."

"Emergency?"

"My dad's not well."

"Sorry to hear that."

Amina shifted, something about Jane's relentless efficiency, her plucking gaze, making her feel like a liar. "It should just be a few days."

Jane turned to her computer, her mouth twitching as she read the schedule. She looked back at Amina. "You've got to be kidding me."

"No, wait—"

"This is unacceptable."

"It's not what you think."

"Sure, it's your father. What does he have? Kidney stone? Diabetes? Lung cancer?"

"No, but—"

"You told me you would see this through." She rapped her desk with her index finger. "If I wanted someone to screw it up, I could have sent in Peter."

"I'd leave on Monday."

"Not to mention that I've already gotten two messages from Lesley expressing concern about your ability to handle her event."

"Monday as in after the Beale wedding."

Jane looked at her, coolly recalibrating.

"Monday through Friday," Amina said, discreetly wiping her palms on her pants. "That should leave me pretty much clear, except for the Johnsons' fiftieth-anniversary dinner on Thursday night."

Jane turned back to her computer, pulling up the next week.

Amina cleared her throat. "Two messages?"

"Both ridiculous. I took care of it. But I need to know you're on top of this."

"I am," Amina said, annoyance creeping into her voice. Jane looked amused.

"Looks like Earl is your best bet for Thursday. Peter is on vacation, and Wanda has an eighth-grade graduation party."

"Eighth grade? Seriously?"

"I told you she's hungry."

Hunger, like loyalty and willingness to work unconventional hours, was a quality Jane valued in her staff. When she started the company ten years earlier, she had worked solo, talking her way into weddings by not charging for her time, just for her prints. It was a strategy that led her to build a devoted base within just a year. Now that Wiley Studios was a twelve-person operation, she was always looking for new growth opportunities. ("God willing," she'd once murmured to Amina in a rare unguarded moment, "we'll be shooting every event with candles on this side of the Cascades.")

Not that Amina needed to prove herself to Jane as much as she had in the early years. If anything, the fact that she'd been given the Beale account was clearly a vote of confidence, even if the reality of dealing with Lesley Beale felt like a demotion.

"So what's the Beales' venue?" Jane asked, writing a phone number down on a Post-it.

"The Highlands."

"Of course. How many times have you been out?"

"Three last week."

Jane raised an eyebrow. "Nervous?"

"I'm not, I just—"

"Of course you are. Lesley is a legendary bitch. But please her and we become the go-to for the lot of them, and that will please *me*." Jane slapped her hands on the desk, signaling the end of the conversation, and Amina stood. "Let me know if you can't get Earl."

Coming to work for Jane Wiley hadn't been Amina's idea. It was Dimple who had known Jane through mutual friends, Dimple who had gotten Amina the interview at Wiley Studios after her career at the *Seattle Post-Intelligencer* had derailed, Dimple who had hustled her out of bed and into the shower five years earlier, claiming she had told her about the job interview the week before.

"Who cares if it's events? You've just got to get out there again. Is this black thing your only suit?" her cousin had said while Amina stood under the pounding water, hungover, hating her.

"Out there" was Wiley Studios in Belltown, where Amina arrived that morning with a tightening forehead, her portfolio and résumé in hand. After a ten-minute wait, she was shuffled down the long hallway into Jane's airy office, where a black notebook lay open in the center of a steel desk with a to-do list that numbered into the fifties. Amina's name was number 14.

Jane had held out a pale hand. "Let's see what you've got."

Amina handed over her portfolio and looked away as Jane opened it, feeling, as she always did, that it was a little like watching a needle go into her own arm. Jane's head bobbed over the pictures.

"What's this?"

Amina glanced over. A smiling young boy's face leaned so close, his features were almost blurry. In the background, his older brother sat in a cement stairwell, wearing a Knicks shirt and smoking a cigarette.

"That's in Brooklyn. For an article on New York's homeless youth."

"Is that where you met Dimple? NYU?"

"Yes. I mean, no. Or, well, we met in New Mexico, but then we also went to NYU."

"And then you followed her here?"

"She followed *me* here," Amina said, bristling a little, and Jane looked up at her briefly before moving on. The next was an old woman with a puff of white hair, slumping into her lawn chair.

"Record heat in Queens," Amina offered.

In the next, a young Asian man in a stained shirt clutched his stomach, his eyes rolled back.

"Bellingham hot-dog-eating champion dethroned."

"Did I see this in the *P-I*?"

"Yes."

The next photo was of a police officer, a mother, and her son. The officer and the young woman faced each other, while the small boy leaned back against his mother, his hands cupping her knees. A dark look hung in the air between the adults, but the boy smiled, gleefully unaware, his mother's hands slammed over his ears. His T-shirt had chocolate ice cream stains down the front.

"This?" Jane's voice was pinched.

"The family of the firefighter who died last year."

"One of the four in the warehouse accident?"

"Yeah."

Jane lay the portfolio down. "Well, all we need now is a picture of someone actually killing themselves, and we'll have a real party."

Amina sat still, her face prickling with heat.

"Why didn't you include that one?"

"I thought it wouldn't be . . . applicable. To this job. Appropriate."

"And you'd have been right." Jane set the portfolio on the desk between them, folding it closed. "But then, none of these are really appropriate, are they? For the job?"

"You haven't seen them all."

"I don't need to. They're not what I'm looking for."

"But there might be something—"

Jane held up her hand. "Do you have any weddings in here?"

Amina shook her head.

"Birthdays? Anniversaries? Baptisms? Bar mitzvahs?"

"No."

"Of course not. Because that's not really what you do, is it?" It didn't seem like a question she wanted answered as much as said out loud, and Amina shifted as Jane smiled coldly at her. "What you do is get the stuff that people watch despite themselves. Meanwhile, I need someone who can take good portraits, who knows how to find the smiling moment and capture it. Someone who can replace me at the events." Amina jumped a little as Jane slapped her hand down on the desk in dismissal. "Thanks for coming. And please tell Dimple I send my best."

Amina did not move. She knew she should get up, say thank you, and head with quiet composure to the nearest bar, but she couldn't. Moving would lead to home, to the bed she was never far enough from anymore. It would mean she didn't have anything else to do in her week. And it was better in Jane's office, better than it had been anywhere else for a long time. She looked at the files and the memos and the calendar separating days into pristine units of time, aware of Jane's growing irritation the longer she sat.

"I understand your hesitation," Amina said at last, her voice coming out softer than she wanted. She cleared her throat. "The thing is that I really can do this."

Jane frowned. "I'm not sure you're hearing—"

"No, I can do it well." Her cheeks blazed. "I can. I have great references from the *New York Post,* and the photo editor at the *P-I* can vouch for me."

"Listen." Jane's voice dropped an octave. "Your cousin told me you were having a hard time after all the hubbub, and I agreed to meet with you, but I can't go giving out jobs to people just because they're having a hard—"

"I wouldn't expect you to pay me," Amina blurted out.

Jane blinked. "What?"

"I . . ." Amina licked her lips and felt the words come out rapidly, hitting her tongue and brain at the same time. "Not until you knew I could do it, of course. Until I proved myself. By shooting a wedding. Or weddings. A month of weddings."

Jane's mouth puckered.

"If you let me shoot with one of your other photographers, you'll see," Amina continued, breathless, terrified. "I wouldn't get in the way, and I would show you the finished product. If you like any of my shots, they can be made available to your clients. And if I'm not what you're looking for, you haven't lost anything." She pitched back against her chair.

"That's ridiculous," Jane said.

"It's free."

Jane looked her over warily.

"Fine," she said at last. "Get to St. Joe's on Capitol Hill on Saturday morning. A nice big Irish Catholic wedding."

Amina rose quietly, quickly putting her portfolio away before Jane could change her mind.

"Thanks," she whispered on the way out the door.

"Ten o'clock sharp," Jane replied.

That weekend, when Amina showed up at the Murphy-Patrick wedding, she saw someone she barely recognized. Gone were Jane's terse manner and the dark suit, replaced by a bubbly woman who gave everyone nicknames and winked like she had a nerve condition.

"Thanks, honeys!" she had shouted, waving a hand to dismiss the bridesmaids. "Now I want one with Snow White and Elvis and the Backup Singers! Yup, in a line, just like that."

The following Thursday had found Amina back in Jane's office, contact sheets spread across the light box in the corner. She listened to the silence of Jane's scrutiny—the woman was unnervingly quiet until she didn't want to be.

"Oh," Jane said finally, with some surprise. "This one is good."

"Which?"

"Bride-fixing-hair-before-ceremony." She glanced up. "Good angle."

She moved on to the next sheet. "Not bad. Most of these with the bridesmaids are decent. You need to watch your shadows a little, though, make sure you always cheat to make the bride look better than anyone else."

"Okay."

Jane paused again over the shots taken during the ceremony.

"Mother of the bride crying works," she said. "She'll think she looks noble."

Amina squeezed her hands together behind her back in a kind of inverted prayer, surprised by how much she cared. Jane moved quickly through the next sheet and the next. She came to the portraits outside the church.

"Oh." She sounded disappointed. "Your portraits are off."

Amina's stomach fluttered a little. "What?"

"They look uncomfortable." Jane pushed the loupe toward her. "Look. See how your group look like they'd rather be somewhere else? My guess is you're coming in late, when the smile gets a little tighter and the shine in the eyes fades. You've got to talk between shots to keep them with you." Amina heard Jane rummaging around next to her. "Look at mine."

The contact sheet Jane placed down on the light box showed bright-eyed, shiny-cheeked, smiling groomsmen, the Irish Catholic version of the Pips.

"Backup singers," Amina said.

"Exactly." Jane took the loupe back, skimming. "Your dance shots are good, but you need to get closer during the toasts."

"I didn't want to get in the way."

"Don't worry about that. Just be quick."

She moved on, nodding at several pictures, circling others with a red grease pencil. On the last sheet, her head stopped abruptly.

"What's this?" she asked.

It was the best picture Amina had taken all night.

"A bridesmaid."

"Obviously. I can tell by the bouquet and the shoes."

The shot was a side view of a bathroom stall. The bouquet lay at the base of the toilet bowl like an offering at an altar. Behind it, two taffeta-covered knees pressed to the ground, followed by calves and feet in scuffed satin pumps. And while Amina had known that the bride herself wouldn't want to see the picture, something—vanity?—had convinced her that Jane would appreciate it compositionally, suddenly understanding the talent she had in her midst.

"What is she doing?" Jane asked.

"Vomiting."

Jane straightened up and looked at her, the skin on her cheeks mottling. "You clicked a puker."

"It happened very fast," Amina said. "She didn't know I was there."

"At a wedding. You clicked a wedding puker."

"It was just a few shots."

"A bridesmaid, no less. Not someone anonymous enough not to care about."

"Well, but—"

"Stop talking!" Jane clapped loudly in front of Amina's face, shutting her up. "Do you have any idea how much trouble that could get us into?"

"I would never have shown those to anyone."

"Damn right you—*those*? Are there more?"

There were two more. One of the girl washing off her face, taken from the stall Amina had locked herself into, and another of her hanging over the hand dryer as it blew up at her face.

"She didn't see you?"

"No."

"How do you know?"

"Because she didn't. Sometimes people just don't."

Jane squinted. "I noticed that about you."

Amina blushed.

"You realize how disturbing these would be to the client?" Jane asked.

"I do. I mean, I do now."

"You didn't then?"

"No, I just didn't think . . . it just seemed like another part of the wedding until I saw the contact sheet yesterday, and—"

"It's unprofessional and asinine."

Amina waited for a scolding, some kind of advice, but when the silence grew until all she could hear was the sound of her own heart slapping in her chest, she understood that she needed to leave quickly. She packed her things with trembling fingers, sliding all the negatives off the light box and into her portfolio, shamed by the sight of the few pictures she'd gone so far as to print. Jane said nothing, sitting heavily behind her desk.

"Thanks," Amina said when she was done, not knowing what else to say. She made her way to the door.

"You can never take those pictures again," Jane said.

Amina stopped, turned around.

"And don't let me get a call from anyone telling me I sent a goddamn voyeur their way. Weddings are about fantasies—you understand? Your job is to photograph the fantasy, not the reality. Never the reality. If I ever see another picture like that, you're fired."

She opened her notebook.

"Does that mean that I'm hired?" Amina asked quietly.

"No. Not until I know you can do good portraits." Jane moved her finger down the page, scanning the schedule. "I've got another wedding coming up the day after tomorrow at the United Lutheran Church up in Queen Anne."

It was a crash course, a month of weddings, two per weekend. Jane and Amina wound their way through teary parents and tense couples, using a half hour during the week to review Amina's work. Jane could move through hundreds of shots quickly, critiquing some, dismissing some, scanning for anything out of line. At the last June wedding they worked together, she sneaked two flutes of champagne out behind the garden tent and told Amina she was hired.

"I've set you up with six weddings for July, and after those, you'll need to drum up your own clients quickly if you want to survive," she had said.

Amina had wanted to thank her but was afraid she'd do something stupid, like cry, or hug her too hard. Jane hadn't been looking at her anyway.

"Five messages?" Outside Jane's office with Post-it in hand, Amina stared at the pink slips the receptionist handed her. "I was only in there ten minutes."

"Four are from the same woman. And Jose came by looking for you, too. He said something about the Lorber print being ready, but didn't I send those out last week?"

Amina ignored the question and the look that came with it, walking down the hallway and frowning at the tight script that dotted the slips. *Lesley Beale, Lesley Beale, Lesley Beale.* "He's in the darkroom?"

"Yes."

"Thanks."

Amina continued down the hallway to the darkroom, stepping into the cylindrical door and coming face-to-face with Jose's rules. Posted on the drum, they specified that there should be no knocking any time, that no one should come in unannounced, or call on the phone between ten and six. While some in the office questioned Jose's definition of "being at work," all of the photographers were far too enamored of his prints to ever tell him so.

Amina knocked softly. The metal boomed around her, and she heard something drop on the other side of it, along with a long curl of something mean and Spanish.

"Jose, it's Amina. I'm sorry," she whispered.

"Well, don't fucking whisper now you made me fuck up!" Jose yelled through the door. "What do the rules say? Fuck Jose up, or leave him alone?"

"I know, I know, it's just I'm going to be leaving in half an hour, so if you have anything for me, I should get it now."

"*Puta!* In your office in ten."

Amina eased out the door and tiptoed into her office down the hall, carefully shutting the door behind her.

Unlike in Jane's office, where the sorted piles and color-coded Post-its gave the impression of a sort of collective organization, the piles in Amina's office left no such impression. She had never managed to make good use of the filing cabinet, preferring to leave her paperwork on top of it, while excess napkins and packs of ketchup lined her desk drawer. A single lamp hung over her desk, and she turned it on.

Lesley Beale. The pile of messages joined several others that lived in a heap at the corner of Amina's desk, and when the phone rang again, she took a deep breath before picking it up.

"Amina!" Kamala shouted. "You'll never guess what just happened!"

"Ma?"

A tumbling sounded on the other end of the line, and Amina heard her mother screeching, "Give me the phone, Thomas! Let me tell your daughter what the genius surgeon did this morning!"

There were more muffled noises and the sound of Thomas's footsteps thundering up what could only be the stairs. He breathed hard into the phone. A door slammed.

"Amina-Amina-Amina, I stole the phone!" he shouted, voice echoing like he was in a bat cave. "I'm in the bathroom! Here she comes!"

"Thomas!" Kamala pounded on the door. "Let me talk to her!"

"No!"

"Coward! Tell her!"

"No!"

"Tell me what?" Amina asked.

"Nothing," Thomas's voice chimed in with false innocence. "Nothing at all. And how are you this fine summer morning?"

"He lost the car!" Kamala yelled. More pounding. "His own car!"

"You *what*?"

"Nothing doing!" Thomas yelled. "Don't fill your daughter's head with such lies!"

There was a pause as he waited for Kamala's comeback, which did not come.

"She must be planning a sneak attack," Thomas whispered into the phone.

"You lost the car?" Amina whispered back.

"Oh, she's buzzing like one hornet's nest today, I tell you."

"What happened?"

"Nothing much, really. Your mother likes to make up stories, what else is new?"

"IN THE SHOPPING MALL!" Kamala yelled into the phone, having found another receiver, and Amina almost dropped hers.

"Bad thing, get off!" Thomas yelled back.

"And guess who had to save him?"

"Oh boy, here it comes. She's a saint! She's a saint!"

"*Lost* it lost it? Like you really didn't know where it was?" Amina asked.

"And it wasn't even at Sears like he said, it was at *Dillard's*!" Kamala snorted. "And then the best part! Tell her what you were doing there."

"I was shopping," Thomas said.

"Bullshits! He was at the hardware store getting keys made because he lost them! First the keys, then the car!"

"*Edi, penay.*" Thomas cut her off, slipping into Malayalam, in which Amina could only pick out a few words. Something about a goat. Something else about idiots. Amina pulled the receiver away from her ear. After a silence, a squeaky "Amina!" came from the phone.

"Yes."

"Did you say you're coming?" It was Kamala.

"My plane comes in Monday afternoon."

"Hey!" Thomas said, delighted. "You're coming?"

"She got some time off from work, so she decided to come see us," Kamala said quickly. "Not like some people's daughters."

"How long?" Thomas asked.

"Just five days. I'm coming Monday."

"Fantastic."

Amina bit her cuticle. She imagined her father in a pool of unfamiliar cars, windshields blank as shark eyes. Alzheimer's? Was this how it started? Thomas's beeper went off, and she heard him fumbling for it.

"Hey, *koche,* I need—"

"I know, I know, I hear it. Talk to you later." Amina listened for a few seconds after he hung up. "Is he off?"

"Mm-hm." Her mother sounded distracted. "My pen's not working; hold on. What time do you come in?"

"He lost the *car*?"

Kamala laughed. "I know! Can you believe it?"

"And you're sure he's safe working?"

"What do you mean?"

"He's seeing Ammachy and then he loses the car?"

"What? No! Not at the same time, dummy. He lost the car this *morning,*" Kamala said, as though that explained everything. "This other thing happens at night."

"But you don't think they have any connection to each other?"

"Of course not. Pish, this girl! Always overreacting to simple-simple things!"

"I'm not overreacting! I'm just saying that if he—"

"Your father loses everything twice every month for the last twenty-five years. It's funny, that's why we told you. Everyone loses the car in the mall!"

Amina pulled at the phone cord. A knock at the door jerked her head, and Jose's half-lidded, reptilian eyes slanted her way.

"I have to go," Amina told her mother.

"You didn't tell me your flight information," Kamala said as Jose ducked through the doorway, a flat yellow envelope in his hands, AMINA ONLY written on the front.

"I'll call you later."

Kamala banged the phone down. Amina stared at the receiver. Jose cleared his throat.

"Right." She looked up at him. "Sorry."

"You okay?" he asked.

"Yeah."

"You don't look okay."

"I'm fine." She glanced at the envelope. "What's that?"

"A beauty. Not that you deserve it." Jose slid the picture onto her desk. They stared down at a white-haired woman laid across a dark tabletop, her arms extending from her sides. The view was from her feet up, her scuffed shoe bottoms giving way to the twisted root of her body. Empty chairs lined either side of her like an invisible audience, and her mouth hung open. The halo around her was barely perceptible, a lightness that made her body rise from the table. A man crouched next to her, his lips pursed.

"Jesus," Amina said.

"That's exactly what I thought!" Jose said, his voice betraying his excitement. "I put in a little bit of light just around her head and body. I brought out the detail of the shoes, you know, like that. And I can go heavier on the man's face in the corner if you want. I just sort of liked it, you know, with her as more of the focus."

"No, I like him soft." Amina looked at the woman's hands, her curled fingers. "The hands are nice, too. This is one of your best."

"*Your* best. Man, I don't know what I'd do around here if you didn't keep me rolling in a steady supply of nasty. She didn't die, did she?"

"No, just passed out from excitement. She was fine when I left." Amina carefully picked up the picture and slid it back into the envelope, then into her bag. "Okay, what kind of filling do you want?"

"Veggie. Also, I need more of the green stuff."

"Chutney."

"Whatever."

Amina wrote the order in her notebook. "My cousin and I are meeting someone in your neighborhood on Sunday, so I can drop them by if that works."

Two years before, when Jose had gone out of his way to print one of Amina's shots in an 18 x 20, he had almost gotten her fired. With just the right amount of light and shadow to enhance just-married Janine Trepolo getting cake pummeled into her face by a slightly too forceful groom, Amina had been sure that it was Jane's version of a pink slip when it arrived in a manila envelope on her desk, AMINA ONLY on the front. She was on her way to her employer's office when Jose asked if she liked it. Only after confirming that no one else had seen the picture could Amina confess that she loved it, and then, not having anything else to offer, had given him half her lunch. When the next print was ready, Jose asked for more samosas. "Trade for trade," he had said, a notion that so clearly pleased him that Amina saw no reason to disabuse him of it, never mind that she bought the food from a well-hidden restaurant in Magnolia.

"You and Dimple are going out in my 'hood? And I'm not invited?"

"Yes, actually."

"Man, when you going to introduce us? Five years you've been here, and I still don't know that girl."

"You're married," Amina reminded him.

"We have an agreement."

"So you say."

"You don't believe me?"

"I believe you'd tell me a lot of things to get to Dimple."

"Dimple," Jose said, licking his bottom lip, "is a human samosa."

"Stop."

He smiled wide, his short, flat teeth making him look like a gremlin. "Go on, gimme that lecture on *sexism-racism-ismism* now, you know you're dying to."

The phone rang, and Amina shooed him toward the door with a hand. "Give yourself that lecture. I have work to do."

CHAPTER 3

There are small blessings, tiny ones that come unbidden and make a hard day one sigh lighter. The weather that greeted Amina on the ride up to the Highlands neighborhood for the Beale wedding on Saturday afternoon was just that kind of blessing. Yes, it was a bit cooler than it should have been in June, but the sky was scattered with a few pale clouds—perfect for everlasting union. The Commodores sang "Easy" on the radio, and she sang with them, *Why would anybody put chains on me* sounding existentially good. She was easy. She could make Lesley Beale happy. At ten minutes before two, she pulled into the Seattle Golf Club parking lot, where one of the many green-clad grounds-keepers waved her around to the back entrance.

"She had some trees rushed in this morning for the long hall," Dick, the bean-shaped grounds manager, explained, pressing a linen handkerchief to his upper lip as Amina passed through the doorway. "No one can go in for the next hour or so."

"Is she here yet?"

"She's been setting up the women's lounge for the girls since ten. Eunice is back there, too."

"What happened to the library?"

"Changed her mind, changed her mind," Dick said, then turned abruptly to answer the question of a woman holding an armload of lilies.

Of course she had changed her mind. Changing her mind was a kind of sport for Lesley, whose clipped charm, equine good looks, and marriage to the heir of the Beale department store fortune had long ago turned her into the exact kind of person whose mind did not worry over how much each change changed. A fleet of handsome catering staff passed Amina as she made her way down the hall.

"Hello?" Amina walked into the lounge.

"Oh, good, I was just starting to wonder about you." Lesley, in a crisp and flawless origami of white linen, watched as an older woman placed a crystal vase in front of each mirror. "To the left, Rosa. More. A little more. Good."

Amina set her bag down, quickly glancing around. The room was a riot of competing pinks. Rose curtains, walls, and carpet glowed under chandeliers. Eight mirrors were ringed with baby-pink Hollywood lights, a peachy wingback chair sitting in front of each like a misplaced cockatoo.

"You'll need to put your stuff in the coat check," Lesley said.

"No problem. Just let me get set up."

"Good idea." Eunice, the perpetually startled-looking wedding planner, stood up from where she'd been squatting on the floor, one hand clutching a spool of white ribbon. "The girls finished at the salon early and are on their way."

Amina nodded calmly, pulled out a light meter, and started taking readings from around the room.

"Where are the lilies, Eunice?" Lesley asked.

"Excuse me?"

"For the vases. They need to be in place before the girls come."

"Right. I just don't, ah, I think because we were going to be in the library and you decided the textures would compete?"

"But we're in the women's lounge."

"Of course! Let me . . ." Eunice's fast walk out the door was a blur in the corner of Amina's increasingly worried eye. Low, pink light. She needed to fix low, pink light before everyone came out looking like fried chicken under a heat lamp.

"Amina, can you put your things down the hall at the coat check? They're cluttering up the room."

"Yup, one sec."

"More to the left, Rosa."

Amina walked to the wall and flipped the few remaining switches up until the place blazed like a flaming tutu. Good God, the mirrors. She might as well be shooting in a funhouse.

"Mom?" The whoosh of the dressing room door revealed the bride-to-be, cutely diminutive in an oversized man's shirt and capri pants.

"Jessica!" Lesley smiled carnivorously. "You're early!"

"Yeah. The other bride was half an hour late, so they took our party first. I felt bad for her, but I mean, whatev, right?"

"Whatev," Lesley echoed with a goofy grin. "So let's see."

Jessica twirled around and Amina ran for her camera just as the door opened again and in came the rest of the girls—tan-limbed, smooth-haired, piled high with bags upon bags, plastic-wrapped dresses, several shoe boxes, a portable CD player. Accessories spread out over countertops. Jackie, the maid of honor, announced that she'd burned a special "love"-themed compilation for the occasion. Amina stepped frantically onto a chair to get a bird's-eye view of the commotion as Madonna filled the air.

"Did anyone bring an extra razor?"

"I did." Jackie held it up like a trophy, which would have been a great shot, but taking the picture sent a blaze of flash through all the mirrors, and Amina's pulse went rabbity.

"Amina, your bag?"

There was a loud knock at the door, accompanied by a deep "Is everybody decent?" Brock Beale shoved through it half a second later, steel-haired and pug-nosed, his buttery gaze falling over the girls. "And how are my favorite ladies today?"

Lesley and Jessica, busy with the clasp of a pearl bracelet, barely looked up, but Jackie turned around with a sweet smile. "Wow, Brock. You look great in a tux."

"You think?" He looked at his profile in the mirror, patting a toned midsection. "I can never quite get comfortable."

This was a lie, a charming one, as there was absolutely no doubt in Amina's mind that Brock Beale was just as comfortable in his tux as he was in pajamas, but it served the purpose of making Jackie all the more adamant in her reassurances, which in turn made him look all the more comfortable. The flash, when it went off this time, made both of them wince.

"Amina, the coat check," Lesley repeated.

"I just need to get a few more shots."

Lesley stepped in front of her camera. "Now would be great."

Amina swallowed a flash of irritation, intently panning across the room, but all the girls had grown too aware of her suddenly, their limbs stiff with the nothing noise of smoothing on deodorants and hairspray.

"Go," Lesley said. "You could use a break."

Cooler air hit Amina's face as she walked out of the women's lounge and back down the hallway. She shivered a little as she turned the corner and headed toward the ballroom, cluttering bags in tow. Lesley's trees stood sentry on either side of her, mummified in plastic. A few men measured the space between them.

"Coatrack?" Amina asked them, not stopping.

"Keep going back," one of them said, and Amina walked faster, past the ballroom, past the kitchen, to the back of the greeting hall. She found the coat check—a few open racks just to the side of a back door—and snatched the first hanger she could.

"Can I help you, miss?" A teenage boy with a blond buzz cut and a face like a ferret seemed to materialize out of nowhere, tugging on the shirt cuffs that peeked out from a short burgundy jacket.

"I'm just hanging my suit."

"I'll do it."

"I already did it."

"Get your number?"

Amina stared at him, not comprehending until the kid reached for the ticket hanging from the neck of the hanger, tearing it off and giving it to her.

"Thanks."

The kid smiled a funny smile at her, like they were on the inside of someone else's joke. "I'm Evan."

"Amina."

He looked past her to the reception hall. "This one is going to be a pain in the ass, isn't it?"

"Pretty much."

"Good luck."

"You too."

Lesley had been right. It both chafed and relieved Amina to admit this to herself, but somehow, the walk to the coat check had reset her. When she returned to the women's lounge, she had found the right perspective, which ended up being right next to any of the mirrors, cheating slightly away from the center of the room.

Now, four hours later, she swayed in the middle of the dance floor. Couples shuffled around her in huddled pairs, smiling at her through the lens. The room was thick with the smell of celebration—lilies, men's cologne, wine, and warm skin.

With the ceremony over and dinner under way, the bride had relaxed into the groom's body, her small frame folded in his tuxedoed arms like a dove between palms. Jessica looked younger and softer than she had during the ceremony, and when she turned her face up to her new husband's for a kiss, Amina knew she had gotten the picture they wanted more than any other.

The shots from the day would be to Lesley's liking, showcasing the Beale style, taste, extravagance. Lesley really had thought of every last detail, from the fruit and champagne and truffle bar to the silk-ribboned seating cards to special games for the kids and the tiny silver Space Needle favors. And while Brock had thrown a stiff arm around his wife for the family photos, holding her as though she were a mini-fridge, the rest of the bridal party was carelessly, casually pretty, the guys tall and just beginning to put on the weight that would make them spread into their fathers, the girls toned and groomed and glossy.

On the dance floor, Amina turned to find Lesley and an older man waltzing slowly beside her, and she moved in step beside them to get a better angle. They bent their heads together.

"We'll be cutting the cake in about fifteen minutes," Lesley said through her teeth. "If you want to take a break or eat something, do it now, okay?"

She was not hungry for anything but air and space. Out in the hallway, caterers walked by with trays full of stacked plates and empty glasses. It was brighter and cooler in the hall, golden light bouncing from cream walls down to burgundy carpet. Amina passed the kitchen with its muted clatterings, its smell of gravy and dishwater.

Lesley had also been right about bringing in the trees. Unwrapped, they proved to be very tall shrubs, pruned to perfect cones as if they'd been uprooted from a gnome's forest. The effect was strangely magical. Amina ran her palm against the bristles of one, then stepped behind it and peeked out to take a picture of the whole row, slant after slant after slant after slant.

The band in the ballroom announced the cover of a special request, and after a pause, the woman's voice sang out the breathy first line of Etta James's "At Last." Chairs barked as guests rose to greet the champion of all wedding songs, the one that always brought indifferent or fighting or estranged couples to the dance floor for momentary reconciliation. If she hadn't already taken too many dance shots, Amina would have headed back, but instead she kept walking, *My lonely days are over* following her down the hall like a forlorn ghost.

The coatracks were filled now, Amina saw as she walked toward them. The arm of her jacket stuck out from the mostly black coats like a drowning victim, and she looked at it longingly. How nice it would be to walk the twenty feet across the carpet, to pull it out and put it on and leave. She nearly screamed when it moved.

The rack moaned. Amina's gut bunched up into her chest as a head rose up from the middle of the coatrack and sank down again.

"Fuck," she heard someone say. She ducked behind the tree to her left.

The rack was moving now, the coats shivering as if cold. The head rose up again, and Amina pulled the camera up to her face, her heart beating staccatos into her fingers. The head bobbed lower, then turned suddenly, roughly, facing her. Amina froze, waiting to be spotted, but the maid of honor's eyes were closed, and stayed closed as Amina zoomed in. Her pink mouth hung in an *O*, lips wet. The girl's head moved in beats, rising and lowering, and Amina focused in tight on Jackie's face, holding her breath to press the shutter. She pressed the shutter again as the girl reached out to steady herself, one manicured hand wrapping around the wire neck of the hangers, her head dipping to the side. When she moaned again, a man's hand covered her mouth. She leaned forward into it. The coatrack disappeared in a thunder.

Through Amina's lens, they were beautiful—pinned like sea creatures on a tide of black coats, limbs flailing against each other in fantastic spasm, white against the dark. The girl lay facedown, the flowers in her hair smashed to pulp. Under her, two ankles bound by pants ran in place, trying to find some footing in the mounds of material. Amina was swallowed by a clean calmness, fingers and eyes and lens suspended in the air twitching, twitching. She watched as two large hands grasped Jackie by the waist, throwing her roughly to the side. Underneath, Mr. Beale clutched his thigh, the whites of his eyes shining as Amina pressed the shutter again.

Jackie moaned.

"Get up," Mr. Beale barked, but the girl did not move. Her breasts dangled out of her dress, and she fumbled, trying to pull the material back up.

"Oh my God," she said.

"Get up *now*," Mr. Beale said again, pushing her shoulder.

The swishing noise just behind Amina sent the camera to her waist, her lungs cinching. She turned to see the coat checker hurrying down the hallway toward them, eyes stuck on the scene in front of him. Amina followed behind him, slinging her camera around her back. Mr. Beale frowned as they approached, and Amina looked away as he stood and yanked his pants up.

"I'll, um . . . take-take-take care of the coats, sir," the coat checker stuttered, and Mr. Beale stepped off of them.

"Jackie, get up," Mr. Beale said again, calmly this time, like he was talking to a toddler, but she didn't stir. She was looking behind him, behind all of them. Amina turned around to see the grounds manager in the hallway, with Lesley and a few guests trailing behind him.

"What's your name, son?" Mr. Beale asked the coat checker.

"Ev-Evan."

"Evan, let's you and me see if we can lift this thing." Mr. Beale motioned to the coatrack. The folly of this was evident by what was on top of the coatrack, namely, Jackie, hands smashed over the bodice of her dress. Amina looked at Mr. Beale, who looked at the grounds manager, who looked at the coat checker, giving him a sharp nod, so it was the coat checker who bent down to the girl, hoisting her up clumsily while the guests looked on. Underneath her, Amina spotted her own crumpled coat.

"Too much to drink," Mr. Beale announced loudly as the help heaved the coatrack up off the floor. "No big deal."

He gave the guests in the hall a knowing wink, and Jackie's face filled with color.

"I'm so sorry about this, Mr. Beale," the grounds manager offered quickly. "Evan is new here and doesn't know—"

But Mr. Beale waved away the rest of this sentence, walking to where Lesley stood with the hollow-eyed look of a cat ready to spring. He put his arm around his wife. "Let's all just go back inside, shall we?"

And how did it happen, the calm turning around, as if there were nothing to actually see besides Brock Beale's unfortunate explanation? Amina could not quite fathom it, and she couldn't look at Lesley again, so she stood still in the wake of receding people, her hand clutching her camera as if it were in danger of being swept away with the easily swayed current.

"You've got to be shitting me." Dimple stood in the back doorway of the gallery, paint fumes and blindingly white walls leaking into the alley where Amina stood. "So you just left your coat there? They'd better goddamn reimburse you."

"Yeah. That's their first priority, I'm sure."

"Well, at least it was ugly anyway."

"It was?"

"Did she know? I mean, she must have known."

"No idea."

They walked to the car, Seattle's Saturday-night Pioneer Square crowd milling drunkenly around them. A few recently emptied beer bottles had been added to the truck bed, and Amina tossed them out, opening the door for Dimple, who ducked her head in and sniffed around suspiciously. "What fucking masala bomb went off in here?"

"It's samosas. We've got to drop them off at Jose's on the way."

"They're on my seat! I can't sit there now."

"Come on. We're running late."

"Great, so I'm going to have curry stink."

"Sajeev's Indian. He won't care."

"I'm Indian. I care."

"You've got issues."

Dimple put the bag of samosas on the floor and climbed in gingerly. She cracked her window and reached under the seat to scoot it up, then stopped. She pulled out Jose's manila envelope.

" 'Amina only'?"

"It's just wedding stuff." Amina reached for the envelope. "Gimme."

Dimple pulled away, opening the flap.

"Wait, don't!"

But it was too late. Dimple was already sliding the picture out, her face lighting up like she'd swallowed a sunset whole. "Holy Christ, what happened to her?"

"Nothing!"

"She OD'd?"

"She's a grandmother!"

"So they can't OD?"

"Dimple, give it!"

"Someone wanted a copy of *this*?"

"It's not—yes. They did. Can you just—"

"Who made the print? Nice work."

"Jesus, Dimple, it's confidential! For a client! Can you not stick your nose into everything for, like, five seconds?"

Dimple loo[...]
of her, then, whe[...]
They rode in silence,[...]

"So what—"

"Dimple."

"I was just going to ask wh[...]
time, you freak."

"Oh." Amina's shoulders dropp[...]
skinny boy they had avoided as kids, th[...]
dunno. The same. Quiet. Bucktoothed. To[...]

Dimple laughed. "That's mean."

"It's true. So, which bar?"

"The Hilltop," Dimple said, and Amina groane[...] Hilltop was frequented by the kind of people who sized one another up by their shoes. "I know, I know, I tried to get him down to the Mecca. It wasn't happening. He insisted on a place where he could get us dinner."

"He's getting us dinner? Isn't it kind of . . . formal?"

"Dinner is nice."

"But for us?"

"Listen, the whole conversation kind of threw me. One minute I was trying to figure out how to negotiate drinks down to coffee, and the next I was saying 'Sure, yeah, dinner on you, great.'"

Amina looked at her cousin. "Are we going on a date with Sajeev?"

"Not even in his fantasies. There's a space."

The Hilltop was bustling, filled with polished faces of women who looked like the "after" images on a magazine makeover page, and men who looked for women who looked like that. Amina smoothed a hand over her own peach-colored dress, part of the wedding-ready work wardrobe that Dimple insisted on calling "Cadbury Couture."

"Holy shit," Dimple said, and Amina's eyes homed in on the long arm waving to them across the bar, the dark eyes and smile just beneath it.

"Holy shit," she agreed.

Sajeev had grown into his nose.

in almost every way, and half an
_____rsation, Amina could not stop shifting her
_____ly white teeth (still slightly bucked) to his toned
_____quinting like he was made of sun. Strangely, the years since
_____n school had turned him *pretty,* the femininity of his thickly lashed
eyes offering strange friction to his button-down shirt, jeans, and tennis shoes just nice enough to let you know they cost more than Italian leather. Something charged with vetiver and sandalwood escaped from the neck of his shirt every time he leaned over, leaving her aroused and suspicious. What kind of a guy wore cologne to dinner with family friends? Certainly not the Sajeev she had imagined they would be meeting. As he detailed where he lived (a few blocks away), what he was doing (programming centered on artificial intelligence), how he liked Seattle (all good but the rain), Amina slipped quietly into a dazed, oversaturated place. Dimple, for her part, was in rare form, her eyes and teeth and fork winking like flashbulbs as she gave him a three-minute life update for both of them.

"And what kind of work do you show at the gallery?" he asked.

He didn't know Dimple well enough to catch the slight flare in her nostril, the disdain for what she often called an "art for beginners" question, but she humored him, saying, "I like all kinds, but what we look for at John Niemen is actually the dialogue between works. We always feature two photographers in every show, and I look specifically for what the works will lend one another. It's a conversation of sorts."

"Is it a conversation other people understand?"

"Just the smart ones."

Sajeev leaned back in the booth, one long arm draped across it. His mouth had a funny way of twisting into a little bow in the corner when he wasn't talking, and Amina wondered idly if he could lift Dimple with one hand. There was certainly enough in the glances over his beer that made her think he wouldn't mind trying. "So who's up next, then? Anyone I'd know?"

Dimple stabbed a tomato wedge on her plate, trying, and failing, not to look self-important. "Are you familiar with Charles White?"

"The guy who makes everything look like a bad acid trip?"

Amina laughed as her cousin set her fork down. Charles White's

work had been a revelation for both of them in college. His most recent photographs, a series taken at a women's shelter and featured in
Art in America, had stayed open on Amina's bed stand for months, its
pointed article about the male gaze much less interesting than the
photographs themselves—lushly colored, taken at angles stark enough
to make the shelter look like Wonderland, its inhabitants modern-day
Alices.

Dimple rearranged her napkin in her lap. "I find his work pretty
remarkable, actually."

"Oh, no doubt! Absolutely remarkable." Sajeev stuffed a French fry
into his mouth. "And so who will Charles White be, ahhhh, convers-
ing with?"

"I don't know yet. I had someone who didn't work out." Stress rose
on Dimple's shoulders, pulling them toward her ears. She'd been in a
quiet panic for weeks now, trying and failing to find the right fit.

"Wow. That's got to suck." Sajeev leaned in, smiling. "I mean, you
don't want to get anything too domestic, right? That would make
Charles White's stuff seem forced, maybe even mean. But anything too
esoteric and you risk mounting a big surrealist in-joke, right?"

Amina looked at him, understanding a little too late that Sajeev
knew, and possibly cared about, photography. She saw a flash of confusion cross her cousin's face, but before either of them could respond,
he settled back farther in the booth, waving a hand at them.

"So you"—and here he indicated Amina—"take pictures, and
you"—his hand brushed Dimple's forearm—"put them up. So when is
Amina's stuff going to go up?"

A pungent silence fell across the table. Amina took a sip of beer,
watching Sajeev over the rim of her glass. Had he really turned into
one of those men who thought asking the uncomfortable question
proved something about his integrity?

"I've asked," Dimple said, just as Amina said, "I don't have anything to show."

Sajeev looked surprised.

"You would if you tried," Dimple said.

"Stop," Amina warned. She looked at Sajeev. "I don't take the kinds
of pictures Dimple needs. I'm a wedding photographer."

His mouth puckered like he had tasted something off. "Wait, really? I thought you were some hotshot photojournalist."

"No."

"Because my mom used to keep your stuff, you know, clippings Kamala Auntie sent. And didn't that one with the guy—what was his name?"

"Bobby McCloud," Amina said softly, eyes darting around the room.

"That's right! That was huge, no?"

Amina nodded, the slow creep of dread filling her lungs.

"And you just stopped? Just like that? I mean, you were really talented."

"Jesus, Sajeev, she's still talented!" Dimple snapped. "It's just a fucking hiatus. You don't need to make it sound like she's dead or something."

Sajeev flushed deeply, looking unsure of himself for the first time all evening. "I'm sorry. I didn't mean it like that."

"Don't worry about it," Amina said, and turned with relief to the waitress who was fast approaching their table.

"How are you guys doing over here? Does anyone need a refill?"

"Please," Amina said. She had no idea.

He walked them to the truck. Amina tried not to laugh out loud about this, a little embarrassed by the chivalry of it all, but Sajeev hadn't asked or offered, he'd just strolled out beside them, turning in the direction Amina pointed to when he asked where they were parked.

"So, cool," he said when they reached it. "You're sure you're good to drive?"

Amina rolled her eyes. "I'm fine. Dimple's the lightweight."

"I am not! I'm just small!"

"Because my mother would kill me if anything happened to either of you," Sajeev said. "And then Sanji Auntie would kill me again."

Amina smiled. "Fair enough."

He had been distinctly nicer since Dimple's cut-down, the little whiff of vulnerability on him making Amina remember him as a kid.

"How is she doing anyway? God, I don't even think I asked about the New Mexico clan. How is everyone?"

"Well, let's see . . ." Dimple held out a hand, ticking off six fingers. "Sanji is probably knee-deep in the annual Indian Association Benefit planning, Raj is cooking himself into an early heart attack, Kamala is inducing guilt wherever possible, Thomas is telling himself stories, and my father is probably frowning at my mother's choice of outfit at this very moment."

Sajeev laughed a deep, appreciative rumble, and Amina watched Dimple grow a little tipsier from it. They reached the truck.

"So, I live here now," he said. "I mean, obviously, I uh . . . but anyway, would love to hang out sometime."

Dimple opened the door, slid in, and rolled down the window. "Amina's leaving for the week. You're lucky we even got her out at all. She's like a ghost during wedding season, always stuck at everyone else's party."

"Where you going?" Sajeev asked Amina.

"Home. Short visit."

"Nice. Well, tell everyone hi for me. And Dimple, maybe I'll stop by the gallery sometime this week? I work right around Pioneer Square."

"Oh yeah?" Dimple asked, a little more excited than she would have let herself be sober.

"Yeah." He bent down, looking her square in the eye for a moment before thumping the door twice, backing up and walking away.

"Now that," Amina said, waiting until he was out of earshot, "is definitely a date."

It was late by the time Amina arrived home, later still by the time she got the truck unpacked. The film and the camera came out first, along with her light meter, and then she went back to pull Jose's envelope from under the seat, holding it flat under her arm. The rain had cleared just enough to let some moonlight into the apartment, and she kept the lights out inside, peeling the dress off and letting it slide to the floor. She put the kettle on for tea.

In her bedroom, she felt around the floor for her sweats, sliding one leg then the other into the sensible black fleece and then looking at herself in the dark, in the mirror. She looked like she had come to rob her own house. In the kitchen, the kettle screamed.

Mint. Always mint, always the red mug. She grabbed the envelope with the photo in it on her way back to her room.

A whiff of cedar rushed out as she opened the closet. She tugged the light on, walked in. Boots and shoes lined either side of her like cobblestones, and she made a path through them, reaching for the pile of coats in the back. She lifted them.

And there it was, smooth and small as a child's coffin. The russet wood glided under her hand; the tiny brass handles were cool on her fingertips. In Montana, the woman who sold her the antique flat file laughed at the two hundred dollars Amina had offered, telling her she could never accept that much for "drawers that won't hold a damn thing." When Amina told her they were for pictures, the woman laughed again, and took the money.

One by one Amina opened the drawers, pulling out the contents in order. She moved methodically, careful not to look down. It was important not to look down. It was important to be ready.

When every drawer was empty she walked out of the closet and back to the window seat, and placed the picture from Jose on top. She looked at it again for a long minute, staring at the scuffs in Grandmother Lorber's shoes before flipping it over.

Underneath was Dara Lynn Rose, on the morning of her second wedding, her hand wielding a large hairbrush. She was screaming, her teeth bared like a tiger's, thin strands of spittle hanging from them. Seconds later she had chucked the brush at her husband-to-be as he fled the room. ("I'm superstitious," she had explained to Amina later. "My first husband had a heart attack chasing a black cat off the lawn.")

The next was Loraine Spurlock, looking up at her stepfather with adoring eyes. He bent to kiss her, his mouth open, his tongue lying in it like a wet animal.

Then came the McDonald sisters, Jeanie and Frances, their four hands gripping a just-thrown bouquet, splitting the baby's breath with determined fingers. They smiled through jaws hard with determination.

Amina moved on to Justin Gregory, the five-year-old ring bearer who had been told he couldn't leave once the ceremony started. He stood behind the bride and groom, staring up at them with a tiny pillow in his hands, a wet stain spread down the front of his crotch. A puddle shimmered at his feet.

Wide-lipped Angela Friedman and her new son-in-law greeted Amina in the next shot, her fingers digging into his neck as he kissed a bridesmaid on the cheek. Then it was the gray coil of Grandpa Abouselman, legs folded like newspaper against his wheelchair while couples danced in the background.

Amina lifted picture after picture, soothed by the rise of a lip, the splay of fingers, the stillness of passing disasters. She knew them well. She felt images rise off the page, the lines of one bleeding into the next until hands turned into flowers and veils became windows. Her heart unbuckled for the familiar faces, their familiar pains. She shuffled through them slowly until at last she was looking at the satin-covered knees pressing the ground next to a toilet, the bouquet on the tile floor. She stared at this one for long seconds, her fingers pressing against the edge. And then the stall turned into the underside of a bridge, the bouquet into a falling man. She was looking at Bobby McCloud.

CHAPTER 4

The George Washington Memorial Bridge, more commonly known as the Aurora Bridge, has been an anomaly in Seattle since its construction in 1932. In a city where eight-lane highways have been avoided in favor of two-lane roads that break for the rise of drawbridges between sweetly named neighborhoods—Fremont, Queen Anne, Ballard—it has always been violently off scale, looking from below like some terrible, sky-slung hammock. Touted as the final link in the Pacific Highway, it became the destination of choice for Seattle's suicidal before it was even completed. The first person to jump off the bridge did so in 1932, one month before its opening to commemorate George Washington's birthday. The 176th person arrived on August 26, 1992.

August in Seattle: an eternity of dusk that hints at Greek mythology, a sun setting so slowly over the Puget Sound that everyone looks like immortal versions of themselves. On August 26, 1992, it made them want their picture taken.

"Just one quick one, okay?" The Korean guy standing in front of Amina was too small for his cargo pants.

She looked at her camera apologetically. "I'm actually on assignment for the *Post-Intelligencer.*"

"Great." He smiled and threw his arms around the two women at his sides. "Cheese!"

Amina did a quick calculation in her head (time explaining job versus time taking picture) and hit the shutter release. Fine. Done. She avoided eye contact with anyone else as she walked across the deck of the *Crystal Blue,* fighting the claustrophobia that crept into her lungs when on a yacht.

This particular yacht was teeming with the young programmers and developers of Microsoft. If it was jarring to see other kids just out of college having their success celebrated with an evening of play on the Puget Sound, it was downright annoying not to understand them. What on earth was a Linux? The very idea that something called C++ existed made her want to drink, but she was not there to drink, she was there to capture Seattle's newest elite, their hoodied shoulders and chipper smiles.

"Give us a *feel* of the event," the photo editor's new assistant at the *P-I* had said, as though Amina would be attending a cashmere sweater. She had wandered around overwhelmed. She hadn't found her shot yet, and now, crawling through the locks and canals on the way back to Lake Washington, she could feel her need to get off the boat as sharply as a full bladder.

"So fucking cool, right?" a guy with orange shorts said to his friend, pointing at the Aurora Bridge in front of them. "I can never get over how cool that looks. It's so, like, Legoland, right?"

"Totally," the friend agreed. "Majorly Legoland."

Amina had slipped behind them, trying to get the right angle on their beers raised in toast to the cantilevered spine, when she saw the man. He was standing in the middle of the bridge, dressed in yellow with white on his face. A clown. This is what she thought at first. She zoomed in and saw a feathered headdress. She took the picture.

The guy in the orange shorts turned around. "Hey, didn't see you. We should turn around, no?" He flashed her a smile.

"No . . . I . . ." She pointed at the bridge. "I was taking a picture of that guy."

Orange Shorts followed her finger. "The guy cleaning the bridge?"

"I don't think he's cleaning it."

"He's wearing a uniform."

"He's wearing feathers," Amina said.

"What?"

The *Crystal Blue* was slipping through the water at a steady pace, gliding closer to the bridge and the man, and now Amina could see him clearly through her viewfinder, his headdress shivering in the breeze.

"Hey, did they arrange for a bungee jumper?" Orange Shorts called out, pointing at the bridge. Heads turned up. The words buzzed over the lips of the crowd.

"Bungee jumper!" Someone yelled. A whoop went up from the boat.

This seemed to startle the man in the headdress, and he wobbled on the bridge uncertainly, eliciting a collective gasp. Amina moved to the edge of the prow, steadying herself against the railing.

The high wail of sirens seeped toward them, growing louder. Police cars were coming down Aurora in a steady line, and an ambulance followed, lights flashing. The whole boat seemed to swell with recognition: *Look! Police! It's a jumper!* People were pressing in on her sides now, and Amina nudged them away, ignoring a disgruntled huff in her ear. She pulled her lens wide to get a better read on the cars, and this is what she was doing when Bobby McCloud decided to take a step forward. Not that she knew his name, or anything else about him at the time—all of those details would come later, as she scoured every last article she could find.

For weeks, months, she would wonder what made her ratchet up the aperture so suddenly, what guided her finger to the shutter release so that when Bobby McCloud flew past her lens, she would capture him. And yet she had done it. She'd gotten the impossible shot. In the photograph that appeared next to the article, her first ever and only to run on a front page, Bobby McCloud would appear forever suspended between the arching underside of the Aurora Bridge and the flat screen of the water, his headdress folding against the air like wings in prayer, his arms flung wide.

"Spectacular," the photo editor had said before rushing the picture to print.

He had pulled a few other pictures from her roll ("Where are the afters?" he had asked, looking fleetingly disappointed when she shook her head) and now turned his attention to the televisions in the far corner of the room. All three local stations were covering the story in as much depth as the few hours allowed, taking statements from eyewitnesses and panning again and again to the railing on the bridge.

Amina watched, wishing she felt sick, or distraught, or anything other than coolly relieved. Even the Microsoft crowd had the decency to be rattled—telling and retelling the last twenty minutes of the ride in shaky voices, as if there were some clue between seeing the man and watching him fall that would reverse the motion. One woman just bawled and bawled until two female colleagues hoisted her to the lower-deck bathroom.

Amina left the office, driving immediately to Linda's Tavern. Forty minutes later, snug in the peaty blur of three beers, she ordered a fourth. When the door opened to reveal a young man wearing a jacket that looked like the one Akhil died in, her hands began to shake.

It was the money that killed him. That's what the papers said, first the *P-I* and *The Seattle Times,* then the *San Francisco Chronicle, The Washington Post,* and *The New York Times* as the story went national. The $162 million settlement for the Puyallup Tribe of Tacoma Indians— the second-largest in history between the Native Americans and the U.S. government—had come for Bobby McCloud like it had for his brother, his cousin, and his uncle before that.

In the library, hunched over the microfiche reader in a sour-smelling sweatshirt, Amina followed the previous years' news. The tribe's decision to give up their claim to the land along the Tacoma basin had been contentious from the start. The land—18,000 acres that were allotted to them in the Treaty of Medicine Creek in 1854 and then slowly poached in a series of "negotiations" that left them on about 33 acres by 1934—was their birthright. Taking money for it was a direct refutation of that right, and of everything their ancestors had stood for. It would only bring harm, even if it did give every member of the tribe twenty thousand dollars right away.

Blood money, Amina heard Akhil saying so clearly that for a minute it seemed the past nine years had not actually occurred. She looked up from the hum of the microfiche, but the only other person in that dank corner of the library was an old man who looked half-asleep. She read on.

Opinions on taking the settlement varied widely within the tribe, as did the imagined uses of the twenty thousand dollars. People said they'd get food, winter clothes, but some expressed misgivings.

"I'm just trying to make sure I don't blow it," Raydene Feaks, a thirty-four-year-old recovering crack addict at the tribal treatment center, said (PUYALLUP TRIBE PREPARES FOR WINDFALL, *Seattle Post-Intelligencer,* February 23, 1990).

"The twenty thousand is not the point," Bobby McCloud maintained. "The one hundred thirty-eight million in social programs, and business start-up money, and land—that's going to be the end to our poverty."

Bobby McCloud did not drink. He did not smoke, and he did not allow smoking in his office at the Tribal Center, where pictures of him with Jesse Jackson and Bill Clinton hung on the walls, along with his diploma from the University of Washington. At age thirty-six, Bobby McCloud was one of the very few in the tribe who had managed to dodge every statistic coming at him, from the eight-thousand-dollar median income to the ninth-grade level of education to the 50 percent chance of becoming dependent on alcohol or drugs by the time he was sixteen.

"Everyone is saying our birthright is the land. Our birthright is to live! It's to succeed, and grow, and watch our children grow," Bobby McCloud said.

A-fucking-men, Red Man.

She must have PTSD. Or maybe it was just run-of-the-mill drunkenness. Or simply the obvious reaction to stumbling into the exact kind of story that would have infuriated her brother. The second time Amina heard Akhil, she was in bed, photocopies of Bobby McCloud articles scattered in piles around her. She blinked down the dark hallway that cut through the center of her railroad apartment. It was empty. She got up and shut the bedroom door.

When the phone rang, jolting her out of a midafternoon nap, Amina knocked over the glass of water on her bedside table. "Shit."

"They are calling because you own the rights," Dimple said. "You've got to do something."

The water spilled over the edge and began pattering down on the last shirt she'd worn outside of the house three days earlier. Amina added a few stray socks to the pile to soak it up. A mostly full bottle of whiskey stood sentry on the nightstand, watching.

"Amina, are you listening to me?"

"Yeah."

It had been a mistake to tell Dimple about the calls. Of course she was going to want to "take advantage" of the offers coming in from agencies wanting the picture. Of course she would see this as an opportunity for them to "cut their teeth" (an expression that always brought the image of a horse bit into Amina's mind) in the world of agencies.

"We've got an open window now," Dimple was saying. "Right now. Not forever and maybe not even tomorrow. All we need to do is make some calls. I guess I just really don't understand what the fucking problem is here."

Stop the presses. Dimple doesn't understand something.

"Shut up," Amina said.

"What?"

Amina pressed her eyelids until circles popped in their meaty darkness. "I just . . . I think the *P-I* might own the rights."

"No. They. Don't." Dimple took pains to enunciate. "Remember when we went back and forth before you signed the contract? That was about owning the rights to your pictures. The *P-I* is *allowed* to use the picture because technically you were on assignment for them, but after that the rights revert to you. Anyone who wants the picture needs to deal with you."

"What if I don't want to be dealt with?"

"That's why I'm saying *I'll do it for you.*"

Surely all that was required was a yes, thank you, a quick disconnection. A roll back under the covers, back to dreams riddled with Akhil. But it was coming again, the cold grip that had arrived with the previous day's paper, the name Bobby McCloud, the stunned grief of the people who loved him clenching over her entire body like some big fist. What could they have felt when they saw that picture? What had she made them see? Amina shivered.

"Ami, are you there?"

"They're never going to be able to unsee it."

"What?"

"He had kids. Did you know he had kids?"

There was a long silence on the other end of the line.

"I'm coming over," Dimple said.

Bad idea.

"Don't!" Amina cast a quick eye at the piles of chaos around her room, the bottles, the butts, the newspapers. "You'll get in trouble at work."

"Just to bring you lunch, okay? We don't even have to talk about it if you don't want to."

"Dimple, I'm fine."

"Yeah, okay. See you in ten."

"No! Stop! Jesus, just give me a moment. I was asleep when you called. I just need to get my bearings and—it's fine, okay? Do it. You should do it. Negotiate it with the agencies or whatever. Go for it."

"Oh, God, I don't fucking care about that now. I wasn't thinking, okay? I know this is about Akhil. Just let me come."

"It's not . . ." Amina heard her voice cracking and swallowed. "Can you just please just take care of the agencies? That would really help."

She held her breath, waiting for Dimple's conscience to wrestle through the moment.

"Really?" her cousin asked after a few seconds.

Amina exhaled. "Yes."

"Okay, but I'm coming right after work."

"I've got plans that might go late," Amina lied. "I'll call you."

After, when the phone was back in the cradle and Dimple was safely held at bay, Amina leaned off the bed, needing to put something between herself and the afternoon light slipping under the shades. And though it was not her style, really, though it reeked of women's television dramas and asking-for-it from some damning God, though it was overblown and overdramatic and more than a little bit disgusting, she pulled the bottle off the nightstand and took a sip, gagging as it hit her gut.

Cheers, kid.

He had underestimated the power of the money. Not the $138 million— Bobby McCloud was right about that portion—which, wisely invested in the Emerald Queen Casino and the Chief Leschi Schools, really would pull the tribe out of permanent poverty. But the effects of the $20,000 settlement checks on individual members of the tribe—that he had misjudged entirely.

"Bobby used his smarts and his place in the tribe to give us away wholesale today," his brother Joseph "Jo-Jo" McCloud told reporters on the Tacoma Sheraton steps immediately after the signing ceremony (TRIBE TRADES LAND FOR FUTURE, *Seattle Post-Intelligencer*, March 24, 1990). "If our parents were alive, they'd be weeping."

From May 1990 to the beginning of 1991, the Puyallup Indians lived what one anonymous tribal member referred to as "a big eight months of the American dream." Cashing a single check worth more money than many made in two years, they bought cars (Firebirds, Z28's, fourth-hand BMWs, a team of pickup trucks), vacations (Disneyland, SeaWorld, Vegas), necessities (diapers, gas, food, heaters, tires, clothes), and nonnecessities (family portraits, dinners out, drugs).

By June 1991, a year and a half after the checks were cut, an estimated 75 percent of those who had received the money had spent it all.

Well, there's a fucking shocker.

"It's understandable," Amina said, folding the paper in half.

No one said it wasn't understandable.

"Don't believe that romantic BS about when you don't have money, you don't realize what you're missing. When you're hungry and broke, you feel plenty bad," said tribal member Gladys Johns (ONE YEAR LATER: THE PUYALLUP TRIBE LOOKS BACK, *The Seattle Times*, March 23, 1991). "But when you have money and it goes? Then it feels worse."

Vacations became a series of photographs. Houses swallowed down payments and spat out inhabitants. Cars were repossessed so regularly that coming out of a bar to find that someone had "stolen your horse" was less embarrassing than it was inconvenient.

"It was killing Bobby," childhood friend and tribal member Sherilee Bean told *The New York Times Magazine* ("Buying Off the American Conscience," October 12, 1992). "All of us, but Bobby especially. Everyone was hit so hard when the money dried up. Even those of us who spent it wisely or invested, we still had to watch our brothers and sisters crash."

In January 1992, Uncle Ronnie McCloud was found in a Las Vegas hotel room, dead from a ten-day alcoholic binge. In March, cousin Michael John was paralyzed from the neck down in a truck crash. In May, brother Jo-Jo McCloud swallowed two bottles of aspirin. He died on May 15, 1992, after spending three days in a coma.

"Aminaminamina!" Thomas crowed into the answering machine. "Wake up, fuzz head! Shake off the day! Rise and shine! Tell us all about it! Your mother's head is already swelling like a balloon, and we haven't even gotten to—"

"But why can't you be telling us anything, *koche*?" Kamala sounded bitterly pleased. "Bala herself says Dimple says some picture of yours is on the front papers and everyone wants it, and now that Queen of Sheba is calling and telling Sanji and Raj and God-knows-who-else like it's *her* daughter who—"

"And she said something about in *The New York Times Magazine* itself?" Thomas asked. "You must send a copy!"

There was a brief pause while Amina's parents, spent, breathed silent elation into the phone line. Then they hung up, Thomas first, Kamala next, and only after reminding Amina to send the picture and also to please rub the coconut oil into her hair once a week to make it blacker.

In the late afternoon of August 26, 1992, Bobby McCloud parked in the parking lot in the back of the Still Life Café and walked up Fremont Avenue to Sally's Party Supply. There he bought the "Cherokee Male" costume for children ages fourteen and up. Seven minutes later, having changed into the yellow plastic fringed shirt and pants in the employee bathroom, he headed out of the store.

The first check of several that would arrive throughout the year was more than Amina made in three months. It was certainly more than she would make in September and October, seeing as how she had all but stopped working. She set the check on the kitchen counter and watched as a patch of sunlight moved over it, half expecting it to turn to ash, and lighting another cigarette when it didn't.

Blood money for blood money, huh?

"Fuck off."

She tried to always keep a cigarette lit now. Knowing that she would burn down the apartment if she slept kept her in a dull panic, ensuring that she stay awake. Sleep was to be avoided, if possible. She had begun to have dreams, and they were obvious, and the obviousness of them infuriated her. Bobby McCloud war-painting himself with batches of tempera. Bobby McCloud reading her the entry for the Spanish-American War from the 1979 edition of the *Encyclopaedia*

Britannica. Bobby McCloud standing in high branches of a cotton-wood tree, showing her the wingspan of a full-grown man.

The protestors were the first nonpublication to use the picture. They marched across the Aurora Bridge, each wearing a single feather, poster boards proclaiming OUR BIRTHRIGHT IS TO LIVE raised high.

Then came the counterprotestors (THE SINS OF OUR FATHERS, AGAIN, *The Wall Street Journal,* September 19, 1992).

Then came the liberal hand wringing (PROBLEMATIC PATRIOTISM, *The New York Times,* October 10, 1992).

But what was there to do, really? What was there to do in a town that had itself been wrested from the Duwamish Tribe, where liberalism was cherished but most of the black population lived behind a Wonder Bread sign, where there were rumors that the university had been built on sacred burial grounds? As debate over the meaning of Bobby McCloud's death built momentum, his figure leapt out of the photograph and onto the silkscreen, showing up like a Rorschach blot on everything from T-shirts to mugs to pins. NEVER FORGET, these items said, and THE CHOICE IS YOURS, and BEGGARS CAN'T BE BOOZERS (this last put forward by the Students for Deliberate Misinformation, a group whose "consciously confusing message" was part of a mission to "expose the unreliability of the media").

Amina had wondered briefly at the irony of receiving the message with a morning beer in her hand before she unplugged the television and placed it on the stoop to be stolen. She had had enough. It would stop now.

And it would have stopped then had it not been for the op-ed piece written by Bobby McCloud's aunt Susan, a comparative litera-ture professor at UC Berkeley. It ran three weeks later in *The Seattle Times* for all to see:

> That we even have this image says a lot about our ability to disas-sociate from the pain of others around us. It takes a certain lack of feeling, an internal coldness, to capture a shot like this. That it

was taken by a photographer covering a Microsoft gathering is a perfect, if horribly sad, metaphor for how quickly we will trade in our humanity for financial gain.

"I'm sorry, but this passes for intellectual discourse?" Dimple fumed, raising the blinds with a rattle. "Blame the fucking *photographer*? Ridiculous."

Amina watched her cousin swoop across the bedroom to the other window, hair pulled into a tight bun, swaddled and cinched into a black drapey dress that made her look like a vampire bat.

"I mean, it's a stupid fucking argument, you know that, right? A free press *depends* on photojournalists providing an unblinking account of what's out there."

Of course she goes straight to censorship.

"And what's Professor Genius going to demand next?" She grabbed the ashtray on the sill and emptied it into a trash can, sending up a puff of gray. "That we put pictures of puppies and kittens on the front page so no one gets their feelings hurt?"

Jesus. She hasn't changed a bit, has she?

"Not really." Amina's voice was a scratchy whisper.

Dimple wrinkled her nose at the mound of clothes by the side of the bed. "I mean, listen, is it a shocking photo? Yes. But it wasn't taken for shock value. And it wasn't orchestrated, for fuck's sake! The whole idea that somehow you're lacking empathy or even *thriving* on this is so—" She picked up the half-empty tumbler on the nightstand, sniffing at it. She frowned. "Wait. Really?"

Amina shrugged. "Our dads drink whiskey."

"Exactly." Dimple laughed uneasily. "So what, you're going to take up the Suriani habit of drinking yourself into a nasty middle age?"

Still hating on the race, huh?

"More or less."

"What?"

"Nothing."

"No, what did you say?"

"I'm not talking to you."

Her cousin's eyes blazed with some combination of anger and concern, and for a minute Amina felt the hot shame of causing it. She shut her eyes. She did not need to look around the room to see it as Dimple must have—graffitied with clothes, bottles, ashtrays, plates of uneaten food lying across the dresser.

"Ami, what the fuck? What's happening to you?"

What does it look like?

Amina shook her head, the prick of guilt between her ribs redirecting into disdain with surprising alacrity. Because really, wasn't it easy to be Dimple? To be able to talk about what was and what wasn't appropriate, to sell it regardless, to live on what you made without thinking twice? To be floating in such a steady stream of self-righteousness that you never had to face the muck under you?

"I took the picture," Amina said.

"So what?"

Don't say it.

"I knew what I was doing."

"Because you're a *photographer.* Because it's what you do."

"Because I wanted it. That's why my fingers tweaked the settings before anything even happened."

"Amina, you didn't make Bobby McCloud kill himself."

"Because it would make a good picture," she explained. "I thought the man falling would make a good picture, that it would be beautiful, like that was the important thing?" She laughed to cover up the way her mouth had begun trembling. "Can you imagine? Like he was some bird for the *National Geographic,* some fucking animal, some—"

"Ami, stop it."

"Because I *needed to see it.* After all these years, I needed to see what it looks like to fall that far down!"

"No."

"And did I tell you I didn't look afterward? I didn't even look! I heard the noise of the hit and turned and walked away because I'd already gotten what I needed."

"Stop it!" Dimple grabbed her arm. "Enough! Stop with this shit and listen to me! *You did not make this happen.* It was a beautiful picture. It was a horrible moment. Both."

Amina began to cry.

"*Both*, Ami." Dimple's nails dug into her wrist. "That's what you have to live with. Okay? That."

Amina pushed her away. "Get off me."

"Are you the photographer?"

"Who is this?" This was not good. The woman on the phone had already said her name twice. Identified the publication she was working for. The *Times*? The *Chronicle*? Why was the phone in her hand? Amina stared at the receiver. The little black dots looked like poppy seeds. They cooed.

"What?" she asked them.

Careful, kid.

"Careful yourself!"

"Excuse me?"

"Hi."

"Am I speaking to Amina Eapen?"

Amina put the receiver back to her head. "You are."

"Do you have a response to the charge that the picture you took exhibits a lack of humanity?"

Oh for the love of—it all lacks humanity! Fucking HUMANITY lacks humanity!

Amina thought about this for a while. About humanity, but also about hubris, that weird word that made her think of a compost made of human souls.

"The checks keep coming, though," she said.

"The checks?" the woman on the phone asked.

"And I keep cashing them!" Amina said, her voice registering her surprise. "So that's something, I guess."

"You are talking about the reprinting fee for the picture you took of Bobby McCloud?" Amina heard the chattering of a keyboard in the background. Robots. Computers were turning humans into robots. The tongue was connected to the fingers to the keyboard. "Do you feel implicated by the money you are making from this?"

YES.

Amina looked around. She found some water, gulped half of it down. "I knew what I was doing."

"Ms. Eapen?"

"I knew he would go."

"What do you mean?"

What did she mean? She saw the high school parking lot, the spray of late-afternoon sun, Akhil walking toward the station wagon, his shoulders hunched under his leather jacket. The words formed loosely in her head and then rolled out her mouth like pebbles. "Hide-a-key."

"Excuse me?"

"I was the only one who knew about him. *Really* knew. I'm the only one who could have stopped it. I guess I just . . . fell asleep at the wheel, you know?" It was a horrible pun. The hideous noise, the laughter, was coming from between her throat and her heart, some place that if stepped on would paralyze her instantly and forever.

Hang up, Ami.

"Did you have dealings with Bobby McCloud prior to his suicide on Wednesday?" the woman on the phone was asking. "Did you know him before this encounter?"

"But are you supposed to believe everything he says? Ben Kingsley, for the love of God!"

"Excuse me?"

Hang up NOW.

"Ben Motherfucking Kingsley," she gasped, her shoulders shaking.

"Ms. Eapen, did you or did you not know Bobby McCloud before his death on August twenty-sixth?"

Amina laughed and laughed and laughed. She needed to hang up the phone, and she did, but not before whispering, "I've known him all my life."

BOOK 3

THE INDIGNITY OF BEN KINGSLEY

ALBUQUERQUE, AUGUST 1982

CHAPTER 1

August 29, 1982, was full of promise. Clear and sunny and just a little too warm for the teal corduroys that Amina insisted on wearing, the day swam brightly in front of the car as Akhil pulled down the driveway, beckoning them toward the first day of school. The air smelled sweet and green; the rearview mirror held their mother at a safe distance at last. Amina watched Kamala recede, small and jittery in a pink nightgown that all but swallowed her.

"Do you think she's going to be okay?" Amina asked. The trees curled in, obscuring the front door.

Akhil frowned, thinking this over. He thought it over the entire length of the driveway, and the dirt road after that, and then the main road. He stopped at the intersection that would lead them to the west mesa, to school.

"Who fucking knows anymore," he said.

———

Mesa Preparatory was unquestionably pretentious. Just what pretense it was operating under was not apparent to most of its inhabitants—the progeny of New Mexico's elite—who, despite their supposedly cosmopolitan upbringings, knew very little about Andover or Exeter or Choate, much less what their brick-building campus, nestled into the west mesa of Albuquerque, was striving toward. What they did know was that they went to the most expensive private school in the state, that the soaring expanse of their green soccer fields drew the envy of other schools choking on dust, and that uttering the word *Mesa* when pulled over by Albuquerque cops had a beneficial effect on anything from a speeding ticket to a DUI.

"Welcome back to Athens in the desert!" Dean Royce Farber crowed at the morning assembly, releasing a flurry of eye rolling but also a sense of self-importance that defined Mesa students for better and worse.

The summer of 1982 had been about as long and hot as any in New Mexico, and the gymnasium sweated scents of overly chlorinated pool, recently varnished floors, new jeans, pencils, erasers, sneakers, notebooks, and hair shampooed with Vidal Sassoon. Under the darkened scoreboard, administrators and faculty sat erect in their folding chairs, legs crossed and ties knotted. Sports coaches stood behind them, green-and-black tracksuits gleaming like beetle shells.

"No matter where you were this summer," Farber said, raising his head and pausing, as though weighing the air with the bridge of his nose, "chances are that if you're a Mesa Preparatory student, you were making a difference."

Amina stared at the legs of her new cords, already hating everything. Why hadn't Akhil mentioned that she was supposed to be making a difference this summer? Memorizing the words to every Air Supply song ever written was hardly interesting. Roaming from one end of the Coronado mall to the other while waiting for Dimple to come home from camp in California was borderline pathetic. Even her outings to the Rio Grande with her father's old Nikon seemed painfully tame for something she had just an hour ago considered adventurous. She scanned the faces framed between upturned collars, the hair side-parted and gelled, the eyes searching out one another's flaws without ever seeming to leave Dean Farber. She looked for Dimple.

"I know that many of you spent your summer embroiled in activities with your family, taking vacation in a variety of locales, and I imagine it is hard to come back to campus. Nonetheless, I'd like to welcome you back to the Mesa Preparatory family, and introduce a few new members of our faculty and staff."

Embroiled in activities? There was a beehivey quality to the phrase that made her think of thin limbs working in unison for some greater, sweeter good. As for her own family, Amina couldn't even remember the last time they had eaten dinner together, much less embroiled themselves in any activity that didn't involve a television set. Which was not to say there were no family activities at all. In June, for example, she and Akhil had witnessed a spectacular fight that left her parents haunting opposite areas of the house (mother, garden; father, porch). All of July there was father hunting, an activity never mentioned aloud but practiced with alarming diligence, whether it was Kamala staring at the clock at dinner or Amina checking for the balled-up men's socks left in the bathroom hamper, or Akhil staring furiously down the driveway. By August there were even sessions of group longing, a sort of inverse Quaker meeting, in which all three remaining Eapens sat on the couch and didn't say a thing about his near-total absence.

Amina looked around the gymnasium to the other dark heads nestled in with the lighter ones. Jules Parker, the black kid, was staring at the scoreboard with an open mouth that suggested hunger. A few rows beneath him, Akhil looked half asleep. It was a blessing, really, the reality of her brother blunted by something as tame as boredom. Akhil had become intensely articulate and demented in puberty. A deadly combination of political conviction, quick temper, thick chub, blooming acne, and antagonistic views he would defend until hysterical had made him nearly impossible to have in the house.

Outside the house was worse. In the previous spring alone, he had become engaged in an "abusive interaction" with the PE coach over the merits of running, a heated exchange with his French teacher over the country's "limp-wristed approach to democracy," a locker room

fight with four boys who called him Tonto, and a time-intensive protest of Reagan's nuclear-arms policy, in which he chained himself to a
desk at school and had to wait the eight hours it took the superinten-
dent to locate the bolt cutters.

"Those of you entering your freshman year might feel uncertain
about your future," Farber was saying. "Perhaps you've heard about
the rigorous course load here, or the demanding schedule we keep, or
our standards of academic and athletic excellence."

A derisive murmur came from a few rows behind Amina, followed by a burst of laughter. Amina turned to see Dimple tucked like
a chick between the preening bosoms of three sophomore girls who'd
apparently decided she was too cool to endure the usual freshman
awkwardness.

"I say this to you: There are times that you will be scared. There are
times when you will question your ability to take on the day. But I
would ask that you remember in those times that more is expected of
you at Mesa Preparatory because *you are simply capable of more*. And
now, I'd like you all to rise for the school motto."

Four hundred Mesa Preparatory students rose to face the flag emblazoned with their school seal. Akhil had at least prepared her for
this much. He had even gone so far as to imitate it, face glazed, voice
psychotically pleasant.

"*Timendi causa est nescire*," the students chorused, and Amina
mouthed along the way she sang church hymns, uncommitted to the
sound of her own voice. It left her feeling like a traitor, though who she
was fooling—God or Dean Farber or herself—was a mystery. *Igno-
rance is the cause of fear,* indeed.

"He's totally been checking me out." Dimple jostled the load of books
in her arms, trying to smooth them into an orderly pile. They were
walking back to the freshman building together, Dimple having de-
tangled from the sophomore girls to catch up with Amina.

"Dirk Weyland?" Amina asked.

Dimple's face slid into the cold look she'd picked up at camp, along
with an entirely new vocabulary, bleached hair, loads of string brace-

lets, a vague disdain for everything but the beach, and familiarity with the bases as applied to the human body (she had been to third twice in July).

"I just didn't know that you guys had talked or anything," Amina said.

"We haven't really, but I've seen him watching me. And Mindy said that he's going to be at David Lewis's party this weekend. So."

Mindy. It was strange that a name Amina hadn't even known until a few weeks earlier could have become a constant pinch in her breathing. Mindy Lujan, the sophomore who'd taken freshman Dimple under her wing; Mindy Lujan with her feathered hair, bullying blue-lined eyes, and potty mouth that rivaled Akhil's, managing to use *fuck* as a verb, an adjective, and a noun, often in the same sentence, as in, "Who the fuck does that fucking fuck think she's fucking with?"

"Doesn't Dirk have a girlfriend?"

"*Ami . . .*" Dimple sighed. "They've been seriously breaking up all summer. You know."

Amina did not know, nor was she under the delusion that she suddenly *would* know if she were invited out with the volleyball team and given the opportunity to glean the kind of details that passed for currency at Mesa.

The crowd was thicker as they neared the building, everyone trying to squeeze through the glass doors like salmon in a fish run. The tide of students pushed them into the locker bay, where Dimple stopped and fished around in her bag with one hand, pulling a crumpled schedule from it. "What do you have now?"

"English, then photography, and biology. What about you?"

"Bio with Pankeridge?"

Amina looked down at the slip of paper on top of her English book. "Yes."

"Oh, thank God. We have bio together."

Amina tried not to smile. Her smiles, she knew, had the opposite effect that they used to on her cousin, placing an unmistakable damper on whatever warmth had summoned the gesture in the first place.

"Did you hear that some girl got kicked out last year for not being able to complete any of her dissection labs? Her life was, like, so over."

Dimple looked smaller suddenly, more like the girl who cried into Amina's hair before she left for camp.

"That's not going to happen to you."

"What if it does?"

"We won't let it." Amina said, and was privately elated by the look of relief in Dimple's eyes. "So I'll see you at lunch?"

"What? Oh." Dimple looked back at her schedule, pretending to see something on it. "Maybe. Let's just see how it goes, yeah?"

"Right," Amina said, and turned to find her way to her next class on her own.

In the car on the way home, Akhil smoked furiously.

"Fucker. What a fucker. Capable of more! And the worst part is he believes it! They all fucking do."

Every window in the car was open, Iron Maiden was screaming from the stereo, and still she could hear him perfectly. The mesa rumbled by in a blur of dust. Amina's hair whipped around her face.

"And you know what the most unbelievable thing is?"

"Can we roll up a window?"

"That he thinks we're on *his* side. As though he can dictate the terms of our fucking mental growth!"

Amina started to roll up her window.

"Not right now! I'm trying to think."

"Can you maybe do it without all the expletives?"

Akhil flipped down the volume, smashed the cigarette between his lips and sucked it, squinting at her. He blew out smoke. "Who do you have for English?"

"Mr. Tipton."

"Goddamn prick."

"I thought everybody loved him!"

"Because they're sheep. Don't start quoting him unless you want me to leave you on the side of the road." Akhil accelerated. Spirals of dust blossomed behind them. He jammed in the lighter and opened the glove compartment. "Who else?"

"Messina for photography."

"I heard she's okay."

Mrs. Messina hardly looked okay, with her deathly pale skin and mud-colored lips and smell of patchouli, but Amina nodded. "Gerber for history."

Akhil shrugged. "Whatever. What about bio?"

"Pankeridge."

"Ballbuster. Don't screw up the labs."

"Great, Dimple's already freaking out about the whole dissection thing."

"She should be. She's fucked if she can't nail it."

Amina stared out the window. She was always messing up with Dimple these days. Not being interesting enough, not getting things that were supposed to be obvious. Her cousin hadn't really wanted to talk about the blurry pictures Amina had taken when she got back from camp, or the ridiculousness of Akhil's "Mad About Mutually Assured Destruction" campaign. She had scanned Amina's room like it belonged to someone else's kid sister, and shrugged at the possibility of walking to the Rio Grande. In fact, the only aspect of Amina's life that seemed worth commenting on was the seethingly quiet Kamala, whom Dimple had immediately pronounced "a serious mental case."

"I don't want to go home," Amina said.

Akhil took a long drag, flicked the butt out the window. "I'm sure Mom's fine."

"All day? Without anyone?"

"Well, maybe she'll get it together. Maybe that will be a good thing."

"So she can be more like Monica?"

"I don't think he meant that."

The words had haunted them, of course. Never mind that outwardly they reassured each other that the fight in June was just one more skirmish in their parents' never-ending battle; inwardly they felt damned by the very sight of it, instantly hardened, their hearts crystallized with shock. What on earth could have prepared them for the late-night return from an office party, the car idling in the driveway, lights on, doors flung open, their mother screaming like her back was on fire? The noise alone had brought them running to the front door, and as all children are riveted by the sight of parental demise, what they saw kept them there. They had never seen their mother drunk before (and, in fact, would never see her drunk again), but there she was, lit from the knees down by the car headlights, sari pooling at her feet, screaming, "Go live with your precious Monica in the hospital then!" like she was a soap opera star.

"Drinking like that in front of the people I work with?" Thomas had shouted, pacing the driveway. "What do you think they think of you now?"

"Isn't that what you yourself told me? 'Monica this and Monica that and why can't you be more like Monica?'"

"Monica can hold her liquor!"

"Monica is a *whore.*" Kamala stumbled a little, frowning down at her ankles.

"She is my assistant, Kamala. You will not talk about her that way."

"Touching you!"

"The Americans do that! It's their way. You would know if you knew any!"

"Now he's going to start again about this job business, and I tell you, I will kill him. I will kill him to tiny pieces!"

"We're not going back, Kamala. You have to at least try to fit in."

"Yes, because there's nothing to do here between cleaning up after your children and cooking them meals and making sure they are doing their homework, right?"

"*Do* something. Volunteer at a shelter. Get a part-time job."

"And now he thinks I am sitting like some fine Mughal princess, counting up my bangles while the bloody servant girls take care of things! Why not wander around all day in some office and come home and cook the dinner and clean the house like some stupid woman in a perfume commercial?" She started to laugh. "Well, Emperor What's-His-Name, I refuse."

"Kamala—"

"I REFUSE." She glared at him. "You think that changing and changing and changing ourselves to fit in with these people is some good thing?" She tilted her chin up, daring him. "Fine then. You do it. Go away and become some idiot who smiles all the time for no reason because I don't care anymore! I really don't."

The surprise was that he had gone away. As Amina and Akhil stood in the open doorway, their father marched straight back to the car, gunning the engine and roaring back down the driveway. If he saw them standing there, it didn't stop him. Nor did he return for dinner the usual one to two nights after a fight. For days and then weeks, their father was not seen during waking hours.

Kamala went into angry, gourmet mourning. She made every meal as though it might be Thomas's last, churning out flaky parathas and paper-thin masala dosas only to watch with fury as they grew limp in his absence. She plucked coriander leaves as *Dallas* and *Dynasty* unfolded on the television, sickened and consoled by the sordid love affairs Americans seemed genetically predisposed to partake in. She borrowed Bala Kurian's Hindi movies and watched them to the exact point where everything fell apart, and then walked around her kitchen, scolding the cupboards.

Amina sighed, tugging against her seat belt. Who knew what they would find when they got home? She knew better than to try to guess. The traffic into the village was at a dead crawl. Akhil sucked his teeth, fiddling with the radio, trying to needle in on the hard-rock station that always faded out as they got closer to home. He sighed and snapped it off. Reached for the glove compartment. Amina kicked her foot up, stopping him.

"We're too close now. You'll reek."

"She won't even notice."

"She's not stupid."

"No, she's just too pissed to care."

Amina sighed. By now she should have been used to the way her mother could perch anywhere in the house, so riddled with fury that she seemed not to see anything in front of her, but it was always disconcerting to walk into the living room and find Kamala smoothing down the same patch of armchair over and over again, or worse, start a conversation in which her mother's reply was an abrupt departure for another room.

"Do you have any gum?" Akhil asked, and Amina reached into the first pocket of her backpack. Juicy Fruit. She handed him a stick before slipping another out of the foil and into her mouth. Then she turned the radio on and inserted the Iron Maiden tape, taking comfort in the sugar and the screaming as they inched their way home.

CHAPTER 2

"So?" Kamala asked. "How was it?"

Amina and Akhil stared, speechless. It wasn't just the plasticky-looking jumpsuit, or the hair she had obviously untwisted from a braid to remold into a high ponytail, or even the tennis shoes Kamala wore on her feet, clean and white and laced in place like intergalactic marshmallows. It was her smile. Somehow in the last eight hours, their mother had become *chipper*. Her eyes and lips glistened with pinks and purples as she leaned against the kitchen counter.

"You like all your teachers?" Kamala nodded.

"Yes," Amina said, automatically nodding back.

Akhil scowled. "What's on your face?"

"I went to the makeup counter at Dillard's."

"Just like that?"

"What *just like that*? I need your permission?"

"What are those?" Amina asked.

"Parachuting pants!" Kamala looked down at her own legs like they belonged to an actual skydiver. "They're the latest things."

Akhil looked so baffled that his mother laughed, giving curve to her bronzed cheekbones. Her eyelashes fluttered like the blackened wings of an underworld butterfly, and Amina wondered at the evenness of the thick black line under each eye until she realized her mother was looking back at her with increasing alarm.

"You look great," Amina said, and a spasm of discomfort flitted across Kamala's features.

"How about your teachers? They're good?"

"They suck eggs," Akhil said, glancing around the kitchen as though there might be more changes hiding in the cupboards.

Kamala shrugged amicably. "Oh well, that's how it goes, right? Win things, lose things."

Amina nodded. Win things, lose things. Sure. Their mother turned from them to a boiling pot on the kitchen stove. She lifted it to the sink, releasing the muddy smell of hot potatoes, and then opened a drawer, rummaging around for something. "Why don't you both get started on your homework? Your father is on his way home, so we'll eat soon."

"Dad?" Akhil's eyebrows shot up. "What's the occasion?"

"First day of school, silly." She fanned the steam from her face.

"So?"

"So? So he wouldn't miss it."

"Since when?"

"Since now, Mr. Curmudgeon!"

"Are you having an identity crisis?" Akhil asked.

"I don't know what you're talking about." Kamala retrieved a potato masher and held it up like a trophy. She smiled. "Now, why don't you and whatever radical leftist policies go upstairs until dinner?"

Akhil said nothing as he left the kitchen. They listened to him stomp up the stairs. Amina sat down on a chair and watched as her mother moved around the kitchen. It was remarkable really. The shiny pants hugged her hips, and from behind, her mother looked like any other Mesa Prep girl.

"You look so different."

"Bad?" Kamala looked at her reflection in the microwave.

"No, just different."

"I wiped off most everything. But I bought myself a lipstick."

"Can I see?"

Kamala pointed to her purse, and Amina opened it and pulled out the lipstick.

"Berry Delicious?"

"Oh, I don't know about that," her mother said with an embarrassed laugh. She opened a drawer and pulled out a knife. "So, you like school?"

"Gina Rodgers is in all of my classes."

"The knows-it-all."

"Yes."

"Ach. Poor thing. No one will ever marry her."

"Mom! She's my age."

"Not now, dummy, *later*. I had a friend like this in college, Ranjini Mukerjee. Such a pill, that girl! And no one wanted to marry her."

"Um-hm."

Queen Victoria, a fat German shepherd with a permanently unimpressed bearing, wandered into the kitchen, sniffing in the direction of the parachute pants before settling on the floor.

"But it's a pretty school, no?" asked Kamala. "So big!"

"It's okay."

"What does Dimple think?"

"I have no idea."

"No classes together?"

"Just biology."

"Well, that's probably a good thing, no?"

Amina sighed. "If you say so."

"Oh, Ami, don't be so tragic. You just need some time apart to grow into your own people." She sliced the top and bottom off an onion and then whacked it in half. She placed the flat side down and cut the rest into colorless rainbows, tears pooling in her eyes. "People need to grow apart sometimes to grow back together, you know."

How did everyone know? Was it so obvious? Amina's throat grew tight, as though someone were turning a bolt in her voice box.

Her mother wiped her eyes with the back of her hand, cursing at the onions. "Anyway, that girl is a little wonky in the head. Comes from Bala's side of the family, you know, delusions of grandeur, excessive vanity. All the women have it. Why do you think they gave her some ridiculous film-star name?"

"Why did you give me a ridiculous Muslim name?"

"Not ridiculous, well behaved! Amina and Akhil are names of good children!"

Amina slid off the stool. "I'll be upstairs."

It was good in her bed. It was soft, warm, and, even smelling of too much Jean Naté, comforting. Amina rolled over onto her back. Her Air Supply poster was deftly wedged between the second and third bar of the canopy, hidden from the disdainful gazes of Akhil and Dimple. Amina loved Air Supply. She loved the album *The One That You Love*, with its hot-air balloon hovering in a ringing blue sky; she loved singing "Lost in Love" even though she had been told repeatedly not to; she loved the way the lead singers, Russell Hitchcock and Graham Russell, shared a name *and* quavering, teary voices, like they had been shattered in the middle of the desert, like they, too, had lost their whole world to a long, hot summer.

"I'm all out of love," she whispered to them now. And then that thing happened that had been happening to her all summer—the hollow ache at the back of her throat went away as she thought of her camera. Her camera! Where was it? And where was her assignment for the week? Half a minute later she had dug both out of her bag, laying them side by side on her bedspread.

Assignment 1: PLACES, SPACES, THINGS
Take this week to show us your world, specifically the places you inhabit, whether that is a classroom, bedroom, or some other place you feel at home. THIS ASSIGNMENT IS NOT ABOUT PEOPLE, rather the rooms and spaces that you move through. Think about the light in each space, and the way it contributes to the mood of the picture. Think about how much honesty can lie in a collection of THINGS. Experiment with shutter speed and aperture (see booklet for details).

Amina picked up the camera and panned around her room. The wall color had been a mistake. Lavender had been in that year, rolling off the tongues of the other fourth-grade girls like a foreign language, and she had mistaken it for her own. The dresser and the desk, bought at two separate garage sales, sat next to each other. Ponytail holders, barrettes, bobby pins, and several Jean Naté products crowded the surface of the dresser, while next to it the desk was empty of everything down to its flat, shiny surface. On the shelves: Indian dolls, records, Rubik's Cubes permanently locked in mismatched colors, the sorrowful plastic gazes of stuffed animals she no longer loved but could not bear to throw away. Clearly, she could not take a picture of anything in her entire room.

"What are you doing?"

She panned suddenly to the doorway, where Akhil stood. "Learning how to use this thing."

"Oh." He leaned into the room, picking up a barrette from her dresser. "Well, you can take pictures of me if you want."

"The assignment is about *things*, not people."

"What *things*?"

"The things that make you, you know, yourself. Your things."

"That's retarded."

"No it isn't. It's honest." She zoomed in on Akhil's face.

"So you're going to take pictures of that gay Air Supply poster?"

"You're breaking out again." She squeezed the shutter.

Akhil frowned. "So what's the deal with Marie Osmond down there?"

"I think she looks nice."

"She looks fake."

"Jeez, Akhil, she put on some makeup. No big deal." She fiddled with the focus until he was just a blur of skin and light.

"The commodification of beauty is an economic trap designed to enslave the modern woman."

Amina shifted two f-stops. The shutter clicked. "I have no idea what you're talking about."

The light swirled where his eye should have been. "Of course you don't."

A few hours later, they sat at the top of the stairs, looking down to the light in the hallway below. The lack of noise from the kitchen assured them that their mother had long since finished cooking, but previous attempts to start eating dinner had been quickly dismissed by Kamala's overly cheerful insistence that their father would arrive *any minute*! Forty-seven more passed. They were ready to eat their pillows.

"I think we should just go down," Amina whispered.

Akhil looked at his watch and sighed.

"Do you think we should go down?" she asked.

"I think he should have been here an hour ago."

"Yeah, I know, but—"

"Mom, can we please eat?" Akhil shouted, cutting her off.

There was no reply.

"Mom! Can we—"

"Sure! Let's eat!" she called back.

Downstairs, the kitchen table had been set with the good china while the crystal water pitcher sweated into a cloth placemat. Silverware gleamed from napkins.

"What is this?" Akhil asked.

"Pot roasts and mashed potato!" Kamala said proudly.

Amina sat down. She picked up a serving fork and poked at the mass of brown. It smelled insistently of American restaurants, of heavy meat undelighted by real spices. She felt her mother watching her and smiled. "Looks good."

Kamala nodded to the main dish. "Try it, you'll like it."

Amina took a stab at the meat. It resisted.

"I won't like it," Akhil said, pushing his plate away. "Can I just have chicken curry?"

"I didn't make Indian tonight."

"What about for Dad?"

"Nope."

Amina and Akhil glanced at each other. It was a point of pride for their mother, always making Indian for their father, regardless of the occasional new dish she might try for the children.

Akhil tried to scoop a spoonful of mashed potatoes, which stretched and thinned as he lifted, as though unwilling to let the spoon go.

"What happened to these?" he asked.

"They're mashed potatoes."

"They're gummy."

"And wait until you try them!" Kamala looked pleased. "I added an extra stick of butter."

Akhil looked at Amina, and she shook her head slightly. *Say nothing.* Kamala walked back to the kitchen.

"Aren't you going to eat?" Akhil called after her.

"No, no. I'll wait."

They ate while she waited. Rather, they tried to eat while the food tried not to be eaten. The pot roast held its shape through vigorous chewing, while attempts to swallow the mashed potatoes left their tongues sealed to the roofs of their mouths. In nonverbal desperation, they split the entire bowl of salad, careful not to alert their mother, who was busily scrubbing the already clean stove and counters. They took advantage of her brief trip to the bathroom to stuff most of what was on their plates into paper towels and bury them in the trash, hurrying back to the table with empty plates as the toilet flushed. When Kamala returned to the kitchen, her hair was freshly slicked back, her lipstick reapplied. She walked to the sink, filled the tin cup she kept by it, and tilted her head back, letting the water fall into her mouth in a thick stream. Her shoulders dropped a little as she set it down.

"How's the food?" she asked, not turning around.

"Good," Akhil said, and Amina murmured in agreement.

"We'll do the dishes," Amina offered.

"No, no. You go upstairs. You both must be tired."

They cleared the table. Akhil set aside a plate of food for their father, while Amina ran a sponge over the white countertops. When they were done, they walked cautiously to the living room, settling down on either side of their mother to watch an episode of *Hill Street Blues* and the ten o'clock news. From the corners of eyes determined not to look directly, they saw the buoyancy leak out of her, first in mood, then in posture. By eleven, she was fast asleep on the couch, ponytail askew, mouth open in a slack grimace.

"Should we wake her?" Amina whispered.

"He should fucking wake her," Akhil said.

Amina leaned over, squeezed her mother's hand. The purple lids fluttered open.

"What's happening?" Kamala sat up, her breath sour with sleep.

"You should go to bed."

Her mother looked around the living room, lingering on the empty armchair.

"What time it is?" she asked.

"Late," Akhil said.

They made a strange processional walking down the hallway, Akhil leading the way, Kamala semi-sleepwalking behind him, Amina following, trying to guide her mother without exhibiting the kind of tenderness that would draw a flinch. Queen Victoria sniffed the floors in their wake. Akhil opened their parents' bedroom door, and Kamala glided through it like an errant canoe.

"Good night, Ma." Akhil shut the door quietly behind her.

Amina looked at him. "Do you think one of us should stay with—"

"No," Akhil said quietly, definitively. "I don't."

Should she go down? Amina lay in bed, blinking into the dark, listening to the screen door open and shut. Thomas was home. He was just sitting down for his nightly drink, she knew by the opening and closing of the cupboards. He would not want company.

She went downstairs anyway. "Dad?"

From the back, she could only see his head rising above the wicker chair like a fuzzy sun on the horizon. When he didn't say anything, she opened the door, stepping gingerly onto the porch. "Dad?"

Her father was sitting in his surgery scrubs, a scotch bottle between his legs. "Did I wake you?"

"No." Amina stood on one foot, not wanting to move or breathe or do anything that might make him tell her to go to bed. She looked around discreetly for something to sit on. Queen Victoria pressed her wet nose to the screen, inhaled deeply, and sneezed.

"Let her in," her father said.

Amina did, and the dog ran straight to Thomas, sticking her face in his belly. He folded over her, rocking. He stayed down for so long that Amina thought he had fallen asleep.

"Why are you awake?" he said into Queen Victoria's neck.

"I . . ." Amina looked at his feet, the dress shoes wrapped with blue booties. "I was just up. Couldn't sleep."

Thomas sat up. "Bad habit. Don't get used to it."

Amina nodded and her father reached next to his chair, to a jelly jar filled with ice. He placed it between his knees and held the scotch bottle up to the light before pouring. He took a long sip. Queen Victoria backed herself into his legs and sat against them, staring tiredly at Amina.

It felt dangerous to see her father so close. For months, he had been a blur coming or going to the hospital. Amina shifted her weight from one buttock to the other, trying to seem at ease.

"So, what's going on with you?" he asked.

"Nothing. First day of school."

"Today?"

"Yes."

Her father clamped his eyes shut, shook his head. "Shit."

The pouches under his eyes were darker than usual, liver-purple and puckered.

"So summer is over," he said, after a few minutes.

"Yeah."

He looked down at his knees. "How was it? School?"

"It was fine," Amina said. "I mean, you know, Mesa. It didn't seem totally horrible, anyway."

"What subjects are you taking?"

"English, history, French, algebra, bio, photography. You can take photography this year if you took regular art in mid school."

"You like art?"

Amina nodded. Her father fell silent. He stretched his legs out in front of himself.

"What's it like?" Amina pointed to the scotch.

Thomas held up the glass, looking at the ice cubes from underneath. "How old are you?"

"Fourteen." She wanted to add that she had tried beer with Dimple already, and an occasional Baileys Irish Cream with Sanji Auntie, but she didn't.

"Hmm." He swirled the glass. "You want to try some?"

She did. He leaned forward, handing her the glass. It was freezing. She looked down, shivered. From the top the scotch looked beautiful, the cracked ice lit up the color of a clean sunrise, the liquid smoking between fissures.

"Hold your breath."

She tilted it to her mouth. Gulped, swallowed. The first hit tasted like sour air, like the hard metallic tang left in her mouth after a visit to the dentist. A warmth spread deliciously from her cheeks to her forehead. When she exhaled, fire rushed up and through her. It moved from belly to brain, out her mouth in a gasp. She swallowed. Breathed again. Her cheeks were numb. She drew a shaky breath and forced her limbs to be still.

Her father smiled. "You like it?"

Amina handed the glass back. "No."

He laughed, startling her. It was a good, deep laugh that rang off the porch and into the night, making the slouching Queen Victoria stand upright, suddenly alert.

"So you like your new school, huh?" He threw one leg over the other, and Amina nodded, not wanting to botch the moment. Her father looked pleased. "What do you like about it?"

She looked around the porch, at the moths' shadows inking the walls. "The campus is nice, I guess. Big. Brick. My teachers seem pretty cool."

"That's good. Wow, high school. You're really getting to be big, huh?"

"Thomas?" The soft voice from the door made them look. Kamala's face was pinched, groggy. "What are you doing?"

The smile fell from his face. "Nothing much. Sitting here."

"Amina, why are you awake?"

Amina shrugged her shoulders.

Her mother sighed.

"I'm sorry I missed dinner," her father said at last. "A young boy came in. They sent him from Grants. Subdural hematoma."

Shuffling, silence.

"Don't give me that look. Kam, I told you I would try, I didn't promise."

Her mother gave a thin laugh. "You never promise."

"What do you want me to say?"

"I told the kids you would come."

"Then I will tell the kids I am sorry."

"When?"

"When? When I feel like it. Don't make a big deal out of it."

"It *is* a big deal."

"Kamala, enough. I've had a long day."

Kamala looked at him, the pain on her face so vivid that it was hard to understand how it erased itself so quickly moments later, her features flattening into regular, everyday disappointment. Her mother turned without another word and walked away, her body disappearing into the dark. Amina stood up.

"Good night," Thomas said as she left, and she waved halfheartedly, not wanting to see his sad face or show him her own.

CHAPTER 3

"What makes someone a good man?" Mr. Tipton asked, placing his copy of *Hamlet* on the desk behind him.

Gina Rodgers raised her hand, triggering a class-wide bristle. Everyone wanted to impress Mr. Tipton, but it was Gina who always raised her hand first, like he was going to fall in love with her for her 4.3 GPA or something.

"Trace," Mr. Tipton called.

"Huh?" Trace McCourt looked up from the F-15 he was drawing across his notebook in exacting detail.

"What makes a good man?"

Trace stared at the gunmetal-gray divot in his finger, then at his pencil. "Someone who stands up for what he believes in. Does his duty."

"What's his duty?"

"To defend his country. And his family." He sniffed like this was something he'd done himself. "His honor."

"What about a man who doesn't have any of those things?"

"Everyone has a country."

"Not necessarily," Gina Rodgers said, her eyes locked on Mr. Tipton. "There are dissidents. And expatriates. And the classic first-generation immigrant caught between the country left behind and the new land. There's—"

"Amina, what do you think?" Mr. Tipton asked.

"What?"

"How would you define a good man?"

Amina chewed the inside of her cheek, all her answers trapped inside a swirl of thinking so thick she had trouble making any words at all. Hands rose on all sides of the room like tulips blooming for the sun. The bell rang.

"You know, you're going to have to speak eventually," Mr. Tipton said as she was packing her stuff to go. "It's English class. Speaking is important."

"I know."

"Don't tell me you're bored with *Hamlet* already." He smiled.

"No. It's just . . . I don't know. One person's good man is another person's, you know, dad." She flushed. "Or ghost or whatever."

"See, now, why didn't you say that? That's exactly what *Hamlet* is about—the complexities of sincerity, the relevance of sanity. In fact, there are debates about whether or not Hamlet is crazy or just pretending to be crazy. I'd be interested to know what you think."

Amina nodded, like *Sure, yeah, I'll do that,* but really, she would have been interested to know what she thought, too.

At least she had her art. Downstairs forty minutes later in the photo room, everyone stared at the board with nervous excitement. It was a thrill, the last twenty minutes of class devoted to critique, the curiosity about what others had come up with and how you measured against it. There was a rule, of course, to look at all the pictures for at least two minutes before talking. Amina's eyes flashed quickly over the others but returned to her own, fascinated by the angle, by the cut of her own face. When had her jaw gotten so sharp? She had done much better with the self-portrait assignment than she had with the last. Part of it was getting more familiar with the printing process; the dodging helped where her own knowledge of the camera fell short. And really, she had gotten the perfect picture, setting her desk lamp at a ninety-degree angle to her body so that most everything around her was blanketed with darkness while the side of her face pressed into the light. She hadn't even bothered to print the more mundane shots—this, she knew, was rare perfection.

"Well?" Mrs. Messina asked. "What do we think?"

"I like Sarah's," someone in back of Amina said, and she turned. Tommy Hargrow, the oldest of seven Mormon kids. While Amina wasn't totally sure exactly what being Mormon entailed, it was always the first thing said about Tommy, the second being that he had six siblings. He studied the board. "I think there's something interesting about it."

Amina looked back at Sarah's picture. It showed her teeth glistening with a goofy smile, her hair weightlessly suspended around her face, like she was underwater.

"I was on the trampoline," Sarah offered.

"We don't talk about our own images unless we're asked a question," Mrs. Messina reminded her. She looked at the photo. "It is interesting to me that Sarah decided to edit out the trampoline, though. Class, what do you make of that?"

Amina made nothing of it. The image was silly, too stagy, too juvenile. She studied her hands.

"I like that there's no, you know, background or whatever," someone said.

"Context," Mrs. Messina said. "What you're talking about is context. We can't place Sarah, exactly, though we know she's joyous. I see at least four pictures on the wall that do the same thing. Take a look at Amina's."

Amina looked down, trying not to smile. There was a long silence.

"Where are the rest?" Mrs. Messina asked.

"I don't have any others."

"You only took one picture of yourself?"

"I didn't like the others."

"Next time, bring them." Mrs. Messina turned to the class. "Listen, you need to keep in mind that we want to see a good sampling of your work. What you like at this point isn't really important because you haven't figured out your own eye yet. This, for example, makes Amina look *pretty*, and maybe like she belongs on an album cover, but beyond that, I'm not really seeing *her* at all. Her other photographs might have shown me something different. Now let's take a look at Tommy's."

Amina sat very still, suddenly aware of how little she was breathing. How dare Mrs. Messina single her out? Sure, she only had one photo up, but at least it wasn't total crap like the ones Missy Folgers had taken, placing all of her horse-riding ribbons in the shape of a horseshoe around her head.

She looked at Tommy's pictures. Three showed him on an abandoned baseball dugout. The last four were of him at dinner, sitting very still while his parents and six siblings swirled around him, in varying degrees of sharpness.

"I love them," someone said.

"Value judgments are useless here. What do you love about them?"

"They're good."

Mrs. Messina sighed. "Why?"

"They make me sad," Missy Folgers said.

Mrs. Messina nodded. "Good. How so?"

No one said anything. Amina stared at the last photograph. It was the loneliness. It was the way Tommy seemed to be talking to the camera because there was no one else to talk to. She stared at the floor miserably, barely aware of the assignment for the next week landing in her hands until Mrs. Messina started reading from it.

"Over the last weeks, you did a portrait of yourselves. Over the next two, I want you to turn the camera on your family. We're learning to tell stories here, so think about action. Okay?"

People were collecting their pictures from the blackboard, and Amina hurried up with them, snapping hers down. She stuffed it into her backpack, not caring as the paper bent and creased under her hand.

CHAPTER 4

"Overpopulation. Truncal obesity. An excess of body hair. This is what we offer the world," Akhil announced the following Saturday. Amina and Dimple sat on rusty lawn chairs on the Stoop, the tiny corner of roof accessible through Akhil's bedroom window, while Akhil himself paced, chain-smoking with one nervous eye on the locked bedroom door. Downstairs, a chorus of parents' voices rumbled with post-meal chatter.

"Speak for yourself, dude." Dimple frowned, pulled at her split ends. "I'm not the fat one."

"Hit puberty and we'll talk."

"Oh, is that what happened? Good to know."

Amina kicked Dimple's ankle.

"Ow. Like it's my fault he's fat and angry about it," Dimple said.

Akhil exhaled a cloud of smoke. "At least I'm not trying to be white."

"I'm not trying to be anything," Dimple sighed, rolling her eyes. "I just *am*."

"Whatever."

"Whatever." Dimple looked up at the sky. "So how long does this take anyway?"

Akhil and Amina were waiting for the annual migration of the snow geese, as they always did in the fall, scanning the sky for the first wave of some twenty thousand birds that made their journey from Canada to Mexico.

"They said on the news that they were in Santa Fe yesterday," Amina said.

"Well, how long is that?"

"You have somewhere better to be?" Akhil asked.

Amina turned the lens on her cousin's ear, the recently pierced cartilage swollen under three silver hoops. She pulled the focus tight. "I think you've got an ear infection, Dimp."

"No I don't," Dimple said.

"It's gross," Akhil said. "Better not let Dirk see it."

"He doesn't give a shit," Dimple said.

"About you? Or about anything not in the immediate proximity of a soccer ball?"

"What is wrong with him?" Dimple asked, head swiveling from Akhil to Amina and back again. "What is wrong with you?"

"Ben Kingsley is playing Gandhi," Amina said, replacing one sore subject with another. She watched her brother's face cloud over. The news, if it could even be called that, had hit Akhil hard. No one had even seen *Gandhi* yet, and wouldn't for three months, but Akhil was already tracking its progress with the nervous scrutiny of a jealous stepbrother, both too close and too distant from its subject matter to be easy with its coming.

"So?" Dimple asked.

"Ben Kingsley is half British." Amina panned down, focusing on her brother's shoes.

"He was *raised* in *England*," Akhil said, sulking.

"So he's not Indian at all?"

"Barely."

"He's half Indian," Amina corrected.

"Oh, for the love of . . ." Dimple rolled her eyes. "Seriously, man, holding on to a grudge over *colonization*? Naming the dog after British royalty? You have so got to mellow."

"Is she speaking English?" Akhil asked Amina.

"Whatever," Dimple sighed.

"Whatever. Right. Never mind the hypocrisy, the insanity, not to mention the corruption of the introduction of our culture to the American mainstream! Mark my words, this movie is going to affect the way every single one of them sees us for the next decade. They'll be looking at you, *but they'll be seeing Mahatma!*"

Dimple slapped her own forehead.

"What's that supposed to mean?" Akhil asked.

"It's not supposed to mean anything."

"It's supposed to mean *something*."

A heavy banging on the door startled all of them, and Akhil looked around the Stoop frantically. Dimple reached under her chair for the bottle of Wonder Bubbles, and Amina under hers for the Stetson cologne. Akhil spritzed wildly as she crawled back into his room through the open window.

"Who is it?"

"Are you going to let me in or what, baby?"

"It's just Sanji Auntie," she told the others, unlocking the door. Sanji entered Akhil's room, fanning her scowling face as she walked across it.

"My Gods, who put on an entire bottle of cologne? Akhil, was that you? You think it's covering up the devil stink of your cancer sticks?"

"We told him. He doesn't believe us." Amina wiggled past her aunt to climb back out the window, and Sanji leaned through it, wrinkling her nose.

"It smells like a bloody billiards hall in here! Really, your parents don't know? Daddy used to be a cigarette smoker, nah? He'll sniff it out."

"That would take him actually being in the house."

"He's in the house now!" Sanji peered around the roof. "Where's the ashtray?"

Dimple held up the jar of Wonder Bubbles.

"Well, if that isn't the height of corruption." Sanji motioned for a cigarette. Akhil gave her one and then cupped the flame on the lighter as Sanji leaned farther out the window, her hot-pink chuni fluttering in the breeze. She exhaled, muttering, "Oh, goddamn lovely thing," and inhaled again. After three drags, she handed it back to Akhil. "So? What's the hot topic on the roof these days? How is the new school year?"

"It's awesome," said Dimple.

Sanji smiled. "I hear you've been invited to Homecoming?"

"You have?" Amina looked at her cousin.

"Yeah." Dimple pinched a stray hair from her sweater and released it into the breeze. "I'm going with Nick Feets."

"Nick *Feets*?" Akhil asked.

"What about it?" Dimple glared.

"So what's he like?" Sanji asked.

"I don't know. I mean, whatever, he's nice I guess. He's a friend of Mindy's."

Amina swallowed, feeling vaguely stabbed all over.

"Fantastic!" Sanji cheered. "Our Dimple is going to her first-ever Homecoming dance! Bala said you were wearing a sari!"

"She *what*?"

"Kathi silk and all that, nah?" Sanji winked at the others. "Hair plaited with jasmine?"

Dimple's face was smothered with horror. "Oh my God, what if?"

"It would be social suicide," Akhil said. "Everyone would know you're Indian, and the next thing you know, you'll be asked to make samosas for the whole school."

"Anyway," Sanji said, clapping her hands together, "I think it will be fantastic, whatever you decide to wear. How I always wish that I had grown up with these American traditions—homecomings, proms, clambakes! You must tell Mummy to take pictures for all of us to see."

Already, Amina could see the pictures: Dimple in some satiny dress with stick-necked Nick Feets, Dimple with the entire girls' volleyball team, curling their arms to show off taut little biceps, Dimple with a corsage bigger than her face. She stared at the top of her camera, slowly shifting from f-stop to f-stop.

"What about you, Ami? Do you have someone you're keen on?"

Sanji asked, and Amina looked up, speechless and aggrieved. She pulled the camera to her face.

Sanji Auntie's breasts lapped over the window frame, the soft folds in her neck streaked with baby powder. Amina panned up to the bleached fur above her aunt's upper lip, and over to the ruby-and-sapphire earring dangling from one fat lobe. Her aunt looked over her shoulder at the door, sighing. "I suppose I should get back before they get suspicious."

"No," all three of them chorused, and Sanji looked pleased.

"I must, I must. Chacko and Raj will pop each other's eyeballs out over this trickle-down theory, and there's only so much good humor Thomas can provide." She looked around the roof. "Where's the horrible cologne?"

Amina reached under the chair and handed her the Stetson.

Sanji sniffed at it gingerly and winced. "*Chi!* Bug spray! Is that the only one?"

"I have some Jean Naté on my dresser," Amina offered.

"That's my girl."

They watched her thump across the room, listening through the door like they had taught her and then opening it quickly, locking it behind her.

"Do you think she'd be as cool if she had kids?" Dimple asked.

"No," Akhil said. "No one is."

Amina leaned back in her chair, reaching behind her for the camera case and her notebook. She flipped open to a new page and wrote down the film speed, exposures, and time of day. She paused at the column she had titled "light quality." She looked up at the sky and wrote down "spitty."

"So what's the deal with your dad, anyway?" Dimple asked.

Akhil scratched his cheek. "Nothing."

"You just told Sanji Auntie he isn't around."

"He isn't."

"Yeah, but why not?"

"Because he isn't," Akhil said. "It's no big deal."

"Then why are you so pissed at him?"

"Who says I'm pissed at him?"

Dimple rolled her eyes. "Clearly you're pissed at him."

"He's not *around* enough for me to be pissed at him."

"Okay, but it's not like he's off, like, gallivanting around the world or having some great romance, right? He's just working."

"It's fine," Amina said. "Akhil was exaggerating. Dad is here a lot. At night, mostly."

"Bullshit," Akhil said. "He got mad at her and he left us."

"What?" Dimple asked.

"Nothing," Amina said quickly, glaring Akhil into silence. "He did nothing."

Dimple looked from one of them to the other, her eyes hard. She leaned back in her chair. "I am so glad I don't have a sibling."

After everyone left, Akhil and Amina returned to the roof and sat, looking up at the disappointing sky. It had darkened to an unimaginative gray, a color so bland that it almost seemed clear, except for the faint and loosening seam drawn by a vanished airplane. Amina thought of the smell of pipe smoke that lingered in the downstairs bathroom even when her father had been gone for days, the dinner plate that sat in the kitchen sink every morning, thin and dry as a bone sucked clean.

"Do you think he'd ever really leave?" Amina asked.

"What?"

"Dad. Us."

Akhil shrugged. "Indians don't leave. They're into the whole live-forever-in-misery thing."

Amina considered this. "You think he's miserable?"

"I think he's a product of his race and time."

She frowned. "You really think he's miserable?"

"Aren't we all?"

"Not really."

"Whatever. I'm just saying, there are things you can't avoid," Akhil said. "It's in the genes—good teeth, bad skin, bad body. Lives of indentured gratitude."

"In-whatered what?"

"You know, bowing and scraping all the time because we're so goddamn thankful just to be in the country. Acting like anyone who talks to us is doing us some big favor."

"When are you bowing and scraping?"

"When am I not? Jesus! Did you know Mom actually *thanked* Mrs. Macklin for kicking me out of French last year?"

"She thanked her for teaching you a lesson."

"She thanked her for being an asshole. I'm surprised she didn't invite her over for dinner afterward. *Oh yes, I make the most wonderful biryani, have you tried?*" He laid the accent on thick, wobbling his head from side to side.

"Shh." Amina pointed toward the sky. She had heard it—the scratchy honk that could only emanate from a trumpet-thin throat, the slightly higher note that it ended on, as though asking a question. She looked up. The wails grew louder, raspy, doubling on one another, rising up into mini-crescendos and bouncing off the cottonwoods and the adobe wall behind their heads. The first goose appeared, piercing the clean wipe of sky above them. The black hull of its wings pitched against the wind, and it floated there, seemingly unmoving, tethered to the clouds. Amina held her breath. Another goose appeared, and another. Each angled behind the next so that they formed an undulating *V.* Sharp cries hollowed in timbre and grew louder in the meat of Amina's heart. Akhil smiled. The birds reeled in wide circles above them.

"Wingspans big as a man," Amina said.

"A lucky man," Akhil corrected. A rare look of unmitigated longing crossed his face. She pressed the camera back up to her face quickly.

"You'll grow," she said.

CHAPTER 5

Why did she decide to photograph an empty classroom the next day? Amina had no idea, just the hope that the empty desks would somehow say something to someone about anything at all. Instead, all it did was make her late to English class.

"Nice of you to join us." Mr. Tipton didn't even look up when she entered the class, while Gina Rodgers, mid-sentence, glared at her over an open mouth. Amina crossed the room hastily, sitting down in her chair. "Act two, scene five. Go on, Gina."

"I just mean that his father was a real leader, so Hamlet has to respect his wishes," Gina said.

Amina stared at the page, catching her breath.

"What do you think, Amina?" Mr. Tipton asked.

"Of Hamlet's father?" she stalled.

"Yes."

"In general?"

"In specific."

"Oh. Uh . . ." She stared at Akhil's scribbling in the margin. "I don't think he's real."

"Of course he's not *real*," Gina said. "He's a ghost."

"I know that," Amina said, feeling her face flush brightly. "But I don't think he's even a real ghost. I think he's, you know, a figment of imagination or something."

"But the guards see him," Gina said.

"A figment of whose imagination?" Mr. Tipton asked. His tone had changed to one of encouragement.

Akhil had written it in bold letters. "Denmark's."

Mr. Tipton smiled. "Say it again. I want everyone to hear."

Amina felt the gaze of the class upon her, and she looked at her book to not lose her nerve. She said it again. Mr. Tipton's eyes crinkled like she'd discovered a lost page of the Bible.

"So you mean a collective conscience?" he asked.

"Kind of, or maybe more like—"

Someone was knocking on the classroom door. Mr. Tipton moved to the door and threw it open with one smooth movement, nodding to encourage her, but Amina's words died in her throat. Akhil stood in the doorway picking at his face, belly pooling over his jeans.

"I need my sister," he said.

"I was afraid you were going to say that," Mr. Tipton sighed. "We were on a roll."

Amina rose, lifting her backpack from the floor. She walked out the door and Mr. Tipton followed.

"Everything okay?" he asked.

"No. I mean, I don't know." He handed the teacher a note, which was read, refolded, and slipped into a lavender shirt pocket.

"Okay then." Mr. Tipton turned to Amina and squeezed her shoulder. "We'll continue our conversation later."

They flew down Coors Boulevard, music off, windows sealed shut.

"What did the message say?" Amina asked again.

"To get you and to come home."

"That's all?"

"That's all."

Amina nodded. They were on a mission. She would be brave. It was exciting, actually, leaving school in the middle of the day, zipping back through the empty roads.

"Maybe they are getting a divorce," Akhil said, passing one of the gated residential neighborhoods.

"What?"

"You know, like they're separating."

Amina dropped her hand. "I thought you said they would never—"

"What do I know? I don't know squat."

"But . . ." Amina searched for something to abate the swiftly growing panic in her. "But why would they make us come home from school to tell us that?"

"Maybe he's moving out today."

Amina's stomach lurched. "No."

"Well, what else could it be?"

Her eyes filled with tears. "You really think so?"

Akhil looked over at her. "Don't fucking *cry* about it, kid. God, I just told you I have no idea. I'm just saying maybe."

"But I thought you said that Indians—"

"Don't you know everything can always change and it always will, probably for the worse?" Akhil shook his head. "I mean, that's basic, Amina. Please tell me you know that."

Amina's nose was filling with snot. She tried to breathe and found she could not. Outside, neighborhood cul-de-sacs spiraled away from them like galaxies, infinitely repeating fractals of driveways and front doors and welcome mats. Could her father do that? Could he really leave them?

"What if he's hurt?" she asked.

"He's not."

"Like, dead or something?" Amina swiped at her nose with her hand. "What if he was in an accident? You know how he drives. What if the car flipped over? Heart attack?" Her voice was edging into hysterical territory.

"That didn't happen," Akhil said, but visibly paled. He opened his mouth as if to say something else but then bit his lip and slipped a tape into the deck.

Twenty minutes later they sat in the driveway, listening to Judas Priest growl out "Breaking the Law" and staring at the cars. Cars because there were two, their mother's hatchback and their father's sedan, neither with any visible damage.

"We should go in," Amina said as the song ended.

Akhil slipped the key out of the ignition, and they walked to the door slowly, taking their time to cross the driveway, to step around mounds of yellow leaves instead of right through them, as though being careful might grant them a reprieve from whatever was waiting behind the front door. When he reached it, Akhil waited for Amina to catch up before reaching for the handle. It opened without them. Their mother looked at them, her eyes and nose soggy shades of pink. They waited for her to say something.

"The Salem house burned down."

"What?" Amina was the first to get her bearings.

It had been three years since they left Salem that horrible morning, but Ammachy's house lived on in her mind, the Wall as irrefutable as the Himalayas.

Kamala nodded. "A few hours ago. We just got word."

"Burned down?" Akhil asked. "Like, it's *gone*?"

Kamala's face trembled a little.

"But how did it—" Akhil started, and his mother waved him silent. A horrible grimace kept penetrating the surface of her face and then getting sucked back in, as if through sheer force of will. Amina watched this happen a few times before her head seared open with a terrible clarity.

"Did Ammachy die?" she asked.

Her mother nodded.

"What about Sunil Uncle?" Akhil asked.

Kamala nodded again.

"Divya?" Amina asked, wishing her mother would stop nodding. "*Itty?*"

Kamala exhaled a shaky breath. "Gone."

Gone. Amina turned around and looked at the car and then back at her mother, whose shoulders trembled as if it were cold outside. *Mittack.*

"Fuck," Akhil said.

Kamala pulled back the door farther to reveal Thomas curled over the dining room table like a question mark, his head in his hands.

"Go," she urged.

They walked to their father. Even from a distance they could see the grief radiating from him. He was thumbing through an old photo album, the one that held the pictures of him and Sunil Uncle when they were kids. Amina knew the album by heart: her father as a fat baby with a thin string tied around his waist; Sunil riding a three-wheel bicycle around a pomegranate tree barely bigger than she; Ammachy and Appachen, two years before her grandfather's heart attack, standing in front of the curving hood of an old Ambassador; Ammachy standing alone on the verandah, smiling in a way Amina had never seen in real life. It was this photo that he stopped at, working it gently from the yellowed corners that held it to the page. He lifted it close to his face.

"Hey," Akhil said. Thomas looked up, his eyes riddled with pink. Amina couldn't recall the last time she had seen her father in daylight hours, but here he was, clutching at the dining table with his enormous grief and aching face.

"Sorry," Akhil said. Amina repeated the word, which felt stupid and scary at the same time, too adult, too full of nothing.

"You don't remember that day." Thomas looked back at the photo.

"No." Akhil breathed tight, feathery breaths, his lower lip glistening with spit.

Their father's face contorted, as though this were a new tragedy.

"What day was that, Thomas?" Kamala asked in the tone she used when the children were injured or sick.

"The first day the clinic opened. She was just thirty-three."

Ammachy wore a sari, probably colored, but starkly black in the picture. She also wore pearl earrings, gold bracelets, and a braid wound with jasmine, but none of her adornments measured up to the wide arc of her lips, the even edges of her teeth hinting at a full smile like the glow of light before sunrise. Behind her, the Salem house rose up gloriously. The verandah gleamed, its walls as white as new paper. A tiny trail of light in the hallway led back to what would later become Itty's room.

Itty's room. Amina's eyes fixed on the dark hallway. Was Itty in his room when it happened? Had he heard the fire coming for him? Had he tried to escape?

She must have made a noise. Kamala came up, hugging her from behind.

"Burned?" Amina said, the word aloud unhinging whatever it is in humans that keeps them standing upright and balanced. She chattered and tilted to the side a little. "Are you sure?"

"*Koche!*" Kamala squeezed hard. A warning.

Amina twisted her head around to look at her mother. "Itty was *on fire?*"

"*Chi!* Amina!" Kamala grabbed her face, squeezed her mouth shut. "Don't say such things!"

Akhil swayed a little on his feet, pale. He took a step toward the stairs. "I need to go lie down."

"Yes. Fine," Kamala said, pushing Amina after him. "Both of you go. We will call you for dinner."

Akhil headed immediately upstairs, but Amina could not move. The roof, hot with tar. The smell of the cows, street fires. Itty, crying on the lawn, clutching his bare feet. She looked at Thomas. He did not look back at her, or even at the picture in front of him, but into the boundless middle distance, a flat plane that did not intersect with any other member of the family.

"Are you going to go back?" she asked, and he flinched.

"Of course he's going back," their mother said, and with this, Thomas's chin began to tremble in a way that made Amina look up and down, anywhere else, so she sensed, rather than saw, how Kamala drew closer, how some part of her must have touched him to release a jag of sobs. When Amina finally looked over, her father's arms were wrapped tightly around her mother's waist, his head pressed deeply into her belly.

The stairs. She had found her way to the stairs. She walked up them needing to stop the flood of images her mind seemed intent on retrieving. The halo of peeling paint around the dining room chandelier. The record spinning on the turntable. Sunil's wrists floating in air as he danced. *Mittack. Mittack. Mittack.*

"Akhil?"

Her brother's door was closed. Amina put her ear to the wood, listening. Was he crying? He would kill her if she opened the door and he was. She twisted the handle and looked inside.

Akhil was on the bed, facedown. He hadn't even bothered to take off his Adidases.

"Hey," she said. When her brother did not answer, she tiptoed into the room. She stood by the bed, watching his back rise and fall in a deep, steady rhythm.

"You're asleep?" she asked, ignoring the obvious.

She didn't want to be alone. She didn't want to sit in her room or even shut her eyes. How could he sleep right now? How could he just turn off like that? Amina stood over her brother, fury rising. Something was wrong with him. She undersood this suddenly, with the same conviction she would understand other strange truths later in life—that Dimple needed her more than she needed Dimple, that her parents' fight was about America, not Monica. Sure, Akhil could talk about whether or not Indians were second-class citizens in the Western world, and how big government was the only recourse for marginalized people, but when something big happened, something so big that neither of them would ever be able to think of India without their own hearts splintering, he bailed. Left. Went out like a fucking light.

"Wake up, asshole," she said, crying now because there was no one left to talk her away from the conversation that had started in her mind, the one that she had imagined she would have had the next time she saw Itty, which wasn't much of a conversation anyway, just some sort of weird shared understanding of how it was to always be outside of everything, even your own family, waiting to be seen. She sat on Akhil's bed and put her head between her knees as blood and the roar of what had been lost filled her ears.

If there was an upside to the disaster, Amina supposed it would have to be the way her parents suddenly united in the face of it. As the hours wore into days, Kamala and Thomas seemed to Siamese-twin, becoming an unrecognizable age (older? younger?) as they shared a child's grief borne by an adult body. As the days wore on, Akhil and Amina felt the strangeness of their own presence in the house, their superfluousness to everything: the phone calls from India, the child-hood stories whispered in Malayalam, the ticket bought, the suitcase packed, their parents, turning and returning to the dining room table to huddle over the old photo albums like caged parrots clutching at a shared axis. On the rare occasion that Amina met her father's gaze, she looked away quickly, shamed by the disappointment she saw there—though what exactly he was disappointed in (her accent? her jeans?) felt as mysterious as it did unfair.

Three days after the news, Akhil and Amina stood together in the driveway as their parents prepared to leave for the airport. Kamala pressed money for McDonald's into Akhil's hand in case she was not back before dinnertime, and their father nodded goodbye, looking right through them like they were the credits of a movie. Amina stepped forward and wrapped her arms around his waist, surprised by the force with which he hugged her back. His beard scratched her head when he kissed it. He pushed her away.

"We should get going," he said, and with that both parents got into the car, driving into the cool October afternoon.

The phone rang a few nights later, just as Amina was drifting toward the heavy blanket of sleep. Her eyes flickered open to the green glow of the digital clock: 11:15. Even Dimple knew not to call after ten. She slid over to the side of her bed and pulled the phone out of the cradle.

". . . so hot, my God. Every night. I can barely sleep," her father was saying.

"Mmmm." Her mother's voice was milky with sleep. "Sounds awful."

"And those theaters! They added three more! Can you imagine? Hindi films, Tamil films, Malayalam films. Nobody in my dreams un-derstands anybody else."

Her mother laughed at this, a soft laugh that was echoed at the other end of the line by her father. A silence followed, punctuated by the wiggling squeals and blips of distance.

"I think I'm going nuts," Thomas said at last.

"You're not," Kamala soothed. "You're just tired. *Pavum.*"

Thomas was silent for another long time, and Amina herself was growing drowsy when she heard him say, "The papers are calling him the Sleepwalking Killer."

Suddenly, she was awake, blinking furiously into the dark. *Killer?*

"Ach," her mother said.

"I guess Mary and the girls talked to reporters before I came, filled them with some nonsense about how he was asleep when he set the fire, how he never would have done it awake. But how do you lock the doors in your sleep? How do you douse the whole house in petrol?"

Kamala's expulsion of breath was swift, as if trying to blow the words, their meaning, far away from herself, but the images bloomed in Amina's mind. Petrol? Fire? *Locked doors?*

"And now it's all the sensation over here, you wouldn't believe. In the *Dinamalar* and the *Janmabhumi Daily* and someone even told me there was a mention in the *Hindu Times*. I can never come back here again."

"*Chi!*" Kamala scoffed. "What are you saying? Of course you can."

"They blame me."

"Who cares what Mary and the girls think? Their opinions are hardly—"

"Not just Mary and the rest of the bloody servants! The town! All of Salem! My mother's old patients. Divya's parents. I saw Chandy Abraham at the funeral, and he could barely look at me."

"People are just sad for you!"

"Bullshit. They are saying it's my fault."

"*It is not your fault.*" Kamala's voice was angry. "You didn't do this! Sunil was unhappy! Nothing could have made him happy."

"Couldn't it have?" Thomas's voice broke. "You know, he wasn't like this when we were young. He was sweet then. This little fat ball, always following me with a grin. Trying to go wherever I went, pedaling his bike with his cheeks puffing as I rode away. I never waited for him. Did you know that? I don't know why, I just didn't."

"You were a boy."

"I was his brother!"

"Oh, Thomas." Kamala made a tiny noise on the end of the line, and Amina realized her mother was crying. "*Pavum.* This isn't going to help."

There was a rustling. Thomas blew his nose, swallowed. "I want to come home."

"Come home," her mother said. "We're waiting."

"Class, any reaction?"

Of course the results of her family-in-action photographs were awful, which meant that Mrs. Messina wanted to talk about them first. Amina stared at the pictures that she had taped up on the blackboard with everyone else's. Why hadn't she realized that she had taken so many close-ups of body parts? Her mother's sneakers (the sole surviving remnant of the Dillard's excursion) curtained by a sari. Sanji Auntie's powdered neck craning upward as she exhaled smoke. Dimple's nostrils flaring. Akhil cupping a flame for Sanji Auntie.

"I like the one with the sneakers," someone said.

"Say more."

"I think it works."

"More."

"Well, like the symbolism," Missy Folgers offered. "The whole Indian American thing. I totally get it."

Amina fought the urge to stare down Missy and whatever she thought she got.

"Tell us about the composition of this one," Mrs. Messina said.

"That's my dad," Amina said.

She had taken the picture the day after he had come back from India, too scared to actually go sit on the porch with him though she had wanted to see him, to make sure he was okay. "I should check on my patients," he had said after dinner, and Amina watched her mother straighten in her chair, whatever part of her had been tenderized by compassion slowly stiffening again. But then he never actually made it to the car. She had watched him drink straight from the bottle for fifteen minutes before setting up the shot. If he noticed her at all, he hadn't said anything.

"It's psycho," someone said.

Why had she superimposed the empty-classroom picture against the back wall? She didn't know. She hadn't even thought that the pictures she took of the classroom were good at all, but somehow, when she was printing, she had reached for the negative, carefully working it into the frame. She had thought it would work on some symbolic level, making it look like her father had been trapped in the hard lines of desks and chairs. Instead, it just mucked up the wall behind him.

"Anyone have anything intelligent to say?" Mrs. Messina asked.

No one said anything.

Mrs. Messina sighed, crossing over to the photograph in three long strides. "C'mon, people. What do you guys feel when you look at this?"

"Scared," said Missy Folgers. People laughed.

"Why are you laughing? She's right," Mrs. Messina said. "It is scary. Why, Missy?"

"I don't know. The way he's sitting, like he doesn't notice anything else going on around him. Like he's in another world."

"A bad world," someone said, and Amina stiffened.

"Exactly. And that's what makes it beautiful," Mrs. Messina said. "We're looking at figures that seem isolated somehow, cut off from the rest of the world. What else gives you that feeling?"

"The porch light," Tommy Hargrow said. "It looks too bright somehow. Which makes everything else look dark."

Amina looked at the bubble of porch light, the shadows tucked around it.

"Exactly. Which, by the way, Amina, is why your mother isn't quite in focus." Mrs. Messina pointed at the blurred corner. "You probably would have gotten her if you had had just a little more light. My guess is she moved."

Her mother? Amina leaned forward, squinted at the portion Mrs. Messina had motioned toward. There was nothing there. She scanned the newspapers on the floor, the door leading to the laundry room, the vigas, the fuzzy lines of classroom behind her father. Then suddenly, sharply, as though the figure itself were rising from the paper, she saw the woman. She was standing in the corner, just behind her father. Amina saw the braid, the jasmine, the sari, the smile buried in her face, and knew she was not looking at her mother at all. She was looking at her grandmother at age thirty-three.

She had to show someone. Not her father. Or her mother. Definitely *not* Dimple. Amina paced the yellow lines of the parking lot, placing heel to toe to heel very carefully, waiting for Akhil. She was sweating. She looked at her watch. Half an hour late. She opened the notebook and peeked inside, both relieved and doubly nervous to find the picture exactly the same.

Maybe they could tell Thomas together. Or maybe they could tell Kamala first, and all three of them could show the picture to Thomas. And what would he make of it? Would he be relieved? Scared? Would he come home more or less?

Fifteen minutes later Amina sat on the hood of the car, watching a thin film of cloud traverse the southeast edge of the mountains. The windshield was hard against her back, the notebook warm on her lap. She turned toward the approaching footsteps. Akhil's forehead creased like a Chinese dumpling.

"It's about time," Amina said.

Akhil looked up at her, eyes glassy, face puckered.

"Are you crying?" She slid off the hood.

"No."

She looked for the telltale bruises. "Did those guys beat you up again?"

"No! Jesus." Akhil hunched his shoulders. He dug the keys out of his pocket, flung the door open, ducked inside, and slammed it shut. Amina watched him through the window. His mouth was twisting nervously. His nose was gleaming and viscous. He wiped a shiny trail across the back of his hand and unlocked her door. She sat down.

"I fell asleep and missed all my afternoon classes," he said finally, his voice sticking in his throat. "Farber said if I did it one more time, I'd be suspended."

"Suspended? For falling asleep once?"

"It's been more than once."

"Oh. Like, how much more?"

Akhil stared at his lap, and another tear worked its way out of his eye, falling onto his chinos. He brushed his cheek angrily. "He thinks I'm doing it on purpose. He said that if I thought he wouldn't expel a National Merit Finalist, I was wrong. Motherfuck!" He was really crying now, his round shoulders shaking under his powder jacket, his head down on the wheel. He lifted it up just to ram it back down. The car keys slid out of his hand and landed on the floor mat with a soft clink.

"It's okay," Amina said lamely.

"On *purpose*? He thinks I'd . . . ? Doesn't he know that the only thing that's going to make anything better is if I get the fuck out of here?"

"You won't get kicked out."

"FUCK!" He kicked the floor. The car shook. "FUCK! FUCK! FUCK!"

"Akhil, stop! It's not going to happen! It's . . ." She looked around the car, as though some piece of clear logic could be found on the dashboard. "He's just trying to scare you. You know that. It's a Farber power trip, man—don't fall for that stuff!" The words felt ridiculous in her mouth, like she was telling a joke with a punch line she didn't understand, and Akhil wouldn't even look at her as he reversed and peeled out of the parking lot.

He was driving too fast for being on school property, but Amina knew better than to say anything about it, so instead she said a little prayer that they wouldn't get spotted by Farber or, worse, his secretary, who loved reporting traffic violations. They caught air over the speed bump and landed with a thump that sent up a little cloud of ash from the ashtray. Akhil screeched to a stop at the gate.

"It's going to be okay," Amina said again, trying to sound a little more official this time, but all this did was make Akhil drop his head to his chest with a sticky gasp. From far away, the dotted line of oncoming traffic swooped toward them like a fleet of planes.

"I mean, you've got, like, a four-point-o," she rushed on, not wanting to see him cry. "You never skip school. Besides, Cheney Jarnet got busted smoking weed in the baseball dugout last year, and he didn't get kicked out, right?"

Akhil said nothing, but let the car inch slowly toward the road.

"Akhil," Amina said.

Silence.

"Hey!" She pushed his shoulder, and when he fell heavily against the wheel, her heart shot up like it was trying to knock her brain out. Little bits of static floated everywhere. *The wheel,* she thought, *turn the wheel,* but when she grabbed for it, the seat belt smacked her back. They continued to slide forward, the cars bearing down on them now, metal grilles gleaming like dog teeth. And everything around Amina felt slippery then, the cool metal of the seat belt clasp in her hand, the rubber mat under her feet, the white line on the road they were heading toward nose-first, like a puppy pushing its way onto a horse track. For one brilliant moment she saw how it would happen, how the cars would crack through Akhil's door and send them up into the sky, how the world would flash through the windows, how the metal and glass would explode into a thousand spears launched from a Lilliputian army. And then the seat belt popped open and she was slamming her foot down hard on top of Akhil's, bringing the car to a lurching stop just as the cars went by them, swerving and honking and releasing the smell of burning tires.

"Jesus fucking Christ!" she yelled, pulling the emergency brake with shaking hands and then scrambling back into her seat. "What the fuck is wrong with you?"

Across from her, Akhil was still, body wedged awkwardly over the wheel. Fear filled her lungs. She lunged at him, pushing him back hard until he hit the seat heavily. She put her hands on his face, his lips. Breathing. He was breathing. And sound asleep.

BOOK 4

YOU CAN ALWAYS
COME HOME AGAIN

ALBUQUERQUE, 1998

CHAPTER 1

Albuquerque greeted Amina with a howling dust storm. Down below the plane, brown coils of sand snaked across the mesas and against the mountains, scattering with the shifting wind currents. They hissed against the windows in the descent, and Amina squinted and held her breath involuntarily as the sky faded from blue to beige. The plane slipped out from under her, and the woman on her side let out a gasp that smelled of white wine. The intercom clicked on.

"Ladies and gentlemen, please check to ensure your seat belts are fastened and your bags are completely under the seat in front of you," said a calm, cheery voice. "It's a windy day here in Albuquerque, and we're going to be hitting a little turbulence on our descent."

Thirty years before, Kamala and Thomas had arrived in a dust storm. Kamala still told Amina about it whenever she felt thwarted by the desert—when a drought shriveled her tomatoes or the mesas caught fire. Once, during a dry summer that drove bears down from the mountains and onto the freeways, she called at six in the morning: *That day we flew in, I looked down and everything everywhere was*

*brown, brown, nothing but brown! I had to walk all the way into the
airport with my eyes closed!*

Amina looked at the swirling ground outside her window and
imagined her parents descending into Albuquerque, their eyes wide
open, India's monsoon season tucked behind them like a shadow.
With Amina not yet born and Akhil in Salem for the eight months it
would take them to make a home, it was the first time they had been
alone in years. She imagined them coming in at sunset, their hands
clasped in a way she'd never seen, their cheeks blazing with orange
light. They weren't distant or shy or awkward in her fantasy; they
weren't a few years into a marriage that Ammachy hadn't approved of.
Instead, they were young and in love and racing into a new country at
twilight. They had things to whisper to each other as the plane descended.

"*Koche!* Here!"

Amina looked behind her to find Kamala struggling down the escalator in a pink cotton sari and running shoes, her huge black purse
hoisted over one arm, hair hanging down her back in the single black
braid she'd worn her entire life. Short, slight-bodied, and bobbing
from side to side like a furious metronome, Kamala made her way
across the floor, entirely unaware of watchers she left in her wake.
Even now, well into her fifties, with a few gray hairs framing the
smooth flute of her cheekbones, she looked girlishly pretty.

"I've been waiting upstairs ten minutes!" she shouted, grabbing
Amina's arm as though she might try to get away.

"That's the departure zone, Ma."

"So?" She looked Amina up and down. "You're looking too thin.
Not eating?"

"I gave it up."

"What?"

Amina squeezed her shoulder, gently guiding her back toward the
escalator. "Of course I'm eating. I just had dinner with Sajeev and
Dimple last night." She silently cursed herself as the information lit up
her mother's face.

"Well, *well*. And how is Mr. Sajeev?"

"Fine." Amina stepped onto the escalator, and Kamala followed, springing forward gingerly, like a cat onto a pile of papers.

"He has some big job now, isn't it? What, exactly?"

"I don't remember."

"I think computer programmer." Kamala smiled.

Outside, the old orange Ford was being pelted on all sides by thick sheets of sand. They watched it for a minute, gathering their breath.

"Okay! Run for your life!" Kamala shouted, and they did, throwing the bag into the back and jumping into the front.

"Hoo! What a business!" she yelled when they'd made it inside, laughing as Amina slammed the door shut. She pulled out from the departure zone, cutting off an approaching car and waving benignly as the driver swerved around them, his middle finger extended. "So the Ramakrishnas want to see you tomorrow. Raj is making jalebis."

Amina winced. "Why can't we tell him that I don't like them?"

"You loved them when you were little!"

It was Akhil who loved them, but saying so would hurt her mother in the way all mentions of Akhil hurt Kamala, the prick of his name silencing her for minutes or sometimes hours. "Well, I really don't love them now."

"Raj loves making them for you, and your father loves eating, so no big deals, right?"

Right. "Where is Dad, anyway?"

"Big case. Your skin is looking good. You've been using the Pond's I sent you?"

"Wait, he's operating?"

"What else would he be doing?"

"I don't know. Resting?"

"He's not sick."

"He's sick enough for you to ask me to come down."

"I said he was *talking*, not *sick*. You're the one who decided you needed to come down."

Amina shook her head but said nothing. Why bother? Once rewritten, Kamala's history was safer than classified government documents. The wind hit harder as they turned north. A few miles away, the hospitals—part of the only cluster of buildings higher than ten stories in the entire town—rose up into the dirty air. Amina squinted at them.

"How was yesterday? You had a wedding?"

Amina pushed away the memory of Lesley Beale's face and the coats and the limbs. "It was fine."

"The bride was a nice girl?"

"Eh."

"What's her name?"

"Jessica."

"Je-see-ca," her mother repeated, nodding to herself. "How old?"

"Twenty-three."

"I see," Kamala said softly, switching lanes. "That's lucky, no? Mother must be so relieved."

"I'm sure she is. Poor you, huh?"

"No one is saying that!" Her mother looked over her shoulder. "So Sajeev is seeing someone?"

"Not that I know of."

Kamala waggled her head from side to side, shaking up and re-evaluating the information as it settled. She flexed her fingers against the steering wheel a few times before saying, "So then you and Sajeev could go on a date."

"No we can't."

"Why not?"

"Because he's not my type."

"Oh, that," her mother snorted.

"What that? *That's* important, Mom! *That's* not a crazy thing to want."

"No need to yell about it." Kamala frowned. "I'm just saying is all."

"Anyway, I'm thirty," Amina muttered. "You don't tell a thirty-year-old who to date."

"Twenty-nine! And your friends don't tell you? Dimple doesn't tell you?"

"That's different."

"Yes, of course. This brilliant country where the children listen to other children about who to spend their lives with."

Amina leaned closer to the window. Up ahead on the road, a herd of tumbleweeds skipped toward the truck, their thorny bodies buoyant with wind.

"Take me to the hospital."

"What?"

"I want to see Dad for a sec."

"Just wait until he's home. Besides, he might be in surgery."

"Then they will tell me that when they page him."

"But why go at all? Hospital is a horrible place."

"*Ma.*"

"Fine, fine," Kamala sighed, squinting into the rearview mirror and shifting lanes. "But I'm not coming in."

Within minutes they were idling in front of the ER, where a few brave nurses sucked down cigarettes, palms shielding their eyes.

"You sure you're going to be okay out here?" Amina asked, pushing a stray lock of hair behind her mother's cheek.

"Yes. I will be taking one nap. Go fast."

Amina pushed her door open and ran.

CHAPTER 2

She held her breath. It didn't matter that the upholstered seats had changed from mauve to green to blue, or that the television had been updated to a more recent model, or that new pay phones stood in place of the ones that had been there when she was a kid; every damn time Amina went into the ER, the fear and hope and worry emanating from the families surrounded her like thick water, filling her lungs with dread.

"AMINAMINAMINA!" Thomas boomed, white curls springing out of his head like daisies as he crossed the linoleum toward her. "I just got the page! What are you doing here?"

"Just wanted to see you," she gasped as his arms swooped down around her, squeezing her air out like wet from a sponge.

"You're lucky I wasn't in the OR!" He pulled back, looking, she thought, no crazier than usual. Graying eyebrows huddled over his eyes like permanent weather, and his dark irises glinted sharply through them. His mustache and beard were as carefully trimmed as ever, outlining his wide, flat lips. "Come, let's walk."

"Okay, but I can't go far. Mom is waiting."

"Fine, fine." Thomas kept one arm over her shoulder as they walked, and she was filled with the smell of him—deodorant and aftershave and the slight masala that always came out of his pores like incense. "So how was your trip?"

"Turbulent."

"I'll bet! A lot of pish and hizoom out there, isn't it?"

"Yeah." A nurse passed them and waved. Thomas nodded at her. "So how are you?"

"Excellent!"

"Yeah?" Amina fought a brief urge to pull back, to study his face like a cop or a shrink or someone else who was paid to know when people were lying.

"Yup. Come, I told Monica I'd bring you to her."

Amina stifled her shiver of repulsion. Over the twenty years Monica had worked as Thomas's physician's assistant, she'd gone from calling herself Amina's "aunt" to her "older sister" to her "buddy," each claim of increasing closeness causing Amina to feel its corollary in claustrophobia. Still, no one spent more time with Thomas. Monica would know if something was really wrong.

They walked down the twists and turns of the hospital corridor, puddles of light guiding them like lines on the road. ("How do you know where you're going?" Amina had asked once, when she was five, and Thomas had tapped his skull and answered, "It's in here," so that now when she thought of his brain, it was a bright linoleum maze, the dead and the dying hidden in corners, waiting for release.)

"Anyan, you still here?" Thomas bellowed at a man approaching them from the far end of the hall. "I thought you would have left hours ago!"

"Dr. Eapen." Small and dark and tucked into his white coat like a check in an envelope, the man came to an abrupt stop when he reached them, smiling with a precision that suggested military training or a sociological disorder. "Is this your daughter, then?"

"This is Amina! Amina, Dr. George."

"Hi," Amina extended her hand. His grip was cold and soft.

"Nice to meet you." His turn back to Thomas was a swift though not unkind dismissal. "You didn't by chance get a moment to look at Mrs. Naveen's MRI, did you?"

"I did."

Amina listened as they exchanged the same words that embroidered her childhood with their unknown specificities—*decompressive, craniotomy, extracerebral*. She studied Dr. George's face for hints of wariness or disbelief, but he seemed to swallow Thomas's opinion whole, nodding at the right points.

"Heyyyyyyy, Amina!"

Down the hall, the steel doors of the ICU swinging shut behind her, Monica came barreling toward them, linebacker thick and squinting from under a pouf of blond hair.

"Amina, nice to meet you," she heard Dr. George say before she was swept up into Monica's embrace.

"How are you, hon? How's Seattle? Things?"

The pens from Monica's lab coat stabbed her left breast. "Great."

"I'll let you two catch up," Thomas said, squeezing Amina's shoulder. "Ami, just say bye before you go."

"Yeah, okay."

He hit a button on the wall, and the steel doors flew open again, the rich darkness behind them unsettling.

"And Dimple?" Monica's mouth was pursed around a breath mint, and cool, sugary air blew over Amina's face. "You guys still close?"

"Yeah, of course. What about you? Things here?"

"Oh, fine, you know. Same shit, another week. You just here for a visit?"

"Yes, until the end of the week."

"Your dad is so excited. You should get him out for some fun. He could use a break."

"What do you mean?"

"Maybe take him to Cochiti Lake for a few days or something. His Thursday and Friday are light."

Amina nodded as two men with stethoscopes rounded the corner, walking toward them. "Is there something wrong?"

"What?"

"Is there a reason he needs a break?"

"No!" Monica bugged her eyes out at Amina with a funny smile as the men passed. "He just, you know, loves to fish with you."

Amina cocked her head, frowning. Thomas did not love to fish with her. Was this some kind of weird code, or just one of Monica's not-that-great-memory moments? Amina was trying to figure out a way to ask when Monica's beeper went off, startling both of them.

She unclipped it, wrinkling her nose. "Crap, I need to take this. You gonna be here for a little while? We should get a coffee in the cafeteria."

"Actually, Mom's waiting in the car."

"Damn. Well, can we get margaritas this week? Have some girl time? I want to hear all about the love life."

The internal shiver was coming back, the repulsion harder to fend off now that Monica was actually in front of her, all hair and nosiness.

"Perfect, call you tomorrow," Amina said, and went to find her dad.

"Over there," the nurse on duty whispered when she entered the ICU, and Amina followed her pointing finger to the far end of the room, where Thomas's feet were visible under a white curtain.

"Hey, Dad?" she whispered when she was just outside it. "I gotta get going."

Thomas peeked out of the curtain, then motioned for her to enter, and she did, suddenly finding herself in a space heavy with the stale breath of a patient. Her father moved aside, and she looked down to find a tangle of silvery hair that fanned out across the pillow like fishing net. The woman was older, maybe in her eighties, her skin thin and tanned and waxy-looking.

"Infection is getting worse," Thomas said, writing something down on her chart. "She won't make it through the night."

"Should you just say it like that?"

"Hmm?"

"You know, in front of her like that."

Her father looked up from his clipboard and smiled at her sweetly, as though she had asked if the Tooth Fairy was making enough money in dental collection. "I'm sure she already knows."

It took three rounds of knocks to wake Kamala up. Amina hopped in the wind, the dust replaced by a cold blast of northern air. She pounded on the windows and, when that didn't work, kicked the doors. Finally, one loud thump sent Kamala shooting up in a puff of sari, her face tattooed with the checked imprint of the truck seat. She looked at Amina and frowned.

"I'll drive," Amina said, and Kamala scooted over wordlessly, unlocking the driver's side. Amina climbed in.

"Put it into gear."

"I remember how to drive, Ma."

Kamala leaned away, resting her forehead against the window. She was quiet as they pulled away from the hospital, quiet as they got back onto the highway, but when Amina checked to see if she'd fallen back asleep, her eyes were wide open, staring out at the service road that ran alongside them.

"He's so happy you've come," she said.

They were heading out of the city fast, into the barren stretches of the Indian reservations, where dried hands of sagebrush crisped in the summer heat. Albuquerque's June sat flat and brown around them, the whole desert parched and waiting like an open mouth for the relief of July's afternoon rains.

Up ahead was the exit to the village of Corrales, where a descent into the valley would bring air that was sweeter and clearer with every passing mile. The road would grow wide, the sagebrush replaced by locoweed and prairie grass, and soon Amina would see the soft line of bosque cottonwoods that enveloped either side of the Rio Grande. She held the wheel loosely, letting it ride out the familiar curves of the road home.

CHAPTER 3

That afternoon Kamala went on a cooking rampage. Revitalized by her nap and the discovery of perfectly ripe rhubarb in her garden, she sat at the kitchen counter elbow-deep in red pulp, churning out a gory chutney while several pots steamed and hissed on the stove at her side.

"GO YE INTO ALL THE WORLD AND PREACH THE GOSPEL TO EVERY CREATURE!" Mort Hinley extolled from the radio.

"Okay!" Kamala shouted, snapping the food processor lid in place.

"RISE UP AND TELL THEM THE TRUTH!"

"Why not!"

"RETICENCE WILL NOT WIN THE WAR OF *MORALITY* AND *TRUTH* IN AMERICA! ONLY THE *FEARLESSNESS OF GOD'S SOLDIERS* WILL DO IT! STAND UP AGAINST THE DEVIL IN HIS MANY FORMS! STAND UP!"

"Standing!!"

The food processor roared to life between her hands, and Kamala threw her head back a bit too rapturously, as though the Kingdom of

Heaven itself were cracking through the kitchen ceiling. Amina watched from the safety of the courtyard until something soft and wet nuzzled her. She looked down to see Prince Philip, an old Labrador with a younger dog's fetching addiction, staring at the stick he had left on her foot.

"Jesus H.," she said, and threw it for him.

It should have been comforting enough that her mother had finally left the Trinity Baptist Church a good three years earlier, shunning their attempts to bring her back into the fold with a haughty disdain that confounded them. It should have been comforting to know that Mort Hinley was just another in a long line of preachers Kamala would love for a day, a week, a series of months, until she had decided (as she had with the Trinity Baptist Church, Oral Roberts, Benny Hinn, and a series of others) that he was getting between her and Jesus. But still, the Jesus-loving version of her mother took some getting used to. And watching Kamala raising her palm to the air above the churning food processor still sent a bolt of nausea up Amina's spine, visions of *Heil Hitler*–ing masses running in black and white through her head.

"Everyone has a *personal* Jesus," a newly saved Kamala had explained when Amina was in high school, believing, apparently, that Amina would greet this news with as much excitement as she would everyone having a personal Porsche. The following week she had forced her to come to a service at Trinity Baptist Church, where the congregants seemed to revel in the fact that Kamala was a saved *Indian,* a sort of born-again Bengal Tiger in their midst. Never mind that the Eapens were already Christians; Pastor Wilbur Walton had explained Amina's presence as a sign of the Lord's work being done. "Back in India," he said, "these folks were following blue-skinned *gods.*"

"You think Jesus cares who got there first?" Kamala had asked when Amina fumed over it on the car ride home.

"But we were Christians while they were still praying to goddamn Odin!"

"Doesn't matter! Jesus loves all equally! And quit quoting your father, you sound like an idiot."

"Mom's a lunatic," Amina told Prince Philip when he returned with the stick, dropping it next to her ankle. The dog looked unimpressed.

Thomas came home a little early, and soon enough Kamala called them for dinner, which comprised not one but all of Amina's favorite dishes—lamb vindaloo and bhindi baingan and chicken korma steaming quietly from the copper pots.

"You made too much, Ma," Amina said, mouth watering.

"Speak for yourself," Thomas said. "When you're not here, she starves me."

"Yeah, you look starved."

Kamala put out several little jars of pickle. "This one Bala made; it's lime but a little too salty. Raj gave us the mango. It's dry. I made the garlic. That's all you're taking for vegetable?"

"I'll get seconds."

"You need the cabbage to keep you from slouching, and the okra will help with your lips."

"What's wrong with my lips?"

"They're getting blackish."

"They are?" Amina looked at her reflection in the microwave. Her entire face looked back at her in different shades of blackish.

"They're fine," Thomas said, helping himself to the food on the stove. "Stop giving her complexes."

"Who's giving anything? Not so much of ghee, Mr. Hardening Arteries."

Thomas put the ghee spoon down with a sigh and set his plate on the table. "Amina, can I get you something to drink? Should we open a bottle of wine?"

"No thanks," Amina said, sitting. "Just water for me."

"Poosh. Party pooper." Thomas grabbed a beer for himself from the fridge.

They ate. The lamb and rice were tender and pungent in Amina's mouth, instantly settling whatever the turbulence had ruffled. Amina sighed deeply, chewing. Her lips buzzed with numbness from the heat. "So good, Ma. Thanks."

"Thanking a mother for cooking is nonsense," Kamala huffed,

looking pleased. "Anyway. Did I tell you my friend Julie's daughter is getting married this weekend?"

Amina gave her father a pained look.

"No talk of marriage," Thomas said.

"Who's talking marriage?" her mother asked. "I'm talking *business*. I told Julie you would have been happy to take pictures, but you're leaving. Unless you can stay?"

"I can't. I work weekends, remember?"

"This is work!"

"Anyhow, I'm sure Julie's daughter has had a photographer picked out for months. That's how it works, you know."

"I know that, silly, I just told her that you were a better photographer is all."

"You don't know that."

"Of course I do," Kamala said, and despite herself, Amina filled with a sudden stab of love, like a breath she hadn't counted on taking. She reached for the jar of garlic pickle, putting a generous portion on her plate.

"You don't need that much," Kamala said.

"I like it," Amina said, and her mother ducked her head to hide her smile.

Evening escape was always necessary. After leaving Monica a message, Amina took a stale cigarette from an empty cassette-tape case hidden in her old desk and wandered down to the ditch just outside the gate at the back of the house. The magic of the smoke and the high altitude sent her head swimming, but when she exhaled, she had one clear thought: *Dad is fine*. The notion surprised Amina with its assuredness, and she turned it over in the coming dark, unsure if she was having a genuine moment of insight or her fear was conspiring to tell her what she most needed to hear.

Coming back to the house, she saw that her father was already waiting for their nightly conversation, the deep yellow of his porch light beckoning like a fire. She walked toward it, wondering once again how anyone could insist on calling the burgeoning mayhem on the back of the house a "porch." Sure, it had started out as a verandah some twenty years earlier, but time and Thomas's endless additions—platforms, nooks, shelves, newspapers, tools, inventions—left it floating in the backyard like a junk barge.

Large, darkened outlines grew clearer as Amina drew closer, turning from monsters to machinery—a router table, two planers, table saw, and drill press. Clamps of varying sizes hung across the back wall, along with several lassos of extension cord, three levels, and two wall-mounted shelves of tiny boxes that held everything from safety pins to masonry drill bits. Three headlamps, a hard hat, a cowboy hat, and a felt touk dotted the wall above a coatrack, on which a lab coat, a yellow rubberized suit, and a flame-retardant jumper were draped. The only actual furniture in the room consisted of two wingback chairs—one made of cracked leather and permanently empty, save for the times Amina filled it, and the other a patchy red velvet, in which Thomas was currently sitting. He shifted, looking vaguely impatient, as she came closer.

"I don't think so," he said.

"You don't think what?"

A lone moth cast a hand-sized shadow across the wall behind him, and he turned to it. He frowned and looked at his watch.

"Dad?"

His eyes zeroed in on her. "Hey, Amina! There you are! I was waiting."

"Sorry. I needed a walk after all the food."

She made her way in, skirting a sawhorse strangled by surgical tubing.

"Where did you go?"

"Just now? Just to the ditch."

"You should be careful out there. High school kids park there now. A whole lot of them are in gangs."

"Like the Crips and the Bloods?" Amina joked.

"Lots of them," Thomas said. "Ty Hanson lost his son last month in a shoot-out in the mall."

"Oh my God, really?" She had known Mr. Hanson in the loose way she knew a handful of her father's patients—more a flash of features and a diagnosis than any real connection. He had a beard of some sort, a recurring meningioma, and a towheaded toddler. "That little kid?"

"Derrick. He had just turned seventeen in April." Thomas's face hollowed with a grief they both knew had nothing to do with Ty or Derrick Hanson, and Amina looked down, her breathing gone tight. The bin at her feet held the double-headed snakes of jumper cables, and she studied their copper jaws until she heard her father standing up.

"You want a drink?" He walked across the porch to rattle around in the old hospital lockers that lined the back wall. "This is the good stuff. Old ER nurse sent it. You remember Romero?"

Amina did not remember Romero. She nodded to avoid being given a full explanation of Romero. A minute or so later, Thomas crossed the porch, holding out one of two jelly jars.

"Cheers," Thomas said, and they toasted without clinking. Amina took a deep swallow. The good stuff tasted like a campfire.

"You don't like it?"

She exhaled. "I don't know yet."

Thomas looked amused, wandering back to his chair and gesturing for her to do the same. "So how is Seattle?"

"Oh, you know. Pretty much the same."

"You're still liking your job?"

She smiled tightly, strangely comforted by how little Thomas understood about her career derailment. "It's fine."

"Do you like the weddings?"

"Yeah," Amina surprised herself by saying, "I guess I do."

"That's nice. Lucky, right?" It wasn't a real question, more an affirmation of what Thomas had taken upon himself as his most important life lesson for Amina—to have a job she felt passionate about. "It's such a crucial business, this liking what you do. Americans get into this idea that you do one thing to make money and then live like royalty when you are away from it—such a strange way to live. Makes you"—his fingers danced around his head—"imbalanced!"

"You never felt that way about work?"

"Never. I had bad days—who doesn't have bad days? But still I look forward to going in every day. Excited and whatnot." His face brightened as he talked, ramping up for his favorite revelation. "I wasn't a good medical student, you know."

"No?" Amina said, like this was a surprise.

Thomas shook his head vigorously. "Terrible, actually. I was such a troublemaker, and Ammachy . . . But going to medical school was a fluke, really. I had the grades, you see, but not the ambitions."

Amina took another long pull of scotch, watching his features soften in the giddy, distant way that fathers in movies did when remembering how they fell in love with their wives.

"Dr. Carter?" she prompted.

"Yes! Exactly. I had never touched a live brain before he came to Vellore, can you imagine? And then the exposition! The surgery! We must have stood for eleven hours that first day alone. People always say time stands still, and it really is that, you know. You find the thing you love the most, and time will stop for you to love it."

He looked at her, clearly pleased with his recounting, and Amina felt a pinch in her heart. She swallowed the rest of her scotch with a gulp. He stood up and motioned for her glass. Prince Philip made a halfhearted attempt to stand, then slid back into position on the floor.

"Oh, I don't know about that," Thomas said, shuffling toward the lockers.

"Know about what?" Amina watched him, body pulsing lightly with heat. The good stuff was apparently a little bit stronger than the regular stuff. Or maybe she was just becoming a lightweight.

"What, Ami?"

"Did you just say something?"

"Nope." He opened the locker. "It's nice to have you here. So you just came home because you had some time off?"

Something about his tone made Amina look up. He held his body still, the bottle poised in midair for her answer.

"More or less." She waited until he was back and had handed her the glass to say, "Mom was a little worried about you, too."

"Worried about what?"

"That maybe something's not quite right with you."

"Pssht." Thomas waved a large hand. "She's thought that forever, no?" Amina conceded with a small shrug, and Thomas's frown deepened. "Anyway, your mother has always been afraid of anything she can't control."

"Maybe she just read the situation wrong."

"Yes, she's quite good at that, too." Thomas cleared his throat. "Did she tell you she sent two thousand dollars to some radio preacher?"

"What? No! When?"

"Last month itself."

"Oh, God. What did you do?"

"Nothing! What to do? She never spends money on herself, now she wants to give it to some quack? Her business." He looked out across the yard for a long time. "I think"—he swirled the liquid around his glass—"she's having a spiritual crisis."

"Really? Mom?"

He nodded, not looking at her. "This business of not belonging to a church, of not having a place for all her beliefs. I think it's affecting her. Making her see evil and whatnot where it isn't." He looked at her, his nose wrinkling with a *What can you do?* shrug. Amina looked hard at him, at his assured posture, his sharp eyes. There were rings around his irises, the pale harbingers of age.

"You're fine," she said out loud. Thomas nodded. She let her head sink into the back of her chair. "Of course you are."

"You really thought something was wrong?"

"I don't know. I mean, it did sound crazy. She said you were out here all night talking to Ammachy or something."

She expected him to laugh, as he usually did when they had weathered another bout of Kamala's insanity, but when she looked at him, his mouth was puckered.

"What?"

"You believed her," he said.

"I didn't know what to think."

"Sure," he said, clearly hurt.

"Dad."

He looked away and she slid her feet across the floor until her sneakers rested on top of his black work shoes. She nudged him, and after a moment he nudged back. Prince Philip shifted in his sleep, rolling until he was all belly and genitals, his canines sharp under a sagging lip.

"Oh, hey!" Thomas jumped up, startling her. He walked toward one of the shelves. "Have I told you about this yet?"

Amina watched as he rummaged in the dark, flipping on one light switch and then another. He pulled out two large spoons tied together and waved them.

"What is that?"

"Come. I'll show you."

"What? Where?"

Thomas nodded to the fields. "You'll love it."

Ten minutes later, Amina stood back in the dark yard with her father, staring into the truck bed.

"And what, exactly, does it do?" she asked.

"Stuns them a bit, when done at close proximity and with soft produce," Thomas said. They had moved Kamala's truck from the driveway to the very back of the field. Two cords of surgical tubing hung between the spoons that were bolted into each side of the bed. In between was a pillow-sized square of leather. Thomas picked it up and pulled it back.

"Holy shit," Amina said.

"Holy *Raccooner*!" Thomas corrected.

The slingshot, if it could still be called that at such enormous proportions, took up the better length of the truck bed when stretched fully backward. Thomas pulled it tight, explaining to Amina, "Thing is, you need to find what works best. We've been doing experiments. Tomatoes, potatoes, that kind of thing."

"We?"

"Raj and Chacko and me. I thought the tomato was something else, but then Raj went and baked an eggplant whole and brought it over and *pshoom!* You've never seen anything like it!"

"You're going to kill raccoons with an eggplant?"

"Not kill! Stun. Stun is what we're aiming for. It's actually a twofer." In the world of inventions, Thomas held the greatest respect for the twofer. A suit made of naturally deodorizing fabric? A bath sponge shaped like a headrest? *Wonderful.* His lips now twitched with anticipation, giving her a full three seconds to come up with it before bursting out, "It will provide a meal *and* a deterrent at the same time!"

Amina looked at the spoons. "You're shooting them with dinner?"

"You make it sound so sinister. It keeps them from getting into the trash. And by keeping it in the truck, we can move when they do."

"How do you know it won't do real damage? I bet a potato could hurt."

"I wouldn't fire a whole, uncooked potato," Thomas said, scoffing. "And stewed tomato barely hurts, really."

"You don't know that."

"I do, actually. Chacko lost the bet and had to stand target. He took two tomatoes in the back."

"Jesus! And?"

"Nothing much," Thomas said, sounding vaguely disappointed. "Nice stain and all, but he said that it wasn't so bad, though he smelled a bit afterward."

Thomas carefully laid the slingshot down and sat on the back of the truck. He motioned for the scotch she had been holding for him, and they toasted silently. The noise of crickets grew slightly louder around her, pressing in with the night.

"If you want, I'll take you to the driving range tomorrow. We made one by the dump," Thomas said. "Those guys let us do it out there, and now we all compete, using each other as targets. Raj thinks we could turn it into a new sport even."

"Raccooning?" Amina asked.

"Exactly," her father said.

It's the altitude, she thought.

Upstairs an hour later, Amina clutched the side of her bed. Her eyes slid dizzyingly around the room, but shutting them was worse, the darkness thick as meat, her head swelling with the sound of the dog barking and the wind through the trees and what might be her father's voice talking under all of it. She sat up, placing her feet squarely on the floor.

In the bathroom she leaned over the sink, staring at her reflection. Her hair was flat and her pupils were wide. She splashed water over her face.

The tiniest bit of light winked from the glass-covered frames that guided her down the hall, and she moved past them like a plane down an abandoned runway. They were pictures, school pictures, hers and Akhil's, each leading to their bedroom doors. Even in the dark she knew which she was passing with every step, her braces in fourth grade, his light mustache in seventh. When she got to the bedroom doors, she turned to his instead of her own. The cool wood pressed her forehead, which she lifted twice and knocked, as if that was a good idea with all the spinning, as if he might have surprised her with an answer. Nothing came, but she was comforted anyway, holding on to the doorknob like it was somebody's hand.

"Hey you," she said.

CHAPTER 4

"Look at this girl!" Sanji Ramakrishna screamed. She threw the door open in a blue silken whirl and streaked down the steps toward Amina, cackling like a fat devil. Pinching hands landed on Amina's shoulders, her cheeks, and Sanji bellowed at the door, "Hey! Fools! Get off your rusty rumps and come and greet our baby! It's taken her all of three days to face us!"

"One day, Sanji Auntie," Amina protested, but her words were lost to the thrum of voices that moved from the kitchen to the entryway, bursting out of the door with the rest of them: Raj Ramakrishna (led by a spatula), Bala and Chacko Kurian (in one of their many silent fights, from the looks of things), and Thomas, whiskey in hand.

Raj greeted her first, the loose girth of him swaddled in stylishly rumpled linen. Plump, cultured, and the wearer of a docile smile that was rumored to have wooed legions of older women in his youth, he double-pecked each of Amina's cheeks before whispering, "There's pani puri and jalebis in the kitchen."

"You really shouldn't have gone through all that trouble."

"Tell me about it!" Sanji said. "All night this one! Clucking about in the kitchen like some mad hen because tamarind chutney wouldn't thicken and how to get done by the time Amina-baby gets here!"

"Come in, come in," Bala Kurian coaxed from her perch on the step, arms clenched in front of her like a tiny prizefighter. Known throughout the Indian community in Albuquerque for her steady supply of gossip, outlandish outfits, and baffling non sequiturs, Dimple's mother was in fine form tonight, glittering under several heavy chains and a saffron-colored, midriff-baring lehenga. (*Straight from Bom!* she would brag over dinner. *Like a dancing girl dipped in ghee!* Kamala would mutter under her breath.)

"Goodness, Ami! But what's happened to you? You're looking so fair!"

"She uses the Pond's every night!" called Kamala, heaving up the driveway with an enormous bowl of rasmalai. "I sent her from Walgreens myself!"

"Or it could be the whole no-sun thing," Amina said, ignoring her mother's look.

"Come, let me see." Chacko Kurian, who had been waiting by the door, now swept the women aside to grip Amina's shoulders with gnarled hands. "You're fairer?"

"Hi. Not really."

He looked down his nose at her as though reading the face of a watch, his eyes glittering from somewhere deep behind heavy brows. "Too old for marrying anyway—why worry about it now?"

"Chackoji, don't start," Sanji warned.

"What start? It's not a conversation, just the plain truth."

Delivered at least twelve times in every get-together, Chacko Kurian's plain truths could have stamped the joy out of any festivity if anyone were to take him seriously. Springing from lost dreams (to pioneer heart surgery with a fleet of like-minded sons) and found realities (a daughter who was as uninterested in his line of work as she was in trying to make him happy), his edicts were always promptly dismissed by the others, giving him the air of a king ruling the wrong kingdom.

"So what all is happening in Seattle?" he asked, clearing his throat. "Your father says you've been busy-busy."

"Yes, well, it's the wedding season."

"How many weddings do you do in one weekend?"

"Depends. Usually two, but sometimes four. Once I even—"

"And Dimple?" His jaw flexed as he asked. "I don't suppose she's given up this silly art business?"

"She's doing great. I saw her right before I left."

"We heard that's not all you saw!" Bala beamed. "What's this about you going on a date with Sajeev?"

"Oh, for the love of God. Dimple and I met him *for a meal.*"

"Dimple went on a date with Sajeev?" Bala looked even more thrilled.

"It wasn't a date. It was dinner."

"A dinner date?"

"Always, I knew that boy would go far," Chacko announced.

"Who cares about that little stick-necked thing?" Sanji asked. "What other news of our girl? And when will she come home? It's been two years already."

"She's really stressed about work right now," Amina said, making the kind of excuses she always had for Dimple, whose teen stint in reform school had gone badly enough to keep her from coming back to see her father, even all these years later. "There's a big show coming up."

"Ach," Sanji sniffed. "Too successful, what to do?"

"Listen, at least she isn't working in a strip club," Bala said, her tone dropping into decibels reserved for gossip-tragedy. "Did you hear about the Patels' daughter Seema? Seems she's in Houston living with an American boy and owning some topless bar where you can only order small dishes of Spanish food! Mother herself told me!"

While the others choked on disbelief ("Seema? The National Merit Finalist?"), Sanji Auntie put a firm hand on Amina's arm, guiding her away.

"You're thirsty, darling? Let's get you a drink."

Amina let herself be whisked up the step and down the green-tiled hall. It was quiet and cooler in the living room, where the bar and the *puja* table competed for attention on opposite sides of the room.

"You need a gin, love? Or are we being good for the parents?"

"No, thanks." Amina took a seat on a leather stool, inhaling the sharp mix of sandalwood and rosewater. The mirrored wall behind the bar showed her pallor. "I'm still feeling the whiskey I drank last night."

"Hair of the dog it is."

"No! God, please."

"Poor baby. Ginger ale? Just sit here and catch your breath."

Amina watched Sanji waddle behind the bar, where she grabbed a tumbler and filled it with ice. Of all the family, it was Sanji Ramakrishna who Amina still loved the most, her thick, meatish body, deep, rumbling laugh, mottled nose, ruddy cheeks, ability to weave equally between the men's and women's conversations, total inability to cook. And then there was the Ramakrishnas' marriage, a subject of continual fascination for Amina and Dimple, having occurred in their unthinkable thirties as Ph.D. students at Cambridge. (*A love marriage,* their own mothers called it, shaking sad heads at the lack of children, though to Amina, that fact itself was unspeakably romantic, as though real love was the substitute for progeny, and vice versa.)

She took the bubbly tumbler from Sanji's extended hands. "Thanks."

Sanji smiled. "So things are fine with you? We didn't know you were coming, you know."

Amina took a sip. "I had some time off."

"Nothing else?"

She put the glass down, took a breath. "I need to ask you about something."

Sanji studied Amina's face for a moment, then leaned in. "It's okay. I know."

"You do?"

"Because Mummy has been so worried, you know. Said you were losing hope about not meeting anyone and needed to come home for a bit to build up confidences. Which is fine, nah? We're always so happy to see you. I just wish it wasn't because you were feeling so down."

Amina frowned. "That's not why I'm here."

"No?" Sanji's concern dipped slightly toward disbelief.

"No! I came home because of Dad."

"What about Dad?"

"Mom said he was acting funny for the last three weeks, so I came back."

"Funny? Funny how?"

"Talking on the porch all night," Amina said, and when her aunt continued to look unimpressed, added, "to his dead mother."

Sanji raised an eyebrow. "Kamala brought you home for this?"

"Well, yeah."

"Oh, I wish you would have just asked me about it, Ami. I could have saved you the trouble."

"You know about it?"

"Of course I know! Raj himself barely sleeps four hours a night anymore—always chattering away like one damn BBC interview. He talks to his father, his uncle, his grandfather. No, really, I'm telling you, it's true! And if your mother would ever just talk to me about anything other than this Jesus business, I would tell her! It's just an old man's disease. Nothing more."

"I don't know. It seemed bad when she called."

"And now?"

"Now he seems fine," Amina admitted.

"Because he *is* fine. Pish, Kamala. She's just missing you is all. Speaking of which"—Sanji stood, motioning for Amina to do the same—"we need to get you back there before those fools accuse me of hogging."

In the kitchen, under a cloud of protest and frying mustard seed, plates of pani puri were being passed around.

"It's only *appetizer*!"

"Amina, come get a plate!"

"I better get more than this!" This came from Thomas, looking down at his portion. "I didn't come all this way to starve."

"Who starves you?" Kamala asked indignantly.

"We're trying something a little different tonight, Amina," Raj explained. "Appetizers and dessert only are Indian. The main meal is Mongolian hot pot!"

"It's a fancy way of saying he didn't cook anything." Sanji pointed to the dining table in the room next to them, where small hills of raw meat and tofu and vegetables surrounded a steaming cauldron. "I told you they wouldn't like it."

"Oh," Amina said. "Wow."

"Wow is right," Chacko said. "Salmonella. *E. coli.* Could be our last supper."

"You Suriani bores!" Raj huffed. "So averse to change, all of you! Remember how you loved the fondue night?"

At this there was a general murmur of agreement, heads nodding over *Yes the fondue was quite good, who knew all that cheese and chocolate but still.*

"Do we get to use the long skinny forks again?" Bala asked hopefully.

"Even better," Raj said, smiling. "We get to use chopsticks."

The chopsticks, for the most part, were abandoned after five minutes. Most found their way back to the kitchen, although one poked out of Kamala's braid, placed there by a frustrated Thomas and either forgotten by its wearer or just tolerated. By mid-meal, three forks had also been lost to the bubbling broth, covered by chunks of meat, cabbage, snow peas, and tofu, and there was a bit of chest puffery from the men over who had made the best dipping sauce.

Bala nudged Chacko. "Tell them about the nurse in the OR!"

"Which?" Thomas asked.

"Sandy Freeland," Chacko said. "You remember how she left suddenly for those three weeks?"

"Yes."

"Turns out she went to find out if her husband, the pilot, was cheating on her."

"And?" Kamala asked, trying unsuccessfully to drag a too-cooked piece of tofu from the pot with a lone chopstick.

Chacko passed her his fork. "She found him in Dubai with not just another woman, but two sons!"

"No! My God!" The gasps came from every side of the table.

"Americans!" Kamala said.

"Not just Americans!" Bala fanned her hands out. "My God, Madras has become a hotbed."

"Ahno?" Kamala motioned for the soy sauce. "Who says?"

"My sister only! She was telling me of one Lalitha Varghese—"

"Lalitha from MCC?"

"Yes, yes! That Lalitha!" Bala said. "Anyway, her husband, the ob-gyn, goes and has an affair with a patient . . . and then moves her into the house!"

Around the table: hisses, nose tuggings, head shakings.

"Poor thing." Sanji tsked. "What did she do?"

Bala held her hands up. "She started shooting the drugs!"

Amina choked on her rice.

Thomas thumped her back. "Heroin?"

"*Demerol.* She took it from his office only."

"Pathetic!" Sanji shook her head. "I would have started shooting the both of them dead and gone to Mahabilipuram on beach holiday."

"Of course you would, darling," Raj said, holding up a plate. "Now, who wants more tofu?"

"No more 'fu!" Thomas said, standing up rather dramatically. He scanned the table, taking a moment to locate his glass before plucking it up and heading out.

"So, Ami, what's this big show Dimple is working on then?" Sanji asked.

"It's Charles White."

They all looked at her blankly.

"He's huge. It's a big deal that she got him."

"So does that mean that if we go to the gallery, someone besides Dimple might actually be standing in it?" Chacko grumbled.

"Chackoji, please don't make me bring out the after-dinner muzzle." Sanji reached for her drink.

"I will never understand what it is she gets paid money to do. Hang pictures on the wall? And this one, with the weddings! What fool can't grab a camera and take some snaps of his own wedding?"

"Ami, baby, a spot of gin?" Sanji said, waving her glass helpfully.

"Yup." Amina snatched it on her way out the door.

"I'm just telling the plain truth; if these girls don't want to hear it—"

"I know, I know, it will be our own undoing." Amina followed after her father as Sanji asked in her loudest, most-determined-to-change-the-subject voice, "Now, Bala, darling, where did this golden getup come from? You look positively radioactive."

Out in the cool hallway, it felt good to breathe. These dinners with the family could get so stuffy, what with everyone sitting on top of her like she might hatch. A quick peek in the kitchen confirmed that it was the kind of wreck that Raj was prone to making and Sanji was doomed to clean up, being, as she put it, "bad in all other feminine arts." In the living room, Thomas was pouring another drink with a scowl-darkened face.

"Hey, Dad."

"Now, that is just not true."

"What's not?" Amina walked up behind him.

"Stop it," he said.

"What?"

Thomas turned around with a start. "Amina!"

"Who were you talking to?"

He blinked a few times before saying, "I wasn't."

"I heard you."

"Really? I must have been talking to myself."

Amina gauged the fumes coming off him. He said nothing as she made her way around the bar, getting a gin and soda for Sanji. "How many have you had?"

Thomas shrugged. "I don't know. Two."

She doubled the number. "I'll drive your car home."

"You don't need to do that."

"I do."

"Whatever," Thomas said, sulking as he always did when she pointed out his drinking, but later, as dinner was finally declared over and everyone stood out in the driveway under the pocketed haze of street lamps, he bragged to the others that his "chauffeur" would be taking him back to his home in the country.

"So you're leaving Friday?" Sanji asked, walking them to the car.

"Yes. Afternoon." Amina unlocked the doors and slid in. She rolled down the window, and Sanji leaned through it.

"How about if I come Friday morning. You'll be around?"

"Like there's anywhere else for me to be?"

Sanji gave her a fat kiss on the forehead. "Good girl." She peered over Amina's shoulder to where Thomas was already settling in for the long ride home, sweater bunched into a pillowish mass behind his head, seat back reclined, large, sock-covered feet on the dash. "Good night, Thomasji. Try not to drive this one too nuts before Friday, nah?"

"Can't drive a nuts nuts!" Thomas said cheerfully, not quite opening his eyes.

Amina slid the car into gear, and her aunt backed up, waving. Soon Raj and Chacko and Bala joined her, their hands raised into the light and flickering like moth wings in the rearview mirror as Amina drove away.

CHAPTER 5

In the garden the next day, Amina and her mother weeded and watered, while dragonflies buzzed overhead and Prince Philip snored into an anthill.

"I don't know where to plant these ones," Kamala grumbled, squinting down at the plastic trays filled with cubed earth. Just a few were beginning to sprout, the thin curls of green reaching out like greedy fingers.

"Can't you put them next to me?"

"No, that's for pumpkins."

"What about back there?" Amina pointed to the fresh mound at the back of the garden. "You've already tilled the soil."

"That dumb dog did it. I gave him a lamb bone the other night, and next thing I know, he's built the pyramid of Giza for it." She picked up the hose, moving it to the bean trellis and releasing the wet, sugary green smell of snow peas and hot soil. Amina breathed deep.

"Nothing smells like the desert." Kamala smiled. "We went to

Texas, remember, for the wedding of that Telegu girl in your high school?"

"Syama?"

"Yes, she married some Houston boy, father arranged the whole thing, but I tell you what about Houston: *too much of smell!* I was so happy to come home. Nice, dry air, everything crisp in the morning." She bent over the eggplant. "What about Seattle? You have a garden there?"

"You know I don't."

"How can you stay in that place? No yard?"

"I don't want a yard."

"Everybody wants a yard!" Kamala knelt to pull a few weeds that were springing up next to the peppers. "Oh, by the way, don't make plans for tomorrow night. I'm making you appam and stew."

"Oh, Ma, you don't need to do all that for me."

"What all that? It's nothing. And anyway, Anyan is coming for dinner and it's his favorite."

"Who?"

"Thomas said you met him at the hospital—the neurologist? He has a son, so he'll bring him, too."

"Oh, right. Dr. George. How old is his kid?"

"Eight."

"Cute. What's his wife like?"

"Foo! Horrible." She pushed a strand of loose hair behind her ear. "I met her last year at some hospital fund-raiser something or other, but then she left him! Can you believe? She's living in Nob Hill with some Afghani now."

Amina stopped weeding. "Wait, what?"

"I know, poor Anyan! Can you imagine? I'm sure he'll meet someone though, hot commodity in the hospital and all that. The nurses are probably plotting over him now."

Amina looked up at the sky, taking pains to breathe evenly. "No. I'm not doing it."

"Doing what?"

"I'm not doing this." Her voice rose slightly as she stood. "You are not doing this to me."

"Having dinner?"

Amina took off the gardening gloves and dropped them in the dust. She turned to leave the garden, willing herself to stay calm until she was in her room.

"Where are you going?" Kamala asked. "We're not done planting!"

"You know, Dimple said this. She warned me you would do this, and I—God!—I didn't believe her. I thought it was too low. Even for you. You're trying to set me up with *Dr. George*?"

"It's dinner, *koche*, not some formal thing where you have to make a decision and—"

"Make a decision?"

"Amina, listen, it's no big deals. I just thought you might like to—"

"Oh my God," Amina laughed, shaking her head. "Is Dad even sick?"

Kamala looked at her for a long moment before saying, "I never said he was sick. *You* said he was sick."

Right. Of course. "So then what was the plan, Ma? You get me back here and Anyan George and I *make a decision* and what? He gets a wife and his son gets a mother and I get a family you can brag about?"

"What's wrong with a family?"

"I don't want one!"

"Yes you do. You need someone, *koche*. Everyone sees it."

It was a soft hit, an unexpected knock that cut Amina's breath short.

"You never try to meet anyone because you think that something is wrong with you," her mother said like it was a simple fact, like she might have been saying *It's a quarter to noon* or *Water the radishes*. "I know, we all know. Sanji and Bala and even *Dimple* says you haven't acted like yourself since you took the picture of that man on the bridge, and—"

"Dimple says nothing! Dimple doesn't even talk to you!"

"She talks to Bala."

"Bullshit! When?"

"When she's worried about something, dummy." Kamala tugged nervously at the bottom of her shirt, and Amina knew it was true suddenly, a thought that made her queasy with shame.

"I'm going," Amina said.

"Oh, Ami."

"No, I mean, I'm *leaving*. Tomorrow. I'm going back to Seattle and going back to my work and my life, and I'm sorry if it doesn't seem like it's enough to you, but it is for me, okay?"

"Hey, *koche* . . ."

Amina unhinged the garden gate and opened it, walking quickly toward the house. Her mother was still calling after her as the screen door behind her banged shut.

That night she could not sleep. At three in the morning, she officially gave up, getting out of bed and walking across to Akhil's room.

It was a different room now—still his, but also all of theirs, claimed bit by bit as the years had passed. His bed and desk and dresser had stayed put, but certain things—the orange beanbag, the chair covered with heavy-metal stickers—had been taken out at some point, coming to what end, Amina did not know. There were also additions to the room—clothes and newspapers and house detritus (an empty water glass, an aluminum-foil-covered flashlight, a December 1991 issue of *American Photo*)—that marked the rest of the family's comings and goings as steadily as a logbook. Akhil's leather jacket—ferried from one holding spot to the next like a paralytic cat—was folded up on his desk. Amina picked it up, sniffing the collar before putting it on.

Thomas had been in last, according to the indent in the bed and the surgical booties curled up like pill bugs under it. Amina lowered herself into his impression like it was a snow angel. She looked up.

There they were, still smiling down at her after all these years. Gandhi still looked like a baby with reading glasses, while Martin Luther King, Jr., and Che Guevara seemed to be connected by the hair. All of their painted faces glowed electrically, a dicey mixture of reality and aspiration. Amina shut her eyes, seeing the coral mouths of the Greats tattooed in pale green across her eyelids.

CHAPTER 6

"Whoa," Monica said the next morning, stopping abruptly in Thomas's office and sniffing like a hound. "What are you doing here?"

Amina looked up from a pile of brain parts, twirling the hippocampus in her fingers. The rest of the model was strewn across her father's desk like a dismembered animal. "Waiting for Dad to give me a ride to the airport."

"I thought you were leaving Friday?"

"She's fleeing the state," Thomas said, not looking up from his computer. "Fight with her mother."

Monica sat on the arm of the couch, looking more stunned than was really necessary. "Really? I was hoping we'd have that girl time tonight. Didn't your mother tell you I called? I called three times."

"Shockingly, she did not," Amina said, ignoring the dark look Thomas shot her. Was it her problem Kamala selectively deleted messages when they came from people she did not like? No, it was not.

Monica looked down at her watch. "Well, what time is your flight?"

"Around two."

"I'll give you a lift."

"You have time?" Thomas asked.

"What?" Amina said, surprised. "Dad, I thought you—"

"Great! It will be fun," Monica said, smiling. "We can sit at Garduño's and have guac and beer until your flight comes. You wanna? I'll bring the car around."

Amina did not wanna, actually, but Monica was already going out the office door fast. Well, then. Amina stood up and looked around the office, feeling let down. She had wanted the drive to the airport with her father, but he had already turned back to his work, his eyes scanning the folder in front of him.

"Well, that's lucky isn't it?" he asked, and Amina nodded, embarrassed by the sudden tears that provoked her eyes. What were they for? Not her father's constant distraction. Not Kamala's predictable meddling. No, this was the feeling that always arose when she left, an unmet urgency, as though she hadn't really done whatever it was she was supposed to do to make home feel like home again.

Thomas's face fell. "Oh, *koche*. Don't be upset about your mother."

"I'm not," she said unconvincingly, and he came around his desk. He rubbed his chin on the top of her head and pulled her into a tight hug.

"It's all going to work out."

"Yeah, I know," she said, giving him one final squeeze before she picked up her bag and walked out of his office, to where Monica's idling car waited.

The woman could not have driven more slowly. On the highway, cars shot by like comets, an occasionally curious head staring back, looking for signs of engine trouble or a flat. Monica flipped open the glove box, removing an emerald pack of menthols.

"What are you doing?" Amina asked.

"What does it look like?"

"I thought you quit years ago."

"Did you quit?" Monica looked at her with a strange, flat gaze.

Amina flushed, and Monica thrust the pack at her with shaking hands. The car lighter popped out. Plumes of smoke filled the car. They were heading down the wrong exit ramp now, the blinker ticking wildly. Monica took a right at the end of it and then another right. She parked outside a Village Inn.

In front of them, the restaurant window showed two worlds laid one atop the other like splices of film: diners hunched into burgundy booths with cheap, brassy chandeliers hanging overhead, and the blank windshields of empty cars fading in and out.

"Your dad tried to save a dead kid," Monica said.

Amina stared at the silhouettes, turning the sentence over in her head, trying to bend it into something that made sense. It did not. Monica cracked a window and pushed in the car lighter again.

"What?"

"Your dad. A few weeks ago." She picked a stray piece of tobacco off her tongue, flicking it out the window. "In the ER."

"A dead kid?"

The lighter popped out and Monica handed it to her. "Massive head trauma. There was a shoot-out in the mall."

"Wait, Ty Hanson's kid?"

"You should light that. Damn thing works for exactly three seconds."

Amina pressed her cigarette into the fading orange coils.

Monica nodded. "He told you about it?"

"He told me Derrick had died."

"Did he tell you what happened in the ER?"

Amina shook her head, and Monica looked out the window on her side.

"We were making rounds when we got the call that they were coming into the ER. Two kids. So we went rushing down to the emergency bay, and he just . . ." She shook her head. "I don't know."

"What?"

"He went to the wrong kid," she said softly, sounding surprised. "The other kid was right there, the team already working on him, and Thomas just ignored him and went to Derrick instead."

"But . . . well . . . he knew Derrick and not the other one, right?" Amina asked. "I mean, why is that such a big—"

"He was talking really loudly. Telling Derrick to calm down, that everything was going to be okay. Telling me to restrain him. And at first I just thought he was seeing something everyone else hadn't noticed, like maybe—who knows—the kid is still alive? Stranger shit has happened in that ER, believe me. But then I see the kid's eyes and he's really gone and Thomas is on top of him, pushing him down like he's fighting to get up, yelling at me to quit just standing there and help restrain him." She looked at Amina apologetically. "I didn't know what to do. I mean . . . I tried to tell him the kid was dead, and he got really angry. He asked another one of the nurses for help. She told him the same thing. He was furious, screaming at everyone. It took us a few minutes to get through."

A few *minutes*? "Shit."

The blur in the corner of her eye was Monica nodding.

"Have you seen that happen before?"

"You mean in a patient or in your dad?"

"Both. Either."

Monica rolled a pocket of smoke around her mouth. "Sure, if someone is delusional. If he has, say, post-traumatic stress disorder or is taking hallucinogens or something."

"You think he has PTSD?"

"Honestly, Amina, I don't know what to think. There could have been any number of things that factored in. Did he eat enough that day? Had he slept well? Were there other things we didn't know about?"

"Like what?"

"I don't know. You know, something like this happens, you revisit a lot of things, wonder if you should have seen . . . I mean, but even that is not particularly useful. I have my theories, but they're just that—a bunch of thoughts, not a medical diagnosis."

"Like what?"

"Oh, Amina, I don't think we should get into—"

"Like *what*?"

"I think he had a psychotic break."

Amina looked down at her lap feeling like she had once when she was swimming in the ocean and something large had brushed against her leg. "What's that?"

"It's a loss of contact with reality."

Heat flared between Amina's fingertips, and she looked down to a solid inch of ash. She lifted the cigarette carefully to the window, tipping the spent end over and watching the ashes scatter through the glass. "He's psychotic?"

"No, he's not fucking psychotic, God."

"Well, I don't know!"

Monica glared at the steering wheel for a few moments before sighing, "Sorry. I just mean people can have psychotic breaks without harming themselves or anyone else, okay? He wouldn't have hurt anyone. I've told them that."

"Them?"

"The board."

Amina's mouth fell open. "They know?"

"They heard about it, obviously."

"From who?"

Monica smiled sadly. "Amina, it's a small hospital. I'm sure they heard it from a few people."

Amina's mind went to the white hospital corridors, the pools of light, the nurses' faces as she and Thomas walked past. Did they know? Had the ICU nurse known? Had Dr. George? She flipped the air vents on the dash open and shut. "And was there, I don't know, disciplinary action?"

"He was talked to. He's knows he's being watched."

"Does my mom know?"

"I tried to tell her."

"And?"

"She hung up before I could get it out."

"Great."

"I know, but what did I expect? No love lost there. And anyway, I'm not sure what we need to do at this point, besides get him to talk to someone."

"Like a shrink?"

"Well, that would be great, but barring that, I mean, anyone." Monica looked at her. "Someone he'd be honest with. You."

Amina thought of her father on the porch, the tumbler in his hands. *Your mother has always been afraid of anything she can't control.*

"Are you okay?" Monica asked, and Amina realized she was gripping her knees, her breath light and shallow.

She gave a quick, reassuring nod. It seemed important to be okay, suddenly. To be a part of Team Okay. "Yes, of course. It's just a lot."

"Yeah. That's why I was trying tell you earlier in the week."

They sat in silence, the sun settling on them like a hot, heavy sheet. The car seemed to grow smaller, the space between them suddenly filled with a thousand twitching anxieties.

"So now what?"

Monica shrugged, dropped her butt out the window. "I don't know. I guess we just have to take what we know and go from there."

"And what do we know?" Amina's voice sounded small.

"We know that your dad had a delusional episode of some sort. We know that this isn't typical behavior for him, and could even be an isolated incident. We know that typically, late spring is a hard time for him emotionally, and that the kid who died was the same age as, you know"—she took a short, sharp breath—"your brother."

"You think this is about *Akhil*?"

"Honey, I have no idea what this is about." Monica paused. "Why did you ask me if he was okay the other day?"

"What?"

"At the ICU. You asked me if something was wrong."

"Oh, I . . . just thought he seemed off or something." It wasn't that Amina wanted to lie to Monica so much as she wanted to buy time, to think through things, to sit somewhere alone until she could put all the pieces together and come up with a plan. "I mean, has he seemed fine to you? Other than this?"

"It's hard to tell. Mainly he just seems really exhausted. A little withdrawn. He sure doesn't laugh as much."

"Has he had any more episodes?"

"Not as far as I know." Monica leaned back and ran her thumb under the seat belt still strapped over her chest. "I mean, look, thirty years with the same hospital, no one wants this to be a lasting mark against him. But he's not there to fix bunions, you know?"

Amina nodded, wanting to get out of the car, to walk around the parking lot until her head came back together.

"Okay," Monica said after a moment, like they had come to some kind of resolution. "Well, so, you hungry?"

"Huh?"

Monica tipped her chin at the restaurant. "I mean, I know it's no Garduño's, but if you want some pancakes or something, we have the time."

Amina shook her head. "I think you'd better just take me home."

BOOK 5

THE BIG SLEEP

ALBUQUERQUE, 1982–1983

CHAPTER 1

Shortly after almost driving himself and Amina into untimely deaths, Akhil went to sleep for three months. It wasn't a straight sleep of course, but a persistent one, a sudden fever of exhaustion that lasted from December through February and found him sprawled over chairs and couches and rugs the minute he came home from school, eyes spinning under the silk of his eyelids. Gone was the constant barrage of words, replaced by an infantile drowsiness, eyes that barely focused, a mouth that opened only to eat or snore. He was too tired to think, he said when asked any question, and it was obvious.

The first week, neither Amina nor Kamala had any idea what to make of it. While Akhil's wordy tirades had been exhausting, his sudden silence was eerie.

"He's like this in school?" Kamala asked, her hand pressed to his forehead.

"I have no idea." Amina tightened her ponytail, crossed her arms. It was paid misinformation. The day after "the car incident," as she and Akhil referred to it, they had come to an agreement of sorts. Amina now woke him after his lunchtime nap, made sure his eyes didn't flutter while he drove, and said nothing about it to anyone. Akhil paid her $4.50 a week. Still, unlike the other brief nod-outs, this kind of sleeping was new. And worrisome. Amina looked at her brother, the stinky cavern of his mouth, his twitching nose.

"Must be the flu," Kamala said, and Amina nodded just so she wouldn't have to say anything incriminating.

During the second week of the Big Sleep, they found themselves conducting strange experiments. On Tuesday, Amina repeatedly kicked her brother's ankles until he opened his eyes and pushed her away. At the Thursday dinner table, Kamala shouted out, "How about this trickling-down theory?" in a desperate attempt to engage him in a conversation. On Friday, they took turns shaking him hard until he woke up.

"What the fuck?" Akhil croaked through a dry throat, eyes goopy with sleep.

"What's happening?" Kamala asked, but the question came out wrong, too full of cheer that did not match her anxious face.

The subtleties were lost on Akhil, who rolled over with such a thump that the couch shuddered a little.

Kamala peered at her son as though he were a jar of something unidentifiable in a fridge. "At least he's eating."

It was an understatement. The sheer amount of food Akhil put away each night at dinner was nothing short of phenomenal. Mountains of rice, stacks of chapatis, flotillas of idlis, and entire chickens disappeared during meals. Amina saw him go through a bag of oranges in one sitting.

At the end of the third week, Kamala perched on the sofa arm. "And what," she asked Amina, as though they had been in the middle of a conversation, "does he say about it?"

"About what?" Amina turned the page of her book, guilt emanating from her upper lip, her armpits.

Kamala pointed a squiggling finger at the space over Akhil's head. "This sleeping-all-the-time business."

"He doesn't say anything about it." This was true. The three times she had tried to bring up his new sleeping pattern, Akhil had either turned up the radio, ignored her, or accused her of trying to "get more fucking money by making shit up."

"You think he's depressed?"

"He's always depressed."

"Not true! He's always *angry.*" Kamala pulled a piece of fuzz from his eyelashes, studied it, and flicked it away. Akhil did not move. "Has something bad happened to him recently?"

"You mean other than Salem?"

Kamala's lip curled inward, her nostrils flared. She blinked at Amina several times before saying, "That didn't happen to Akhil."

"No, I know, but we just—"

"Not Akhil. Not you." Kamala walked to the chair Amina sat in and bent down, surprising her with a kiss on the head.

"You both are *fine,*" she said, squeezing Amina's arm quickly before heading to the kitchen.

Strangely, saying the words out loud changed something in Kamala. As week four turned to five and the holidays rounded the corner, she was lighter suddenly, bustling about the kitchen, making tins of cookies and halwa that Akhil would devour by the handful before passing out, crumbs lining his lips. Once, when she caught Amina hovering over the couch, she prodded her away, saying, "Enough," like Amina was pinching him.

"Maybe he's fucking possessed," Dimple suggested on Christmas Day, channeling Mindy Lujan to the best of her ability, though the holiday had wrenched them apart for an entire twenty-four hours. She and Amina stood in Akhil's room, looking down at his sleeping body. "What does your dad think?"

"He's been really busy with work. And it only really happens in the afternoon like this, when Dad isn't around, so it's really just me and Mom who see it."

"And what does Our Lady of Supreme Intolerance say?"

"She thinks he's fine because he's not depressed."

"Cool." Dimple's eyes wandered toward Akhil's window. "Do you know where he hides his cigs?"

But it was not cool. As the cars of the Kurians and the Ramakrishnas receded down the driveway, as Thomas mumbled about needing to make rounds and Kamala divided the leftover idlis into Ziplocs for freezing, Amina sat in Akhil's beanbag, peeking at her snoring brother over the pages of her book. The next week she grew more agitated. Was it normal for anything that wasn't a cat to sleep for sixteen hours a day?

"I think he's sick," she announced loudly after dinner the following Monday. Enough was enough. Winter break was over, and Akhil was getting worse instead of better, heading for the couch like a drunk rushing to the bottle the minute they came home.

"You said yourself he is doing fine in school," Kamala said, scrubbing the stove with gusto.

"Look at him, Ma. Does he look fine to you?"

They looked at Akhil. Truthfully, Akhil did not look *un*fine so much as uncomfortable, one arm folded under him, the other hanging bent over the edge of the sofa.

"This isn't normal," Amina said.

Her word lingered in the air, spreading like the smell of smoke. Amina saw her mother's shoulders dip and rise. Kamala went to the kitchen, picked up the phone, dialed.

"Come now! Your son is sick and won't wake up!" she announced after a beat. She slammed the phone down.

It rang back almost immediately. She listened.

"No ambulance!" She slammed the phone down again.

Half an hour later Thomas gunned down the driveway in a whirl of dust. He left the car door open and the lights on, running in the front door.

"Where is he?" he asked Kamala, not breaking his stride.

"The living room." Kamala, Amina, and Queen Victoria followed him down the hall.

"What exactly is wrong?"

"He won't wake up."

"How long has he been out?"

"Not out, sleeping! Since he got home!"

"Did he suffer any kind of head trauma today? Falling, getting hit, anything like that?"

Kamala looked at Amina.

"Not that I saw," Amina said.

By now they had entered the living room. Thomas took a sharp breath and knelt down on the shag rug. He shooed away the dog and pulled at Akhil's eyelids, revealing the white, swirling custard of both eyes. He grabbed a wrist.

"Akhil?" His voice was loud.

Akhil rolled over. "Mnff."

"Akhil, wake up."

Akhil frowned but didn't open his eyes.

Thomas looked at his watch. "Pulse is steady and breathing looks fine." He placed his hand under Akhil's nose, then reached into his pocket, pulling out a thermometer. He placed it in Akhil's ear. "So he's been asleep for about five hours?"

"No, he was awake for dinner," Kamala said.

"I thought you said he's been asleep since he got home."

"He woke for dinner and then went right back to sleep," Kamala said. She leaned forward, whispered knowingly, *"Maybe drugs."*

"Did he have a healthy appetite? What did he eat?"

"Five helpings of chicken curry, nine chapatis, two spoons of salad, one bowl of rice and dahl, one bottle of RC Cola."

Thomas's eyes widened. "Really? All of it?"

"What, all of it? He likes my cooking."

"And dinner ended when?"

Kamala glanced at the clock in the kitchen, held up her fingers calculating. "Two and a half hours ago."

"He's not on drugs," Amina volunteered.

The thermometer beeped and Thomas pulled it out, looking at it for a long moment. "So he was totally coherent during dinner?"

"Not at all," Kamala said with the barest note of triumph in her voice. "I said 'Good for Star Wars,' and he said nothing!"

Thomas looked at Amina for translation.

"You know, Reagan's new defense-policy thing. Mom said she supported it, and Akhil didn't argue."

Amina watched this information filter through her father's mind, his brow growing heavy. "Kamala, you do realize I was with a patient."

"And?"

"And this could have waited."

"I've waited two months! How much longer should I be waiting?"

Thomas pulled the stethoscope from his neck, placing the white tips inside his ears. Amina and her mother stood still as he cocked his head, shut his eyes. When he was done, he pulled the earpieces out and rocked back on his heels, taking in the room. He looked at the book bags flung on the floor, the shoes and papers covering the carpet, the television broadcasting game-show applause. His eyebrows raised slightly at the "snackument"—a tower of crackers and spray cheese that Amina liked to build and eat—before landing on Vanna White turning over a row of white *s*'s.

"Well?" Kamala asked.

Thomas stood up, pulling a big antennaed block out of his pocket and setting it on the table in front of the couch. "We'll just have to see."

"Don't you think we should take him to the hospital?"

"Not yet." He walked across the room to the liquor cabinet.

"When? Tomorrow?"

"I think we should just watch him for a bit." He took out a tumbler.

"We've been watching! I'm telling you! He's not himself anymore!"

"Kamala, please." The liquid splashed down. "We can't send him to the hospital because he isn't fighting with you. Sleeping for a few hours in the middle of the evening is hardly unusual for a boy of his age."

"But it's not just that! Amina, tell him!"

Her parents' eyes shifted to her, pleading separate cases. Amina looked from one to the other.

"Something is wrong with him," Amina said at last, and her father looked plainly disappointed. "No, really, he's been sleeping all the time. And he . . ." She struggled to think of something that wouldn't get Akhil into trouble. "Even when he is awake, he's really out of it. Sometimes he has to pull over when we're driving. He sleeps during lunch. And then he comes home and eats like some crazy starving animal. And Dimple thinks he's possessed."

Her father sighed. "Is that everything?"

Amina nodded, feeling foolish.

"Not everything!" Kamala interjected. "He needs to see another doctor! Right now! Take him!"

"I told you he doesn't—" Thomas started.

"Yes HE DOES. I AM TELLING YOU HE DOES."

"Does what?" Akhil asked, his voice cottony with sleep. They turned to him, but no one said anything.

"What's going on?" Akhil asked.

"You're awake." An unsurprised Thomas took a sip of his scotch.

"Yeah."

"What day is it?"

Akhil stared groggily. "What?"

"Day of the week. Monday, Tuesday—"

"Thursday."

"What's the date?"

Akhil frowned. "Is this a test?"

"Yes," Thomas answered.

Akhil blinked several times before saying, "January 12, 1983."

"Why are you sleeping so much?" Kamala demanded.

Akhil looked at Amina, his face darkening with accusation. "Am I in trouble?"

"No, of course not," Thomas said.

Akhil slumped back into the chair. He looked at his father, frowning. "What are you doing here?"

"What do you mean?"

"It's early."

"Your mother called me home."

"Why?"

No one said anything. Kamala bit her lips together, blew air in puffs through her nose.

"What is going on?" Akhil looked warily from one to the other. Amina shrugged.

"Something is wrong with you!" Kamala shouted.

Akhil's eyes rounded. "What?"

"Kamala!"

"*Wrong* with me?"

"Your mother was just worried, and now she's not," Thomas said. "Don't worry yourself."

"Don't say how I am!"

"Kamala, enough. You're scaring him."

"I'm not scaring anyone! Reagan could be deporting all of us to-morrow, and he would sleep like a baby!"

"We're being deported?" Akhil asked.

"Listen, he's fine—"

"He is not fine! He's sleeping all the time like some kind of infant! His brain is going soft! He's turning into furniture! You're too busy in the hospital all the time with your precious patients—strangers!—and here your own son is dying and you won't even—"

"I'm DYING?" Akhil sat up.

"HE'S GROWING!" Thomas bellowed, his voice slapping the ceiling. "My God, Kamala, nothing is wrong with him. He's a regular boy in the middle of a growth spurt! You and your ridiculous wringing your hands and good Lord, it doesn't take a doctor to know these things—just *look at him*! LOOK AT HIM!"

Amina followed her father's arm, an arrow of accusation tipped by a trembling finger, pointing straight toward Akhil. She looked at her brother. She really looked at him. And for the first time, she saw that his arms had grown thinner and longer as if stretched, knuckles grazing the carpet as he slouched into the chair. And his legs. Bulkier in the thigh, hard-looking, like twin benches attached to his torso. Her eyes moved up to his scowling face and saw that the acne had sucked back into his cheeks, leaving tiny craters in its place. And his cheekbones. They were too huge suddenly, swollen into arcs that hardened his face into a new, lunar topography. He blinked. He stood up. Amina backed up.

"Done?" Her brother's voice was tight with fury.

"Yes," Thomas said.

Akhil stalked across the room. Moments later, his feet trampled the stairs. A bedroom door slammed above them. Kamala stared at her husband. She opened her mouth to say something and then shut it.

"Kamala, you were scaring—"

The flat of her palm silenced him. She turned and left the living room, sari swishing against the bare floor. Another door slammed.

Thomas tipped the rest of the scotch into his mouth, swallowed. He walked over to the couch and sank into it. "Go if you want."

Amina stayed.

Her father placed his elbows on his knees, his forehead in his hands. A face mask hung loosely from his neck. His scrubs were dotted with blood. He looked up at the television. "What's this show?"

"*Wheel of Fortune.* They're trying to guess a word."

"Huh." He looked confused.

"Or a saying. You know, like 'tears of a clown.' Or 'from dusk till dawn.'"

She sat down next to him on the couch and turned up the volume, but her father had lost interest.

"What's that?" she said, pointing to the box with the antenna.

"It's a telephone."

"Where's the cord?"

"It doesn't have one. It's a new thing, a phone that can go where you go. Soon they say they'll be making them for cars."

"Why would anyone phone someone from a car?"

Thomas shrugged. "For directions?"

"Huh."

They were quiet for a moment.

"What's that?" he pointed at her plate.

"It's a snackument. Ritz crackers and cheese in a can. You can eat it."

"What kind of cheese comes in a can?"

Amina grabbed the can. "Hold out your finger."

"The sun will come out tomorrow!" a cheery voice announced, and a flurry of lit tiles *ding-ding-ding*ed on the television.

Her father held out his finger, and Amina decorated it with swirls of yellow cheddar. Vanna turned the lit tiles over. The winning contestant got a new car and a vacation to Phoenix, Arizona. When Amina was done, her father held his finger to the light, turning it this way and that so that it glistened.

"The wonders of America," Thomas said. He placed the finger in his mouth and sucked it.

CHAPTER 2

Two days after Thomas had pronounced Akhil's sleep nothing more than a growth spurt, Kamala settled on a cure for it. Amina, curled into an armchair with a copy of *Heart of Darkness,* barely noticed as her mother lifted Akhil's legs and settled herself under them on the sofa. Kamala opened the first volume of the *Encyclopaedia Britannica* and cleared her throat.

"Anguilla," she announced.

"What?" Amina said.

"The most northerly of the British Leeward Islands," Kamala read, underlining the words with her extended middle finger. "Area, about sixty square miles."

"What are you doing?"

Kamala jerked her head at the sleeping Akhil.

"Oh," Amina nodded.

Her mother squinted, refinding her place. "The first inhabitants of the islands were—"

"Wait," Amina said. "Why Anguilla?"

"I'm starting with *A*'s."

"You're going to read them all?"

"No, dummy, just the good ones. I skipped Akrotiri, Afghanistan."
Kamala cleared her throat and resumed: "The first Amerindians settled on Anguilla about three thousand five hundred years ago. Ar-
chaeological finds indicate that the island was a regional center for the
Arawak Indians, who had sizeable villages at Sandy Ground, Meads
Bay, Rendezvous Bay, and Island Harbor. The Caribe Indians, who
eventually overpowered the Arawaks, called the island Malliouhana.
Early Spanish explorers named the island Anguilla, which means
'eel.'"

"You think he's going to wake up for this?"

Her mother looked over her reading glasses. "Of course not."

"Because he can't hear you."

"Not true. I read they can hear you and they understand and it
calms them."

"They?"

"Coma patients."

"Akhil isn't in a coma."

"Doesn't matter. His brain will be stimulated."

"By Anguilla?"

"Amina, I do not have all day. Someone has to make the dinner
and set the table, and you can either shut up your mouth now *or you
can go to your room*!" The last part came out in a yell, and Akhil's eyes
cracked open. They blinked twice in the land of the awake like a sea
mammal penetrating the surface of the ocean and then shut again.
Kamala watched and turned to the encyclopedia with renewed fervor.
"The British established the first permanent European colony on Anguilla in 1650."

Amina stared at the glossy green cover of *Heart of Darkness*. She
did not want to go to her room. She did not want to listen to her
mother read about Anguilla.

"Despite a few invasion attempts by the French, Anguilla has remained a Crown Colony ever since. Then in 1969 the British Royal

Marines were going to go in and kill everyone for order and it would have been a bloodbath, but those people treated it like an independence day parade."

"It says that?"

"No, I just remember that part."

Amina put *Heart of Darkness* down. She listened to the brief history of Anguilla, watching the lines on her mother's face soften, her cheeks grow fuller, suddenly plump with purpose.

"The currency is the Eastern Caribbean, though the dollar is widely accepted," Kamala said, closing the book with a muffled thump.

Amina looked at her. "That's all?"

"That's all for now." Kamala struggled to lean over Akhil's legs and placed the unwieldy book at the foot of the couch with a thump.

"Legs," she said. Amina stood up and walked over to the couch, wedging her arms under Akhil's legs and lifting them up. Kamala slid out, stood up, wobbling a little. She took off her reading glasses and smoothed down her sari, pulling it tight over one shoulder.

"Now what?" Amina asked, dropping her brother's legs. He rolled farther into the couch, burying his face in the seam.

"Now dinner. Come and set the table."

The next night was asteroids. The next was Athens. Amina went to her room for Australia (she had done a report on it in fourth grade, using the same encyclopedia) but came back the next night armed with her camera.

"The Aztec calendar utilized a 260-day year and a 52-year time cycle," her mother read, and Amina crouched so that she was taking in the full length of her brother, his feet growing like strange roots out of Kamala's sari.

By John Wilkes Booth, Amina was on her sixth roll of film, and the family had entered an entirely new phase, one that would fill her with peace when thinking about it later. It wasn't just the muzzle on Akhil's vitriol that sent calm down the hallways like the scent of summer, it was the soothing sound of Kamala's reading, the triumph that bloomed in her eyes with each finished passage. January's snowstorms began, settling thin white blankets over the cottonwoods and ice over the ditches, and Amina wandered outside to get pictures of her mother and brother through the living room window, tight in their coziness. The days began to grow fractionally longer, Kamala moved on to Catholicism and cicadas, and, as though responding to the incantation of a spell, Akhil's eyes began to crack open for increasingly longer intervals. He would listen wordlessly, watching the ceiling as though it were another galaxy.

CHAPTER 3

Akhil woke from the Big Sleep during da Vinci. Kamala was just launching into the sad account of the rapidly eroding *Last Supper* when he said his first full sentence.

"I want to paint a mural." His tongue darted out, licking dry lips.

A mural? Amina leaned forward to see if his eyes were really open. They were.

"On the ceiling," he clarified. "In my bedroom."

It was early February. Outside, the prairie grass had flattened into grayish yellow slicks, and a northern wind blew against the tin roof, making the house creak. Kamala put the book down and turned to him.

Akhil looked at her. "Can I?"

"Okay."

"Really?"

Kamala nodded slowly. When he smiled at her, she patted his legs and he lifted them. Open sesame. Kamala stood and walked toward the hall with a sleepwalker's disregard for her surroundings. "Let's go, then."

"Now?" Akhil asked.

"Now?" Amina echoed.

"Ben Franklin's closes at eight."

In the store, under the glare of fluorescent lighting, Kamala and Amina pushed the cart forward while Akhil gathered big tubs of powdered tempera paint. He strolled the aisle ahead of them, pants hanging slack around bony hips, three inches of sock exposed at his ankles.

"So much of white?" Kamala asked, peering into the basket.

"It's for mixing."

"Ah." She smoothed her braid down one shoulder, glancing at the tubes of oil paints hung like bats from the displays on either side of them.

"I've got to find the brushes," Akhil said, turning left abruptly and wandering into the fluorescent haze.

"Ma," Amina said anxiously when he was gone.

"Mmm?" Kamala had pulled one of the tubes down and now cradled it in cupped palms. "Cadmium yellow! Should we buy it?"

"What? No! That's oil paint! It's expensive!"

Kamala turned over the tube, eyebrows shooting up at the price tag. "My God, no jokes!" She placed it back on the shelf. "Oh well."

"Ma, what are we doing?"

"We're buying Akhil paint for his mural."

"Akhil doesn't have a mural."

"Because he doesn't have any paint."

Amina moved the cart to the left as a woman with half a cart full of pink yarn passed. "But he's never painted anything in his life!"

"So? First time for everything, nah?"

Amina bit a little of her thumbnail off, spit it into the aisle. "Well, can I get more film?"

"We just bought you film last week."

"One roll. I need more."

"You're using it too fast."

"No I'm not! Ma, seriously." Amina pulled into the model-plane aisle. "And besides, how do you know he's even going to do anything with this stuff? That he's not going to fall back asleep tomorrow until June?"

Kamala didn't answer her, marveling at a bin of sea sponges.

At the register, they bought one full set of tempera paint, three extra tubs of white, six paintbrushes in various sizes, a stenciling kit, and a sea sponge.

"Really, Mom, I don't need it," Akhil protested about the sponge.

"You might!"

"For what?" Amina glared at the entire contents of the basket.

"For effects, dummy!" Kamala handed the clerk at the register her credit card, smiling in a conspiratorial way. "My son is an artist."

"I told you why Guevara, right?"

"Yes."

They were taking a detour across the west mesa, driving at a thundering pace, the graded dirt road under them making Akhil's voice vibrate.

"Because, you know, the prophecy wasn't totally clear on who to pick. So that part is up to me. And I recognize that Che comes with certain complications, but I think it's important to recognize the spirit of a true revolutionary."

By "the prophecy," Akhil was referring to a recurring dream he had had during the Big Sleep, giving him a glimpse into a future in which he was destined to be "a great leader among other greats." ("Like Madonna?" Amina had asked. "Like Mandela," he had answered.) While the hard details of exactly what Akhil saw in his future were never revealed (Was he strolling through the U.N.? Flying Air Force One? Sitting in an expensive leather desk chair that swiveled?), the way he would reach his destiny was clear: He would paint a mural of the Greats. It would harbinger change. And now, one week later, he had already fashioned a collage that would serve as the basis for the mural, reimagining the Sandias as a sort of Rushmore-esque homage to Gandhi, Che Guevara, Martin Luther King, Nelson Mandela, and Rob Halford.

"I told you why Mandela, right?"

"Yes."

"It's just such a crime, what they've done to him. I mean, if you really think about—"

"You told me. I have."

Contrary to Amina's belief that he would buy all the paints and pass out from sheer exertion, Akhil had woken up with a bang, rejoining the Mathletes, rephrasing his political convictions, and stalking from one end of the campus to the other with newly hewn limbs. He was big now, man-sized, a fact that was not lost on Mindy Lujan, of all people.

"Hey, Amina, is that your brother?" she asked one afternoon as they sat on neighboring benches in the quad. Amina, startled by being personally addressed for the first time all year, almost didn't understand the question. She looked where Mindy pointed. Akhil was striding out of the science building in the first pair of jeans that had fit him since November and a leather bomber jacket, recent gifts from an overjoyed Kamala.

"Yeah."

"He's fucking *sexy*. Like, the Indian James Dean or something."

Akhil dug his hands deeper into his pockets, appearing to mutter to himself.

"Gross," Dimple said.

"What?"

"He's my *cousin*."

Mindy crossed her legs. "So you can introduce us."

"No way."

"What, you want him for yourself?"

Dimple snorted. "Dis. Gus. Ting."

"Then what's the problem?"

"The problem is that I'm not doing it."

"Fine."

Three days later Amina found them sitting on the hood of the station wagon, Dimple with legs and arms crossed, Mindy with bare legs in front of her, as though it were not February and barely warm in the direct sunlight. She waved as Amina approached.

"Hey! Where've you been?"

Amina scowled at Dimple. "Getting my prints from the dark-room."

"Oh yeah, Dimple said you're totally into your photography class or something." Mindy eyed her notebook. "Can I see?"

"Amina is sort of private about her work," Dimple said, flashing Amina a look. "I haven't even seen them, right, Ami?"

"Here." Amina handed Mindy the notebook.

"Cool." Mindy thumped the small space between her and Dimple, who looked visibly uncomfortable. "Come on up. Let's see."

The hood of the car was warmer than Amina thought it would be, pressing into the backs of her thighs with the promise of spring and soft grass. She opened the notebook. The first photo was all hands and feet: her mother's gnarled fingers clutching the B–Bi volume; Akhil's feet oddly flexed forward and backward, like he was performing a bal-let in another world; Akhil sleeping with a pillow over his head; Akhil eating dinner with his head in his hands. The last picture was Akhil in what Kamala had called the "Our Lord and Savior" position, head hanging over the edge of the couch, mouth open, back arched over the armrest, arms flung apart as though to embrace the ceiling. The hol-low of his stomach disappeared into jeans that Amina now realized were unzipped.

"Shhhhhhhit," Mindy breathed.

"He's got a breath issue," Dimple said. Mindy flipped the picture over. "So, I can have it?"

Amina felt herself warm, though she wasn't sure if it was because she was pleased to be asked for the picture or because she didn't want to give it away. Mindy leaned closer, her eyes reflecting the burgundy hood of the car, the shadow of Amina's head. Her glossy lips parted to reveal rows of curiously small teeth, and Amina felt an astounding urge to rub noses with her, or purr, or roll over.

"Fucking *finally*," Dimple said. Amina turned to see Akhil walk-ing across the parking lot, head ducked to his chest, one hand dug deep into his jeans pocket. He looked up suddenly and came to a halt.

"What are you doing here?" It wasn't exactly clear whom he was asking, as he looked from Amina to Mindy to Dimple and back to Amina.

"Looking at pictures of you naked," Mindy said.

"Not naked," Amina said quickly. "Just sleeping. I have ones of Mom, too. And Dad," she lied.

"Pictures?"

Before Amina could protest, Mindy grabbed the photo from her lap, thrusting it at Akhil. Amina watched her brother take it in, her gut sinking as his brow furrowed. He looked up at her again but didn't say anything. He unlocked the car door, threw his books into the back.

"I told you he's a freak," Dimple said. "He flips out all the time for no reason."

Mindy slid off the hood as the engine started. She opened the passenger door and leaned down. "Can I get a ride?"

"To Corrales?" Dimple asked.

"Yeah." Mindy swayed slightly. Akhil's gaze, trapped in the crease between her breasts, swayed with her. Mindy smiled, drawing his eyes to her face.

"Do whatever you want," he said, and Mindy eased into the passenger seat. She unlocked the back door for Amina, who got into the car, feeling a little sick and thrilled with the oddness of it all. Dimple's mouth was a hard slash through the window as they drove away.

Amina wasn't totally sure where one should be when one's brother was being seduced, but she was pretty sure the backseat was not the right place. She stared into the rearview mirror, trying to catch Akhil's eye, but her brother wasn't looking back or even at Mindy. He was slouching behind the wheel, his right knee at an odd angle, as though it were being magnetically drawn to the passenger's seat.

They weren't two minutes into the drive when Mindy reached into her bag and pulled out a cigarette. She turned to Akhil. "Do you mind?"

Akhil glanced down. "Is that a joint?"

"Yeah. Do you smoke?"

"Yeah."

"No you don't," Amina said, but if they heard her, they didn't answer. Mindy pulled out a lighter and sucked in, pinching the tip before
handing it to Akhil. He took it.

"So, fucking Corrales, huh?" Mindy exhaled. The car filled with a
rich, funky odor, and Amina coughed.

Akhil took a tiny puff and held it in, nodding. He handed it back
to her.

"You want some?" Mindy turned around.

"No!" Akhil said. "She's a fucking kid."

"Oops! Sorry."

"It stinks," Amina said.

"It's skunk," Mindy replied, and Amina sat back, baffled.

"So how long you guys lived in Corrales?"

"I don't know. Nine years."

"Cool. I have an aunt that lives in Rio Rancho."

"Uh-huh."

"Rio Rancho sucks," Amina said.

Mindy looked over her shoulder and laughed, her hand landing
on Akhil's knee. "Doesn't it? It's like the old-person capital of the state."

"TB survivors," Akhil said, taking the joint back.

"What?"

"A lot of them are tuberculosis survivors. The climate is easy on
their lungs."

"Fascinating." Mindy turned so that she was leaning against the
passenger door, her body facing Akhil's. "So what else do you know?"

"About what?"

"About other things."

"Other things?"

"About Indian things."

"Indian things?"

Mindy squeezed his knee. "Kama Sutra?"

Akhil looked like he'd been hit with a bad smell. He knocked her
hand away, and a nervous swell rose in Amina's stomach. Would they
pull over right there, on Coors Road? Would he yell furiously, or talk
extra slowly to make each word hit harder? Would his speech be about

racism or appropriation, or would he just tell Mindy she was a big fat nothing? Anything was possible. Amina imagined the heat-blurred silhouette of Mindy in the rearview mirror, waiting for some low-rider to pity her and give her a lift back to school.

Akhil said nothing. Mindy slid her hand to his upper thigh, squeezed again. He did not remove it.

"Where's your brother?" Kamala asked, some forty minutes later.

"Dunno."

"What do you mean don't know?"

"I'm reading," Amina lied. She fanned the pages of the book with her thumb. She hadn't really been able to read at all, had only circled the words *Kurtz, green,* and *river.*

Kamala frowned. "Did he go somewhere?"

"He's out."

"Out where?"

Amina shrugged. After they dropped her at the head of the driveway, Amina had watched the car roll fifty yards down the dirt road.

"Hey! Idiot!" Kamala snapped oniony fingers in front of her face. "Where did he go?"

Amina sighed. "Jesus."

"What Jesus? I'm asking you a simple question, and you're sitting like some deaf-mute."

"I'm trying to read."

Kamala grabbed Amina's left ear, twisted hard.

"Ow! God! He just went to Ben Franklin's for paint! He'll be back soon!"

Kamala let go. "Why didn't you just say so?"

"What the hell does it matter? He's out doing whatever he wants, and it's not like we have to keep track of him every shitty second of the day!" Amina rubbed her ear.

"No cursing!"

"Leave me alone, then!"

Kamala scrunched her face and abruptly held a cool palm to Amina's forehead. "You're having a hormonal episode," she announced.

Three hours later Akhil sat at the dinner table looking like he'd gotten a once-over from an industrial-strength vacuum cleaner. Hair stuck out from his head in charged puffs, a half-inch circumference around his mouth was swollen and pink, and his left ear glistened gooily. His hooded sweatshirt was oddly bungled around his throat, as though hurricane-level winds had whipped it into a knot. Kamala passed the potatoes.

"So you're the team captain again?"

Akhil took a spoonful of vegetables. "Uh-huh."

Kamala scooped two more spoonfuls onto his plate. She followed with a leg of chicken, three spoonfuls of yogurt and cabbage, and two chapatis. "How many people are on the team?"

"Can I have one?" Amina asked.

Kamala reached for the water pitcher, filling their glasses. "Ten? Twelve?"

Akhil's fingers pressed tenderly at his ear before migrating to his mouth. "Six."

"And all are National Merit semifinalists?"

"Yeah." Akhil rubbed his nose, then stopped, sniffing his fingers.

"I tell you, in India we competed in maths all the time, but there was never a real tournament—such a good idea! A sport that tests the mettle of the mind!"

"That's not really a sport," Amina said.

"Not true! What do you think chess is?"

"Not a sport either."

"Shut up, idiot box! You know your grandfather was the champion chess player of Madras Christian College and went on to become the—"

"Semifinalist for the All-India Chess Championships. Yeah. You told me."

"Well, you're in a fine mood today, Miss Impressed with Everything. Maybe you should try using your brain for something instead of criticizing everyone. Maybe you should try leading a team of—Akhil, what's wrong with your ear?" Kamala pointed a serving spoon at him.

"Nothing."

"You keep fiddling with it. It's infected? Come, let me look."

"No." Akhil leaned back. "No, it's fine."

"But it's swollen, no?"

Akhil shook his head, and the sweatshirt around his neck slipped to reveal a pulpy bruise.

"Oh my God!" Kamala stood up. "Oh my God, you've been hit!"

"What?" Akhil looked at Amina, who pointed a finger at her own neck.

Akhil slapped a hand over the bruise. "No. Nothing. It's nothing, Ma."

"Who did this to you?" Kamala demanded. "Those boys?"

"No one, Ma, it's nothing—"

"What nothing? You've been beaten! Was it the same boys as last year? Mr. No Good Martinez and his thuggy band of *goondas*?"

"No, I swear—"

But she was already rising from the table. "Mesa Preparatory code of honor my foot! They said it wouldn't happen again, and now this! Why didn't you say anything? When did this happen? I'm calling your father."

"No! Don't!"

But Kamala was already walking quickly to the kitchen, hand held in front of her like a weapon.

"Do something!" Akhil whispered, hurrying after her.

"Like what?" Amina followed.

In the kitchen, their mother punched the buttons on the phone with her middle finger, pointing it at them when she finished dialing. "Thugs! I saw it on the *Eyewitness News,* gangs coming to Albuquerque with their initiations and putting ideas in the heads of teenagers! Yes, operator, can you have Dr. Eapen kindly call home? His son has been beaten to a bloody—"

"It wasn't a boy!" Amina shouted.

Kamala stopped talking, her mouth puckered over her next word.

"It wasn't a boy," Amina repeated.

Her mother put the phone back in the cradle. "A girl?"

Akhil nodded.

"A girl beat you?"

"He wasn't beaten," Amina said. "It's a hickey."

Kamala's eyes widened. "Who?"

"The thing. On his neck. It's like a kiss, but sort of hard. Like a sucking kiss. He was with Mindy Lujan. That's where he was when you asked. That's why—"

Kamala waved a frantic hand and Amina stopped talking. Her mother stood dead still, palms flat against the counter like she was holding it in place. She looked at them, her mouth twisting at the corners, and Amina realized she was trying not to cry.

"Oh, Mom . . . ," Akhil started, but Kamala's lips just stretched tight and thin and paper-flat, as though they could be torn. She walked around the counter to her purse and picked it up, stuffing it under one arm. Then she went out of the kitchen and down the hall and out the front door, opening her car door and slamming it with a thump. They watched her pull out of the driveway.

"Thanks a fucking lot, Amina."

"You said to do something."

"Shut up."

It took four hours for Kamala to come home. Amina knew because she was awake, wondering if it was possible to lose both parents to the difficulties of living in America. Could their mother really just leave them, too? Was that all it took, one good fight and members of her family would drive off down the driveway forever?

But then came the noise of the car, the keys landing on the countertop. Kamala hushed the dog's whining with the low hum of Malayalam. Footsteps and paw steps made their way across the house and the bottom stair creaked as Kamala climbed up to the kids' landing. Amina hurriedly arranged herself into something she thought a mother would feel good about coming back to—back straight, nightie smoothed. A good girl. A Girl Scout. But Kamala didn't knock on her door. She didn't knock on Akhil's either. Amina stared at the brass knob, listening to what sounded like rustling and fleeing, Kamala's steps softer on the stairs as she hurried *slipslapslipslapslip* down.

Amina got up. She tiptoed across her room and opened the door as silently as she could, peeking into the hallway. Nothing. No Kamala, no Queen Victoria, no one to look intrepid for. But wait. She squinted. Yes, there was something. A paper bag. It sat outside Akhil's door, as familiar and mystical as a lawn gnome. Amina slid across the floor in her socks and knelt in front of it, dumping out the contents. A box fell to the floor. Small, neat, not much bigger than her hand. She turned it over, looking at the picture of a couple silhouetted by the sunset. LATEX, bold letters proclaimed, and with the proclamation, Amina understood that she had no business with it whatsoever. She shoved it back into the bag and half ran back to her bedroom, diving under the covers.

The next morning the bag was gone. Akhil did not say anything about it as they ate their toast alone in the kitchen. And Kamala did not come out at all, even as they washed the dishes and packed their bags for school, though Amina thought she caught a glimpse of her mother's dark head looking through the dining room window as they pulled out of the driveway.

CHAPTER 4

Nobody at Mesa Prep was prepared for the mid-semester arrival of Paige and Jamie Anderson. By late February, any luster of new lives or new possibilities had been dulled into the routine of schedules and cliques. Students clustered in the quad in the morning, bored to death with one another and staring sullenly toward the parking lot, as though daring it to spit out something worth looking at. So there was a pause as the two figures crested the asphalt horizon, a round of glances exchanged. Bodies turned slightly on benches. Words trailed off into the morning. Were they real?

Wearing down coats, hiking boots, and blank faces that gave nothing away, Paige and Jamie arrived like orphans, a hint of tragedy, bravery, and unmentionable events following them with the persistence of a shadow.

"Who's that, Snow Fucking White and the Disco Dwarf?" Mindy said, watching them cross the lawn that first morning.

"Shut it, Mindy," Akhil said, proving that while Mindy's remark was overzealous, her move to ostracize the Andersons was actually highly instinctual, the tactical response of one species whose time has been eclipsed by another. There was a palpable knowingness, along with several other features, on the approaching Andersons that would wipe the likes of Mindy Lujan off the Mesa Preparatory map, including:

1. Paige's thighs (curvy)
2. Paige's breasts (hidden by her white jacket, but clearly visible in outline, like croquet balls covered in snow)
3. Paige's neck (long)
4. Paige's cheeks (ruddy)
5. Paige's mouth (large and slightly blurry at the edges, as if the lips hadn't been told where to end themselves)
6. Paige's hair (shiny, black, bobbed)
7. Jamie's Afro (huge)

To be clear, Jamie's Afro (yes, he was white, but what else to call it?) was not in itself attractive, but somehow the sheer wildness of it, with outer limits reaching a blond radius twice as wide as his actual head, served as a brilliant counterpoint to his sister's tidy black locks, baby's breath to her rosebud. It made her, if possible, more perfect. No one said anything else as they walked past, disappearing into the dean's building.

"What's their deal?" Akhil said as they were lost to the bright glare of the closing door.

"Only one way to find out." Dimple slid her books off the concrete bench and followed them.

Unsurprisingly, it was Dimple who broke the first legitimate scoop on the Andersons, some four hours later in biology class. She walked in past the chalkboard, where the words *interphase, prophase, metaphase, anaphase, telophase* swirled yellow against green, and winked at Amina. When Ms. Pankeridge stepped out of the room five minutes later to find more pipe cleaners for the mitosis models, Dimple announced, "They're intellectual refugees."

"What?" Hank Franken asked, working his pinkie finger steadily into a Styrofoam ball.

"The Andersons. They got kicked out of St. Francis's."

"Bullshit. Says who?"

"Says them."

"Hicked hout?" Gina Rodgers asked, her lips clamped over two pipe cleaners.

"That's why they're here now. Apparently their grandfather had to bribe the school or something so Paige could graduate on time."

"Kicked out for what?" Amina asked, and Dimple smiled like she'd won the $25,000 question.

"Atheism."

A small murmur went up in the room, followed by a few nervous glances. While everyone knew better than to actually believe in God, the outright denial of one seemed dangerous and possibly gauche.

"Can they really kick you out for atheism?" Amina asked.

"They'll kick you out for anything," said Hank, his fingers now deeply rooted in five separate balls so that when he raised his hand, it looked like half a solar system. "Those nuns are relentless."

"What exactly did they tell you?" Amina asked.

"Well," Dimple began, looking coolly around the room, "when I asked him why they were starting here in the middle of the second semester, he said because legally, the U.S. required schooling until the age of sixteen, and that St. Francis's had become untenable for him. So then I said, well, thank God they had room for you here so late in the year, and he said God had nothing to do with it, his grandfather's checkbook did."

"And that makes him an atheist?" Amina asked.

"Pretty much," Dimple said.

After dinner, Akhil stood stoned on an aluminum ladder, head, hand, neck, and wrist all craned toward the ceiling. Downstairs, they could hear Kamala cleaning the dinner dishes, bursting with the first bars of "The Sound of Music" every few minutes.

"Dimple says they got kicked out for being atheists or something," Amina said, lying on Akhil's bed.

"That's a load of crap."

"How do you know?"

"Because Paige is in Mathletes."

"So you talked to her?"

He looked from the piece of paper in his hand to the ceiling, studying it for long seconds before drawing a single long, skinny line. "Does Che look like a girl?"

"Is he the bald one?"

"Fuck you. The bald one is Gandhi. You can tell because of his glasses." Akhil climbed back up. "And anyway, of course I didn't talk to her."

"Why not?"

"Because she's, you know." Akhil mashed the paintbrush down in the can. "Pretty."

"And Mindy will get jealous?"

"No. We broke up yesterday anyway. I mean, we're still, you know, seeing each other, but we've decided not to be exclusive. But anyway, Paige told Mr. Jones that her father didn't think St. Francis's was academically rigorous enough. You really don't think that looks like Gandhi?"

"It looks like a baby."

"But the eyes are good, right?"

"Kind of, but they're in the wrong place."

"Oh, that's all? Fucking great."

"Make them lower." She went to his desk, opened up his history spiral. She drew an egg on the paper and then drew a light line across the middle. "Like this. Everyone always thinks eyes go high on the head but they're usually more in the middle of it."

Akhil was quiet, pink eyes scanning the paper. "Hey, Ami, maybe you could—"

"No."

"I'll pay you."

"No. How much?"

"Two bucks a night."

"Three."

"Please? I'll take you to Coronado mall this weekend."

"Two seventy-five."

Akhil groaned. "Seriously. Please."

Amina considered it. This money, combined with what she was making on Akhil's "flash sleeps," as she'd begun to think of them, would put her in fine contention for getting at least an extra roll of film a week. "Fine, two. But just the drawing. I'm not painting anything."

"Deal." He looked back down at the paper. "Where do the mouths go?"

"Dunno." Amina took the pencil from him and started up the ladder. "I'm bad with mouths."

CHAPTER 5

"The river is crucial to understanding every other element in these pages," Mr. Tipton said the next day, holding up *Heart of Darkness*. "Who can tell me what it signifies?"

The door opened, sending in cool air and swiveling heads from the board to the doorway. Amina saw the fuzz of the blond Afro, then studied her notebook as the rest of Jamie Anderson materialized. Mr. Tipton crossed the carpet to shake his hand.

"Welcome," he said with a broad smile. "We were expecting you yesterday. Jamie?"

The Afro bobbed.

"Well, come in. Dean Farber tells me you've transferred in from St. Francis's?"

"Yeah," Jamie said. His voice was slightly muffled and husky, as though he was getting over a cold.

"And before that you lived in Chicago?"

"My dad was a professor at the University of Chicago."

"Ah, I see," Mr. Tipton said, his eyes sparkling with appreciation. "Well, welcome. Take a seat."

Jamie looked around the room. He looked at the empty seat next to Amina and then chose the one directly across the classroom, sliding into it. His eyes flicked up. They were a deep, unnerving green, protected by ferocious eyebrows.

"So, Mr. Anderson, in the last two weeks, we've plunged straight into *Heart of Darkness,*" Mr. Tipton said. "Everyone else has read the first hundred pages, so you'll need to catch up over the weekend. Meanwhile, I don't suppose you brought a copy?"

Jamie lifted the paperback. The cover was different from the one available at the Mesa bookstore.

"Great," Mr. Tipton said. "So who in the class can fill Jamie in on the broad themes in the book? Amina?"

"It's okay, I've read it," Jamie said, to her utter relief.

"Really? I was told St. Francis's doesn't cover this particular work until senior year."

"I read it on my own over the summer."

"Oh! Great! So I expect you've got some insight into some of the prevalent themes."

"Maybe," Jamie said.

Amina's stomach clenched with nervousness, as though she were being ratcheted up a ramp on a roller coaster. *Maybe?*

"So we were talking about the river," Mr. Tipton said, hands jamming back into his pockets. He rocked on the balls of his feet. "Who can tell me what the river is?"

"Life."

"Death."

"A journey."

"Obsession."

"Good!" Mr. Tipton said. "These are all good thoughts. Jamie, anything to add?"

Jamie tugged at his left ear. "A river."

The collective titter gave way to a tingling silence. Mr. Tipton did not smile. "That's all?"

"In a sense."

"In what sense, exactly?"

Jamie shrugged his shoulders.

"No, no," Mr. Tipton said, "go on, I'm interested. Please tell us in what sense the river is just a river."

Jamie muttered a little, his ears reddening, and Amina shifted in her seat.

"No? Okay, let's move on," Mr. Tipton said, resuming his pacing. "So. A journey. What kind of jour—"

"In the sense that in order to experience this book, really experience it, the best thing anyone can do is to get rid of the need to label every symbol in it." The flush spread fast over Jamie's face, covering everything but the white half-moons under his eyes.

"Excuse me?"

"I mean, if you're really plunging—you said plunging, right?— into this book, then tethering yourself to every single guidepost along the way isn't really going to make that happen."

Mr. Tipton's mirth was palpable. "So you think critical reading is a useless activity? That your classmates are just, what, not *experiencing* the book?"

"I think the best way to experience this book is to let it happen to you and think about what it all means later."

"Later when?"

"Later when you're a high school English teacher."

Amina was sure she wasn't the only one who gasped audibly, but somehow it was her face that Jamie locked onto. She swallowed.

"Mr. Anderson, let's take a minute in the hall, shall we?"

Jamie got up and walked out first. Mr. Tipton carefully placed down his chalk and walked out after him.

"Holy shit," someone laughed, and someone else let out a low whistle, the kind reserved for pretty girls and danger.

The mouths were disastrous. Every single one of them. She hadn't drawn them well, to be sure, but the mural had taken a turn for the

worse when Akhil insisted that all the lips be shades of pink or peach.
The Greats had the smiles of country club mothers.

But if the failure registered at all with Akhil, he wasn't showing it
as he led Kamala down the halls to see the progress.

"Let me see, let me see," Kamala said giddily, as though Akhil
wasn't doing just that. The door to his bedroom swung open, and
Amina let her eyes rise to the ceiling, seeing, for the first time, how the
mural darkened the ceiling like a gargantuan spider. Kamala circled
under it, hands clasped over her heart.

"Fantastic!" she said.

Akhil, too pleased to hide a smile, looked away.

"Who are they?"

"In order, they're Nelson Mandela, Martin Luther King, Mahatma
Gandhi, Che Guevara, and Rob Halford."

"Of course they are! Which one is Gandhi?"

"The one with glasses."

Kamala squinted.

Akhil sighed. "The one on the left."

"Yes, yes, of course." Kamala smiled enthusiastically. "And who is
this baldy fellow over here?"

"Rob Halford."

"He's lead singer of Judas Priest," Amina explained.

"Lovely," said Kamala. She looked so tiny in Akhil's room, gazing
at the ceiling and hugging herself tightly, as if to keep her joy close to
her. "And now what? You'll do more? Or something else?"

"I don't know."

"Maybe the sky?"

Akhil frowned, looking at the ceiling. "The sky?"

"You know, for background. Use the sponge!"

"Oh, yeah. Good idea, Ma."

"Good idea," Kamala repeated. She and Akhil studied the ceiling
together, heads turning this way and that while Amina watched from
the bed. "It's really good, Akhil. I can't believe you did this whole thing
by yourself." Kamala hesitated before reaching out to gently squeeze
Akhil's shoulder. She let go of it quickly, walking out the door before
he could turn to see the tenderness on her face.

The sky began that night, tattered clouds making their way across an orange and red sunset. Below them, a crucifix-shaped flock of snow geese flew into endless twilight. As an afterthought, Akhil also labeled each of the Greats, block letters making clear what artistic longing could not.

CHAPTER 6

Had she known it was going to be an exercise in complete humiliation, Amina would not have come to the dance at all. As it was, she sat in a whirlpool of disco lights trying not to watch every single person in the entire school (including Akhil, including Dimple) make out with someone else. It wasn't easy. God knows she had already scrutinized the streamers scaling the gymnasium walls, the monster-large speakers floating over sweet-smelling smoke, the disco ball spinning like the eye of a Cyclops. "Only the Lonely" blared through the speakers like some kind of cosmic taunt.

She hated it. She hated the lights and her shoes and her hair and the fact that the wistfulness of the singer's voice made her wish for a nuclear war or an earthquake or really anything that might make someone else want to kiss her.

"What are you thinking about?" A face spinning with white stars leaned over hers, and Amina shot up straight, almost smashing into it. Jamie Anderson stood beside her, jean jacket collar turned up, some sort of velour shirt underneath. Colored lights illuminated his enormous puff of curls, making him look like a candied dandelion.

"What?"

"You look like you're thinking about something."

"Bombs," Amina said, wishing instantly she hadn't.

Jamie nodded, like of course she was thinking of bombs. "The ones in the mountain?"

Amina looked at him warily.

"By Kirtland Air Force Base," he said. "You know what I'm talking about."

She had no idea what he was talking about, or why he was even talking to her at all, considering that he hadn't said word one to anyone in English class after his initial outburst. He surprised her further by sitting down. A little breath of him escaped from the jacket. He smelled like denim and deodorant.

"One of the Manzano Mountains is hollowed out and filled with nuclear warheads. I thought everyone in the city knew that."

"I guess no one told us retards."

Jamie winced and smiled at the same time, looking over his shoulder, and Amina covertly wiped her hands against her jeans. Sweating. She was sweating.

"So what are you doing here?"

"It's a school dance."

It wasn't a great answer, but Jamie nodded. "Cool."

Amina tried to ignore the couple in front of them, noses nuzzling necks, hands locked onto asses.

"You know if a war starts, we'll be the first to go?" Jamie said. "And the thing is, I bet the Russians wouldn't even want to kill us if they could. You know? I bet they're just like us over there, just at the mercy of their leaders—"

Amina stood up. "Do you have a cigarette?"

He smothered a look of surprise. "Yeah, sure."

She turned and started down the steps. "You can just give it to me. You don't have to come if you don't want to."

He followed her. "What if I want to?"

"Can you stop talking about bombs?"

"Because it scares you?"

"Because you sound like my brother."

He didn't say another word as they thumped down the rest of the bleachers. They reached the bottom just as the song ended and the mass of conjoined faces in front of them split apart, looking alternatively dreamy or just wet.

"C'mon," Jamie said, grabbing her hand. She looked down, mesmerized by the sight of his pale hand on hers, and let herself be led through the heated bodies, the sweat and Polo cologne and fruit-flavored lip gloss and hairspray. The wood floor turned to linoleum under her feet and the air cooled as Jamie pushed the gym door open. She followed him to a set of arches a few hundred feet from the gym and looked away as he fished into his jean jacket and then the back pocket of his pants.

"So what's up with your brother?" he asked, putting two cigarettes in his mouth. "He's a pretty cool guy, right?"

"You know him?"

Jamie blew on the end of one, handed it to her. "Not really. I just see him around. He went to that nuclear-waste protest at UNM last week."

"You went to that?"

"My whole family went."

Amina looked away, dumbfounded. Was that what other families did? A car skidded into the lot. The door opened and three girls uncrumpled themselves from the front seat, cooing their way across the parking lot.

"So you're from Chicago, right?" she asked.

"Yeah. We just moved here last summer."

"Huh." Amina flicked her cigarette, the way she'd seen Akhil do it, thumb on the filter. "Do you miss it?"

"Yes. Not as much as my sister, but yes."

This made sense. The few times Amina had seen Paige during lunch break, she was staring intently off campus, as if there were a whole world waiting on pause just outside the gates.

"Why did you get kicked out of St. Francis's?"

"Who says I got kicked out?"

"You didn't?"

Jamie blew at the end of his cigarette. "I got busted getting high at the Christmas Pageant."

"Oh." Amina tried for nonchalance, but she didn't personally know any freshmen who had gotten high, or at any rate, high enough to get kicked out of school. Something about it excited her terribly. She wanted to lead Jamie back into the light and check his pupils and reflexes, maybe test his memory.

The gym door opened, and the high wail of an electric guitar slipped out before it shut.

"Anyway, I'm sure she'll go back next year," Jamie said. "She's trying to get into Northwestern."

"Why don't you like Mr. Tipton?" Amina asked.

Jamie shrugged. "It just seems like everyone kisses his ass."

"Well, if you are trying to get kicked out again, it won't happen. The worst they'll do here is have you sit in the corner and not get to participate in the discussion."

He snorted. "Yeah, that would suck."

What was it about him that was so hard to stop looking at? In a school of razor-jawed, short-haired boys, he was hardly handsome. His eyes were too deep set and his eyebrows too present. And yet these, together with his ruddy cheeks and too feminine lips, gave him an oddly androgynous face that Amina had to fight to ignore in class. Now the sneer on those lips sent a small flare up her spine.

"I'm not an ass kisser," she said.

"What?"

"I'm not an ass kisser just because I talk in class."

"I didn't say that."

"Yeah, right."

"No, really. I *like* what you say in class," he said. "I mean, it's smart."

"No it isn't."

Why had she said that? She didn't even know what she was saying anymore, or what exactly was going to loosen the knot that was hardening in her throat. She looked across at the parking lot, where one of the trucks appeared to be bouncing slightly in a disconcerting way.

She felt Jamie's gaze travel with hers, and the hair on the back of her neck stood up like it was being brushed the wrong way. She let herself look right at him. His hair radiated from his head in a beautiful nimbus, and she felt his face coming closer, the center of some oddly beautiful flower.

"What?" she said, and he jerked back in surprise.

He looked down at her hand. "Are you going to smoke that?"

Her cigarette had a thumb-tip-sized ash growing on it. She flicked it, stuck it between her lips like a straw, and sucked. A cat with its claws out skidded down her trachea. For one moment she held it in, looking at the curious expression on Jamie's face, and then she choked and everything came out at once, smoke and tears and spit exploding out of her face. Jamie jumped back.

"Holy shit!"

She gasped, and began coughing again, this time jamming her face into the crook of her arm so he couldn't see her. She wheezed, hacked. She felt his hand thumping her back like it would do any good, and she cursed silently through the rest of it, which ended with a few shaky breaths and a swallow.

"Are you okay?"

She nodded, not trusting her voice. She needed to burp and wasn't sure if it would be smoke or air.

"You don't smoke, do you?"

She shook her head, which made him laugh out loud. She dropped the remaining cigarette and stamped it out.

"Why did you ask for one?"

"I just wanted to get out of there."

"Oh. No shit." He looked back at the gym and took a step toward it, then turned around again. "So do you want to go for a walk?"

"No."

"Around the soccer field or something," he said, pointing past them like she didn't know where it was. "And then we can go back inside."

The sprinklers had gone off recently, and the wet grass tickled her ankles as they followed the lime boundary. Jamie walked a little ahead of her.

"So what did Paige do?" she asked.

"What?"

"To get kicked out?"

"Oh, she didn't. She asked my parents if she could transfer because she thinks the Catholic curriculum is actively regressive."

They approached a corner, and Amina's shoulder brushed his as they rounded it. His hand swung close to hers, leaving a little comet trail of heat, and Amina thought of how if she were Dimple, she'd just grab it like it was some normal fucking thing to do.

"So you guys are Hindu, right?"

"What?" Amina startled. "No. We're Christian."

"Oh." He sounded disappointed.

Amina walked a little faster. "Yeah. I mean, not that anyone in my family is anything, really. Our mother has taken us to church, like, twice. But we're not Hindu. Although apparently the converts to our kind of Christianity were probably, like, Brahmins when Saint Thomas came down to India in 50 A.D., which is when our religion started, although everyone just, like, assumes it was some British colonization thing."

Was she babbling? She was babbling. She fought down the inexplicable urge to tell him about how she and Akhil had once found a viper in their grandmother's garden, or how Thomas used to see dead bodies burning on the banks of the river when he was little. They turned another corner, and Amina noticed with disappointment that the lights were on in the gym. Groups of kids were starting to come out the doors.

"We should go back," Jamie said, walking across the field. She followed him.

"Fu-uck. Fu-uh-uh-uck."

Akhil was knocking his head against the windshield repeatedly as they approached the station wagon, his hands gripping the roof.

"What is wrong with you?" Amina said, wanting more than anything for her brother to retain at least a whisper of the cool that Jamie had attributed to him earlier.

"Kee-ee-ee-eys," Akhil said, not missing a beat. "Ssee-ee-ee-eat."

Amina pushed him out of the way. Sure enough, there they were, glinting behind the sealed window and locked door.

"Oh my God."

"You locked your keys in the car?" Jamie asked, and Akhil looked confusedly from him to Amina and back again.

"Apparently," he said.

"Be right back," Jamie said, and turned and walked toward the gym doors, where people were still coming out in sweaty clumps.

"What are you doing with that guy?"

"Nothing. How are we going to get home?"

"Dunno."

"What about Mindy?"

"I dropped her off at her house. We were done."

Amina looked at the car, wrinkled her nose. She hated getting in with the overheated smell of Mindy (Giorgio of Beverly Hills, menthols, yeast) clinging to the upholstered seats. "Great."

"You locked your keys in?"

Amina and Akhil turned to see Paige walking briskly toward them with Jamie behind her.

"Yeah."

"And you don't have a coat hanger on you?"

Dimples cupped either side of her smirk.

"No." Akhil scowled.

"Joking," she said. "I was joking. I think I've got one in my car."

"Don't worry about it if it's a hassle."

"It's not," Paige said. "I do it all the time."

"She's good," Jamie said, as they watched her walking across the parking lot to a yellow van. "Faster than anyone."

"I'm Akhil, by the way," Akhil said, reaching forward to shake Jamie's hand. Jamie returned the introduction, and then they dropped hands and stuffed them into pockets, awkward with the sudden formality.

"We have class together," Amina volunteered. "English."

"Oh yeah, with Tipton?" Akhil smirked. "What do you think of that guy?"

"I try not to."

"Good answer."

Paige reemerged from the van, waving a triumphant hand.

It was nothing short of riveting, really, watching Paige Anderson untwist the neck of the hanger while she studied the lock on the door, taking in the dimensions and calculating the geometry that guided her hand to the tip of the hanger. She bent it into a tiny *u* and then slid it first up, then down through the window crack. She bit her tongue between her front teeth and hooked the hanger around the lock. It slipped.

"Crap." She shook out her hands. "Gimme a minute."

"We're not going anywhere," Akhil said, and she took a deep breath, wedging the hanger again, this time pulling it at an angle. The lock popped up.

"Nice." Akhil smiled.

"Thanks," Paige said, looking a little pleased. She opened the car door and handed him the keys.

"Amazing." Akhil wasn't even looking at the keys; he was looking at Paige, his face stretched into emotions Amina had never seen— wonderment, desire, and raw happiness riding over its surface.

"We should go," Jamie said, breaking what had become a too long silence.

"Right," Paige said faintly, backing up. "I've got to get my bag from inside. Can you grab the car and meet me?"

"Yep." He held out his hands. Paige threw him her keys.

"You can drive?" Amina asked.

"Around the parking lot," Jamie said, and started off, already ten feet away before Amina could say goodbye.

"Well," Paige said to Akhil. "See you on Monday, I guess."

"Yeah." Akhil watched her go, grinning that crazy grin that made Amina want to kick him or cover his head with a paper bag. "Wait!"

"Yeah?" Paige stopped.

He cleared his throat. "So . . . what's your name?"

Paige looked at him for long, increasingly painful seconds. Finally she said, "We're in Mathletes together, I just picked your lock, and you're going to pretend you don't know my name?"

"Well . . . ," Akhil started, but she was already walking quickly away, fingers sprinkling a wave behind her. She was halfway to the gym, her dorsal softness jumping in and out of puddles of light before Akhil let out his breath. His features pooled with panic. "Shit. Should I . . . ?"

"Don't ask me—" Amina started, annoyed, but he was sprinting before she even finished, his shirt filling with wind, his legs slowing to a jog and then a very quick walk that would catch Paige just before she got to the gym door. Amina watched as he tapped her on the arm and then recoiled, running a hand through his hair and saying something she couldn't hear. There was a beat. A pause. A moment of silence between them that Amina would later recognize as the forgettable turning into the extraordinary. Then Paige threw her head back and laughed, revealing a white slash of teeth, the long curl of her neck, and a fate that Akhil never stood a chance of resisting.

BOOK 6

WE BURY WHAT LEAVES US

ALBUQUERQUE, 1998

CHAPTER 1

If her mother had been surprised at all to see Amina come home from the airport, she had not let on, frowning briefly at Monica's car idling in the driveway before walking straight back to the kitchen, opening the fridge, and pulling out the dosa batter and potato masala for lunch.

"So you're staying?" Kamala ladled white batter into a flat pan, slowly circling it into a thinner and thinner round.

"Yes, for a little while." Amina sat at the kitchen counter, starving, her bag at her feet. "A few weeks, at least. I just talked to Monica, and she said—"

"Then I will get some beef and some chicken." Kamala straightened her braid with a sharp tug.

"What?"

"You need to eat, don't you?"

"Yes. Right." Amina sipped at her water, as though it could satisfy her roiling gut. The hunger was making it hard to think.

"And then you can photograph the Bukowskys' wedding, too," Kamala said.

"What?"

"Julie's daughter! I told you about it! The wedding this weekend?"

Amina looked at her mother blankly.

"Jenny Bukowsky is one of the nurses in the OR. Her wedding is Saturday and we have to go anyway. You can take some pictures. We'll buy them for them as a present." In one smooth move, Kamala flipped the thin pancake onto a plate, adding a fist-sized clump of potatoes in its center and folding it in half. She handed it to Amina. "Coconut or tomato chutney?"

"Yes, please."

Kamala spooned a generous amount of both onto her plate before turning back to the stove. As she placed the ladle back in the batter, she said, "I canceled the dinner with Anyan. Eat."

The pancake cracked under Amina's fingers with a burst of steam that smelled of turmeric and chilies, filling her with relief so sharp that it erased everything but itself. She ate one dosa and then another, dimly aware of her mother spooning more chutney onto her plate and refilling her glass with water. Finally, in the middle of the third, she sat back to breathe, mouth tingling. She knew she should tell Kamala about Monica, the car, the conversation, and instead found herself saying, "Ask him if Wednesday works."

Her mother took a quick glimpse over her shoulder. "What?"

"For dinner. Dr. George."

"Really?"

"Yes." Amina felt momentarily guilty at the pleasure that fanned out over her mother's face. "This is really delicious, by the way."

"I'll make you one more."

"No! Jesus. You're going to get me fat if you keep feeding me like this."

"No Jesus," Kamala scolded lightly. She lifted the pan from the stove and placed it in the sink, turning the water on so it hissed as it cooled. One by one, she replaced the chutneys in the fridge door and turned around. She walked over to Amina, hugging her so briefly and furiously that she was five steps out of the kitchen before Amina thought to hug her back.

Half the village of Corrales and most of the OR staff of Presbyterian Hospital turned out for the Bukowsky wedding the following Saturday night. Just-shined cowboy boots escorted broom-skirted ankles first across the horse-patty-strewn parking field, then to the dance floor, a patch of dirt stamped level in the middle of some cottonwoods. Up on a nearby trailer bed, the Lazy Susannahs played bluegrass at top volume under a ring of Christmas lights, while dogs and small children hurtled through folding chairs and Johan Bukowsky clutched his shirt.

"I'm all right!" he proclaimed loudly at several intervals, drawing hoots of appreciation from the crowd. "It had to happen sometime, right? I just didn't think so soon."

This got a good laugh from everyone as his daughter's seven-year engagement had been made much of during the ceremony, and Jenny herself ducked a shaking head into the groom's neck. Amina stepped lightly onto the dance floor, snapping a photo and then receding as the hired photographer popped into her frame.

"Did you get it?" Kamala asked anxiously from behind her. "Do you need to get another?"

"Nope." Amina turned the lens on her parents, who were looking particularly dashing and out of place in their best silks, like Bollywood actors who had wandered mistakenly onto the set of a western.

"Not us!" Kamala dabbed her upper lip with the tip of her sari. "You need to get the bride and groom standing and kissing! And then one of all those people that stand at the altar in fancy clothes and do nothing. And the cake! Don't forget the cake!"

"The real photographer will do all that," Amina reminded her. "I'm just here as a favor, remember?"

"It won't be a good favor if you don't get any nice pictures."

"Isn't this wonderful?" Thomas crowed. "Can you believe it?"

At least his inability to stay tear-free during a wedding was still firmly intact. Amina took a few quick shots of the Christmas lights reflecting in her father's eyes, his hands rising as he danced at the side of the floor. It hadn't been hard to convince him that a few weeks of her events had canceled, suddenly opening up her schedule. Harder was convincing Jane she needed to stay, and to get freelancers to cover the gaps for three weeks of work. Or, as Jane called them, "people who really want your job." The laugh that she had inserted to take the sting out of the threat only made Amina more nervous.

Amina pushed through the ring of people watching the dance to the backyard.

Tubs of beer glistened like buoys across the evening. A smattering of chatty groups had settled in for the night, and she tried to take a few candid shots of each before they grew aware of her. A dark-haired girl, one good year away from being self-conscious, was trying to make a black Labrador dance with her, paws to shoulders, and Amina backed up to get the right angle, not realizing until after the picture was taken that her ass was pressed into someone's very still hands.

"Jesus!" She whirled around to find a tall old man in a huge suit looking vaguely stricken. "I'm so—"

"S-sorry about that," the man stammered, looking down. "I wasn't trying—"

"No, no, it was me. I wasn't looking." She felt herself blushing and held up her camera like it had pushed her. "Pictures!"

"Right. Yeah, okay."

He was not old at all, she realized, on closer inspection of the man's face. It was the baldness that had thrown her. His face was actually youngish, all thick eyebrows and rocky lines. The man smiled apologetically, and Amina automatically looked into her viewfinder, liking something about the shape of his skull and the curve of the cottonwood trunk behind him.

"Oh no, don't do that," he said, stepping out of the frame but not before she caught something. A flash of deep-set eyes. The girlish mouth. The cover of her high school copy of *Heart of Darkness* veered sharply into her mind, and she lowered the camera.

"Jamie Anderson."

His smile was the same, a wince. "Hey, Amina."

"I didn't recognize you."

"I know."

"You're bald." Her shoulders jumped Tourretically. "I'm sorry!

That's not—I just, uh, you know, you used to have"—Amina held her hands out from her head a foot in either direction—"hair."

"I shave it in the summer." Jamie rubbed his ear, which was burning pinkly. "Less hassle."

His head glowed like a porcelain dish, and she fought the absurd urge to lick it. Time had rendered him taller, a little thicker, fuller in the face and shoulders. But that mouth. It had not changed even a little—heavy-lipped, petulant, hanging open slightly as if ready for argument. Amina stared at it, dimly aware that it was asking her something.

"What?"

He pointed to the camera. "You're the photographer?"

"Yes. I mean, not *the* photographer, like *the wedding* photographer, but a photographer. In the world. For a living." Was she speaking English? She looked down and patted her camera like it was a lap dog.

"Ah." Jamie took a sip of beer. "So what do you photograph? In the world. For a living."

Amina colored, cleared her throat. "I can't believe you still live here."

"I just moved back six months ago. Position at UNM."

"You're a professor?"

"Anthropology."

"Seriously? I mean, that's great."

Jamie looked at her curiously, half grinning. "So you're back, too?"

"Visiting. Just for a little while. A few weeks. Something is wrong with my dad." Why on earth had she said that? Amina's face grew warm as Jamie looked at her with a little more concern than she felt comfortable receiving from near strangers. She looked away. Across the courtyard, a thin woman sat alone in a folding chair, a full paper plate of enchiladas on her lap. Amina lifted her camera and took a quick picture.

"Is it serious?" Jamie asked.

"I don't know." Amina shifted uncomfortably.

"I'm sorry, I don't mean to pry—"

"You're not. I mean, you are, but it's fine." Amina fiddled with the flash on the top of her camera. "Anyhow, I should get back to it. I promised my mom I'd get pictures for her."

"Oh. Right, sure." Jamie backed up to let her pass, and she moved swiftly toward the bar.

"Good to see you," he called after her, and she waved behind her, too unnerved to turn around.

Ridiculous. She had been ridiculous. Talking nonsense and still undone by the lower half of his face. The wine the bartender handed her a few moments later was a little too sweet, but she sipped it steadily, not daring until it was mostly gone to turn around and look at the party. Jamie had walked clear across the lawn, where he was bending down to give the bride a kiss on the cheek.

"Kiddo!"

Amina turned to find Monica coming at her, arms pinwheeling, hair spooling out of a French braid. She spilled a little white wine down Amina's back as they hugged.

"Shit! I got you?"

"A little."

"Forgive me, hon. It's been *quite* a week." Her intonation begged for elaboration, but Amina let it pass. "How are you doing?"

"Fine," Amina said. The band kicked it into high gear, banjos ringing, and out on the dance floor a circle formed, thick with clapping hands.

Monica leaned in close, dropping her voice. "Any news?"

"Not yet, but I've got a plan. I'm talking to Anyan George about it."

"Dr. George?" She looked worried.

"I know, but listen, we need help. And better him than anyone else."

"Yeah, I guess you're right. Smart. Man, I'm glad you're home." Monica threw an arm over her shoulder, covering her in the smell of flowery deodorant and white wine.

She whooped suddenly in delight. "Oh my God! Will you look at him! How long has it been since you've seen him look like that?"

Lunging from haunch to haunch, Thomas had moved into the center of the circle, arms crossed in front of him like a Russian folk dancer. Three kicks drew three glorious cries from the crowd, and he rose up with the last, his palms opened to the air, chin tilting toward the sky, curls bouncing. Amina found him through her viewfinder. A smile broke across her father's face, charming it.

"He'll be okay, you'll see," Monica said, taking a swig of wine, and Amina let the shutter fall over and over and over, willing her to be right.

CHAPTER 2

How had she forgotten how the flat light of a desert afternoon could suck the dimension out of anything? The first of the Bukowsky wedding photos were complete tossers. Garbage. The newlyweds looked like line drawings, gashes for mouths and empty sockets for eyes. Amina flipped through them quickly, leaving the worst in a pile on Akhil's desk. At least by the time the evening light rolled in she had found her rhythm. She lingered over the shot of Jamie Anderson, glad to be able to stare at him without having to make conversation. His features, once soft and strange, had hardened into deep crags and furrows. He had turned just as she was taking the picture, his eyes cast down, his mouth beginning to purse in a way that made her feel a little sex-starved and desperate. True, the actual conversation with Jamie hadn't gone so well, but conversations with men almost never did, for her.

The phone was ringing.

"Ami, get that!" Her mother called from below.

She reached for it on the desk, but the cradle was empty.

Amina stood and looked around the room. The phone rang again. "Ami!"

"Hold on!" She turned to the bed, lifting up one pillow and Thomas's blazer before her arms understood what her brain could not, throwing open the closet door. Inside, the phone trilled at her maniacally, as though delighted to be found. Amina picked it up, brushing a film of dirt from the mouthpiece.

"Hello?"

"I think I'm choking." Dimple did not sound like she was choking. She sounded like she was lighting a cigarette. Pioneer Square's morning hustled around her, the drunks and the bike messengers and the ferries floating through the phone line. "I don't think I can get this show up."

"Of course you can."

"No I *can't*," she said, sounding irritated. "And I don't need a fucking cheerleader right now, Amina, I need a realist."

Amina walked back to the desk, phone in hand. "What happened?"

"I still haven't found someone to pair with Charles White. I swear, I've looked everywhere. Nothing fucking works."

Amina flipped through a few more wedding shots. Red chili enchiladas did not photograph well. Guests hunched over white paper plates, looking like they were devouring piles of bloody flesh. "Isn't it getting late?"

"That's not helpful."

"You asked for a realist."

"Yeah, not an asshole."

"Jesus, Dimple."

"I'm sorry. It's not your fault. Or, well, it is, but not really."

"What did I do?"

"I want to show your work."

Amina swallowed. "Oh."

Dimple snorted. "*Oh*, she says."

"What do you want me to say? I don't have anything."

There was a short, unsettling silence, the kind that precedes fights between family like a growing electric field precedes lightning.

Dimple cleared her throat. "Okay, listen, I found the pictures in your closet."

"You what?"

"I found—"

"You went into my closet?"

"Yes, I did. Listen, I was at your house for the plants and then I needed a jacket, so I—"

"Bullshit."

Dimple was quiet for a second. "Okay, fine, I was looking through your stuff. I don't actually know why. I know that sounds weird. But I found them and I fucking love them. And listen, I know this isn't a great time to ask, and I hope you know I wouldn't unless I felt really, you know, desperate. Well, no, desperate and *compelled*. Because your work is compelling." She took a breath, changing her tenor to one Amina had heard her use with others too many times to feel flattered by. The honeyed tone, the easy pump of ego. "You know, the thing is, I can't stop thinking of how great it would be, actually. It's a good pairing, a really spot-on counterpoint to Charles's selection. I think we could actually go small with this—make it concentrated. Eight or ten—"

"No."

"Wait, stop, just listen for a second, okay? You know we're exploring the idea of domestic accidents, and it's, like, perfect. So if we go with the fainting grandmother, the peeing ring bearer, and those two bridesmaids fighting over the bouquet—"

"Are you listening? No."

"—lead with the picture of Bobby McCloud jumping—"

"No!"

"The puking bridesmaid. We've got to show that, obviously."

"Dimple, it's not happening! Period. And if Jane ever finds out anything about those pictures, I'll be fired instantly. There's a reason they were hidden."

"Wait, these are hidden from *Jane*?"

"Yes! But also the clients. They don't know about them, either. And this isn't the way they're going to find out."

"I'm not sure why Jane's opinion really matters," Dimple said.

This was not a good path to go down. "Look, you asked. I am saying no. Clear?"

Exhale. Silence.

"Dimple, do you hear me?"

"Yeah, yeah, I hear you. I know what you're saying. And I know we've had this discussion before, but somehow, Amina, I'm just never quite convinced that you don't want me to keep bothering you about it. I mean, right? You do, a little, don't you?" Dimple took another sharp drag. "I mean, you don't, like, lose ambition because you switch tracks for a little while."

"Switch tracks? I'm a wedding photographer!"

"So what? What if showing your stuff was, like, what you needed to get past it? You know, like on fucking *Oprah*. Scared-of-her-shadow housewife remembers her inner fire, starts a multimillion-dollar business, takes care of orphans on the side. Full circle!"

"I've gotta go."

"Wait! No! Okay, look, I'm sorry. I don't mean to do that. I just hate having to beg you for something you should be thrilled to give me. I mean, this is business. It's an opportunity. You took these pictures, the best fucking pictures I've ever seen you take, by the way, and what? You think if you show them, you're somehow worse off?"

"When did this become about me? Your job gets hard and I'm the jerk?"

There was a brief pause on the line, punctuated by the anxious bleat of a ferry.

"Okay, fine, that's fair," Dimple said. "Yes, I'm stuck. I don't have a good match, and even if I did, I wouldn't have a pristine set of prints that I love all ready to mount! But you do. And you're here, so we could bang this out fast. And I really do think you're a great fit for the show. *Please.*"

She sounded like a junkie. Like a photography junkie. The saddest, most pretentious thing in the world.

"I'm not there," Amina said.

"You're coming back this week."

"No. I need to stay here for a little bit."

"You've got to be fucking kidding me."

"Something is really wrong with my dad."

"What?"

It should not have felt so good, or easy, to tell Dimple everything, given the preceding conversation, and yet it did. It felt like taking off a tight helmet.

"Oh God." Dimple's shoes clacked as she paced. "Does the family know? I mean, obviously my mother doesn't, or everyone would, but the others?"

"I don't think so. It depends on how far it got around the hospital. But don't say anything about it yet, okay? I need to figure some stuff out."

"Of course. Right. I won't mention it to Sajeev."

Amina frowned. "Why would you tell him?"

"What? Oh, just because he asks about everyone from home when we talk."

"You talk?"

"He's been coming by. Talking about digital cameras, blah blah blah. Not important. How long are you going to be out there? Like, a few days or what?"

"Maybe another few weeks." Amina leafed through the remaining pictures on the desk, trying to channel Monica's strange, flat tone from the day in the car. "We just need to get him checked out and then take things step by step."

She stopped on a picture of her parents. She laid it flat on the desk. Dimple was telling her she'd keep picking up the mail, watering her plants, but Amina barely heard her. Technically, the photograph was beautiful. Taken at that moment when the sun pulls all the color in the desert to the surface, it showed Thomas at his radiant best, mid-dance, his arms thrown to the sky, a ring of blurred, smiling faces surrounding him. Except for Kamala's. Even slightly out of focus, Amina could see the wary pinch of her mother's brow, the look of someone assessing a traffic accident.

For half an hour after she and Dimple hung up, Amina sat at her brother's desk, listening to her parents tumbling around the house, banging into and out of it at regular intervals, opening and closing cabinets and drawers and doors without ever seeming to run into each other. It was amazing really, a dance so intricate it felt choreographed, executed to perfection through years of practice.

And what would they do if something was really wrong with Thomas? How could they possibly face it any better than they could face each other? Amina looked at Kamala's blurry face in the picture. It was useless, really, to fear whatever was making its way toward them, its slow progress dismantling the familiar routines of their lives, but that did not stop her from sitting as still as she could in the brightening day, as if stillness could keep the worst of it at bay.

CHAPTER 3

Anyan George was endearing in his own way. It wasn't a way that made Amina feel like reproducing with him, or even getting close enough for a friendly hug, but his offer to help in the kitchen, his attempt to appear casual in a button-down shirt and a horrible argyle sweater vest, his inquiries about Kamala's many sisters, and the tittering laugh he released generously at anything even resembling a joke made dinner the following night somewhat less of a chore than she had imagined it would be.

"More cabbage?" Kamala asked, pushing the bowl toward him. "Amina, hand him the cabbage."

"Oh, no thank you," Dr. George said, patting his sweater vest. "I am finally stuffed. It was absolutely delicious."

"We'll send it home with you! Don't want you becoming skin and bone!" Kamala smiled a bit too hard, her eyes darting across the table. "Amina will be quite a cook someday, you know."

"You must take after your mom in the kitchen?"

"God, no. The only thing I can do in the kitchen is try not to hurt anybody."

"Amen to that!" Thomas said.

"Oh, *pah*. What for dessert, Anyan?" Kamala asked, annoyed. "We have ice creams and we have cookies and we have ladoo."

"Much as I hate to, I should go. Early-morning call and whatnot."

"Sure, sure." Kamala was already walking toward the kitchen with hands full of dishes. "Let me just get your leftovers together. Amina, come."

In the kitchen, her mother's smiled vanished. "Can't cook! Who tells people the worst thing about you first? Why not let him get to know you?"

"You think *that's* the worst thing about me?"

"I'm just saying, let him get to know you! All night you and your father are acting like clowns so he will laugh." Kamala threw open a cabinet, whipping out two empty Tupperware containers. "How will he take you seriously?"

"We were having a good time."

"Well, there are times to have a good time and times to put a good shoe forward."

"Ma, stop. It was a perfectly nice night, and you're about to ruin it."

Kamala spooned heaps of potatoes into one bowl and cabbage into the other, sealing the lids with a tight mouth. Amina took them from her, walking back into the dining room.

"Are you sure there's not too much?" Anyan smiled when he saw the food.

"Take, take," Kamala said. "When you are ready, we'll have you back for more."

"Thank you so much. I really had a lovely time."

"I'll walk you out," Amina said, reaching for the door.

"Oh." Thomas, on his way out the door, stopped, looking confused.

"Good, good, excellent!" Kamala snaked her arm through Thomas's to keep him back, and for once, Amina was relieved by her mother's enormous will. "Good night! Nice to see you, Anyan! Bon voyages!"

The door closed with a gaudy thump, and Amina, too embarrassed to look at the doctor's face, turned and walked down the steps. Their feet were loud across the gravel in the drive. Anyan kept a careful distance between them and seemed relieved when they had reached his navy blue BMW without incident.

"Well, Amina, very nice to see you again."

"Yeah, you too." She looked at him expectantly, wishing he could read her mind, and the silence around them grew fatter.

"Listen," he said at last, softly, apologetically. "I feel I should tell you that I am, in fact, seeing someone."

"You are?" Amina asked, before remembering that she didn't care.

"A nurse, actually. She's very nice, really, and though of course we've been a little less than public about it due to our work life, I'd be remiss if I didn't mention it."

"I need to talk to you about my dad," Amina said.

"Excuse me?"

"I mean, that's great, about the nurse. I'm happy for you. But I need to talk to you about my father. I've been hearing some stuff about him."

Even in the fading light, she could see Anyan stiffening, his eyes traveling back to the house.

"Don't worry, they can't hear you," she said. "You can't hear anything from the front yard when you're inside, just the back, for some reason. And I can talk to you at your office if that's easier; I just didn't want to show up in the middle of a workday without you knowing what it was about."

"And what's it about, exactly?"

"What happened in the ER," she said. "Did you hear about it?"

"Yes."

"And?"

"And . . . ?" He looked at her blankly.

Was he trying to irritate her? Amina gestured impatiently. "What did you hear?"

"Oh." Anyan straightened, smoothing his mustache. "You know, that there had been some kind of miscommunication."

Miscommunication? Amina almost laughed out loud. "I heard that he tried to save a kid who had died."

The doctor gave a short nod. He had apparently heard that, too.

"Look, Dr. George—"

"Anyan."

"Sure." Amina felt the heat rising to her face. "Can you just level with me? Give me some idea of what's going on?"

"I'm not sure I know what you mean."

"I want you to tell me what's happening to my dad. People know, right? That's what Monica said. And if something is really wrong with him, then I should know."

"I'm sorry," Anyan said, shaking his head as if to clear it. "I'm just surprised that you're bringing it up. You seem genuinely worried about him."

"Aren't you?"

"No."

"Why not?"

"Because he's fine." He paused, waiting for her to accept that, and when she didn't, he continued: "Look, I know Thomas very well. I've seen him under great duress, and I recognize that this was an anomaly, not a pattern of behavior. And even if no one wants to come out and say it, things like this do happen in hospitals. Medicine's a human practice, with human errors. Thomas made an error, that's all."

"You really think that," Amina said, unable to keep the wonder out of her voice.

"I do."

"But then why would he try to work on a kid who was already—"

"Who knows? It was a friend's son, right? It must have touched off something in him momentarily. At any rate, it was one incident in an otherwise sterling career, and no one was harmed by it. We don't need to make it into something bigger." He patted her awkwardly, the gesture fumbling between bedside manner and brush-off.

"But it wasn't just one incident," Amina said.

"Excuse me?"

"He's had other incidents. Here. At home. I think he's been hallucinating regularly."

Anyan smiled thinly, as though waiting for a punch line. "What are you talking about?"

"That's why I came home. My mother called and told me that he was on the porch all night talking to his mother, who has been dead for years."

Anyan's smile faded. "Talking?"

"Yes."

"You saw him do this?"

"My mom has. And to be honest, I thought she was overdramatizing until I talked to Monica the other day. Now I'm not so sure."

"But what . . ." Anyan shook his head at the car in disbelief. "What does Thomas say about it?"

"He doesn't. That's why I'm talking to you."

It took a few moments for this information to find purchase in the doctor, moving, against the current of mentor and friend, to patient, to illness. Disbelief redirected to concern. Anyan turned from her, pacing a few steps before looking back at her. "Do you know how long these episodes last? Their duration and frequency?"

"No."

"Is there any sort of manic or depressive behavior immediately before? Do you notice that he's in a heightened state of activity, or—"

"Honestly, I have no idea. And I know you can't just make a diagnosis with a bunch of sketchy details, but . . ." Amina trailed off hopefully, willing him to disprove her. He didn't. She sighed. "I think I should bring him in to see you. I know it's not totally kosher, and I'm sorry to put you in that position. But if it's nothing, or, you know, even if it's something, I'd just rather figure that out with you first before word gets out."

"But he won't come. I already suggested it to him once, right after the ER, when it was just due diligence. He said no."

"I'll get him there," Amina said with an assurance she did not feel.

Anyan smoothed his mustache. "And what about Monica? What does she say?"

"She doesn't know about everything. I wanted to talk to you first. But she's on board."

"Okay then, I'll talk to her tomorrow. See if she can switch his schedule around for the time being so that he's not doing surgeries."

"Yeah?" Amina said, relieved. "You can do that?"

"I have to do that," Anyan said. "If what you're saying is true—though I think we should give that a wide improbability, considering that you haven't seen the behavior firsthand—then he shouldn't be practicing."

Amina nodded, feeling acutely ill at ease, as though she'd just sold classified information to the enemy, though she was unclear of who that enemy was, really. The disciplinary board at the hospital? Anyan George? The world at large, in which her father saw everything through the lens of his work?

"Your mother is watching us," Anyan said, sounding a totally different kind of upset now.

Amina turned around just in time to see the curtain falling back across the dining room window. "I should go back in. So is there some way for me to set up an appointment without, you know, alerting the entire medical community?"

"Call me directly. Do you have my number?"

"Mom does."

He opened the door to his car, putting his leftovers behind the front seat before folding himself inside. He moved slowly, as though the air around him actually weighed more, and Amina fought off the urge to apologize. No, she had wanted this, had sought him out specifically, guessing his admiration for her father would make him want to shelter Thomas a little while they figured things out. She waved as he started the car, and moved out of the way so he could leave.

CHAPTER 4

Moldy eggplant. Curried potatoes. Something that looked like a pile of slugs but turned out to be decomposing okra. The following Saturday, as Kamala headed out to the garden and Thomas tinkered on the porch, Amina pillaged the refrigerator, rounding up its worst offenders. A few rutty-looking tomatoes sat on the back of a shelf, and she set them carefully on the counter. Then she went to the gardening shed, pulled out the wheelbarrow and loaded everything in, wheeling it back to the porch.

Decked out in a headlamp and overalls, Thomas was hunched over a clamp as she walked in.

"I'm making a chest," he told her, not looking up.

"I brought you some things."

"What things?" He looked up, blinding her.

"Ow. Come see."

She led him outside to where Prince Philip hovered over the wheelbarrow.

"Leftovers!" Thomas said, opening a container. "My God, why didn't I ever think of it?"

"Because you're not the genius in the family."

"Pssht!" Thomas thumped her on the head, pleased. "Meet me out back."

She walked the wheelbarrow to the backyard while Thomas ran and got the truck, driving it through the tall grass and into a clearing. Kamala, weeding ferociously a hundred yards away, stood up, hands on her hips.

"Raccooner!" Amina shouted, and she went back to weeding.

"Did you see? I made a target." Thomas pointed to a piece of plywood fifty feet away, emblazoned with the black outline of a raccoon.

"Holy hell."

She helped him set up the Raccooner this time, and when she was done, she lined up the leftovers, smallest to biggest.

"Potatoes first?" she asked.

"You got it."

They loaded it in and Thomas pulled the slingshot back. "Ready?" She nodded.

"*Psshooom!*" he yelled as a clump of mustard streaked a wide arc across the yard, missing the target by a generous amount. Prince Phillip dashed after it.

"Oh, man, should we worry about that?" Amina asked.

"He's eaten worse."

The okra were the next to go, slimy fingers shot one by one across the yard, two of the dozen actually hitting the target, though not within the raccoon outline. The beets fared worse, which disappointed both of them if only for the promise of a bloody-looking hit. Prince Philip dutifully hunted them down, returning with horrible pink teeth.

"You do a biggie," Thomas said.

Amina lifted an eggplant from its Tupperware, shuddering at its cold, soft weight in her hand.

"Okay, so you're going to try to get the sling back as far as possible, but don't worry about that so much. Put it more in the center, okay? Right. That's pretty good."

Amina pulled back another three inches, grunting.

"Strong girl," Thomas said approvingly. "Good. So once you feel secure, try to angle it toward the—"

"Shit!"

The sling sprang from her grip, hurtling forward with a horrible whipping noise. They both ducked and, when nothing happened, straightened up, looking hopefully at the target. It was clear. Amina looked at Prince Philip, who looked anxiously back at her. The eggplant had disappeared.

"Jesus, kid!"

"Goddamn it. Give me the other one."

"Are you kidding?" Thomas laughed. "You're dangerous!"

"Give it!"

"Yeah, yeah, fine." Thomas bent to retrieve the other half of the eggplant, just as a high, thin, keening cry pierced the afternoon. It left a wake of silence behind it, and Amina looked fearfully at the sky.

"What the hell was that?" she asked.

"No idea."

And then they heard it again, a cry so wild and raw that they stood up on the truck bed. Prince Philip shot out an alarmed bark, and they turned to each other, eyes widening in recognition. The third cry sent them jumping into the open field and running through the tall grass, Amina's legs chasing her father's toward the garden.

And what was there to say about Kamala's figure huddled in the dirt, her fingers covered in mud, her face streaked with it, the howls that exploded from her throat? Amina and Thomas ran toward her, hurdling compost bins and piles of mulch. Kamala had fallen down. She was on the ground. Prince Philip barked angrily at the closed garden gate.

"Ma!"

The ground had been ripped apart, black clumps of soil strewn everywhere. A garden shovel lay where it had been dropped. Next to it, Kamala clutched herself, rocking, rocking. Amina bent down, touching her mother's shoulder.

"Ma? Are you okay?"

Kamala jerked upright, the cuff of a jacket spilling out of her arms.

"Oh my God," Amina said. "Mom what are you doing with—"

"You!" Kamala shrieked. "You get away! Get away, you filthy devil!"

But she was not talking to Amina. She was looking with burning eyes at the garden gate, where Thomas stood.

"Dad? Dad didn't . . ." Amina turned to look at her father, who was staring at Akhil's leather jacket with the sad, stunned recognition of a dreaming man returning to the waking world.

"Dad?"

Thomas shut his eyes.

"Dad, what did you do?"

"I'm so sorry," her father said.

BOOK 7

AKHIL THE GREAT, THE LATE

CHAPTER 1

Paige and Akhil could not get enough of each other.

Yes, it was a cliché, one that Amina had often heard describing the kind of love that required couples to sit on each other's laps when the whole couch was available, but with Akhil and Paige, it was literal. From the start, it seemed to her like they'd plunged into an underwater world in which the only way to breathe was through each other.

It was a shock, of course, seeing Akhil—only recently minted into fuckability by Mindy—approach Paige in the quad the following Monday with a notebook that he'd emblazoned with her name in black Sharpie. No one expected Paige to blush any more than they expected Akhil to reach out and tuck her hair behind her ear before walking quickly away. But then notes were exchanged in lockers. A hide-a-key box was left wrapped on the hood of the station wagon to prevent future lock-outs. Less than one week later, when they were kicked out of the library for talking too loudly about the drought in Ethiopia, it seemed strange that it had taken them two months to get together.

She was perfect for him. Yes, another cliché, but there were times when Amina felt that somehow Paige Anderson had been pulled out of a very specific dream that no one but Akhil would have bothered to have. It wasn't just that her upbringing on one of the finest university campuses in America had left her with a carefully curated collection of protest T-shirts (it had), or that she referred to her parents as "Bill and Catherine" (she did), or that she was leading a student coalition to campaign against the nuclear-waste site just outside Socorro (she was), or that her thighs and breasts and blurry mouth were primed for constant, prolonged attention (they were)—it was that every part of Paige, from her conscience to her politics to her grown woman's body, was suffused by an optimism so assured that to stay with her, Akhil had to stop being such an angry dick.

"So what?" Amina overheard Paige saying to Akhil one morning during one of his poor-Indian-me rants as they walked across campus. "We're a country of immigrants, and you're the first wave. At least you've got an opportunity to set your own stereotype."

Paige believed that changing the world for the better was a reasonable goal, that racism could be unhinged by education, that nuclear disarmament should be embraced in their lifetimes, and that equality between the sexes would surely occur as women integrated into careers dominated by math and science. She also believed every act of consensual sex released positive energy into the atmosphere.

Most important, Paige believed in Akhil. Or at least gave him the benefit of most doubts. In her eyes, Akhil's political tirades became evidence of great passion. His neuroticism belied a big heart. His tendency to pick fights was a desire for honest communication. His pot habit was introspective.

And strangely enough, with Paige's eyes on him, Akhil began to transform. Amina watched with marvel as her brother's rants became less didactic, his worries developed rich humanitarian undertones, and his endless baiting turned into invitations for "discourse."

"Do they ever stop talking?" Dimple asked some weeks later, as their dark heads crossed the campus, ducked to the world outside of each other.

"Not really," Amina said. But she had listened in on enough of their phone conversations to know that it wasn't so much what they talked about (Van Halen, apartheid, Riemann sums) as the charged pauses in between, the reevaluating and rethinking, that was truly remarkable. In fact, it wasn't until Akhil stopped driving Amina home altogether, and started returning from "after school activities" with lips rubbed to pulp, that Amina began to worry that the union might be too intense.

"We're just driving to the top of the mountains and back down," he told her when she hinted as much. "We do some of our best thinking at higher altitudes."

And where was Jamie during all of this? Right there, and yet, somehow, not. He still showed up for English class, and he still seemed interested when she was talking, but beyond catching eyes once or twice, neither of them knew what to say to the other. It wasn't a lack of interest so much as an eclipsing of one—a mutual embarrassment that their own odd exchange could be overshadowed by something as potent as their siblings' connection.

"I am stone in love with her," Akhil said to Amina a month after the dance, in one of the only direct exchanges they would ever have on the subject. They were just starting out for school. It was spring and everything was rain clean, and new, tiny shoots of green just beginning to dapple the fields. When Amina sneaked a look at his face, she saw that spring had come to Akhil as well, his insides finally catching up with his outsides, leaving him altogether reborn. He had finally found an America he could love; an America that would love him back.

CHAPTER 2

Thomas was home for dinner. What exactly the occasion was, neither Amina nor Akhil knew, but they had come home from school to find him chatting in the kitchen with their mother, stealing pinches of carrots from her cutting board as she grated them.

"What are you doing here?" asked Akhil, never one to wait for a reveal.

"Case finished early. Thought I'd get some rest."

"Oh."

"Carrot halwa!" Kamala announced, like anyone had asked.

"How was school?" Thomas smiled and the children mumbled vaguely at him, a little scared of his enthusiasm.

"Wash up!" Kamala commanded. "We've got lamb curry and rice."

Half an hour later, they sat at the table, Kamala ordering everyone to try everything, as though they had never had her cooking before.

"So I'm going to prom," Akhil said, trying not to look pleased.

"You are?" Amina said.

"What's a prom?" Kamala asked.

"It's a dance. A formal one. That you go to. With a date."

"Neat!" Thomas said. "And you're going?"

"A date who?" Kamala asked.

"A girl in my class. Paige Anderson."

"Paigean?"

"*Anderson*, last name. *Paige*, first."

"Oh." Kamala nodded. "How do you know this Paige?"

"Through Mathletes."

Kamala smiled. "A nice girl!"

"Well, yeah."

"You asked her?" Amina asked.

"We asked each other," Akhil said haughtily, as though she had missed some essential point he had made earlier.

"We should meet her," Thomas said. "You should bring her here before the dance."

"Dad, it doesn't work like that."

"What do you mean? Shouldn't the parents always meet the date before the outing?"

"Only if you're the girl's parents. It doesn't matter for the guy's."

"Oh." Thomas looked fleetingly disappointed. "Well, no matter, we could simply meet her afterward."

"No, no, no." Akhil shook his head. "Afterward is the casino party, and then after that is . . . another party."

"So many of parties?" Kamala asked. "Who is having them?"

The parties after prom, Amina knew (well, not knew firsthand, but knew in that Dimple had told her), were always conducted in hotel rooms on the side of the highway. Akhil put a chunk of lamb in his mouth, chewing and stalling. He swallowed and said, "Just some friends of mine in the class. Nice kids. Mathletes."

The last line blew it a little, Amina could see, her father's features darkening slightly. "We should talk to the parents."

"What parents?"

"The parents of the kids with the parties. Just to make sure it's okay."

"What do you mean, make sure? Of course it's okay."

"We'll see," Thomas said.

"What do you mean?"

"I mean that unless we feel good about it, you're not going any-where."

"You can't do that!"

"He's going to need to rent a tux, you know," Amina said, to change the subject. "It's required."

"Tux?" Kamala asked.

"Tuxedo," Amina said. "They're, like, required. All the boys have to wear them."

"One of my patients has a tuxedo rental shop!" Thomas said, sounding pleased. "We can go see him together. Bill Chambers. Nice man. You'll like him."

Akhil said nothing.

"Eh, Akhil? We can go see him?" Thomas stopped eating, his cheek bulging with a pocket of unchewed rice. "Akhil?"

Across from him, head tucked to his chest, Akhil didn't stir. His breaths were light and shallow.

"What's wrong with him?" Thomas asked.

"Nothing. He's asleep," Amina said.

"What?"

"Don't worry, he's just tired," Kamala said.

"What do you mean? He was just asking us if he could stay out all night. He was getting upset."

"And now he's sleepy," Kamala said. "So what? Growing boy, you said it yourself."

"He's done this before?"

"He's always tired during dinner," Kamala said, wiggling her hand for the curds, which Amina handed her. "He needs to get more sleep."

Thomas rose from his chair, walking around the table. He hovered over Akhil, peering at his face, but when he moved to pick up his wrist, Kamala slapped him away.

"*Chi!* Let him have some rest."

But Thomas would not be deterred. He leaned over Akhil, first waving his hand across closed eyelids, then pulling them up, one by one, exposing two pockets of white. He lifted his wrist and pinched it between two fingers, listening to his pulse. He turned to Kamala. "How often has this happened?"

"How often has he fallen asleep?" Kamala snorted. "At least once a night."

"Fallen asleep in the middle of doing something else."

"He hasn't! He just sleeps a lot. My God, I told you that months ago! But he's getting better. Ask Amina."

"Have you seen him do this?" he asked Amina.

Amina looked at him uneasily. "Yeah."

"During normal activity? When he should otherwise be in an alert and stable condition? Are the triggers usually emotional?"

"I . . ." What was he asking her? "I don't know."

"How often has it happened?"

"I don't remember. A few times."

Thomas tugged at his beard, frowning at his watch. "And when did it start?"

"I'm not sure. Six months ago, maybe."

Thomas kneeled down, his brow furrowed into dark canyons. He held Akhil's hand, stroking it lightly. Watching them, Amina realized it had been years since she had seen her father do anything so intimate as touch any of them. When Thomas pressed his brow to Akhil's sleeping face, she had to look away.

"What are you doing?" Akhil asked, jerking awake.

Thomas backed up. "Hey. Are you okay?'"

"Why wouldn't I be okay?"

"You just fell asleep."

"No I didn't." Akhil looked at Amina, who tried to nod with just her eyes. "I just shut my eyes for a second."

Thomas sat back on his heels.

"Finish eating," he said. "We'll talk after."

Two days later, they left for the hospital.

"What are they going to do?" Amina asked as she watched Akhil place his pillow and his backpack in the backseat of Thomas's car. They would not be coming back until late the next afternoon, Thomas had explained, checking his pager mid-sentence. Now her father was in the driver's seat, his mouth moving over words that Amina could tell were directed not at her brother at all but at whoever was on the newly installed car phone.

"Who knows? Some stupid dream-monitoring nonsense." Kamala frowned.

"But why does it take so long?"

"Measuring nighttime and daytime activity or some idiot thing."

"But what does Dad think is wrong?"

"Nothing! Nothing is wrong, he just wants to perform some tests to make sure nothing is wrong."

Did Kamala hear herself when she said things like this out loud? Amina's annoyed disbelief was abruptly tempered by her mother's face, the fevered anxiety of someone treading water with no shoreline in sight. She squeezed Kamala's shoulder and went upstairs to read.

CHAPTER 3

The problem with talking to Paige was that Amina had never really talked to her before. Or certainly not more than a few sentences, with Akhil nearby making sure the communication remained short and sweet. Still, the next day at school, Amina found herself walking toward the picnic table behind the senior building where Paige sat alone, reading a book.

"Oh, hi," Paige said, looking up. "What's up?"

"Nothing."

"Yeah?"

"Yeah, um." What was she supposed to say? Amina smiled nervously. "Akhil isn't here today."

"I noticed."

"Yeah. He's, uh, did he call you? About why he isn't here?"

"No." Paige closed her book. "Is something wrong?"

"No. Nope. Nothing."

Paige squinted at her with that same look Jamie would get sometimes in English class, like he thought you were trying to trick him when you were really just trying to figure out what to say. Amina stared at Paige's jeans, which were blue and slightly bell-bottomed and hugged her thighs.

"Have you ever seen him fall asleep?" Amina asked.

"What?" Paige stiffened.

"I mean, I just . . . has he ever fallen asleep around you suddenly? Like, maybe when he's emotional or excited or something?"

Paige blushed slightly, pushing a lock of black hair behind her ear. "I don't know."

"Never mind. It's silly. I'm just, you know, trying to figure something out. It's not a big deal. My dad just asked about it, and I thought—"

"Wait, your dad's worried about it?"

"What? No, no. I mean, kind of. He just . . . he asked me, and I don't really even see Akhil that much anymore, I mean, not that there's anything wrong with that, but you're sort of the person who sees him most now, so I thought that maybe you . . . but it's no big thing. Thanks."

She had no idea what she was thanking Paige for, or even really saying at all. She spun frantically and walked toward the sophomore building, daffodils blurring together in the corner of her vision as she sped away.

"Hey, Amina!" Paige called after her, but she just waved, pretending they were finished with a conversation that they'd never actually started.

"What's for dinner?" Amina asked, coming into the kitchen late that afternoon.

Kamala sat on a stool sorting red lentils. "Meen curry, rice, cabbage. I'm making dahl too, but for tomorrow."

She put her backpack down and headed into the pantry.

"Is Akhil back?"

"Yes."

"Cool." She grabbed a fruit roll.

"Don't bug him, nah? Poor thing was woken up all night."

"Yeah, okay." Amina headed up the stairs, kicking her shoes off before going across to Akhil's room. His door was half open, his socked feet dangling off the edge of the bed. Amina watched the rise and fall of his back from the doorway.

"Get out."

"You're not even asleep."

"Get out anyway."

She walked around his bed to his desk, pulling out the chair and sweeping a collection of ripe-smelling T-shirts to the floor. "So what did they do?"

"Tests."

"Yeah, no duh, but, like, how was it?"

"How do you think?"

"Did they give you a brain scan?" she asked.

"They monitored my sleep. Put some sensors on. Woke me up a few times."

"Was Dad there?"

"Mostly."

"Did it hurt?"

Akhil said nothing.

"Well, anyway, it's over, right? I mean, did they find anything?"

Her brother was silent except for the socked foot wagging at the end of the bed.

"Hey," Amina said. "Do you remember that *That's Incredible!* about the guy with the twin stuck in his head? Remember, the guy with the headaches?"

"GET OUT!" Akhil yelled, head rising from the pillow, and she sprang from the chair, heart thwacking.

"Jesus, psycho, I'm just asking!"

But he was up already, up and coming at her and taller, if possible, than he had been just the day before. She tried to dodge him, but Akhil grabbed one of her arms, twisting it behind her back and jamming her wrist between her shoulder blades.

"Ow! Ouch, Akhil, stop!"

He threw her into a headlock, dragging her across the floor. When he reached the door, he threw her out, slamming it behind her.

"Dickwad!" Amina yelled at it, cheeks burning. What the hell had brought that on? It had been years since he had put her in a headlock, and she was pissed to find out she was no more able to get out of it than she had been when she was eleven. She kicked the door, hard.

"Fuck off!" Akhil yelled.

"You suck!" she yelled back.

"Amina!" Kamala called from downstairs. "What in God's green name are you doing? Leave him alone! He's had enough for one day."

It was Paige, of course, who would give him the comfort he needed. Amina watched them at school the next day out in the parking lot at lunch, clearly in too deep of a conversation to bother going off campus. Akhil sat on the hood of the station wagon, and Paige stood in front of him holding both of his hands while he talked. When he leaned into her, Amina looked away.

The dinner Kamala made the next night was just short of delicious. The culmination of two days' work, it had started out of familial love but met with anxiety in the final hours of preparation, as Thomas came home and spoke to her in low tones in the kitchen.

The result was a botched favorite family meal. Kamala's idlis, usually light, now sank into slightly-too-smokey sambar. A strange tang infected the coconut chutney. The mango lassi for dessert was much too pulpy, but still everyone made sure to swallow every last drop, as if tipped off by their own organs to avoid the coming conversation. Finally, Thomas folded his hands.

"You can't drive for a while," he said.

"What?" Akhil frowned. "For how long?"

"It depends."

"On what? What did I do?"

"You didn't do anything."

"Then why are you punishing me?" Akhil leaned back in his chair, glaring at his father.

Amina saw her parents' gaze meet, retreat. Silence.

Akhil leaned forward. "Dad, you can't just say it depends and then not tell me. You have to tell me what so I can know what the rules are. I mean, it's only fair."

"We have to do some more tests."

Akhil's lips hung open. He blinked. "What?"

"We need to do a few tests at the hospital, starting next week." Thomas took a deep breath, spreading his palms wide. "Your sleeping patterns show evidence of adolescent-onset narcolepsy."

Akhil stared at him, the color leaking from his face.

"There's a possibility that you need to be treated," Thomas said.

"Narcolepsy? Like I fall asleep?"

Thomas nodded.

"But I don't do that anymore." Akhil looked at his mother. "Mom, tell him."

"I don't think it's such a big deal," Kamala said.

"What?"

"I don't see why this sleeping is so different from the other sleeping," she said to Thomas. "So he sleeps! Last time, I told you, it was nothing, *no big deal, growing boy, in my head,* nah? Now he's better, and you think it's some big crisis."

Akhil turned to Amina. "Tell Dad that I don't sleep like I used to. Apparently he hasn't been around enough to notice."

Amina looked at her father. Akhil kicked her under the table.

"Ow! Jesus!"

"Tell him!"

"It's . . ." Amina cleared her throat, scared. "You do, though."

"What?"

"It's different now. It's not that weird long sleep-forever thing. Now you just pass out for just a little bit. Sometimes. Anywhere."

"*What?*"

"Something is wrong with you! I don't know!" Amina looked at her father pleadingly. "I'm not the doctor."

Akhil turned back to Thomas. "So that's why you took me in for those tests? You said you were looking for sleep apnea!"

Thomas nodded. "We were looking for everything. Apnea was a possibility. Narcolepsy was also a possibility."

"But you didn't tell *me* that."

"I wanted to be sure."

"Oh, so now you're sure?"

"No, not entirely. But we need to look into it if we're going to treat you—"

"Treat me? Like I'm your *patient*?" Akhil's voice shot up a scale.

"Not mine. Dr. Subramanian's."

"You're going to let that guy fuck with my brain?"

"Akhil, we're not going to do anything to your brain—"

"Bullshit! You're going to fucking lobotomize me! You're going to . . . what do you think? That you can just change me?"

"What is he talking about?" Thomas asked his wife, but Kamala shrugged, arms crossed tightly over her chest.

"God only knows what things you and your son will say to each other. So? Now he's angry. Brilliant, Thomas."

"I told you, this isn't something we can ignore—"

"Of course it isn't. When I tell you, it's some silly joke, right? Some silly woman with her head on outwards. But when you decide, *then* it's a problem."

"This has nothing to do with that. How many times do I have to say—"

"I'm not going," Akhil announced. His parents looked at him. "To get more tests. I'm not going to do it."

"You have to," Thomas said.

"You're not touching my brain."

"Of course I'm not; the testing isn't invasive—"

"I'm telling you, I'm not going."

"Son, don't make this worse than it is, okay? All I'm saying is that we need to figure out what it is. That's all."

"And then what? We find out I've got narcolepsy, and then? What's the cure?"

"Why get ahead of yourself? We'll just have to take it slow. First figure out what we're dealing with."

"We? *We?* What, you're going to stick around for this like you care?"

"Of course I care! Don't be silly!"

"Bullshit. You're never even fucking here. You don't even . . ." Akhil looked at his mother, at Amina, at his father's mouth, which was already opening in rebuttal. "You don't even like us."

Thomas's mouth snapped closed. Akhil's eyes turned bright pink, and for an awful moment Amina thought he might start crying, but he said nothing else.

"You think I don't *like* you?" Thomas asked, almost laughing, but then he stopped, a deer in the forest listening to an unwelcome stillness. He looked from Akhil to Kamala to Amina.

"You think I don't like you?" he asked them.

No one answered. The question blew through the kitchen, over Akhil's pained eyes and crossed arms, brushing a stray strand of hair from Kamala's furrowed head, and finally pressing against the base of Amina's throat, so that even if she could have figured out what to say, she wouldn't have been able to say it.

Thomas's head dipped. He took his plate to the sink and stood in front of it, his silhouette buzzing in the fluorescent light.

"Someone has to work," he said quietly.

Amina looked at the table, its glaze of crumbs and splotches, the arced footprint of oil left from a jar of mango pickle. From the corner of her eye, she saw her father lean heavily into the kitchen counter.

"You need to get the testing," Kamala said.

"What?" Akhil asked.

"You do."

"Mom, you *just* said—"

"And now I am saying different."

"Based on *what*?" Akhil said, spit flying across the table. "Dad? His fucking . . . *patriarchy*? You're just going to sit there and take it like some goddamn pushover? IT'S THE 1980s, MOM. YOU ARE ALLOWED TO HAVE YOUR OWN OPINION."

Kamala shut her eyes and exhaled slowly, as if to expunge every last trace of the sentence. "No driving until you do."

"*What?*"

"It's not safe."

"Since when?"

"Since now." Kamala stood up from the table, her eyes scanning the living room, then marched to the couch, where Akhil's backpack lay.

"Wait!" Akhil shot up. "Wait, what are you doing?"

"I want the keys."

"No! I mean, you don't have to take them. I won't drive. I promise. I swear."

"Then it won't matter that you don't have the keys."

"But when do I get them back?"

Kamala hovered over the bag, looked at her husband.

"Once we know the severity of your case," Thomas answered.

"And what if it's severe?" Akhil asked.

Amina saw her parents look at each other again. Kamala licked her lips. "Then you don't drive, but that's not the end of the—"

"I don't drive *ever*?"

"Not until we know that you won't hurt yourself or someone else," Thomas said.

Kamala reached for the backpack, but Akhil cut her off, grabbing it with one hand and fending her off with the other. His eyes were wide and white in their sockets, his face sweaty.

"Not on weekends? Not even to prom?" he asked.

"Give it to me," Kamala said, motioning.

"No."

"Give it."

"No!"

The tug-of-war that ensued was brief, silly, catastrophic. Kamala latched on and yanked the bag in her direction, while Akhil pulled it in the other. Amina watched from the kitchen table as her mother leaned away with all her weight like some sort of sari-clad warrior. Akhil leaned back. There were grunts, groans, curses, and just as Akhil began to get a better grip, his mother redoubled her efforts, straining harder, her whole person intent on winning, so much so that she failed to see the decision when it flickered across her son's lips in a cruel smile. He let go suddenly, and the bag slammed into her face, sending her backward, hard. She landed flat on her back. For a moment, the rest of the Eapens were silent, staring at her arms and legs akimbo, sari splayed, the backpack where her face should have been.

Amina was standing, though she didn't remember standing up. Her father moved quickly, shoving Akhil away and lifting the backpack. Under the nylon and the zippers, Kamala lay blinking, one eye shut in dismay.

"Don't move," Thomas said. "Just sit there for a moment."

Kamala raised a hand to her cheek, pressing it gingerly. She stared at the blood that dotted her fingertips.

"It's a small cut," Thomas assured her. "Don't touch it. Amina, get the hydrogen peroxide."

Amina turned and ran to the pantry on legs shaky with heat. It was cool in the pantry, full of the smell of soup and pickle, and she wanted to stay there for a moment, hidden, until whatever needed to happen out there had happened. Her mother groaned. Amina stepped on a bag of basmati to reach for the cotton balls, Band-Aids, and peroxide.

"Oh my God, Mom," she heard her brother say.

Amina walked past him on the way back and almost felt sorry for him, kneeling on the carpet, looking like he wanted to melt into it.

"Get ice in a bag," Amina's father barked as she handed him everything, and she ran back to the kitchen, opening the freezer. She grabbed out two trays of ice and then looked frantically around the kitchen.

"Where are the plastic bags?" she shouted.

"Oh God, Mom."

"Under the sink," her mother said, her voice weak, and Amina grabbed one. She emptied the trays into it and ran back. Akhil hadn't moved an inch, but Kamala's hands were roaming her face, patting her features as though they were Braille.

"What else?" Amina asked breathlessly, feeling suddenly important.

"Do we have a steak?" her father asked.

"Lamb only," Kamala said.

"Get me the lamb."

"I'll get it," Akhil said.

Kamala flinched as the cotton ball was pulled away, her cheekbone swelling fast into a bulbous arc. Her eye jerked in its socket, red and bloody-looking. Amina gasped.

"It's okay," her father said. "There are some broken blood vessels, so it just looks bad. Can you see my fingers?" He held up two and cupped his hand over her mother's other eye.

Kamala nodded.

"How many?"

"Two."

"Good."

Akhil returned, lamb in hand. When his mother's bloody eye fixed on him, he began to cry.

"Can you sit up?" Thomas asked gently. "We need to check your head."

She sat up. She held her head in her hands like a bowl full of something that might spill easily, while Thomas felt up and down her neck and around the back of her skull.

"You've got a small bump here," Thomas said, pressing, and she let out a little cry. "I want you to follow my fingers with your eyes."

The checks turned up nothing. Kamala's vision was fine. She did not appear disoriented, or even upset, really, just deeply, deeply quiet. She sat on the couch, head buffeted between ice and meat, eyes closed. Akhil sat with her. He still could not look at her without his mouth trembling, so he sat with his face turned away. For their part, Amina and her father kept busy by cleaning up the kitchen, finding Tupperware to match the leftovers and scraping the turmeric stains from the stove and countertops. They stacked and lined the dishes up by the sink, and while Thomas swept the floor, Amina filled the basin with hot, lemony soap-water.

"I'll do it," her father said, setting the broom to the side.

"It's okay, Dad, I'll—"

"Sit."

It was hard to tell from his tone whether he meant it as an act of kindness or punishment, but she knew better than to argue. Amina looked at the couch and knew she did not want to sit in the pained current between her mother and brother. She walked instead to her book bag, still resting on the kitchen counter where she had set it earlier, and pulled her camera out.

Would Thomas even appear with all the bright light bouncing off

the tiles in front of him? Amina had no idea, so she adjusted the settings a few times, hoping she would catch the S-shaped shadow curling up his back as he washed dishes, the few suds that rose in the air
like bits of dander. She turned around, walking into the dining room
to take a picture of the splattered and stained tablecloth. From that
distance, she took a few shots of her mother and brother on the couch,
faces flashing blue with the changing television screen. She pulled her
focus tighter and saw that Akhil's mouth was moving. Then Kamala's.
Then Akhil's again. Who knew what exactly it was that he was saying,
or what Kamala replied, or why, ten seconds later, they looked at each
other and laughed a little before settling back into silence. All Amina
knew was that by the time her father was done with the dishes, they
had turned to *Hill Street Blues* and were watching it side by side, the
bright brass of the keys held safely in her mother's hands. Thomas
stood in front of them, wiping his hands dry on a dish towel.

"I see you've come around," he said to Akhil, who said nothing
back, his gaze hardening. Amina took the picture.

"I understand it's very difficult, these moments," Thomas continued a little too loudly, as though he was being recorded for posterity.
"Nobody likes these things life hands us. But part of becoming a man
is understanding how to face them head on instead of running all the
time. It's time you knew how to do that."

Why is it that fathers so often ensure the outcome they are trying
to avoid? Is their need to dominate so much stronger than their instinct to protect? Did Thomas know, Amina wondered as she watched
him, that he had just done the human equivalent of a lion sinking his
teeth into his own cub?

Akhil's gaze broke away from his father's, shifting to the driveway
in one beat. His mouth pursed, as if sucking on a secret, and with a
flash of clarity, Amina knew what it was. It popped into her head
cleanly, like a blade so sharp she couldn't even feel the cut. She stood,
the camera pressed to her face. Akhil looked at her through the viewfinder, fury swirling around him like invisible wind, daring her to say
anything. She shut her eyes and took the picture.

CHAPTER 4

The next afternoon, Amina stood in the space between the door to her room and Akhil's, clenching and unclenching her fists. She couldn't take it anymore. It was a horrible sound, and its showing no sign of stopping in the ten minutes she'd waited outside made her brave enough to just go in.

Akhil was crying in his bed. *Really* crying. Crying in a way that she hadn't seen since they were kids and he'd accidentally dropped his *Star Wars* light saber out the car window, all that would-be heroism shattering into plastic junk on the highway.

"Get out," he said, but even this was whimpered so weakly that she couldn't take it seriously. She sat at the bottom of his bed, not knowing what to say. The Greats smiled down at them maniacally.

"Paige is going to dump me."

"What? She said that?"

"She will when she finds out."

"What do you mean? You didn't tell her?"

Her brother took a sticky breath, trying to swallow before he said,

"Not really. I can't. There is no treatment that works. I looked it up today; it's all just a bunch of shit they try on you and almost none of it changes anything."

Could that be true? Amina thought of their medicine cabinet, all the pills and candy-colored syrups. "Well, maybe Dad knows of something that will—"

"Dad can't do shit about this! It's a disease!"

"But . . ." Amina licked her lips nervously. "I mean, you don't even know that you have it for sure."

"You're the one that said it! I fall asleep all the time for no reason, right?"

Amina found a cuticle and bit it, wishing she'd never said anything to anyone ever as Akhil started crying again. "Well—"

"Well, nothing! Don't you see, you stupid kid?" he gasped. "It's never going to change for us! It doesn't matter how much we grow, or change, or try to become like everyone else, in the end, we're fucking deformed, and they will know it. We're too fucked up to love."

Amina thought of her father standing in front of the sink, of Kamala's uneaten pot roast, of Akhil's twitching face during the Big Sleep, of the Salem house that kept getting taller, story by slanting story, in her dreams. She thought of the moment she could have grabbed Jamie's hand but didn't.

"It's going to be okay," she said loudly, mainly to stop the thinking.

Akhil didn't say anything.

"She'll still love you," she told him, her voice strong in the place of any real conviction, and when he still didn't say anything she realized he'd probably fallen asleep again. Great. Another failure on top of a failure. She looked up at the Greats. *You bastards,* she thought. *Do something for him already.*

"You think?" Akhil asked softly, startling her. "You think she'll still want me?"

"Of course she will," Amina said, relieved. "Just tell her."

Thank God for Saturday mornings. A reprieve from the familiar, a day unworn by routines. Anything was possible. The week might still be redeemed. Amina made her way down to the kitchen, surprised but not unhappy to see her father staring into the cupboards.

"What are you looking for?"

"Coffee."

"Next to the spices. With the red top."

Thomas pulled down the tin of Nescafé and opened it, taking a hesitant whiff before nodding. "You want some?"

"Gross."

"Right." He took the tiny plastic cup out of it, ladling a spoonful into a mug. "What are you looking for?"

She was looking through the paper for the horoscopes for any indication that Dimple missed her, or barring that, that someone was on the verge of falling in love with her. Thomas watched the kettle with remarkable concentration.

"Know what we need?" he asked a few moments later, and she looked up, the line *Someone special has taken notice of you* momentarily disorienting her.

"Huh?"

"A coffeepot with an alarm clock attached. You know? So that when the alarm clock goes off, the coffee starts brewing. So by the time you get to the actual kitchen, there it is—a full pot of coffee!—just waiting for you. Neat, huh?"

"Sure." She looked down at the paper to read his horoscope. "Okay, Dad, today for Leo says—"

The phone rang, cutting her off, and Thomas answered it.

"Cindy!" he said, as though to a long-lost friend. It was the way he always talked to the nurses who called. "What's going on?"

"What?" Thomas said. "No, he's home, why?"

The voice on the other end said something, and Thomas covered the receiver and turned to Amina.

"Check the driveway for the station wagon," he said, his voice calm. He spoke back into the receiver. "What time did you say they came in?"

Queen Victoria was sitting in front of the door as she approached and made no effort to move as she turned the handle.

"Let's go, Your Majesty," Amina said, and the dog got up with some canine groaning, shuffling aside as Amina opened the door. She stood blinking in the morning, the heat of the coming summer warming the tops of the trees and chasing puffs of cotton down from the branches into the driveway.

Akhil's car was gone.

"How bad are the burns?" Thomas said as they drove, phone jammed between his shoulder and ear, and Amina heard a burst of static in reply. He was driving fast, his arms shaking, and the pack of traffic they were moving in dropped back like dogs until there was nothing but clean road and sky in front of them.

"Okay," her father was saying. "Okay. Was he at all responsive when he came in?"

Next to him, Kamala read every movement of his face.

Amina looked out the window, staring at the fence of green poles that divided the highway until they blurred together to reveal the cars driving in the opposite direction on the other side. They zipped by at an astounding speed, and she counted them frantically as she heard her father hang up, as her mother said, "What? What is it?"

"Let's just get there," Thomas said.

Sanji Auntie came barreling through the sliding glass doors like a maddened hippo, salwar bunched around her hips, wet hair clumped to her forehead. When she saw Amina she walked quickly across the room, shouting, "Are you okay?" and smothering her with a hug before she even had time to answer.

"Are you okay?" Sanji said again, holding Amina firmly back and looking at her.

"I'm fine. It's Akhil."

"Daddy said something on the phone about a car accident?"

Amina nodded. "The ambulance brought him in. The ER recognized him and called Dad."

"So they're inside? You've been waiting out here alone?"

Amina nodded again, suddenly feeling very teary. Sanji sat down in the chair next to her and pulled her onto her lap, which should have felt ridiculous but didn't. She shut her eyes tightly and pressed her face into her aunt's neck.

"Poor thing, must have been scared, no?"

Amina nodded and let herself cry a little as Sanji Auntie rubbed her back in circles, talking up a storm.

". . . almost didn't hear the phone ringing because I was just getting out of the shower, but then I thought I'd check and your father told me and I came running. Uncle is on the way, and Bala and Chacko are at home with Dimple, who is so worried about you. I told them we would call as soon as I heard anything. Poor thing. But don't worry, nah? Akhil is okay. Mummy and Daddy are just scared right now. But he'll be fine."

"Okay," Amina whispered.

Sanji Auntie didn't say anything but kept rubbing her back, which helped a little. Out the window Amina saw more flashing lights, and another ambulance pulled up. This time, when the EMTs hopped out to open the back she made sure to look away. Sanji Auntie inhaled and sighed, shifting Amina on her lap. She started to say something and stopped.

"What?" Amina asked.

She sighed. "I'm just thinking, this is a bad place, no? How about if I take you to the Kurians'? You can wait there instead?"

"What about Mom and Dad?"

"I'll tell one of the nurses to tell them. They can come and pick you up later. This is no place for you to sit."

Amina sat up and looked at the steel doors, feeling a little guilty.

"It's fine, Ami, Mummy and Daddy would want you there instead anyway. Shall I just call Bala?" Sanji scanned the waiting room. "Come, there's a pay phone."

They walked across the room to the far corner, where two of the three pay phones were occupied. Sanji picked up the third and, after listening to a dial tone, dropped in a quarter. Amina watched a man sink into the chair she had abandoned, checking his watch.

"I have her," Sanji Auntie was saying into the phone. "Shall I bring her over to see Dimple? I don't want her waiting here with so much of awful things in this place."

Bala Auntie's voice squeaked over the line, and Amina thought she heard someone saying her name. She looked to her side.

"Ami." It was her father. Amina caught a blurry flash in his eyes, and he looked away. Pink. His eyes were terribly pink. Behind him, Amina's mother stood, holding something in her arms. A cat. A baby. Amina squinted and saw Akhil's leather jacket.

"Kamala, what happened to your eye?" Sanji Auntie said, and Kamala looked through her like a window. And something stopped then. It might have been her breathing or the sirens or every beeping monitor in the hospital, but in those seconds, Amina saw how smooth and hollow her mother's eyes had grown, how stripped of perception. When no one said anything else, Sanji Auntie hung up the phone.

"There was an accident," Thomas started to say, then didn't say anything else.

One hand covered Sanji's mouth, and the other flew to Amina's shoulders, as if to steady them. Someone somewhere was saying *no, no, no, no.*

"What?" Amina heard herself ask, even as her father looked at her, even as she knew. "What?"

Kamala held the car keys in front of her like a flashlight, guiding herself across the parking lot to the car door with steady steps. Behind her Thomas followed, and behind him, Amina and Sanji.

"Kamala, Thomas, let me drive you all home, please," Sanji Auntie said again, and Kamala shook her head.

"We're fine."

"You're not fine, *ben,* how can you be fine? It's nothing to me; Raj and I will come back to pick up your car this evening—"

"No," Kamala said firmly, unlocking the door. "No, thank you."

Sanji stepped away from the car, watching as they got in. She pulled up the tip of her salwar and tugged the bulbous fruit of her nose with it. She bent down to place her palm against the backseat window, staring at Amina as the car started up.

"Call me," she mouthed, and Amina nodded. She backed up as the car pulled away.

It was instantly worse without her there. They weren't out of the parking lot before Amina felt the silence slam down swiftly between them, smooth and relentless as concrete. Kamala shifted the car into gear, and Amina watched her father through the passenger seat mirror. Strangely, he looked normal to her now—calm and fatigued, as he always did when he came back from work, but okay. She could not see her mother's face.

"We need to call Chacko and Bala," he said as they got on the highway.

"Sanji will."

"We should call them ourselves."

"You call."

Outside, the cars passed blurrily, buffeting against them with a pop of wind before breaking away into the horizon. Kamala moved into the left lane.

"Where are you going?" Thomas asked.

Amina looked out the window and saw they were headed up I-40.

"The car," Amina's mother said.

"Later, Kamala. We'll see it later. They haven't gotten it off the mountain yet."

"Today."

Amina felt her father's gaze through the rearview mirror. He leaned over her mother and whispered something to her in Malayalam, but she shoved his head away.

"So? She'll stay in the car. So what."

"I need you to stay in the car," her father was saying. He had opened the backseat door and was kneeling next to her, looking into her eyes. "I need you to stay here, okay? Can you do that, Ami? Will you do that for me?"

The car was parked at the side of the road. Outside, the mountain air smelled like pinions and rock and gas and ashes, and Amina nodded. She watched as he turned and ran to catch up with her mother, who was already stalking up the bend toward the guardrail, her black braid bouncing against her back.

Watching her parents through the window, Amina was sure they were in the wrong spot. The road looked much too itself, the same twisted vein of asphalt they always rode to the peak, the same low guardrails that held the tops of the evergreens at bay. Two white pickup trucks and men in orange jackets greeted her parents, pointing below with gloved hands. Her parents turned and looked.

What was it that they saw that day? What had happened to Akhil's car that rooted her father to the spot as her mother turned around, first walking toward the road, then carefully kneeling on it, her eyes flickering shut? And were they forever lost to each other in that moment, completing the severing that had begun on the last trip to Salem, or did their connection fray more slowly, as the everyday weight of what had happened came to bear down on them? Amina would never know, but for days she could not close her eyes without seeing her parents as they had been right before they looked down, the tips of the evergreens spread out before them like waves, the New Mexico sky blank and white as eternity.

BOOK 8

HIDDEN PARK

ALBUQUERQUE, 1998

CHAPTER 1

Getting Kamala out of the garden and into bed was no easy feat. The shock of finding Akhil's jacket buried among the vegetables was one thing. The mud, another. She had been covered in it—streaks drying on her forehead, black lining her fingernails, clumps falling from her sari as she followed Amina back to the house like a zombie. In the end there was nothing to do but strip her to her underskirt and blouse and hose her down while Thomas slunk off to find her some Valium. Dried and dosed, she had fallen into bed without a word, turning her head away on the pillow when Amina asked if she was okay. Amina lowered the blinds and closed the bedroom door.

Outside, Thomas was waiting, his hands clamped in front of him. "Well?"

Amina put a finger to her lips, guiding him into the kitchen. She left him on one side of the counter and crossed to the other, needing the hard slab of white between them.

"How did she seem?" Thomas asked.

"Tired."

"Good." Her father paused. "Your mother is very strong, you know."

"So you put the jacket there?"

Thomas nodded once.

"Why?"

"I apologized to your mother. I apologize to you. It was inappropriate."

"But I don't understand why you would do that." She was starting to shake and trying to stop shaking because it felt stupid to be so undone, so upset over a goddamn piece of clothing. She crossed her arms trying to shore herself up.

"Hey, *koche*," Thomas soothed. "It's not some huge thing. I had a bad night. I've been working a little too much. I might need to slow down for a bit."

Amina looked at him, his glasses tucked into the front pocket of his overalls, and for a moment his explanation felt like it was not only true but right, like a newly paved road or a toothpaste-commercial smile or a horoscope you really wanted to believe in.

"Go get yourself a glass of water," her father was saying, "and drink it slowly."

"What happened in the ER with Derrick Hanson?"

She watched his face move quickly from surprise to something else, the skin around his mouth tightening. His eyes grew sharp, and Amina felt a flush spread from her throat to her scalp.

"That's not your concern," he said.

"If something is wrong, then I should know. To help."

"I don't need your help."

"Or get you to the right doctor."

"Goddamn it, Amina, there's nothing medically wrong with me!" Thomas shouted suddenly, and Amina's heart clattered around her rib cage.

"B-but how do you know that?"

"Because I do!"

"But did you talk to someone afterward? Did you get tests done? Are you taking medication? Dr. George said he tried to get you to come in and—"

"You talked to Anyan about this?"

"I . . . it . . . yes. But—"

"You talked to a *co-worker* of mine?"

"Yes, I just thought if—"

"Do you have any idea what you've done?" Thomas's face drained of blood. "No, of course not! Why think through anything when you and your mother can sit here wringing hands and pointing the blame at me? Haven't you grown tired of that yet?"

Amina's eyes filled with tears. It was a distinctly feminine humiliation, the kind daughters close to their fathers go to great pains to avoid, as betraying of their fragility as a stain on the back of a skirt.

"Oh, stop it." Her father plucked two napkins from the holder on the counter and shoved them at her. Amina breathed into the napkin, aware of the pressure gathering against her skull like beads of condensation. She blew her nose. It did not help.

"I think it's time for you to go back to Seattle," her father said.

She squeezed the napkin into a damp ball.

"Your patients," she said.

There was a moment, a snap between them, and then a long corridor of silence with Thomas's stricken face at one end of it. Amina put the crumpled napkin on the counter.

"I'm calling Dr. George tomorrow." She took a quick breath and exhaled. "You are going in to see him, and whomever else you need to see. If you don't, I will go and tell the board at Presbyterian what is going on myself."

Then she walked out of the kitchen, through the porch, and out the screen door to the garden, to where Akhil's jacket still lay in a clump, pill bugs racing through its ruined folds.

CHAPTER 2

At least he was right about Kamala's resilience. As the next morning dragged itself over the Sandias, sky gray and faded as an old nightgown, as Thomas headed to work and Amina sat groggily in the kitchen, Kamala rose, cracked a coconut in the kitchen sink, and shrugged off any questions with a steaming batch of hoppers and chutney. Afterward, she cleaned the dishes, organized her spice cabinet, and pickled a batch of limes.

"You want tea?" she asked.

"Sure," Amina said. She was exhausted. Her dreams had been full of shouting. She waited until the chai was brewed and in front of her to say, "He's going to go see a doctor."

"What?"

"Dad. We talked this morning." *Talked* was putting a fine point on what amounted to a curt nod from her father, but Amina leaned across the counter, trying to project some measure of confidence. "He's going this week."

Kamala rummaged around the fridge, pulling out a voodoo-doll-sized piece of ginger. "What for?"

"Did you want to sit down for a second?"

"Ginger chutney!"

"Well, so . . . there was an *incident* in the ER." Amina was getting to hate that word, its false officiousness like something a middle school principal could rectify. She cleared her throat. "Apparently Dad thought Derrick Hanson was alive when they brought him in and tried to save him."

"So?"

"He wasn't. Alive."

"Oh."

"Yeah. So he's being watched now by the hospital board. And now with this . . . I just think he needs to go to the doctor. To see if there's something, you know, really wrong."

"You think there is?"

"I don't know. I wonder if it's depression or something."

"Pish! Thomas doesn't get depressed."

"Everyone gets depressed, Ma," Amina said, her face warming. "And it can definitely affect your perceptions."

Kamala stopped cutting. When she turned around, her face was anxious and tired, as if all the morning work had just taken its toll. "What if something is wrong with him?"

She was so small, Kamala. In the daily onslaught of opinions and accusations, Amina almost never noticed it, but now, in the kitchen, she saw again how slight her mother could look in certain lights.

"Or maybe he's being tempted by bad spirits," Kamala continued, so softly and thoughtfully that it took a few seconds for Amina to understand what she was saying.

"Ma, stop."

"It happens! Mort Hinley says people like your father are susceptible to all kind of devilry—doctors *especially*. All this playing-God business makes them think—"

"Please. I'm begging you."

"But what if he's the one letting them in? All they need is one crack"—Kamala daggered a finger into the air—"and they will infest an entire soul! Heads go spinning! I've seen it myself on the *Oprah*. Fine, don't believe me, what do I care? You have your depression-shmession theories, I have mine!"

Amina rubbed her skull. "He's going to see Dr. George tomorrow. I thought we could go with him."

"Oh."

"What?"

Kamala smiled over her shoulder. "Sure. If you'd like."

"It's not a date, Ma."

"Yes, of course." The phone rang, and Kamala dried her hands on her apron, pulling it from the cradle. "Hello?"

Amina let her forehead drop onto the countertop, liking the way the cool shushed her mind. Devilry? Was that even a word?

"She's busy right now," Kamala said. "She'll call you back."

"Wait, me? I'm right here. Who is it?"

Kamala held the phone out with a pinched face. "American."

Amina took the phone from her mother.

"Hello?"

"Amina?"

It was Jamie Anderson. She knew it instantly, and then felt silly for knowing it, like she'd been caught waiting for him. She walked into the pantry, avoiding Kamala's displeased look. "Yeah, it's me."

"Hey. Hi. It's Jamie. Jamie Anderson. From Mesa—"

"Yeah, I know. Hi."

"Hi."

There was a long pause.

"Hello?" Amina asked.

"I'm really bad at the phone," Jamie said. "Did you want to get dinner?"

"What?"

"I said I'm bad at—"

"No, I got that. Dinner?"

"Yes. Or, I mean, if you're still around by then."

"By when?"

"Tonight."

"Oh," Amina laughed. "Yeah, I'll be here tonight."

"No going out tonight!" Kamala shouted, throwing open the pantry door. "Nina Vigil wants to see your photos before she hires you. I told her we'd come!"

"What?"

"Quinceañera! Her granddaughter's! I told her we'd bring by the Bukowsky photos this evening." Kamala squinted at the phone. "Who is that?"

"A friend." Amina shooed her mother from the pantry, shutting the door behind her. "Hello?"

"So . . . not tonight."

"No, it's fine. Maybe we can just grab a drink somewhere at nine?"

"Are you sure?"

"I'm sure I'll need a drink by then," Amina said, and he laughed.

"How about Jack's Tavern? It's on—"

"You think I don't know where Jack's is?" she teased.

"Oh. Right, of course."

Amina hung up. Outside the pantry, her mother stood like a tiny sergeant, arms crossed over her chest. "Who was that?"

"Who is Nina Vigil?"

"The Vigil family up on Toad Road! You met them at the Bukowskys'! She saw you taking photos and asked me if you'd do her granddaughter's—"

"Fine. How much?"

"What?"

"What is she paying me?"

"I told them you would do it for free."

"You *what*?"

"And then they will pay you if they want to order any prints, same price as Jane."

"I don't work for free, Ma!"

"Oh, *pah*! What else are you doing? And besides, you can make it up to Jane by giving her the cut. Get her back on your good sides, right?"

The worst part, Amina realized, was that Kamala was right, but admitting that was akin to negotiating with a terrorist. What would stop her the next time?

"You know, it would be helpful if you'd actually run these things by me before you did them. It's a good idea to tell the person doing the actual work."

"I'm telling you now, silly. Don't get all bent into shapes."

"Fine," Amina muttered. "But listen, I'm just shooting this as a favor because you already promised. No more after this."

"Just the Campbells'," Kamala agreed.

"Ma! Jesus!"

"No Jesus! It's their anniversary. And hold on." She went to her purse and opened her wallet, pulling out several twenty-dollar bills.

"What's this?"

"Maybe go to the mall today and buy some clothes."

"What?"

"So you don't look like a man all the time."

Amina shook her head and left the kitchen.

"Bright colors!" her mother called up after her. "Everyone likes bright colors!"

An hour later, Amina stood at a pay phone in a mall hallway, where poop and perfume and the grease from the food court formed the kind of atmosphere you might find in Jupiter's red spot.

"That kid with the Afro?" Dimple was asking. "Paige's brother?"

"Jamie, yeah."

"Is it a date?"

"No." Amina stared at the red Exit sign at the end of the hall. "He's bald now. I mean, not bald, but he shaves his head in the summer."

"That's weird."

"It isn't really."

"So first of all, stay away from pastels. They make you look chalky."

"You never told me that."

"You never asked. Okay, and then what shoes do you have out there?"

"My sneakers."

"What else?"

"I was only going to be here for a week, remember?"

"So get some nicer shoes. Something a little more feminine."

"Why does everyone think I dress like a man?"

"Like a sandal. Or a flat."

"I just don't like dresses. It's not like I'm some transvestite."

"Are you sure this isn't a date? Because you sound nervous."

"I haven't talked to humans besides my parents in a week." Amina heard a cough in the background, followed by Dimple's quick shushing. "Who is that?"

"What? Oh, just Sajeev."

"Just Sajeev?" Amina started to laugh but then stopped. "Wait a minute. Are you *dating* Sajeev?"

"Hold on a sec," Dimple said, *clackclackclack*ing across the gallery floor quickly, and then, from the sound of things, into the bathroom, where she whispered, "Yes."

"*What?*"

"It's not like it's a big deal."

"Not a big—are you fucking kidding me? *Sajeev Roy?* Your mother is going to hold an international press conference!"

"Shh! I've been trying not to think about that." Dimple paused. "I really like him."

"Really?"

"Is that so surprising?"

"Well . . . *yes.*"

"I know." Dimple sighed. "It's totally fucking weird. Sometimes when he's asleep I just stare at him and think, *What the hell is* he *doing in my bed?* But then when he wakes up and I don't know . . . he's *nice* to me. I feel like I don't have to try so hard with him."

"Huh," Amina said, feeling a little nick of jealousy. "Wow."

"Anyway, do me a favor and don't tell the others. I just want to enjoy this without everyone, you know."

"Planning an all-Albuquerque ticker-tape parade?"

Dimple laughed. "Exactly."

Amina hung up a few moments later and headed back down the white corridor, a little disoriented. Dimple and Sajeev? Was that kind of oppositional attraction possible in anything other than a romantic comedy? She made her way through the food court with its faux hot-air-balloon landscape and back into Macy's, where she skipped the horrible dresses that had sent her to the pay phone in a panic and stopped at the first set of shirts. She pulled one up, frowning at its twinkly curviness. "Can I help you?" a hen-faced saleslady asked, smoothing her plump waist.

"I need to buy a shirt."

The woman drew up short in surprise. She recovered quickly. "Is it for a formal event? Gala? Black-tie wedding?"

"No, just a regular old dinner."

"Oh, great." She smiled nervously in a way that put Amina at ease. "So let's get out of the formalwear."

Twenty paces and a few turns later, they were surrounded by decidedly less ball-worthy clothes. "Anything in particular you're looking for? A tank top? A button-down?"

"I have no idea."

"A color, maybe?"

"Something bright."

"Gotcha." She moved with surprising deftness for her girth, lifting and plucking shirts from the racks like they were ripe fruit. "You open to yellow?"

"Yeah, sure."

"Most people can't wear it," she said, lifting up a sunflower-yellow blouse. "But it's great for your skin. And green?"

"No green."

The woman motioned for Amina to follow her back to the dressing room, where she hung the blouses in a tidy row. "Anything else right now?"

"No, thanks. This is great."

There were reasons that Amina didn't like to shop, her too long, thin-in-odd-places torso among them. The fuchsia shirt hung on it like a sail. The blue button-down made her look like a high school lesbian. She pulled on the yellow tank top, gasped a little as she looked in the mirror. It worked. She looked healthy, glowing.

"You doing okay in there?"

Amina opened the dressing room door. The saleslady smiled. "That's really great."

"You think?"

"Absolutely. It's the right color and the right fit. Shows off your neck and arms."

"Yellow isn't weird?"

"Not a bit."

Amina closed the door, turning her back to the mirror and trying to see what she'd look like to Jamie. Minutes later she stood at the register, flushed with an unusual amount of pleasure. Was it a purchase high? Minor-task accomplishment? She took the receipt and folded it.

"Thanks so, so much," she gushed. "You've been really helpful. That was so, you know, easy."

"Oh, sure." The woman hesitated before handing her the bag with her shirt. "I'm Mindy."

"Hey, Mindy, I'm Amina."

"I know."

Amina looked at her for a moment before the trapdoor in her brain released. "Holy shit."

Mindy laughed a little, shifting nervously. Her fingers reached up to straighten her necklace, a small silver cross on a thin chain.

"Hi," she said, and Amina tried to find some vestige of the girl who seduced Akhil with a joint and cleavage. Was it always this way? Did everyone from high school end up looking like weird facsimiles of other people's parents?

"This keeps happening," Amina said.

Mindy nodded. "So you're back visiting?"

"Yeah. Parents."

"Oh, nice. I live here. Obviously." A slight blush rose to her cheeks. "Remember Nick Feets from school?"

Amina didn't. She nodded.

"We got married a few years ago. We live in the valley." Mindy took a quick breath. "Yep, three kids, dogs, the whole nine. Our oldest is probably going to start at Mesa next year. They've opened a middle school, you know."

"Wow." Amina had the distinct feeling she was supposed to say something more. Congratulations? Hallelujah?

"What about you? Last I heard, you and Dimple were in New York or something?"

"Seattle," Amina said, distracted by that funny, bubbling-up feeling of thought rising from her subconscious. "We moved to Seattle."

"Oh yeah? You like it?"

"Mostly."

The girl Akhil lost his virginity to has a hen face and three kids. This was the thought, whole and uncharitable, and with it came the subsequent thought that Akhil himself might have looked old by now, which was so obvious that Amina felt stupid for never having thought of it before. And yet she hadn't. The tiny corner of her imagination reserved for what-ifs had always brought him back more or less as he was, maybe a little taller, or broadened in the chest and waist, the way boys tended to be after college.

"Oh no," Mindy said. "You look upset. I didn't want to upset you. I just thought . . ." She was really blushing now, red patches blooming on her cheeks and chest like an allergic reaction. "I mean, I didn't know if you recognized me and were just being nice or something."

"Oh," Amina said, backing away from the counter. "No, I didn't."

"I mean, it's a job, you know?"

"Yeah, sure. And you're really good at it."

Mindy's eyes narrowed, and for a split second Amina thought she saw the old Mindy, the one who would shred her with a sentence, but then she just shrugged. "Thanks. Well, we're having a thirty-three-percent-off-all-red-tag-items starting Wednesday—everything except housewares."

"Okay." Amina raised the bag awkwardly in salute and backed away. She walked quickly down the aisle in front of her, taking one turn and then another, racing through the golden-hued jewelry/perfume section until she was finally, thankfully, spat out into the dark cavern of the mall. On one side of her, a few bodies pummeled at unseen forces in a video arcade, and on the other, a collection of massage chairs were entirely empty, save for a lone, undulating salesman. At the farther end of the mall, a shoe store specializing in designer names for less promised relief. Amina walked toward it.

CHAPTER 3

Jamie Anderson was with another woman. Why this should feel so bad was not anything Amina wanted to dwell on, though she was sure that the shower and the shirt and optimistic leg shaving had something to do with it. She stood in the doorway of Jack's Tavern, her breath lodged in her chest as Jamie smiled at a pretty redhead, the kind of girl who turned playing with her hair into performance art.

"You going in?" A pie-faced guy behind her asked, and Amina stumbled into the bar, trying not to feel self-conscious as the girl watched her approach.

"Hey," Jamie said, catching sight of her and standing. The suit had been replaced by a shirt and shorts and flip-flops, giving him the air of a surfer.

"Hey." Amina turned to the girl. "Hi, I'm Amina."

"Hi." The girl regarded her coolly.

An awkward second passed.

"So I'll see you soon, Maizy?" Jamie prompted, and the girl looked from Amina to him and back again before slowly standing up. Her hand tugged Jamie's T-shirt briefly, and she leaned into him. "You didn't tell me you had a date."

Jamie backed up. "Have a great night."

"You got it." She turned her head in Amina's direction, not quite looking at her before walking slowly back to the bar, where, Amina now saw, a small group of girls was waiting for her, the corners of their eyes taking in everything. She slid into the vacated spot. "Sorry to interrupt."

"You didn't. She was just a student in my Intro to Anthro intensive."

"Oh."

"Yeah." Jamie shifted in the booth seat, his knees knocking the table. "I kind of forgot that this was a student hangout."

"Is it weird for you?"

"Nah." He rubbed his head a little, looking around the bar. "Yeah, maybe a little."

The girls at the bar were making no secret of looking at her now, and Amina tried to relax, or at least to look relaxed. Of course he had a female following. Was there anything college girls found sexier than being told what to think?

"What do they call you?" she asked.

"Professor Anderson."

"Wow."

Jamie raised an eyebrow. "Was that sarcasm, Amina Eapen?"

"No, not at all," Amina laughed, crossing and uncrossing her legs. "I'm impressed."

"Yeah, you look impressed." His eyes fell to her collarbone. "Nice shirt."

Her face blossomed with heat. "Thanks."

Just then, the group of girls at the bar erupted into laughter, the redhead the loudest among them. She laughed with her head thrown far back, her hand nestled into her cleavage, and even without looking around the room, Amina could sense collective relocation of the male gaze, the beery, smitten hunger behind it.

"Hey." Jamie leaned in, his foot bumping hers. "Do you want to get out of here?"

"What?"

"Go to another place down the street? Or maybe just on a walk? There's actually a pretty nice park a few blocks away if you—"

"Yes."

It was much better outside. Deep-blue evening was settling over Albuquerque, erasing the mountains and bejeweling the traffic lights running up Central. The air smelled sweet and diesely, like the promise of a road trip. Some minutes ago there had been a decision that involved leaving her car where it was, buying beer, and heading to the park, and since that time they had been walking steadily uptown, Jamie filling her in on details about his life that she wanted to know but was too nervous to absorb.

His walk was the same. Not that there was anything so remarkable about the way he leaned back on his heels, hands jammed into his pockets, talking to some midpoint in the sky like it was a floating amphitheater, but it did give Amina a déjà vu of sorts, the newness of him (definitely bigger out of the suit, with an equal amount of stubble lining his scalp and jaw) cut by an unnerving familiarity. He still had that weird, slightly dismissive tone, and that funny way of squinting while she talked, as though he couldn't quite hear or believe what she was saying.

"So it seemed like the right time," he was saying now, wrapping up the trajectory of his last twelve years, the highlights of which included graduate work at Berkeley, a few years living in South America, the offer of a tenure-track position at UNM, and a divorce.

"You were married?"

"For about three years."

"Oh." Amina felt strangely embarrassed about this, though less for him than herself. What had she been doing with her life? She'd never even tried hard enough at having a relationship to have it fail.

Jamie pointed his chin ahead. "There we go."

There was a 7-Eleven, replete with red-orange glow and shelves of brightly colored products that looked like they could survive a nuclear winter. Jamie held the door open and followed her in, tagging her hip when she started walking down the wrong aisle.

They stood in front of the glass case, sizing up the beer options.

"So, Rolling Rock?"

"Yeah."

Two minutes later they were back out the door, corn nuts, beef jerky, and M&M's thrown into the bag. ("Trash picnic," Jamie had said approvingly of her last-minute additions.) They turned onto one side street, then another, winding through a residential neighborhood where small stucco houses hovered behind dusty-looking lawns.

"Where are we going?" Amina asked.

"It's a surprise. Hold up a sec." He stopped at a station wagon and fished his keys out of his pocket.

"Wait, this is your car?" Amina asked.

"Yep." He opened the hatchback and pulled out a blanket. He handed it to her, along with a small cooler.

"You just park it here?"

"In front of my house? Yeah."

Amina turned around. The house that greeted her was not particularly different from the others, though it did look like someone had recently swept the porch.

"Wow. Don't look so disappointed," Jamie laughed.

"No! I'm not." But she was, a little. Somehow, all the talk about tenure and anthropology had given her visions of a thick-walled, libraried adobe, the kind of place that was covered with kilim rugs and fertility sculptures. The white stucco in front of her looked only slightly more substantial than a roadside weigh station. She laughed. "So the surprise is that you're taking me back to your place?"

Jamie looked confused for a moment, then alarmed. "Oh, no! We're not! I just, uh, I wasn't thinking that, actually, I just . . ." He shut the trunk, walking quickly away from both the house and car, as if to shed them. "C'mon. Follow me."

Amina followed Jamie's lumbering back down a tiny, dirty alleyway, growing more curious with every step until they stumbled into a bowl of green. Old, tall trees that were rare anywhere that far from the river rose up to greet them, the tops of their branches inked with night.

"Oh. Holy shit," Amina said.

Jamie flashed her a sly look of pride. "Hidden Park."

Amina turned back to the houses that spun a ring around the park, no fancier-looking than their fronts, but now infinitely more charming because of the secret they guarded.

"So this is your backyard?"

"More or less." He walked a few paces and set their bag of goods down, reaching for the blanket. He unfurled it, and Amina, feeling pleasantly chastened, helped settle the edges, slipping her sandals off before stepping on it. "Not bad, huh?"

"It's beautiful. I'm a little jealous."

"Yeah, Corrales sucks as far as outdoors goes." He handed her a beer. "Here you go."

"Is that a . . . ?"

"Beer cozy? Sure is."

"You keep them in your car?"

"I keep a lot of things in my car. What?"

"Nothing."

"Are you knocking the cozy? Because I'll take it right back, you know."

Amina smiled, clinking her bottle to his and taking a sip. Jamie slipped off his own shoes and scooted back until he was even with her, his legs hanging off the blanket into the grass.

"So you never did tell me what you took pictures of," Jamie said.

"Oh. Right. Well, I used to be a photojournalist."

"No kidding. Like wars and jungles?"

"Eh . . . more like street fairs and methadone clinics, but yeah."

"That sounds like fun."

"Was that sarcasm?"

"Only a little bit. The rest was me being impressed."

"Oh, you shouldn't be." Amina shook her head. "Anyway, I'm kind of on a break. I'm doing events now—weddings, anniversaries, quinceañeras. So do you just teach, or do you . . ." Jamie looked at her oddly. "I mean, not *just* teach," she corrected hurriedly. "I've always heard that teaching is really hard. I just meant, do you work in the field too or something?"

He took a sip of beer, and it left a little foam wake on one side of his mouth. "It's part of the reason I moved back, actually, to study the effects of the Sandia Casino and gaming culture on the authority of tribal elders."

"Is that as sad as it sounds?"

"Not always. You'd be surprised. Either way, I try not to let it get to me."

"And does that work?"

He leaned in and whispered, "I'm a trained anthropologist, you know."

Soap and saltines. That's what he smelled like, and something else, something she couldn't quite name, but wanted to, the want itself such a persuasive force that she found herself guzzling half her bottle of beer to keep her face away from his neck.

"So what does it mean, you're on a break from photojournalism? Was it a planned thing?"

"Uh, no." Amina shifted.

"You got fired?"

"No." She cleared her throat. "Actually, I kind of fired myself."

"What do you mean?"

What did she mean? Amina looked at the grass beyond his shoulder, surprised by the foreign feeling of wanting to tell him the truth. Like many people whose lives had formed around a particularly painful incident, she had grown used to providing ellipses around the event of her brother's death to keep conversations comfortable. At some point, the subconscious logic of this had spread to the rest of her life so that she rarely talked about things she had been deeply affected by. It wasn't hard to do. She'd certainly never felt bad about it before. And yet sitting here with Jamie, she had a pressing feeling she would miss out on something important if she didn't at least try.

"I didn't mean to," she said. "Or, at least, I didn't think it would be such a long time. I just took a picture . . . some pictures . . . they were hard for me. I guess I needed a little bit of a break afterward, but then the longer I didn't do it, the harder it became to start again, so, you know."

"But you're still taking pictures."

"Yeah, but they're . . ." Amina stopped herself. He did not need a catalogue of her disappointments. "Yes, I am."

"You seemed like you really enjoy it. The other night, at the wedding, I mean."

"Oh, that was just relief. I think by the time you saw me I was pretty much done."

"I saw you at the church."

It took a moment for this to sink in. "You didn't say hi?"

"I didn't know if it was cool."

There wasn't a ton of light in the park, something that was only obvious now that night was settling in. A warm yellow, domestic glow emanated from some of the houses, but other than that, there was just a lone street lamp that buzzed on and off intermittently, casting Jamie, when she looked at him, in a sharp silhouette. He looked nothing like his sister. The thought sneaked up on Amina, and with it, the faintest flicker of Paige's face, those cheeks that held the curve of stone fruits, Ming vases. She was on a date with the brother of the girl Akhil had loved.

"I can't believe you're a professor," she said.

"My dad was a professor."

"I know. But you hated teachers in high school."

"*Hated* is a strong word."

"Mr. Tipton?"

"Oh yeah, I fucking hated that guy."

They laughed. It felt good to laugh. It pushed the pressure from her head out into the cooling night, where it rose up through the branches to the two stars that had just become visible. Amina finished her beer and stared at it a second before deciding to lie back on the blanket.

Jamie bent over the bag. "You hungry yet? Want some corn nuts?"

"I'm good."

"Okay." He rustled through what seemed like the entire contents of the bag, while Amina prickled beside him. What was he doing? She should sit back up. She would count to five and then sit back up.

"I guess I don't really want any either." Jamie glanced back at her and then lay down, too. A cottony field of heat emanated from his forearm, pulling at her like gravity. She imagined herself rolling over, on top of him. She imagined the heat from him moving under her.

"So is it weird for you that I'm divorced?"

"What? No. Why?"

"You seemed a little freaked out earlier."

"No! I mean, I haven't been married before, so I don't know. I guess it just seems really grown-up or something."

"More grown-up than getting married?"

"Definitely."

Jamie laughed. "Yeah, I guess that's true."

"Is it weird being divorced?" What was she doing? Amina bit her lip too late.

Jamie paused, thinking. "I guess sometimes it's weird. I don't know. A lot less weird than being married to the wrong person."

"How did you know she was the wrong person?"

"Wow, you're really just sticking to the easy questions tonight, huh?"

Amina sat up, embarrassed. She was killing the moment. And for what? She needed to get ahold of herself.

"Do you want some M&M's?" she asked.

"Sure." Jamie stayed flat and she reached over him, feeling around the damp bottom of the paper sack and staring inadvertently at the zipper of his shorts, which protruded slightly. A pale seam of skin peeked between his waistband and T-shirt. Jamie cleared his throat. "We didn't fight well."

"What?"

"Me and Miriam. We were too mean."

Amina tried not to smile. She did not like the name Miriam. She held up the M&M's. "Hold out your hand."

"What about you?" Jamie asked.

She wiggled a few candies through the wrapper into his palm, then her own. "What about me?"

"Are you seeing anyone?"

Amina felt herself blushing in the dark. "Not really."

Jamie popped the entire handful of candy into his mouth, crunching loudly. "You ready for another beer?"

"Yeah, sure." She didn't actually want another beer, but it didn't matter. She took the cool bottle he offered, setting it in the grass. They lay back at the same time, and this time their shoulders touched. Above them, the stars were soft and plenty.

"Hey." Jamie's voice vibrated through her collarbone. "How's your dad?"

She had forgotten she had told him. "We don't really know yet."

"Tests?"

"Yeah."

"I went through that a few years ago with my mom."

"Oh yeah? How is she doing now?"

"She had stage-four breast cancer when we found it. She died a few months later."

"Oh God, Jamie, I'm sorry."

"I'm not. I mean, I hate that she got it, but I don't mind that she went fast."

There was something in his voice—a brittle tidiness—that made her uncomfortable. "My dad's not really sick that way. I think it's more of a depression thing with him."

"So does that mean you'll need to stay awhile?"

"I don't know yet."

"Got it."

Did he? Amina did not know and then it did not matter, because in the next second, Jamie propped himself up on one elbow and looked down at her, the park light fanning around him like a halo. He pushed a strand of hair off her cheek, and in a blink she finally recognized him, the boy who used to sit across from her in English class, scowling into a paperback every time she opened her mouth.

CHAPTER 4

The rubber duckies were a surprise. The next afternoon, as the Eapens sat in Anyan George's office, Amina stared at a row of yellow bodies, carefully arranged bill to tail. Everything else in the office—from the neat row of diplomas to the green plaid armchairs to two frames filled with the face of a sweet-looking boy who had aged at least a year between photos—had been expected. But the ducks across the desk were as distracting as live acrobats. Amina picked one up, sniffing its sweet body before carefully replacing it.

"Adorable, no?" Kamala asked.

Amina frowned to discourage her. All morning, her mother had been too cheerful, tucking herself into her best teal sari to accompany Thomas to the scans, trying to slip gold bangles onto Amina's arms as they were leaving the house. Now, waiting for Anyan George to come back with the preliminary results, she was practically giddy.

"A real sense of humor!" She indicated the duckies with her chin. "Like you!"

Thomas uncrossed his legs and recrossed them, checking his watch.

"I'm sure he's on the way," Amina said soothingly. Poor Thomas— the clichéd bad patient, all walnut wrinkles and testiness, imaginings of the worst. She wished she could just squeeze the worry out of him, or better yet, suffuse him with the heady benevolence that swam through her veins like sweet tea, leaving every part of her that Jamie had touched feeling blessed and anointed. She rubbed her fingertips across her lips.

"It's so nice for men to be in touch with their, you know, feminine side," Kamala trilled on. "*Good Morning America* had one whole show on it! This one bakes cookies, that one sews his daughter's Halloween costume each and every year." She smoothed her sari against her lap, fingered the coral earrings she had put on that morning. "Are you sure you don't want to put your hair down? It looks much nicer when it's down."

"It's fine, Ma."

"You're sick?"

"What?"

"Why does your voice sound honk-honky?"

"It doesn't."

It did. Too much talking. Amina blushed.

"If Anyan's not here by one, we'll simply have to reschedule," Thomas announced.

"He's only a few minutes late," Amina said, ignoring the way her father set his jaw against her. Beyond coordinating the basics of time and place, Thomas had done his best to avoid her over the past few days, walking out of rooms as she entered them, grunting away any attempt at conversation. It was to be expected, of course, but still unsettling, and she found herself looking forward to the end of the appointment, when they could begin to right what had become disjointed between them.

"Here, *koche*!" A ChapStick appeared in front of Amina's face, held between Kamala's fingers like a winning lottery ticket. "Lips are dry."

Amina swiped it across her lips and handed it back. She looked down at the spiral notebook on her lap, "Dad's Test Results" written across the top of a clean page, and added the date in the margin for good measure.

He had his sister's mouth. She had understood this the night before as a child does a textbook optical illusion, eye bending between the revelation of white birds and black birds, the old woman and the young woman. Jamie's face, Paige's mouth.

The office door opened and Dr. George stepped in. He was smaller than Amina remembered, or maybe just overwhelmed by his lab coat and pleated pants, by the oversized manila envelope in his hands.

"Hello, hello. Good afternoon, sir. Whole family came, I see." He smiled a little shyly at them, settling into his seat. "I apologize for the tardiness."

"Oh, please." Thomas smiled with no trace of his former irritation. "We should be thanking you for making time on such short notice. I hate to pull you away from your real patients."

"How is Anjan?" Kamala beamed.

"Well. He's well, thank you."

"He's looking so grown-up, you know. What grade is he in now?"

"Second," Dr. George said. "He's just a bit tall for his age."

"I'll bet." Kamala patted Amina's leg.

"Are those mine?" Thomas asked, pointing to the envelope.

Dr. George nodded. "Yes, and the blood work is being sent over right now."

"Well, let's have a look. We don't want to keep you."

"I hope you don't mind, I also had Dr. Curry take a look before I came."

"Oh, good. How is Luther?" Thomas stood. "Back from Hawaii, then?"

"Yes, sir." Dr. George walked to the light board, and Thomas stood in front of it, his arms crossed. Amina got up and stood there too, doing her best to look focused as the fluorescent light popped on, bathing them in a cool, white glow.

The scans were beautiful. They always were, whites and grays spreading out between the thin curves of skull like weather patterns from some distant planet. When she was younger, Amina would try to find shapes in them—flowers, dragons, boats.

"I wanted to get a second opinion before I came over, of course," Dr. George said quietly.

Two seahorses met in a mirror, their snouts just touching. One had wings and the other carried an egg.

"Glioma," Thomas said.

Dr. George nodded.

Amina looked back at the fanning waves of gray, the dark curls and symmetrical lakes. "What?"

Her father did not answer. She looked at his blank face, which seemed waxen suddenly, as if it had never known motion. A phone was ringing somewhere.

"Curry agreed?" Thomas asked.

"Yes."

"His approximation?"

"Between two and three."

"I see."

"Wait, what?" Amina asked, louder now, panic edging into her voice.

"And the EEG?" Thomas asked, holding a hand up to silence her.

"That's on the way," Dr. George said.

"Yes, but was there—"

"A good amount of focal slowing," Dr. George said. "Yes."

Thomas nodded. His eyes dropped to the carpet and did not move.

"Who?" Kamala asked, pushing her way between them to look at the scans herself. "Something is the matter?"

No one answered her. Amina felt something cool on her arm. She looked down to find Dr. George's hand on her elbow.

"Shall we sit?" he asked.

There was something about his tone that made Amina want to be on her best behavior, and she turned at once, almost running into Kamala, who looked just as determined to get back to her own chair. Dr. George sat down across from them. Thomas stayed standing.

"There appears to be a mass in the occipital lobe," Dr. George said.

"A mass? Is that the same thing as a tumor?" Amina asked.

"Yes."

"No," Kamala said.

"Is it bad?" Amina felt stupid asking. Weren't all tumors bad on some level?

"We need to do a biopsy to know more," Dr. George said.

Her notebook was on his desk. Amina pulled it off and onto her lap, and slowly wrote "tumor" at the top of the page. She immediately crossed it out. She wrote "biopsy" instead.

"I realize this is a shock," Dr. George was saying. "For all of us. Though of course this does explain some of the symptoms. Amina, you had mentioned the hallucinations. Audio and visual inconsistencies are common for this type of—"

"Shut up," Kamala said.

"Ma!"

"It's okay," Dr. George said. "It's understandable."

Kamala sat very still in her chair, her face tilted upward like a child bent on not receiving punishment. Behind her, Thomas was all back, the light from the board turning the tips of his curls an even whiter white.

"It's a terrible shock," Dr. George explained to Amina, as if she needed the explanation. Amina looked out the window at her car. It seemed strange that it should still be out there, waiting, in one piece.

"But . . ." Amina cleared her throat. "I mean, what's the treatment? Do you operate? Take it out?"

"We will know more when we get more tests, but the location and the size would indicate—"

"No," Thomas turned around. His face was pale and he smiled sadly at her. "It's inoperable."

"So then, like, what? Radiation? Chemo?"

Thomas shrugged.

"We've had some success in preventing growth with radiation," Dr. George said, but now he was talking to Kamala, Kamala whose head tilted farther back, glaring at the ceiling. Tears leaked from the corners of her eyes. Amina watched in surprise as her father stepped toward her and reached down to brush one, then the other away.

"Kam," he said softly, and her mother pulled his hand forward until it covered her whole face.

There was a knock at the door, and it opened to show a slight Asian woman who held two more folders in her hand. She smiled when she saw Thomas. "Hey, Doc."

"Thank you, Lynne," Dr. George said, rising to take the envelopes from her. "We'll be a minute longer."

"Oh. Sure." She closed the door quickly behind her, and Thomas motioned for the envelopes. He slid them out and flipped from one page to the next, reading for what seemed like twenty minutes, though of course it could not have been. Amina looked blankly in front of herself. She counted the yellow bodies until she lost count, and started over. Her father handed the papers back to Dr. George.

"I should go," he said. "I have a patient waiting."

"What?" Her head snapped up. "Dad—"

"Sir," Dr. George said, rising, "I'd like to schedule you for a biopsy as soon as—"

"That's fine. Please make the necessary arrangements with Monica. My schedule will be cleared."

"Wait!" Amina half-shouted, and Thomas turned to her, stone-eyed. "Can we—I mean, we need to talk about this, right?"

"I'm late as it is." Thomas swiveled to find the doorknob, avoiding looking at Kamala, who wasn't looking at him anyway, but at her own lap, as though she couldn't imagine who it belonged to. "Please make sure your mother gets home safely."

BOOK 9

A FATHER OF INVENTION

ALBUQUERQUE, 1983

CHAPTER 1

The morning of Akhil's funeral, the remaining Eapens sat in the car, looking at the glass doors of Love's truck stop. Outside, an eighteen-wheeler glided by like a cruise ship, and the car rocked gently like they were on water.

"Okay," Thomas said, a reassurance to no one in particular. "Okay then."

Amina watched her father open the door and stand up. He shook his legs so that his pants fell smoothly, and when he took out his wallet, she looked away. It wasn't that she expected the world to stop for the funeral. But certain things, like the country music blaring from the car next to them, or needing gas to get to the church, or having to pay anyone for anything, seemed cruel.

In the passenger seat, Kamala readjusted the pleats on her white sari, smoothing them down with one hand. She leaned her head back into the seat cradle, and Amina watched her through the rearview mirror. The bruise was spectacular. A large purple poppy bloomed over Kamala's cheek and eye socket, her red-rimmed eye in its center.

Strangely, the bruise had the effect of making what was beautiful on her face more so, her nose more patrician and lips more full and the good eye somehow better than it had been before, so that the sum of her parts gave her the air of a harrowed starlet, of glamour all lit up with tragedy.

"These were the biggest they had," Thomas said as he opened the door and sat down. A cloud of diesel and dust floated in, and he handed the sunglasses to Kamala before shutting the door. Amina watched her open them and pause. The frames were purple and spar- kly and as big as tea saucers. Kamala put them on gingerly.

"Let me see," Thomas said, and she turned her head toward him. He placed his thumb on her chin and rotated her head from one side to the other.

"Fine," he said, and started the engine.

She would not cry. At the funeral, Amina kept her eyes closed for fear of seeing any one image that would stick too deeply inside, turning the day into something real. She ran her fingers along the edge of the card stock in her hand, digging the corner under her thumbnail. Already she had seen too much of it, the white program with Akhil's senior photo and the numbers 1965–1983 underneath. Already it had sucked her air out, replaced it with a buzzing numbness. The room, she knew, was thick with Indians, doctors, nurses, patients, parents, teachers, and the throngs from Mesa High, unrecognizably adult in their suits and black dresses. *Prom,* Amina thought when she first saw them. It was like they were practicing for prom. And in truth, there was some- thing prom-ish in their manner, some terrible mix of dread and cool and hunger for the unknown that washed over their faces like sun- light.

"Two, Samuel, chapter twelve, verse twenty-two to twenty-three," the minister said. The rustle of opening Bibles sounded like a flock of birds rising through the church. Kamala, face hidden by the sun- glasses, did not move.

"While the child was alive, I fasted and wept; for I said, 'Who can tell whether the Lord will be gracious to me, that the child may live?'

But now he is dead; why should I fast? Can I bring him back again? I shall go to him, but he shall not return to me." Pastor Kelley exhaled and looked up. "This morning is a difficult morning for you. It is a morning filled with questions and despair, when the young have seen one of their own taken by the hand of the Lord. And so you have come here for comfort and I can only say to you . . ."

Amina kept her eyes shut as Pastor Kelley went on to deliver a sermon about God's favorites, apparently believing that Akhil was one of them. She did not see Mrs. Macklin rising to the podium to give, at Kamala's request, an odd testimony to Akhil's courage in the face of French. She did not notice how Mindy Lujan looked at the coffin and stifled sobs, surprised and terrified by her own grief; how a group of young Mathletes stared at their just-shined dress shoes, wondering what it felt like to fly over a cliff and exactly how fast Akhil had been going at the moment of impact; how everyone kept looking around for no-show Paige, as if she was supposed to be the North Star of their mourning, something they could fixate on and guide themselves by.

Instead, buffeted by the darkness of her own eyelids, Amina saw her mother's face so clearly that it seemed for a minute that time had been kind enough to reverse itself. She saw the orange cut of the kitchen light on her mother's cheekbones, the rise of steam from the idlis and stew, how Kamala's mouth had softened watching Akhil eat, how in that moment everything extraneous had been erased. Two mouths, one eating, one hiding a smile. She opened her eyes to see her brother sitting on the choir bench.

She blinked. He blinked back. She sucked in, trying to make her mouth move, make anything move. He waved. She couldn't breathe. She tried to yell or shout or scream or just say anything, but Akhil winked at her and put his finger to his lips, a dodgy smirk rising on them. She shook her head. Up on the podium, Mrs. Macklin leaned in and whispered, *"L'esprit est éternel pour les enfants,"* and Akhil flipped the woman the bird, kissing his middle finger before raising it high.

"Stop," Amina said, and a chastened-looking Mrs. Macklin stopped talking.

"He's right there," Amina said, but her arm felt suddenly too heavy to lift and no one looked anyway. Dimple's hand was cool on her wrist.

"He's there," Amina said to her mother's sunglasses, and watched Kamala's lips curl in until they disappeared completely. Her father's eyes were stones.

"Bathroom," Dimple whispered in her ear, and Amina stood up, letting herself be led down the center aisle, past the Indians, past Jamie Anderson, who stood trapped in the middle of his row as she walked by, silent and aggrieved. By the time she thought to look back, Akhil was standing too, stretching at the side of the podium. He waved at her lazily and strolled toward an open window. No one stopped him when he climbed out.

"Ami?" The tips of Dimple's black shoes pointed into the bathroom stall.

She had asked to be let in before. She would ask again. Through the crack in the stall door, Amina could see the bathroom mirror, the reflection of Dimple's head pressed to the metal door, listening. Outside, mourners were singing some flat and lousy hymn that managed to make them sound like children and insects all at once.

"Please?" Dimple shifted her weight. Amina leaned forward, slid the lock open. Her cousin came in, locking the door behind her, and Amina scooted over on the tank of the toilet. Dimple climbed on, nervously eyeing the toilet water. When she leaned back, it was Amina who sighed. It was better with Dimple there. They sat next to each other, a pocket of warmth growing between their touching shoulders. Their feet ringed the toilet.

"I'm not crazy," Amina said after a few minutes.

"I never said you were." Dimple flicked a piece of lint off her skirt.

Amina flexed her fingers in front of her, counting them silently.

"What did you see?"

Amina shrugged. The bathroom smelled of disgusting pink soap and talcum powder that made the back of her throat itch. Ten. All fingers were accounted for. Dimple splayed her own hands out, raising them to cover Amina's, squeezing them into tight fists. Amina ducked her head to her chest to keep herself from crying.

"It's okay," Dimple said. "No one can see you."

Amina shook her head. How to explain that she felt like if she cried, if she actually started, she might never stop? That it felt too bottomless, like jumping into one of those cave pools that was the size of a pond but actually thousands of feet deep? No, there was no explaining this to anyone, even Dimple, who held her in a clumsy half hug as the service ended and the mourners rose to leave.

They made an uneasy knot in the kitchen. Long after the reception had ended and the rest of the guests had parted, the Ramakrishnas and the Kurians curled tightly around the kitchen counter, watching Kamala. It had been hours since the burial service, hours since their arrival at the house, whereupon Thomas immediately excused himself for the bedroom and his wife took up a post at the stove. A hissing cloud of ghee billowed across the ceiling, and under it Kamala flipped and folded yet another golden crepe, its thin edges perfectly browned.

"Who's ready for another?" she asked.

Bala and Sanji shook their heads, while Raj and Chacko exchanged hesitant glances. They had all eaten as much as they could, and certainly more than they wanted. Even Dimple, for once willing to accept anything Kamala had to offer, had stuffed herself beyond reason.

"Amina?" Kamala trilled.

"No, Ma."

"I'll take it, Auntie," Dimple said, shuffling forward.

Kamala nodded curtly, slipping it onto the plate before returning to the batter bowl. She lifted the ladle with a quick hand.

"No! No, Kamala," Bala said, standing up. "Really, no need. We're all so full. Make it for yourself only."

Kamala stared at her through glassy eyes. "I'm not hungry."

"Of course not. It's okay. Don't eat, then. Why don't you come sit?"

Kamala was silent, considering this. She looked away. "Have you seen the mural?" she asked.

Bala looked desperately at Sanji.

"Kamala, come sit for a moment," Sanji said.

"Come, I'll show you," Kamala said, walking quickly out of the kitchen.

The others looked at one another, too anxious to move.

"You think maybe we should sedate?" Sanji asked Chacko and Raj, but the latter's eyes flashed nervously toward Amina. They all turned to look at her.

"It's upstairs," Amina said. "The mural."

In the stairwell, the rustling of silk against silk, the thick press of kitchen spices and the day's stunned sweat. Amina followed her relatives up. It was strange enough to see the Kurians and the Ramakrishnas on the stairs, since they usually just called up when it was time to go, but when they entered Akhil's room, all eight of them crammed around the bed, Amina felt distinctly ill. She stared at the floor while Kamala flipped the desk lamp up to light the ceiling and the others craned their necks. A sharp silence filled the room.

"It's the Greats!" she heard her mother say. A flurry of motion dotted the corner of her eye as her mother extended an arm. "You see?"

"Yes," Sanji Auntie said at last, and the men shuffled in assent.

"Gandhi is the one with the glasses," Kamala continued. "Gandhiji, Che Guevara, Martin Luther King, Nelson Mandela, Rob Halford!"

"Rob Halford?" Chacko asked.

"He's a singing priest," Kamala said, and the others nodded quickly. "Akhil admired him very much."

"I want to go home."

The voice, soft and shuddering, stopped them. Amina looked up to see Dimple standing in the corner, her elbows cupped in her arms.

"I want to go home," her cousin repeated, her lip trembling. Her face scrunched into a ball and she held herself tighter as tears leaked out of her eyes. Bala Auntie moved quickly across the room, putting one arm around Dimple and the other forward, as if to stop anyone who tried to interfere with their swift turn toward the door.

"We should take her home," she told Kamala, who nodded mutely, the light in her own face suddenly leaden.

"We'll stay," Sanji said, but Kamala shook her head.

"No, you go," she said. "We're fine."

———

"Call us. You need anything, nah? Just please call." Sanji Auntie wrung her hands in the driveway, looking at Amina and her mother as if to absorb their pain with her eyes alone. Kamala nodded, already walking back into the house. The doorway faced them, its squared light empty.

"Amina baby, you hear?" Sanji Auntie asked, cupping Amina's chin in her hand. "Call me when you're missing him, okay? Call me when you miss him too much."

Amina nodded, felt Sanji's fingers slip from her face, replaced by two wet kisses on either cheek. She turned and walked through the front door, shutting it.

CHAPTER 2

As it turned out, it was not Akhil whom she missed in those first weeks so much as her family, or the family they had been before. As her mother slept straight through dinner and her father wandered through the house like a horse that had slipped into an aquarium, Amina warmed bland casseroles, doused them in Tabasco, and turned on the news even though she had no intention of watching it. A few times she even took the stairs back up to her room, shutting her eyes and listening to Tom Brokaw through the floorboards and pretending that nothing had happened at all. It was amazing how easy it was to do, how utterly convincing. Oh, she wasn't so dumb as to pretend it had all been good then, with Thomas at the hospital and her mother talking to the television for company and Akhil and Paige dreaming up a better world while Amina watched the empty driveway. But they were better. That much she was sure of.

She had forgotten about the picture entirely. It was only after arranging all her barrettes in order of size, turning her bedspread over to the plain white side instead of the tiny-flowered side, and placing her rolled-up Air Supply poster in the trash as some sort of peace offering to Akhil, that Amina remembered. Her book bag, unopened now for more than two weeks, lay under her desk chair. She tugged it out.

Schoolbooks. They spilled out of her bag like old friends from a town she'd moved away from. The hardbacks of algebra and biology slid out first, cheerfully jacketed in green and yellow, followed by two spiral notebooks, the copy of *On the Road* that Mr. Tipton had recommended she pick up, and a pencil case. And there it was at the back, her white photography binder, photos held in plastic sheets. Amina pulled it out and sat on her bed.

She steeled herself as she flipped it open, blurred her vision by almost crossing her eyes. Yes, these were Akhil. She would not really look, she would not see. She flipped quickly, turning past more of him, then her mother and Sanji Auntie, some dark shadows she knew for sure were her attempt to make a still life out of her mother's perfume bottles, then Dimple blowing a bubble, then a study of her own foot. Fast, fast, fast, she stopped only when she saw the picture that looked almost pure black. She focused. There it was. She pulled it out.

It would be another few hours until dawn and another few after that until Kamala rose from her dirty bed to take a shower, or rather, sit in the shower, black hair matting against her breasts and the yellow tile until Amina handed her a towel. But Thomas, the night owl, had to be around. The TV was on mute in the kitchen, bright color flashing over the empty couch.

"Dad?"

Her father's slippers were paired in perfect position in front of the couch, as if being worn by an invisible man. Sections of newspaper slid from the table to the floor.

"Hello?"

The refrigerator door shut behind her, and Amina spun around, guts in her throat.

"Jesus, Dad!"

Thomas blinked at her from behind a tumbler of scotch. "Amina? What time is it?"

She looked at the clock on the microwave. "It's three. Well, three-fifteen."

"What's going on?" There was an edge of panic in his voice, one that had been growing since the funeral. He put his drink down. "Are you okay?"

"Yeah, I just . . ." Amina stepped back, a little unnerved by the fear and worry and protectiveness spreading out of him and diffusing through the kitchen. "I just wanted to show you a picture."

"Picture?"

"Photograph."

Thomas looked at her like she was speaking dolphin. Amina waved the sheet in her hand.

"Oh," he said. "You mean a *photograph*."

"Right."

He found a steady look of interest and managed to hold on to it. "Let's see it."

Just like that? She hadn't thought this through. She should have warned him, maybe, prepared him for it a little bit. Amina looked at her father, pants hanging loosely from his body, beard and hair fanning out from his face. He did not smell good. What if it scared him? Gave him a heart attack? Amina saw herself and Kamala growing old alone in the house together, the trees swallowing up the driveway. She put a hand on Thomas's arm, and he swayed a little.

"The thing is, I took it a while ago, like, after Ammachy died?"

She paused. Thomas seemed to understand a second too late that something was required of him. "M'okay."

"So. It was kind of this thing for me, and then I forgot about it, and then I remembered. Just now."

"Uhn."

"And the thing is, Dad, this wasn't even in a single photograph, it was two, you know? I mean, I used two negatives. So I probably couldn't even print it again. But it came out this way."

She handed him the photograph. Thomas flipped it over, and they were looking at him six months earlier, newspapers scattered around his ankles, a white bulb glowing in the corner of the porch. Her father's eyes skidded all over the frame, bouncing from light to shadow.

"What is it?"

"It's you." She put her finger on his figure in the chair. "See?"

He raked his fingers deep into his beard. After a pause he looked back at Amina. "It's very nice work. Lovely."

"Do you see her?"

"Who?"

"Ammachy." She tapped the figure in the picture. "Look behind the chair."

Thomas stared at her, confused.

"Here," Amina said, pointing again. "In the picture."

But he was not looking at the picture. He was looking at her face. Curiously, repulsed, as though she were a bug that had found its way into his shower.

Amina's pulse quickened. "I know. I mean, I know it's weird, but you know, maybe she knew you were sad, maybe she just came to be—"

Thomas let the picture drop out of his hands. He was trembling. Amina tensed with dread, suddenly understanding how large her father was, how quickly he could knock her to the ground. He lurched at her. He clutched her head so tightly to his chest that her ears were flattened and she could hear his heart crashing against his ribs like rough waters against a dock. To her horror he began to sob. He was trying to say something.

"What?" Amina asked, muffled by his shirt. She pushed her head back for a pocket of air. "What did you say?"

"S-s-sorry."

"What?"

He pushed her back, hands clamped hard around her biceps. Tears swam down his cheeks. "I'm sorry, Amina. It shouldn't . . . shouldn't have happened. I should have s-seen it. Coming. I should have been h-h-here, I know."

"What are you saying?" She was scared. "Why are you saying that?"

"You can be mad. I don't expect you to forgive me right now. I don— . . . I don— . . . I really don't." Thomas tried to compose his face but instead succumbed to a new round of choking and gasping.

"I'm not mad at you!" Amina's voice broke and now she was crying, too. She pushed him away. "I'm just showing you, I thought you would . . . I thought it would make you happy, or something."

"It's okay if you need to hate me right now, I understand that it might—"

"No, wait! Stop!" Amina swooped down to the floor, picking the photograph up and thrusting it at him. "*Here,*" she said, pointing to her grandmother's sari. "*That's* her body! *That's* her head. See?"

Thomas shut his eyes, face quivering. He inhaled deeply, exhaled a night's worth of scotch. When he opened his eyes, they were dull, focused. "There's nothing there, Amina."

"You're not even looking!"

"There is no reason to look. There is nothing in the picture."

"But we saw her in my class! We saw her and my teacher said—"

But he had closed in on her again, smothering her into a hug so tight that her voice box crushed against his shoulder. He was saying sorry again, whispering it desperately like a man at confessional and adding to the indignity by rocking her from side to side like she was some kind of baby.

"They don't come back, *koche,*" he murmured into her ear. "I'm so sorry, they don't come back."

"Don't!" She pushed him and his arms dropped instantly to his sides. His face was a jag of despair. She wiped the wet off her face with her sleeve.

"Ami, please—"

"Jesus, just forget it, okay? Forget it!" She left the kitchen, pounding up the stairs as loudly as possible. Who cared? Her mother would never wake up, and her father was a scotch zombie. Back in her room, she shoved the books off the bed with one hand, letting the photography binder crack open as it hit the floor. She turned on her desk lamp, slid the picture under it, and looked.

Yes. She was still there. Right there. Ammachy's teeth and eyes were the only bit of white in that corner, but the happiness that radiated out of them pushed up from the photograph like starlight. Well, then. Amina placed her thumbs on the top edge of the picture and ripped it clean down the middle. She stacked the halves and ripped them again, and then one more time, until they were inch-big scraps on the desk table. She picked up her trash can and swept the whole pile in, piece by piece. When she was done, she pulled out her Air Supply poster.

Back at school a week later, the whispers were everywhere. They followed her from English to biology, moving from the back of her neck to the space behind her ears as she opened her locker. A few of the kids in her class had tried to talk to her on the first couple of days back but soon gave up with an air that suggested they had just been doing her a favor in the first place. Crowds parted as she walked through them, heads ducked fast to homework when she entered classrooms without teachers. Kids whose brothers and sisters were in Akhil's class talked to everyone else like they had extra insight.

"What?" she had shouted at Hank Franken that Friday, when he was staring at her. He dropped his pen and Dimple had also glared at him then, but later, sitting on the deserted track field with Amina, she looked uncomfortable.

"No one is trying to make you feel bad, you know. They just don't know what to say. That's what they tell me, anyway."

"Why are you even talking about it?"

"What?"

"Don't ever talk about my family with anyone again."

Dimple blinked, looked confused. "Right. Okay. Listen, I only say anything when people tell me that they're sorry or something, and even then I barely say—"

"What are they sorry to you for? You aren't even really related to us."

It shouldn't have felt good to see the naked hurt in Dimple's eyes, but it did. It felt like sunlight on cold fingers. Amina leaned into the air and felt something snap between them. She watched Dimple's mouth tremble.

"Maybe you should sit alone if you need to cry," she suggested.

Dimple jumped up, and she was yards away before Amina stopped smiling. She watched until Dimple turned and walked across the parking lot, taking a seat on the low wall there. And for the first time since his death, Amina felt the urgent need to talk to Akhil.

A few nights later the doorbell rang. Up on the Stoop, Amina dropped her cigarette across the laces of her Adidases, which began to smoke immediately.

"Shit!" She whacked at them.

The whole smoking thing was not going well. Despite diligent practice every evening, she was no better at inhaling than she had been in the spring, and she was actually worse at holding the damn things. Why did they always insist on jumping out of her hands? What was she doing wrong?

Fucking Akhil, she thought, climbing in through his window. It was another new habit, always thinking *fucking* before *Akhil. Fucking Akhil should have taught me how to smoke, and how to do fucking trig, and how to pack a fucking bowl. Now I am fucked by everything I don't fucking know.*

Amina walked down the hallway, flipping on lights and trying to wipe the smell of smoke off her hands. Sanji would not care, of course, but if it was Raj or Bala, or worse, Chacko, she was sure to get a kind-but-stern talking-to that the others seemed determined to give her, as if to reassure her and themselves that there were still rules worth following. The doorbell rang again.

"Coming!" she yelled loudly, passing her parents' bedroom door and halfheartedly hoping Kamala would come out with some level of concern about who was at the door or why. But no, of course not. Charles Manson could be ringing with the entire Family and a bag of knives, and Kamala would probably just wait in bed for them to dismember her. Amina opened the door.

"Hey."

It was not the Manson family. It was not any member of the Ra-makrishna or Kurian family either. It was Paige Anderson, looking beautiful and out of place, like a deer at the edge of a paved road. Amina stared at her, every normal-sounding greeting drying up in her throat. It wasn't so much that she hadn't seen Paige since the accident (she had, alone at school, sitting with various books plastered over her face), but somehow the reality of her—bob grown past her shoulders, body tucked into a somber navy dress, cheeks still permanently flushed—felt disconcerting. She was so real, standing there, so fraught and insistent and *alive*. It was like looking at a bare, beating heart.

"Can I come in?" Paige asked.

Here? Amina thought. *To this house?* But her body moved to the side like it was some normal thing, and Paige walked in. Behind her, Amina caught a glimpse of a figure in the passenger seat of the Andersons' Volvo in the driveway.

"Is that Jamie?"

"What?" Paige looked anxiously over her shoulder. "Oh, yeah. He didn't want me to come alone."

"Does he want to come in?"

"Oh, no. He's just keeping me company. I, uh . . ." She cleared her throat. "I was hoping I might talk to your parents."

Amina shut the front door. "My parents?"

"Your dad?"

"He's still at work."

"What about your mom?"

"My mom?" Amina said, face hot from catching what felt like some sort of repeating disease, one in which you were doomed to echo someone else's bad ideas instead of strenuously objecting to them. "She's in bed."

Instantly, whatever had been powering the light in Paige's face—nervousness, anticipation, bravery—was snuffed out. Her shoulders dropped and she looked lost, the foyer rising up around her. When her eyes moved from the stairs to the darkened landing above them, Amina felt sorry for her.

"You want to go up?"

"What?"

"To his room. It's upstairs."

"Oh . . ." Paige blinked several times, considering it. She took a deep breath and looked at Amina. "Okay. Yes."

If it was strange to have the Ramakrishnas and the Kurians upstairs, it was doubly strange to have Paige there, staring at the row of Akhil's school pictures in the hall with the intensity of someone trying to find the YOU ARE HERE stamp on a mall map. She studied his younger photos (third grade, buckteeth; fifth grade, buckteeth and mustache) before stopping at his senior picture, the one taken after he'd woken from the Big Sleep and before he'd met her. Her forehead pleated.

"He never invited me over here," she said, and then looked at Amina like that fact was important somehow, like it was a mark against her instead of the Eapens.

Amina motioned to Akhil's room. "You can go in if you want."

Paige nodded, walking past her quickly, but when she entered the room, she stopped suddenly, as though she'd hit an invisible wall.

"Oh," she said, covering her face with her hand.

It was not an oh of disappointment or an oh of surprise but an oh that Amina had never heard before, scraped raw with an emotion Amina would not know herself until years later, when she understood what it was to long for someone, to ache for their smell and taste on you, to imagine the weight of their hips pinning yours so precisely that you crane up to meet your own invisible desire. She watched as Paige crossed Akhil's room, undistracted by all the usual things that stopped people—the Greats, his desk, the leather jacket hanging from his chair—and moved straight for his hamper, which she opened up, pulling out a forgotten T-shirt and crushing it into her face. "Oh," she said again, muffled. *Oh*. And even if Amina didn't yet know what it was to love like that, to burn until your spine has no choice but to try to wind itself around an empty shirt, she understood for sure that the people who said it was better to have loved and lost than never to have loved at all were a bunch of dicks.

"Amina?"

How had she not even heard Kamala coming up the stairs? Amina turned around to find her mother walking down the same hall Paige had just stood in, yesterday's nightie bunched around her knees. She looked at the open door to Akhil's room, and her face darkened.

"What are you doing in there?"

"N-nothing," Amina stammered, willing Paige to put down the shirt and step away from the hamper, but it was too late for that now, Kamala was already pushing past her and into the bedroom, suspicion pressed deep into her face. Paige turned, her face filling with panic before she seemed to get ahold of herself. She placed the shirt on the bed, smoothed her dress down, and stood tall.

"You must be Kamala," she said, offering a hand to shake, and Amina flinched. "I'm Paige."

Kamala looked at her hand, confused.

Paige swallowed, tried again. "I'm . . . I was . . . I'm Akhil's girl-friend."

Kamala looked at Amina.

"The one he was going to prom with," Amina said.

At this, Kamala stiffened a little, the needle of connection between prom and everything that had followed pricking some corner of her mind.

"I was—I am so sorry to not come to the funeral," Paige said, hand lowered, cheeks burning with pink circles. "That's why I'm here. I wanted . . . I just . . . I wanted to come by to see you both. You and Thomas. To tell you how much I loved your son."

Kamala looked at her for a long time, gaze brewing with some-thing Amina couldn't quite place, until she said, "Loved?"

The word was spoken neutrally, but one look at her face was enough for Amina, who reached for Paige's elbow.

"Yes." Paige brushed Amina away, looking puzzled. "Yes, of course."

Kamala laughed once, hard, like a shovel hitting cement.

"Paige," Amina said evenly. "Let me walk you down."

Paige straightened at this suggestion, taller than either of them.

She looked from one to the other, her face suddenly ripening with an expression Amina had seen her give Akhil a thousand times before. It was a look of hope, of compassion, of—God forbid—love.

"Amina, I'd like to speak with your mother alone."

"I really don't think that's a good—"

But it didn't really matter what Amina thought because Paige was already saying, "I loved your son more than I've ever loved anyone," in a low and steady voice, one sweet with the belief that there was something left for her to hold on to in this house, that two people in pain could find common ground. It was an opinion that was probably welcome across the Anderson dinner table, or at least taken seriously, but it was not welcome in this room, where Kamala's rigid face slammed away every word and Amina turned silently and fled, going back down the hallway, down the stairs, and through the front door like a shot. She shut the door behind her with a thump.

Fucking Paige. Fucking Kamala. Fucking Akhil.

"Hey," she heard from her side, and she nearly screamed. Jamie waved from her periphery. He was standing awkwardly next to one of the planters, his face drawn with worry.

"Are you okay?" he asked.

She was not okay. Amina knew this for sure as she charged toward him, shaking like a comet and ready to flatten him, so she was surprised by how easily he caught her, his arms opening just enough for her to fit between them, his shoulder landing firmly under her chin. Warm. He was warm. His heart thumped against her chest, and Amina shut her eyes, wanting to keep pushing forward until she somehow disappeared all the way into him.

Why wasn't it weird to be held by Jamie Anderson? It's not like she had ever been held by anyone not related to her before, and none of them felt even a bit like Jamie, who was exactly her size and skinny, with skin hotter than she would have thought healthy. But it wasn't weird, even if she was half stepping on one of his feet and his Afro was scratching against her ear. It wasn't even weird when he said, "How's it going?" like they weren't already plastered together.

"It's horrible," she said.

He hugged her tighter and whispered something. It sounded like

I'm sorry, but it also sounded like *I'm worried,* and she wanted to ask which he meant, because it seemed like a pretty big distinction, but just then the door opened and Paige came flying through it, eyes wet, mouth trembling.

"Go," Paige said to Jamie as they sprang apart. "Go, go, go!"

"What?" Jamie asked as she stumbled down the steps. "Wait!"

But Paige was not waiting. She was running toward the Andersons' Volvo, her dress flapping at the backs of her knees. Jamie looked at Amina, his face clouding.

Well, what did they think was going to happen? Where did they think they were?

"You shouldn't have come," Amina said, and watched as this registered with Jamie's slight flinch, a tic behind his gaze that then turned into his backing away from her and running after his sister.

Long after their taillights had disappeared into the darkening trees and the traces of Jamie's heat had evaporated from her skin, Amina stood on the porch, trying not to think about what Jamie probably thought of her now, or how good it had felt to be hugged, or how Paige hadn't even looked at her on the way out. Her feet felt heavy going upstairs, and heavier still as she walked down the hallway toward the slight stir of air and light that came from Akhil's room.

Inside, Kamala was praying. This is what Amina thought at first when she saw the unlikely Pietà of her mother sitting on Akhil's bed, the T-shirt strewn weakly across her lap. Kamala's head was bent over it, and something about this—not being able to see her face—made Amina realize suddenly how much she missed her mother. She missed Kamala banging the cupboards in the kitchen. She missed her shouting "Hey, dummies! Rise and shines!" from the bottom of the stairs in the morning. She missed her saying "Oh, really?" when Queen Victoria burped too loudly, like they were having an actual conversation, and how sometimes she would come up and squeeze Amina's shoulder out of the blue, which used to feel like a poor excuse for a hug but now, in memory, felt like sitting in front of a blazing fire with a world of snow falling outside.

"Ma?" She took a step into the room.

Her mother's head snapped up, and with a stab of fear Amina realized her mistake. This was no noble sorrow, no reverential Mary. Kamala glared at her like a tiger hunkered over a fresh kill, and Amina found herself thinking, *She will kill me now, too.* Not that Kamala had killed Akhil. No one had—not Kamala, not Thomas, not Akhil himself, not even Amina. Except that standing there, looking at her mother, Amina suddenly understood that they all had, in some way. They all had.

Kamala opened her mouth, dark eyes glinting.

"Shut the door," she said.

It got better after the Andersons' visit. Not better in that anything actually good happened, but better in that Amina stopped waiting for it to. It was as though a punctuation mark had been put on the event of Akhil's death, giving it an exact shape for her to size up. She stopped waiting to feel normal. She stopped expecting anyone to understand. She stopped keeping an eye out for Paige at school, and when Jamie talked in class, she looked right through him, daring herself to feel less and less for either of the Andersons until finally they slipped back into the Mesa masses, their bodies moving in a steady line down the hallway, avoiding her without even trying.

"Amina?" Her father opened her bedroom door on the last school night of the year. "Can I come in?"

Why do fathers always look ungainly in their daughter's bedrooms? Like mythical beasts wandered in from the forest of another world? Thomas made an effort to steer clear of Amina's piles of clothes, of the desk and bookshelves, but he still managed to rattle everything on the surface of the dresser and knock his head on the canopy over the bed.

"Hello," he said, peering under it.

"Hey."

She had been lying there since she had come home, looking at the picture she'd taken of Akhil on the couch the night of the fight over the keys and playing the reverse time game. It was a simple game; all it required was her imagining how far she would go back to change what had happened. How many days would she live over—minute by minute, not making any choices that would mess with the order of the universe the way they did in *Star Trek*—to change that one? Would she go back to seeing her parents fighting in the driveway over the summer? Easy. Back to Dimple on her first day home from camp? It wasn't even a question. Back to breaking her arm in sixth grade, to being called a nigger by all the boys in her class in fourth? Harder. But yes. She was in third grade, during the class where she'd laughed so hard she accidently wet her pants, when Thomas had knocked.

"What are you doing?" he asked.

She shrugged.

He sat on the bed, the weight of him tilting it dramatically to one side. He was all knees and shoulders, too low to the floor. "How are you?"

"Fine."

When she had done it all, when she had relived every moment without changing a thing, she would get to come back to that night. It was the best part of the game. That night, she would go through minute by minute, slowing everything down to remember exactly how it happened. She would talk to Akhil in his room. Go down to dinner. Eat the idlis and sambar. She would watch her father grow sad at the sink without interruption. She would know exactly when to go—after the fight, while Kamala and Akhil watched TV and Thomas cleaned the kitchen. She would do it perfectly, silently slinking out the back door, across the driveway. She would lower herself down under the car, letting the gravel dig into her knees. The air would be thick with the smell of tires and oil as her hand reached under the wheel hub, fingers searching until she felt the metal at their tips. She would empty the hide-a-key box.

Thomas's eyes slid to the picture on her lap and then away. "I thought maybe you'd like to do something."

"Like what?"

"Like go to a movie."

"Tomorrow's the last day of school."

"Ah. Right. What if we go get dessert somewhere?"

"Dessert?"

"Yes. Heidi Pies. You like Heidi Pies, right?"

"I'm not hungry." She saw his face drop and felt a pang of guilt. "Thanks anyway."

Thomas opened his hands, read his palms as though there was a pamphlet resting on them. "You need to get up now."

"What?"

"You can't do this, *koche.*"

"Do what?"

"Amina." He leaned over and squeezed her leg awkwardly. "I know you miss him. I miss him, too. We won't . . . we won't ever . . ." He cleared his throat. "But you cannot sit in bed for hours like this. It's not right."

"Me? Mom is the one who is in bed all day!"

"Mom will do what Mom wants to do. She will get up, too. Soon. But you are too young for this."

"What about you? You've just been sitting around all night on your porch doing nothing but drinking scotch!"

"Not true."

She glared at him.

"Drinking scotch, yes," he corrected. "Doing nothing, no. I am very much doing something."

"Yeah, right."

"I'll show you." He stood up, banging his head on the canopy. He wiggled his fingers for her. "Come."

Once she had emptied the hide-a-key box, Amina would let herself open her eyes. *Akhil is in his room,* she would think. And maybe a noise would happen, a hollow tap across the hall, the click of what could be the light going on in the bathroom, and her gut would shimmy and she'd think, *I've done it. I've fucking done it. I've brought him back.*

"Come with me," her father said.

———

"What is it?"

"What does it look like?"

"A garbage bag."

Thomas smiled. "Exactly. Except this one, I made."

This was obvious from the pile of deflated garbage bags all over the porch.

Amina looked at him. "You've been making garbage bags?"

"Special garbage bags. Here, take it." Thomas handed her the one he held in his hands.

She took it. It was not particularly special, except that he had cut slits in the top, and run a long piece of more garbage bag in and out of the slits.

"Wait." He looked around the porch and grabbed a pile of newspaper, a soda can, a bottle. "Ready?"

She held the bag open and he dropped everything inside. She looked in after them. Nothing happened. She looked back at her father.

"Pull the ties!"

"What?"

"The things on the side! The handles!"

She held the bag away from her. Yes, there were long loops on either side. She pulled them, and the bag cinched at the top, the opening shrinking to a small *O*.

"You've made a garbage bag with handles?"

"I've made a garbage bag that closes easily! Ties shut! And then watch." He motioned for the bag, and she handed it to him. "It's a handle. So you can carry it. See?" He walked across the porch with a bit of jaunt to his step, the star of his own infomercial. He put the bag down and leaned back, hands on hips, like he was surveying the frontier ahead instead of just the screen door.

There was a moment, a longish moment, actually, where Amina imagined walking straight out of the house and down the dirt road to the main road, where she'd thumb a ride into town and show up at Raj and Sanji's with a full suitcase and clear instructions to adopt her. She could become their daughter, their instant joy, the crucial part of a family that had suddenly expanded instead of contracted. Would she be happier in the long run? It was impossible to predict. But what

Amina did know, what she was suddenly quite sure of, was that, unlike
Raj and Sanji, her parents from this point on would need her to be
more than she had ever been, and along with their need would come
her inability to fill it. Even in her best moments, she could only be a
reminder of what they had lost, the stain of her missing brother all but
blotting out her own features, and really, what was it to be the object
of affection for such permanently disfigured hearts? What would be
left of her own shape? Then she realized that Thomas was looking at
her with a face so full of hurt and hope that there was nothing to do
but ask, "What else have you made?"

It was the beginning of something. The projects that she and her
father would work on together, obviously, but also of Thomas's return
home. Not to the car, or the hospital for days on end, or even the
porch, but the house, where he would eat dinner almost every night,
or barring that, wake her up for an early breakfast. And though at first
he asked too many questions about her schedule and interests and
teachers, soon enough they settled into the work, remastering everyday objects into something new. They installed a heel-operated fan in
a tennis shoe, created rubber grips for toothbrushes, and, inspired by
sprayable cheese, tried to make an aerosol face cream.

When Kamala woke up, went to the mall, and found Jesus through
the scalding proclamations of the Trinity Baptists, they built a recep-
tacle to catch rainwater and funnel it into her garden. When she began
to cook dinner again, they attached magnets to her most frequently
used spices and stuck them to a metal sheet just next to the stove.
When she turned the radio on to WEXD, Exodus in the Southwest,
and stood on the kitchen table one Sunday morning, shouting, "He
will rise again!" with desperate rapture on her face, they slipped into
the fields, taking measurements of tree trunks to decide which might
be most suitable for a family of hammocks.

She was right about the crying. When it came, it seemed like it would
never stop. Amina lay shaking on Akhil's bed, whispering *Please,*
please, please, God, please, because she hadn't asked God for help yet,
and now it seemed like the only thing left to do. *Please, God.* It had

been too long now. Akhil had been gone for three months, and if those first days were hard because remembering things about him hurt, these days, the days of forgetting things about him, actually hurt worse.

But wouldn't he come back? It seemed impossible that he wouldn't. There was still the smell of him in his room—a pungent combination of dank socks, cigarettes, marijuana, and Vaseline. There were his shoes in the closet, looking like they could be stepped into at any moment, and his bathrobe hanging in their shared bathroom. His car keys, left on his desk by Kamala the day of the funeral. Surely he could not just be gone. Maybe it would take a season or a year, but Amina felt sure she would see her brother again.

She wasn't entirely wrong about that. For almost a year after his death, she caught glimpses of her brother everywhere. Once, he had disappeared into the back room of the post office just as she walked in. Another time, he sat with a group of migrant workers in the chile fields on the edges of Corrales as the car whizzed by. Later, when she was standing in the ethnic-foods aisle at Safeway, she saw him strolling by the dairy section, his body dark against all those jugs of milk. And once, just once, she had woken up to the sharp smell of cigarette smoke floating over her bed, the air living with someone else's breath.

BOOK 10

OCCASIONAL/ACCIDENTAL

ALBUQUERQUE, 1998

CHAPTER 1

Thomas did not come home the night of his diagnosis. Though he called at regular intervals, assuring them he would be home within hours, he somehow managed to never actually arrive, leaving Kamala and Amina to fall asleep on the couch, each eventually rising to take to her own bed for a few hours, and meet the other back in the kitchen at dawn, mute. Finally, in the morning, he arrived in the middle of breakfast, downed a glass of orange juice, and announced he was going to bed.

Monica called shortly after, hoarse and eerily wordless. *We're taking care of it,* she had said, and then wept so softly and steadily that Amina found herself in the odd position of remaining optimistic, as if the ubiquitous movie premise that hope was every bit as important as reality was something she actually believed in; as if she understood which *we* and which *it* were being referenced.

But wasn't there reason to hope? No one had said *dying,* after all, and Thomas was still scheduled for tests, which meant that whatever had been discovered in Dr. George's office still held the possibility of being treated. Eight hours later, as her father arose, stood in the kitchen, and delivered a short, detailed plan about going forward (more scans and a biopsy, a temporary hiatus from work, and the immediate start of radiation), Amina found herself thinking that he actually seemed, if not better than before, then clearer somehow, pulled from a murky pool and rinsed clean with purpose.

"Waiting for results can often be trying on families," he told Kamala and Amina, as if they were the patients. "My advice is to keep yourselves busy, and try not to dwell too much on what-ifs. Eat regularly. Try to get some form of daily exercise."

Shortly after this speech, Thomas started cleaning out the porch with the zeal of a newly arrived tenant. Several months' worth of newspapers were hauled out, cords were redoubled and hung in neat rows, three bags of miscellaneous screws, nails, and nuts were parsed into plastic trays, making them useful again.

For her part, Kamala bought an unlikely copy of *Mastering the Art of French Cooking* and began the even less likely task of following the recipes to the letter, resulting in a beguiling array of foods so layered in cream and butter and flour that she seemed to be baiting a familial heart attack, even as her family shunned the change. ("You're trying to kill me?" Thomas asked without irony one evening, frowning at a pot of béchamel sauce.)

Even Amina, propelled by the distinct need to do *something*, shrugged off her career limbo, clearing her new plan with Jane and charming the guests at Nina Vigil's daughter's quinceañera with such success that she lined up two more gigs before the night was over. She rifled through her room looking for every last hidden cigarette, flushing them down the toilet as a kind of karmic payment for Thomas's health. She would quit smoking and he would get better.

Through all of this, the family kept a complicit silence about Thomas's condition, which itself started to feel oddly progressive as the second week bled into the third. More imaging was done, a month's worth of patients rescheduled, and then Thomas lost a half-dollar-sized patch of hair to the biopsy. Sure, it felt strange, smuggling him in and out of the hospital and ignoring phone calls (Bala, Sanji, Dimple). It felt especially weird to ignore the two messages from Jamie, or rather, to listen to them five times apiece and never call back, but somehow every time she picked up the phone she found herself putting it right back down. It was too much. Too heavy. It would be better to wait and call everyone after, when she could tie it up into a tidy bundle of *the past*.

By the third week, their handling of Thomas's diagnosis actually seemed proactive, as though by refusing to acknowledge the tumor, the Eapens had quarantined it from spreading into their actual lives. More than once over that week and the next, and usually when driving her father to his appointments, Amina found herself looking at their present from a twinkling vantage point in the future, sure that once this stage was over (the details for how it would become over being vague but surely possible), they could return to the life they knew before as unremarkably as tourists reentering their own living room. And so it all went on, cleanups and chicken a l'orange and appointments layered thickly enough to keep fear of what the future might hold from penetrating until exactly four weeks after the original prognosis, when out of the blue, Thomas sat down in his chair on the porch and began a long, gentle, occasionally exasperated conversation with Cousin Itty.

"Still?" Amina asked. Kamala nodded, looking through the screen porch with a frown and crossed arms. A timer set to announce when the beef bourguignon next needed tending ticked quietly behind them.

At least he was no longer sitting down. Something about coming home and finding Thomas prattling away to the empty chair beside him had made the situation seem much more dire than it did now, some nine minutes later, as he wandered around the shop, explaining things.

Amina glanced at her mom. "Does he still think—"

"DON'T TOUCH THAT," Thomas boomed, springing forward, and both mother and daughter jumped. "You'll lose a finger! Do you want to lose a finger?"

"Jesus Christ!" Amina hissed.

"No Jesus," Kamala said.

The worst part was that there seemed to be no stopping the talking. Amina had tried to interrupt when they first came home, and

Thomas had just stared at her blankly until she left the porch. Five minutes later, armed with the notion that he couldn't possibly have lost his grip this suddenly or showily, Amina had confronted him again, only to be completely ignored. He did not answer her questions. He did not acknowledge her at all. He just waited until she ran out of words and continued his tour of the shop.

"To cut boards," Thomas explained now, tapping the leg of a table saw. "Big ones. Bigger than that."

He was talking to Itty, no doubt about it. Even though she hadn't heard it in decades, Thomas's flat, loud cadence was instantly recognizable, like a foreign language.

"You called Anyan?" Kamala asked.

"I left a message with his service."

"And what did they say?"

"They said he'd call me back."

"But what did they say about *Thomas*?"

"They didn't say *anything* about *Thomas* because I didn't tell them about *Thomas*. They are not doctors, they're operators."

"So then what? We just sit and wait?"

"What else?"

"Go talk to him."

"You go talk to him!"

"Chi!" Her mother snorted to cover up the fact that even now, in the midst of illness and disaster, she was unwilling to set foot on the porch. "What nonsense! Leaving your own father to wander around like some yakking idiot?"

"I don't think we leave him at all, not when we're not sure if he's . . ." Amina watched her father lift a level into the air, reading the fluorescent bubbles like they were measuring something. "Anyway, I think we should keep an eye on him."

"I am not watching this man like one television! You think I have nothing else to do?"

"Oh, that's right, you're busy cooking food that *no one likes to eat*."

"I am cooking food that will fatten him up! You want him to waste away to nothing? He needs reserves for radiation!"

"So go back to the kitchen, if that's where you want to be!"

Kamala gave her a long, cold look. To Amina's surprise, she threw open the screen door, marching straight onto the porch. It seemed to curl and shrink around her, like wood chips spent by flame, and she paused for a moment, getting her bearings. She thumped through the machinery with her fists clenched, little puffs of sawdust gasping at her heels. "Thomas!"

He took no notice of her, bending to adjust the radial dial.

"Thomas!" Kamala shoved a pointer finger between his shoulder blades.

"*Cha!*" he yelled, wheeling around to face her. "What!"

"What are you doing?"

Thomas looked around nervously. Whether it was the simple fact that she was on his porch for the first time in fifteen years or that her clenched, fuming face was doubled up on him like a fist, Kamala had him spooked. He took a quick breath before saying, "Talking to Itty."

"Why!"

Why? Amina blinked from the laundry room. She would not have thought to ask why.

"Because . . ." Thomas looked behind him, presumably to where Itty stood. "Because he's *here.*"

Kamala took this in with a frown, then dodged to the side suddenly, as though she might catch a glimpse of Itty if she were fast enough. She straightened, looking back up at Thomas. "You see him?"

"Yes."

"Right now?"

Thomas nodded.

"Then tell him to go."

Thomas looked stricken. He began to tremble visibly, dropping his eyes to the floor.

"Thomas, you hear me? Stop this now."

Thomas shook his head, lost, it seemed, to the shavings and filings and occasional winking screw or nail.

"Hey!" Kamala barked and he looked up at her. "What are you doing?"

"I . . . I don't know." He swallowed, his eyes filling with tears. He looked behind him and then back at Kamala. Amina watched from behind the screen, her eyes and nose suddenly liquid with grief. He should not go like this. He should not lose his dignity.

Thomas's shoulders tented up and down with the effort of trying to speak, but Kamala stopped him, squeezing his forearm. She spoke so softly, Amina had to stop breathing to hear her.

"Never mind. Not important. I am going to be in the kitchen cooking. I will not leave unless I tell you first. Come get me if you need. Okay?"

Thomas's head dropped. Kamala turned and strode back toward Amina, who only now realized that the droning she had heard in the back of her mind was not just some by-product of too much emotion, but the live and urgent trill of the telephone. Anyan George was calling back. Kamala opened the screen door and walked into the kitchen, past the still-ringing phone.

"It's for you," she said.

Jamie Anderson had not swept his entryway recently. That afternoon, as Amina rang his doorbell and paced, she almost crushed a tiny cluster of anthills dotting a seam between bricks and had to do a funny hop-skip to right herself. But no, even breathing hard, even disturbed by Anyan George's lack of help ("Keep an eye on it," he'd said, as though looking away were an option), she would not destroy another creature's carefully wrought world. If she were God, she'd be a little fucking kinder.

A few seconds passed. She rang the doorbell again. She had hung up the phone with Anyan George and driven straight there, not admitting to herself that she knew exactly where she was going until she had pulled up behind Jamie's station wagon.

Could he really be out? Amina banged on the door. She stepped forward, letting her forehead drop against it. If this were a movie, Jamie would open it right now. She'd fall into his arms. They would make love. She wouldn't know if she had an orgasm because women in movies never touched themselves during sex, and it made her suspicious of their climaxes.

It was not a movie. He really wasn't home. Amina backed up, willed the pressure in her chest to ease up. It was probably a good thing. What was she doing there, really? She did not know this man. She did not know his temperament, his cleaning habits, and the haste had been a ruse, a trick to keep from thinking clearly. By now her hand had found the doorbell and she rang it over and over again, not for any real hope of summoning Jamie, but to feel the power of her own cause and effect. There was a bubble in her lungs, the kind that happened when she stayed underwater for too long. *Air Supply.* She gasped with understanding. They really were such a better band than anyone knew.

Without warning, the hair on her arms stood on end, her animal brain understanding a split second before the rest that someone was behind her. Amina turned around to see Jamie stopped on the sidewalk a full house back. His park blanket was tucked under his arm, football-style.

"Hi," she said. Jamie nodded at her once, the kind of nod you give across a room when you have no intention of getting closer. A neighbor switched on a radio that briefly blared rap before it was turned down and rerouted to NPR.

"You're here," he finally said.

"Yeah."

"You didn't go back to Seattle?"

"No."

He waited for her to say more, but she couldn't, unnerved by the reality of him, his 94 ROCK T-shirt, the wariness on his face.

"Can I come in?" she asked.

"I left you two messages."

"I know. I'm sorry."

Jamie's eyes did not leave her face, and though nothing in them looked vulnerable toward her, she remembered their first kiss, how strange and eager they had both been, like two mutes trying to describe a freak storm.

"I had a funny week," she said.

This seemed to release him from whatever paralysis he'd fallen under. He walked to his car, opening the hatchback and putting the blanket in, shutting it with a neat slam. She backed up as he made his way to the front door.

"How long have you been here?" He smelled sweet and chlorinated, like a day by a pool.

"Not long."

"Huh." Jamie unlocked the door and pushed it open, motioning
for her to enter first. She walked through a foyer to a sunny, sunken
living room with two couches. Amina walked toward the smaller one
as Jamie set his keys down.

"Nice place."

"Have a seat."

She had not been so far off about the rugs and fertility sculptures. A
huge kilim calicoed the floor, and earthen pots of various sizes nestled in
niches. Pillows dotted the sofa, and in one corner a surprisingly ornate
wooden desk held neat piles of paper. Other than that, though, it felt like
a man's house, plantless, dusty, and with a barrenness she couldn't quite
place until she realized there was nothing hanging on the walls.

"Nice artwork."

"Want something to drink?" Jamie ducked through an archway,
and she heard the fridge door open. "I've got seltzer or beer."

"Just water is great."

The soft thud of cabinets turned into a running faucet, and a
cheerless, robotic woman's voice announced three messages. The first
beep was followed by a reminder from the dentist's office. The second
was a husky-voiced girl. "Hiii, Professor Anderson, I'm really sorry to
have to call you at home, I just have some questions about next semester," she said, sounding stoned and possibly naked. Jamie hit the fast-
forward button.

"James Mitchell Anderson," a laughing voice said after the third
beep, and Amina's stomach lurched with recognition. "Your nieces
would like to talk to you. We've made up this game with that photo
from the Quinns' party where we draw you new hair every week and
tape it on, and this week Cici—"

"Mohonk!" someone clearly little and delighted screamed in the
background.

"Yes," Paige laughed. "You have a Mohawk this week. Green, actually. But I think you'd totally dig it. Anyway, call us back. We'll be
around all afternoon."

"Paige has kids?" Amina asked as Jamie walked into the room with a glass of water and a Corona.

He tossed her a coaster before sitting on the opposite couch. "Three daughters. The youngest is six months old."

"Does she live here?"

"Yup."

Amina nodded. "Cool."

Jamie took a long swig of beer. His gaze bounced toward her and away.

"So how have you been?" she asked.

"Fine."

"Working a lot?"

"Yup."

A light-blue sedan pulled up in the driveway of the house across the way, and Amina watched it, breaking into a sweat. Did he want her to leave?

"I'm sorry I didn't call," she said. "I had a kind of weird week."

"No big." His fingers drummed against the bottle. "Four weeks."

"We got my dad's test results back. He has a tumor." She was too nervous to look right at him but sensed his flinch from her periphery. "In his brain. A brain tumor."

"When did you find out?"

"The day after I saw you."

"I'm sorry to hear that."

Was he? Amina looked at Jamie's face for comfort or sympathy and instead saw reticence, like he did not want to catch what she had.

"So anyway, he's starting treatment next week." Her voice pinched with an effort to keep calm. She took another sip of water, her hurt blossoming quickly and more substantially than expected, like some stupid sponge toy that grows to five times its original size in water. So this was what it felt like to tell other people the truth. It felt like shit.

"Anyway." She stood up. "So that's what has been up with me. What about you? Seen any of your former students? How is Maizy?"

Jamie frowned. "What are you doing?"

She was pacing. Amina shrugged.

"Are you mad at me?" he asked.

"Are you mad at me?"

"A little."

She stopped. "Wait, really?"

"Yeah."

"Because I didn't call? I just told you we found out—"

"I know. I know that."

"Then what—"

"I don't know. It's not like you don't have a good reason. But you asked if I was mad, and I am, kind of."

There was something about the reasonableness with which he said this, the entitlement, that made her want to reach over and throttle him. Amina spun on her heel, heading toward the front door.

"Don't do that."

"What?" She turned around. "What am I doing?"

"Don't turn me into some asshole."

"You're doing that all on your own."

Jamie put his beer down. "Sit down."

"What for?"

"Can you please sit back down?"

Amina wavered in the middle of the room, momentum shooting off to equally impossible outcomes. She wanted to be back in Seattle. She wanted to be in her car already, driving back to Corrales. She wanted to be back to the night in the park, with his collarbone on her tongue. Jamie motioned to the spot next to him on the couch. She walked toward him and sat stiffly. A fresh puff of dust motes flew into the air between them.

"I just thought you had left," he said after a moment. "And that sucked, but then at least I had something to tell myself. Man, she felt so much she just had to *leave*." He laughed self-consciously. "And then it turns out you were here ignoring my messages."

His face turned toward her like a bruised flower, something sad and too delicate in its dark center, and she shrank a little.

"I didn't want to talk about it," she said.

He did not look particularly moved by this information.

"I just . . . I kept thinking once we knew for sure what we were dealing with, we could just tell everyone at once and get it over with.

But every week it seems like we know less, and now it's just . . ." She leaned back against the couch, the fight in her replaced with a calmness bordering on exhaustion. "The biopsy showed low-grade cells, but the problem is that might just be that small area of the tumor, and it might be worse somewhere else. My dad thinks it is, anyway. And then he seemed totally fine until this afternoon, and now he's . . ." Amina snorted, gesturing into the air. "And honestly? I don't want to talk about this with you. Not now. This is like the biggest boner killer I could think of."

She watched a piece of fluff wander through the air in front of her, horribly aware of the silence that descended.

Jamie cleared his throat. "Did you just say boner—"

"Yes. I don't even know where that came from. Fourth grade."

"It's sexy."

"Really?"

"No. But it's sweet. That you were thinking about that, I mean."

She pushed her leg against his on the couch, thinking about how saying a small, true thing for the first time felt much scarier than not saying anything at all.

"I don't know," Jamie sighed. "It's not like I'm some expert at this. To be honest, I was a total dick when my mom got sick." He shook his head. "But I think you go one of two ways with this stuff—you either try to be good to the people around you, or you give yourself a free pass to act however badly you want to, you know?"

Amina nodded. He was right. Even if she hadn't been appallingly close to his neck, the smell of his skin filling her with relief and arousal, she would have had to cop to that.

"I'm sorry," she said.

His hand was on her leg. Amina watched as it slid down to her knee and back up, his fingers stroking the inside of her thigh.

"So what happened today to finally get your ass over here?" he asked, and she shook her head. She pulled his hand higher and watched gratefully as it disappeared under her skirt. She would tell him later, when they rose from the couch parched and flushed, ready to guzzle down the entire fridge's worth of beverages, but for right now, she was ready to stop talking.

———

The entire household was asleep by the time Amina got home that night, which made the next thing she needed to do infinitely easier. She found Prince Philip curled up against the coolest patch of the dining room floor and tugged at his collar until he stood up.

"Come," she said. He padded after her, through the living room, kitchen, and laundry room, out onto the porch, where they stopped just long enough to pick up a flashlight. Amina opened the screen door that led to the yard.

"Go," she said.

She stumbled after him in the dark, trying to stifle the feeling that she was playing the part in the movie where the well-meaning woman gets murdered in her mother's eggplant patch.

"Stay away from the beans," she hissed once they were between the rows of vegetables. The dog went down the row that led to the trellis, and she walked down the other row, passing beds of lettuces, cucumbers, and snap peas, as she made her way to the back of the garden. Kamala's bucket of garden tools waited mid-row, and she picked a small shovel out of it before continuing to the back.

"So what did he say about the jacket?" Jamie had asked as they sat on his kitchen counter that evening, passing a bottle of seltzer back and forth.

"He said that he was sorry."

"That's all?"

"What else would he say?"

"Well, why did he put it there in the first place?"

Amina frowned. "Did you hear the part about the tumor?"

"Yes," Jamie said, squeezing her leg reassuringly. "But that's medical. The doctors will deal with that. But what was he trying to do? That's the part you've got to figure out." There was an earnest, Hardy Boy–ish glint on his face that made her uneasy.

"I just told you he won't talk about it," Amina said.

Jamie scratched his neck. "Is the jacket the only thing he buried?"

Now, in the dark, she scooped through the damp soil, trying not to think too hard about the snakes that roamed the garden regularly or made temporary houses from sun-warmed spades and bags of blood meal. Her hand brushed something hard, and she recoiled, fumbling for the flashlight.

Glass. Not a shard, but a nice, rounded edge, which when pried loose appeared to be a jar of something. For one horrible moment, she thought she was looking at human organs, but a longer, calmer look revealed nothing more terrifying than Kamala's homemade mango pickle. She put it down next to her and kept digging. Not ten seconds later she hit a cardboard corner, which turned into a warped copy of Nat King Cole's *Love Is the Thing*. Just under that, the gilded cup of Thomas's BEST DOCTORS IN THE SOUTHWEST 1991 trophy lay on its side. A few minutes later, as she stared at the glittering clump of Thomas's car keys, Amina shut her eyes, submerged by the panicky feeling that the objects had not been hidden so much as they'd been biding their time, waiting for her to find them. She stood up, feeling sick.

"Fucking *fuck*," she said out loud, and across the garden Prince Philip wagged his tail guiltily, sending the bean pods into silvery applause.

"Let's go," she said, walking toward the gate with everything jumbled in her hands. Prince Philip did not follow her. She shined the flashlight on him. "Hey, move it."

He walked toward her reluctantly, one long bean disappearing under the soft curtain of his lip, but stopped, looking dolefully back at the trellis. She did not have patience for this. Amina stalked the twenty feet toward him, grabbed his collar, and wheeled around. A flash of white burst into her line of vision. She gasped. There, waiting politely at the side of the path she had just walked down, was a brand-new pair of white Velcro tennis shoes.

CHAPTER 2

The next morning, the pounding would not stop.

"Hullo? Ami? Hullo?" Fattened through the fish-eye lens, Sanji's nose had turned into its own island of sorts, as craggy and pockmarked as any dotting the South Pacific in recent millennia. Her eyes, in comparison, were hard, distant stars. She turned her head, blinking rapidly into the peephole, and rang the doorbell again.

"Who is it?" Amina stalled.

"Surely you are not pretending that you haven't been staring at me for the last half minute?"

Amina opened the door. "Hi, Sanji Auntie."

Cool, flabby arms squeezed her around the middle hard, more a Heimlich than an actual greeting. She peered behind Amina to the empty hallway. "So? Where are your parents?"

"Running a few errands."

"Really? Where?"

"I'm not exactly sure. They didn't tell me."

Sanji tugged her ear sharply. "Liar!"

"Ow!"

"They are in the hospital itself! Bala called me half an hour ago saying Chacko called her and your parents were checking in for some scans! Are you people going to talk to us or what? Because if you aren't, we would like to know right now and be done with it!" Sanji breathed hard, dabbing at her upper lip with her chuni.

"Done with it?" Amina asked skeptically, but her aunt's glare was unrelenting. She shifted tactics. "How did Chacko Uncle know it was a scan?"

"Excuse me?"

Amina raised her eyebrow.

"Well, of course he snooped around!" Sanji bellowed, incredulous. "You think that is some problem? One month and we haven't heard one word from any of you, and now you want to talk patient-doctor confidentiality nonsense? Really?"

Really, Amina did not. Really, she wanted to shut the door and go back upstairs, to try to get a handle on what she would need to shoot the Lucero wedding that weekend, or maybe just not think about anything at all.

"Well, don't just stand there looking pathetic," Sanji ordered. "Give me some tea."

They walked back to the kitchen. Amina motioned to a counter stool, and Sanji took it, fluffing herself up and resettling like a pigeon in an airshaft.

"Caffeinated okay?" Amina asked.

"Decaf is for children and Americans."

The cabinet was stocked like a bunker, Typhoos, Red Labels, Darjeelings, and Assams packed tightly. Amina wiggled a box loose. "Dessert?"

"No, thank you."

"Mom made a crème caramel."

Sanji sniffed suspiciously at this information. "Just a bit, please."

Amina found the right Tupperware, spooned a generous amount into a dish, and handed it to her aunt, who was frowning at Amina's hips.

"Looking too thin, Ami."

"Am I?" Amina looked down in surprise. "Weird."

"Weird." Sanji snorted. "My God, what I would eat with your no-tummy tummy! Pastries! Villages!"

Amina turned toward the stove, adjusting the kettle and watching Sanji eat the crème caramel through the reflection in the microwave oven. It was actually nice to have her in the house, her solid, shouty anger a relief from all the other, undirected craziness.

Milk, sugar, a bowl of mixture, two spoons, two mugs of tea. A minute later Amina set everything on the counter between them and sat down, instantly more jittery, like there was a panic button on her ass. She watched the cream cloud the tea and stirred as slowly as possible.

"Ami?"

She looked up, surprised by the reciprocal nervousness in her aunt's face. "You're okay, baby?"

"I just don't really know how to start."

"Perhaps the beginning?"

There was a crack in the wall behind Sanji's head. Amina watched it and said, "Dad has a brain tumor. He's been undergoing radiation for a few weeks, and now he's getting another scan to see if it's helping. He can't work because he's seeing things that aren't there."

Sanji's face did not move. The rest of her did not move, either.

"Brain tumor?" she repeated.

Amina nodded.

Sanji clapped a firm hand over her own mouth, but not before a gasp escaped, stabbing the air in a way that made Amina not want to breathe, for fear that the feeling was contagious.

"It's a glioma," Amina continued after a moment, partly for clarity and partly to sop up the shocked silence seeping from her aunt. Couldn't she just say something? Offer some twitch of reassurance? Several seconds slid by, each more damning than the last.

"We're taking care of it," Amina added in desperation, and at last her aunt responded.

"Oh, baby! Oh no!" Sanji lunged across the counter toward her and was bounced back by her breasts twice before she jumped out of her seat and just came around. Her hug was swift and brutal, a punch of perfume tinged with slight body odor. She stroked Amina's back manically. "You poor girl! My gods, and I came here yelling at you!" She pulled back, patting a thick hand over Amina's face. "Are you okay? Of course you're not, all alone with this! Oh, why didn't I just listen? Of course it wouldn't be some simple-simple thing! Chacko himself said it must be bad, and Raj said no, Thomas would of course tell us, and then Bala said one of her sisters only told her last month itself about some lump in her breast five years ago—can you imagine? But then again, what does one hope to get from a far-away sister in that situation? Not like family in the same city, no? Where we can all take care of each other?" She looked beseechingly at Amina.

"We didn't want to worry anyone."

Her aunt was nodding before she could even finish. "Yes, yes, of course. And Mummy? How is she?"

"Hard to tell."

"Ach." Sanji squeezed Amina's elbow. "Must be a terrible shock."

"I don't know. I mean, part of me thinks that must be what it is, but after that first day, she hasn't really talked about it, either. I think she just thinks he's going to be okay."

Sanji's eyes filled with worry. "It's bad?"

"That's what Dr. George said."

"Anyan George? That young fellow?"

"Yes," Amina said, confused about whether this was an accusation of some sort. "And the radiologist."

"My gods," Sanji whispered again, shaking her head. "And you, baby? How are you doing?" Amina shrugged, and Sanji kneaded her arms like they were dough. "Pish! What am I saying? Of course you are not okay! All this horrible business and no one to shoulder the burden! And now your mother has gone off and made French foods!"

"It's fine," Amina said miserably, and Sanji squeezed harder.

"But I don't understand why you didn't just call us. Not wanting to bother? Must have been terrible, all this testing and waiting without anyone else to help! We would have been there!"

"Dad wasn't up to it, and I just felt . . ." Amina shook her head, suddenly claustrophobic. She pushed back from Sanji, taking a deep breath. "Anyway, there's not really much you can do."

Sanji tugged her own nose, looking perplexed. "And you say he's seeing things?"

"Yeah."

"What things?"

"Just, you know." Amina shifted. "Like, hallucinations."

"Rabbits?"

"What? No, people. His family in India."

Sanji's mouth fell open. "The ones who burned up in the fire?"

"Yes. Although not just them. Apparently he had an incident at the hospital, which is part of the reason he's not working for right now." Amina stopped talking, wanting to tell Sanji about the previous night's findings and yet feeling protective of her father's standing in the family. What if Raj and Chacko thought less of him? What if Bala couldn't keep her mouth shut?

Sanji looked at her watch. "So they will be there all morning?"

"Yeah."

"Good." She looked around the kitchen and as if checking off an item on a to-do list, shoved one last good bite of crème caramel in. "So I'll just go sit with them."

"Wait, now?"

"Of course!"

"But . . . well . . . I mean, they don't know you know. I'm not sure if they want anyone to—"

"Too bad! I'm going. And when the others know, they will come, too. Enough is enough. One more month hiding and you'll all be mad, no? And then where will we be?"

"But Sanji Auntie—"

"No *but*ing! You really think they will be so upset? Ridiculous!"

"I just think—"

"No thinking! Amina Eapen, you listen to me, okay? We are all we have here. Do you understand? That is *it*. And we can all talk about old times and Campa Cola and wouldn't it be nice if we could go back, but none of us ever want to go back. To what? To who? Our own families can't even stand us for longer than a few days! No, we are home already, like it or not, and that's how we . . ." Sanji gulped furiously. "*Your parents,*" she began again, her voice trembling. "They welcomed us, no? Raj and I, all those one million years ago. Didn't give one sticky fig who we were or where we came from, just invited us over for samosas and tea, and poof! Instant family. Bond made! And like that we'll go on, nah?" She turned abruptly and began walking to the door, leaving Amina to follow. "So I will go and call later. And I'll talk to Raj and Chacko and Bala, and don't worry, I will tell her to keep her mouth shut for the sake of all involved. You've told Dimple?"

"Not yet. I will."

"Do it today, okay? She should know. It's not good to shut everyone out this way."

They had reached the door, and Sanji tugged it open, squinting into the flat midday light. She turned to Amina, folding her into one last hug before making her way down the stairs and back to the car she had left stranded in the middle of the driveway.

Back up in her room, Amina looked out the window to the yard below, acutely aware of how quiet the house had grown. Lately, with Thomas not working and Kamala trying her hand at puff pastry, there was almost always someone around, someone shuffling below and making it feel like even if they weren't quite in sync, they were a team of sorts, a little tight unit. Now, with Sanji on her way to the hospital, Amina was alone with the unease of having brought the others into the mix. It wasn't that she doubted their love or intentions, but the weight of that love would be no small thing. What would they do with everyone else's worry on top of their own? Thomas did not weather other people's concern well. He was not going to be happy with her.

She missed making her father happy. The realization came to her whole, like an egg dropped into a waiting palm, and she turned it over, surprised and embarrassed by its familiarity. For years, she had banked on being the person her father kept closest, but now, with her parents at the hospital while she hid in the house, she had to admit that this was no longer true. It had been weeks since Thomas had invited her onto the porch, and longer since she had seen him relax in her company. And while she knew he wasn't petty enough to blame her for his diagnosis, she also knew that getting him to the doctor had tainted her somehow, leaving her outside his confidence. She chafed at the memory of the day before, his sullen look on the porch, the way she had kept hammering questions at him, as though that would have worked. And then Kamala, of all people, doing the right thing.

The phone rang, startling her. She stared at it for a moment before picking it up.

"We need to talk." It was Dimple, sounding, if not frantic, then breathy, like she had just gone for a jog for the first time in thirty years.

"Hey. Good. Yes."

"Good?"

"No, not good. I just mean, good that you called. I was going to call you. We need to talk."

"I know." Dimple hesitated. "Wait. Do you know?"

The other line beeped. "Shit, can you hold on, Dimple? It's probably my parents."

"No, wait—"

"Just a sec." Amina clicked over. "Hello?"

"YOU LYING SHIT!"

Amina's heart skittered. "Jane?"

"Are you fucking kidding me?"

Amina's mind raced, her pulse beating uncomfortably fast. "You don't like the quinceañera pictures?"

"Don't be coy with me, sweetheart. It doesn't suit either of us."

"Jane, wait, just hold, okay?" Amina swallowed whole words, trying not to sound as scared as she felt. "I'm not sure what—but—can—let me just get off the other line."

"Don't you DARE fucking—"

She clicked over, the silence a welcome foxhole.

"Ami?" Dimple asked. "Is that you?"

"Holy crap."

"What?"

"It's Jane. She's pissed. I've gotta call you back."

"NO! Talk to me first."

"What?"

"We need to talk."

"Later, Dimple, she's—" Jane hung up, the sound of her disconnection sending a flare across the murk of Amina's confusion. "Wait. Why is Jane yelling at me?"

"Well, first of all, Jane needs to calm down and understand that—"

"WHY IS JANE YELLING AT ME?"

"Because she thinks the show is bad for business. Okay. So." Dimple paused. "I went ahead and had ten of your prints matted and framed. I'm showing them with Charles White."

"*What?*"

"Occasional accidental, the everyday tragedy."

The panic that filled Amina was both swift and unexpected, like stepping in a puddle and getting caught in a riptide. Her legs shook. She looked down at her knees and then up at her hand, which had locked around one of the bedposts.

"Occasional *slash* accidental *colon,* documenting the everyday tragedy," Dimple clarified.

Amina squeezed the bedpost harder. "You . . . ?"

"Stop. Please don't panic. It's going to be amazing."

"You can't do it."

"Of course I can."

"No, you *can't.* She'll kill me. I promised."

"No you didn't. Not in writing."

"What?"

"I checked."

Checked? Amina's eyes spun around the bedroom. "Dimple, I told her I wouldn't even *take* them. It will kill her business."

"Oh, c'mon. Is that what she told you?"

"She's right! People don't want to see their bad shit memorialized—not by the hired help! What were you thinking? Oh my God, she's going to sue me."

"She can't sue you. I mean, she can, but she won't win. They're not her pictures."

"Yes they are."

"No, they are *not.* Jane doesn't own the rights if the clients have bought their negatives. So as long as the clients sign the release, we've done nothing wrong."

Amina blinked, stunned. "You can't really believe that."

"Why wouldn't I?"

"She took me *in,* Dimple. She trained me."

"Oh Jesus. You're not going to, like, recite the entire script for *The Color of Money,* are you? Because the whole rookie-screws-the-master thing is played out. She didn't teach you shit about taking these kinds of pictures. This is what you do. This is what you've *always* done. Jane doesn't want anyone to see your best work? Fine. That's her business. But it can't be yours."

"They're her clients. They'll never use her again if they see them."

"That's not what Lesley Beale says."

It felt like years since Amina had even thought about the Seattle socialite. "What the hell does Lesley have to do with it?"

"I went to your office to see if there were more photographs, and found the one in the manila envelope on your desk. The naked brides-maid on the coats with Brock Beale? Holy fucking hell. *Amazing.* The grimace on his face. It might actually be my favorite."

"Oh my God." Amina sat on the bed. "What have you done?"

"Stop acting like it's bad, will you? I've gotten the permission to show your work from the clients who own the negatives."

"You showed Lesley that picture?" Her throat felt hot and vomity.

"Yes, obviously. I had to. She *loved* it, by the way. I mean, are you kidding? And we can talk all day about her art history degree and the 'truth of vision' and the 'integrity of the moment'—which we did, by the way, and which I might actually agree with if agreeing with that woman didn't make me want to drive a stake through my own heart—but make no mistake: That photo is the best thing that could have ever happened to her claim to the Beale fortune, and she knows it. She wants it up. She wants the whole fucking show up so it doesn't look like the vendetta it is. Why do you think she's helping us?"

"Lesley's getting a divorce?"

"Oh, right, you missed that. Yeah, it's big news out here. Apparently that douchebag has been screwing half of the—"

"*Helping* you?"

"Us, Amina, she's helping *us.* She's calling the clients personally. Talking about the value of art, the honor of honesty, the exclusivity of being included, blah blah blah. Honestly, who fucking cares what she's saying? It's working. We've gotten six out of ten permissions so far. We just need to—"

"No. Stop. I'm not going to do it."

"Because of Jane?"

"Yes, because of Jane!"

"So take her out of it. What's she going to do to you?"

"I am not getting fired over this!"

"Amina," Dimple said, taking a breath. "You're already fired."

"That's not true." She knew even as she said it that it probably was. Dimple was a bully, not a liar, and more to the point, it felt inevitable. Didn't she always know Jane was going to find out and fire her? Wasn't it exactly what she had feared every time she got another print?

"She told her staff," Dimple said. "Apparently there was some kind of shakedown over there this morning. She's trying to figure out who else knew."

Amina hunched over, riding out the fresh wave of guilt that crashed over her. Had Jane sniffed Jose out, found evidence of his prints? "Did she fire anyone else?"

"No idea."

Her hand hurt. Amina let go of the bedpost, slowly unclenching her fingers. "She's going to hate me."

"She might. Then again, she might not, once she calms down. That's why I'm saying take her out of the equation. A, because you're already fired, and B, because you don't actually know this is going to hurt her business. Neither does she. It's just an assumption. I mean, let's say this show goes up and absolutely nothing bad happens to the business. Do you still feel like shit?"

"That's not the point."

"Fine. Then why did you keep them at all?"

"What?"

"The prints. Why bother?"

"I . . . I don't know."

"Really? You don't? You don't know that you've been hoarding them in your closet—your *closet,* by the way, worst metaphor come to life—because you secretly wish other people could see them? Because I know that. It seems pretty obvious, actually. And why wouldn't you? They're fucking good. They're your best work. I mean, listen, you can tell me that isn't true, and that they were really just for your own viewing pleasure and you want things to go back to the way they were, with you pretending that your life doesn't suck now that you've traded your ambition for America's belated goddamn moral crisis, and you know what? I will give them back. I really will. I will give them back and you will just have to forgive me at some point in the future, because no matter how right I am, I'm actually not willing to have you hate me over this. Okay? But you have to tell me that that's really what you want, not just some sad shit you like to play out because you weren't loved enough as a kid or whatever."

Amina was silent, lying back on the bed, the phone next to her head. Her cousin's voice no longer filled her entire ear, just the space near it. It felt much less personal this way; the difference between getting blood drawn and getting a mosquito bite. It also allowed her the distance to admit that something was happening every time Dimple said *best work*. It felt like eating or fucking or otherwise having the right thing go in the right place. It felt primordially good.

"Who else's permission did Lesley get?" she asked.

There was a pause, and then the sound of shuffling paper. "Okay, so the Lorbers, obviously. The passed-out grandma reminds me of Snow White in the coffin. Dara Lynn Rose is fine with us using the one where she looks like she's going to kill her husband with the hairbrush. And Caitlin McCready signed off on her sisters wrestling over the bouquet. She wanted a signed printed copy, too, which is what I'm offering people if they seem hesitant. Um, what else . . . Oh! Lorraine Spurlock looking up at her father all moon-eyed. Is that as gross as I think it is?"

"It's her stepfather."

"Disgusting. But good for us. Lila Ward is fine with the ring bearer wetting his pants, the Abouselmans signed off on sad wheelchair grandpa on the dance floor, the Freedens are pretty close to releasing Dad handing the check to the caterers, and the Murphys haven't decided on the best man pissing in the corner of the tent."

"That's eight."

"Yeah." Dimple took a breath. "Jane owns the puking bridesmaid. I thought she might want to share it. It looks better for the business, ultimately, if she's on board."

"Let me guess how that went over."

"Mmm."

"And the other?"

"Bobby McCloud."

"No."

"*Yes*. It's the reference point. The catalyst. It makes everything that follows make sense."

"But it's not even a wedding photo."

"No, it's a Microsoft party-boat photo. It works, trust me. I will make it work." Dimple shut what sounded like a filing cabinet. "Listen, we are going to retell that story, okay? Do you get that? This is your chance to set the record straight."

She had switched tones again, imbuing her voice with the kind of self-importance that had served her well in the gallery community, those trusted to be the arbitrators of meaning when the artists behind the work had lost track of their own narratives. A pulse beat between Amina's eyes. She eased it with her thumb.

"Ami? You there?"

"Kind of."

"I'm sorry I didn't call you this week," Dimple said after a moment. "I got your messages and all this stuff was going down and I just wanted to get some of it sorted before I talked to you. Anyway, how are things? When are you coming home?"

It seemed impossible now to have a conversation about anything else. Amina took a deep breath, trying to gear up. She turned her head slightly, her father's trophy sneaking into the periphery of her vision, and waited for the news to find its way out of her.

CHAPTER 3

"I think," Jamie said that evening, his heart thundering under her ear, "you just raped me."

They were on the floor in between the foyer and the living room. Overhead, ceiling fans spun in lazy circles.

Amina rolled off of him, onto the tile, where her underwear found her ankle and clung to it. "Really? You seemed like a willing participant."

"No ma'am." Jamie let his hand fall against her belly. "I swear to God, I just answered the door."

Amina laughed. She hadn't meant to come at him that way, so fast, so grabby. She turned her head to look at him. Dots of sweat lined his upper lip and hairline. He looked a little overwhelmed.

"Was it . . . too much?"

"No way. I just wasn't expecting you."

She sat up, found her shirt, and slipped it over her head. "So you want me to go? Maybe come back later?"

He cupped her calf, squeezed it. "Don't be a freak."

Amina smiled to show him she was not a freak. She stood up and stepped over him, walking toward the kitchen.

"Can I get you something to drink?" she asked. "You have seltzer and beer."

"I don't have beer, actually. We drank it all last night."

"Do you have seltzer?"

. "Yeah. You hungry? I could make us something."

She did not want to eat, possibly for months, but Amina made the appropriate noises of enthusiasm. Ever since her parents had returned from the hospital, shrunken like old apples and unable to say anything beyond the fact that the results weren't looking great, she had felt weirdly high. Not stoned, but toxic—the kind of high you get on gas fumes in your own garage.

Jamie walked down the hall toward his bedroom, taking off his shirt. "Just let me jump into the shower real quick."

Amina got herself a glass of water and sat down at his kitchen table, an old red Formica job from the late sixties, red with a slightly lighter harlequin print. A single paper napkin lay on it, and she folded over an edge.

"So how have you been?" Jamie called from the bathroom, peeing. She shuddered. Pee talkers baffled her. How could they do that? Give you no opportunity to not listen?

"Fine. You?"

"Fine. Good, actually."

He had a good view of the park from his kitchen, the tops of the trees, the lush, interlaced branches that seemed to hold the darkening sky up behind them. Amina tore a bit of the napkin off, listening to the screech of the shower turning on, and wondering what it meant about their future that Jamie showered with the door open. She was a closed-door showerer, a hoarder of steam and privacy, and for a minute it seemed like that meant something, then the sweet, rich smell of deodorant soap wafted down the hallway, filling her with a satisfaction so complete that even ripping up the napkin felt rewarding. Jamie turned off the shower and went to his room. A few minutes later he emerged, wearing the same shorts but otherwise clean in a way that made her want to get him dirty again.

"You're getting tan." She tapped the bridge of his nose, where the contrail left by sunglasses made his eyes look greener.

"I was out at the pool all day."

"Oh, yeah? What pool do you go to?"

"Paige's. She'd love to see you sometime, by the way."

"Yeah." She looked back down at the napkin, folding the remains into a tidy square. When she looked up, Jamie was studying her with a funny look.

"Is that weird or something?"

"Not, it's not that, just that I'm . . ." There was no good finish to the sentence, Amina realized, *uncomfortable,* and *nervous,* and *scared to see Paige as a grown-up* not being feelings she wanted to share. "Hungry. I'm hungry. You're making dinner?"

Jamie nodded slowly, as though unwilling to break from his thought. "Actually, I was thinking in the shower—what do you think about going to the Frontier instead?"

"I think you're a genius."

Of all the things Amina loved about the Frontier Restaurant (its tacky faux-barn exterior, the walls jumbled with bad desert paintings, the tortilla maker spouting fat gobs of flour like something out of a Mexican Willy Wonka's), she loved the orange vinyl booths in the front the best. Right across from the ordering counter, they offered a steady view of the kitchen and the clientele of doctors and gallery owners and car salesmen and students and junkies who came in all day, every day.

"Who do you think gets the bigger socioeconomic cross section of Albuquerque: this place or the DMV?" she asked, stealing an onion ring off Jamie's plate.

"Here for sure. You sure you don't want to get more to eat?"

"I'm not that hungry."

"You ate your dinner and half of mine."

"I did not!"

"A third. Definitely a third."

"Wow. Territorial. Did you count the actual onion rings I took?"

"Ninety-seven." Under the table, Jamie's knee brushed against hers; it felt hairy and slightly damp and strangely not off-putting. "So you're going to do it?"

"I guess so."

"You haven't decided?"

"No, I've decided. I just feel funny about it."

Jamie grabbed a stray onion ring and dragged it through ketchup. "When is the opening?"

"September."

"Huh."

"Yeah. Hopefully I can go." She tried not to think of her parents' faces as they emerged from the car that afternoon. They hadn't been mad about Sanji showing up, or at least they hadn't said as much to Amina, but then they hadn't said much at all.

"How's your dad doing?" Jamie asked.

Amina shook her head, not trusting herself to talk about it without getting upset.

"Any word on the prognosis?"

She shook her head again.

"So you don't want to talk about it."

"I just don't have a lot to say about it."

Jamie took a sip of soda. "Just using me for the sex, huh?"

"That's not true," Amina said, realizing too late that a serious answer turned it into a serious question. Jamie said nothing, rattling the ice around in his cup.

She took a breath. "It's just my whole life, you know, I just thought doctors knew things the rest of us didn't. Like they were privy to some metaphysical library or something."

"Metaphysical library?"

"Just go with me here."

"Are the books there written in invisible ink?"

"No, dummy, ghost blood."

Jamie looked at her appreciatively. "Go on."

"And now, I'm just so, uh"—she laughed to cover up the way her eyes had begun to tear up—"I'm just so fucking disappointed right now. I mean, seriously? Nobody knows *anything*. It's all just tests and results and more tests, but where's the part where they take you into a room and say *He has two months to live* or *That was a close call, but it looks like he's going to make it*? Where is the part where I stop making deals with the universe like it's some karmic pawnshop that will let him get well if I'm a better person?"

Jamie handed her a napkin, and she pressed it over her face, willing herself to pull it together.

"Shit," she said. "I'm sorry. Are we making a scene?"

"Nope. Just you."

She laughed and crumpled the napkin into a ball. "You were right, by the way. There were other things in the garden besides the jacket."

"Yeah?"

She told him, careful to keep her tone even but watching his face like it was an emergency weather report. The keys, she explained, had been lost right before she came back home. She had no idea about the mango pickle. But the rest of the items were definitely for members of her family—the trophy for Ammachy (Thomas had always joked that he should have sent it to her), the album for Sunil, the shoes for Itty, and of course the jacket for Akhil.

"Wow," Jamie said, looking more impressed than concerned. "So he's seeing your brother, too."

"I guess so. I don't know. It's sad."

"Is it? Whoa, don't give me that look, I'm just saying that it could be worse. At least he's seeing people he loved."

Amina looked at him. Really looked at him, at the light skein of wrinkles at the corners of his eyes and the little patch of stubble he'd missed by his sideburns and the unnerving way he was squinting at her like *she* was the one who had somehow overlooked the central truth about what was really happening. "Jamie Anderson, how did you of all people become such a Pollyanna?"

He picked up an onion ring, shoved it into his mouth whole. "Must have been the divorce."

The family descended the next day. First came Raj, hurrying up the steps with pale blue rings stamped under his eyes and a cardboard box that smelled several kinds of delicious, then Sanji, huffing under a bright red cooler.

"Hello, baby," she said, sticking out a cheek for Amina to kiss.

Bala came next, looking nervous and slightly corrosive in a bright yellow-green sari. She handed Amina a pack of store-bought cookies as Chacko parked the car.

"His brain? You're sure about this?" She said it as though it were a bad decision Amina was in the middle of contemplating: *You're sure you want to drop out of college? You're sure you want to give your father a tumor in his brain?* "Because Sanji said she saw them yesterday and he seems fine, but then of course she said he's been seeing things, so he must have been putting on a good show for her benefit, isn't it?"

"He's in the kitchen." Amina motioned to the doorway. "Go see for yourself."

Chacko inspected his way across the driveway, taking note of the encroaching yard like it was a traffic violation. He marched up the stairs and squeezed her shoulder before stepping inside.

In the kitchen, Kamala and Thomas pulled dish after dish out of Raj's box, snapping and unsnapping lids.

"Chapati and beef *and* appam and stew?" Kamala frowned. "It's too much. We don't need."

"Speak for yourself, woman." Thomas pulled a chapati straight from the warming dish. "Between all your truffles and trifles, I haven't had a normal meal in weeks."

"You've had some nausea from the radiation?" Bala asked.

"Surprisingly little," Thomas said.

"I'll get you some beef." Raj motioned to Amina for a spoon. "You can also have the stew, of course. I just thought the beef would be nice and rich in irons. I also made a tomato carrot salad, for vitamin C. It helps with the absorption, isn't it?"

Thomas popped open another container. "My God! Samosas, too? You must have been cooking all night, Raj."

"No, no, I just made a few things. I also brought a little homemade yogurt in case you're having indigestion. Sanji says you're thinking of starting chemotherapy?"

"Looking into it. Just spoon some salad, too, nah?"

"Excellent, yes, absolutely. Sanji, can you look in the cooler for the kichadi?"

"Ho ho!" Thomas looked more genuinely excited than Amina had seen him in weeks. "Yes, please, and thank you!"

"He should be eating only bland foods," Chacko announced from the other side of the kitchen counter, where he had settled in. "Bland foods are better for nausea. Rice and curds, maybe a bit of dahl."

"Kichadi!" Sanji held up a Tupperware.

"Actually, though, what you can eat differs from person to person." Bala hovered uneasily in the doorway of the laundry room. "My sister with the breast cancer told me that everyone will say one thing or another about what you can eat and what you can do and how you will feel, but really it's the individual body."

"You have more plates?" Raj asked just as Amina was reaching for more. "Oh, good. Maybe get some bowls too, for the payasam."

"Payasam!" Thomas crowed, and even Kamala had to smile.

Half an hour later they sat around the living room with plates that had been filled and emptied twice, the ladies and Chacko perched on the couches while Amina, Thomas, and Raj tucked themselves against stray couch cushions. Poor Raj. Coming down from whatever high had enabled him to cook thirteen separate dishes, he looked particularly spent, the crepey skin under his eyes pouching. Sanji squeezed his shoulder and leaned back into the couch.

"So then, I suppose we should all just take turns at the hospital?" she said.

"Hmm?" Bala fiddled with her bangles.

"I was just thinking one of us should always be with him."

"*I'll* be with him," Kamala said.

"Of course, of course," Sanji said. "I'm just saying that one of us should be there for you, too."

"What me? Nothing is wrong with me!"

"Just to help," Amina said, nodding to Sanji. "I think it's a good idea, Ma. And you and I should take turns going, too."

"And you like this Anyan George?" Chacko asked Thomas.

"Yes. Bright kid."

"Never mind all that, can he *handle* this? I was a little surprised that you went with him over Rotter or Dugal."

Thomas's jaw tightened slightly. "I've shown my slides to Rotter as well; he agrees with everything Anyan has said and done so far."

"And what about here?" Sanji asked. "At home? Things are manageable?"

There was a long silence as the Eapens took pains not to look at one another.

"We just mean if there's something we can do—" Raj started.

"We're fine," Kamala said.

"And what about these hallucinations?" Chacko asked. "Are you having them regularly?"

Thomas hesitated, then nodded.

"And they're primarily auditory or visual?"

Amina watched her father shift on the floor, as if something was poking into his back. "They are both."

Chacko's mouth puckered like he'd tasted something sour.

"What's wrong with that?" Amina asked.

"It's unusual to have both," Chacko said. "The tumor is in the occipital lobe. As such, visual hallucinations are more common, but *hearing* things is highly unusual, unless it has spread to the—"

"We're looking into that," Thomas said quickly.

"It might also be bad spirits," Kamala said. "What? It happens. Oh, don't you look at me like that, Sanji Ramakrishna, this is a true and documented fact. You think all those monks in the sixteenth century were lying? Sometimes a toll in the body can be a portal to unwelcome forces."

Amina sighed. "It's a tumor, Ma. You saw the scan yourself."

"No one is saying there is no tumor! I'm just saying that it is entirely possible that he's being taken advantage of by dark forces *pretending* to be family. Why else would they be coming to see him? It's not like they saw each other so much in real life."

Thomas stood up, walking out of the room. "Anyone want something to drink?"

"Perhaps I was unclear." Chacko frowned. "I did not mean to suggest that hallucinations are uncommon at all, Kamala, I merely mean that seeing *and* hearing things at the same time is unusual, although if the brain is seizing—"

"My sister had hallucinations!" Bala said, nodding earnestly. "Every night, she would dream of an old ayah we had when we were girls, the nasty one with the crooked fingers who used to pinch us."

"That's a *dream,* not a hallucination," Kamala fumed.

"Can we get back to matters at hand?" Sanji bounced a little on the couch. "I think we should set up some sort of a schedule."

The others did not hear the latch of the front door clicking open, nor did they notice, as Amina did, how the floor in the dining room lightened with a sweep of sun. She rose and muttered "Bathroom," as if anyone was listening, and headed for the hall.

The front door was wide open, and through it, she could see her father standing in the driveway, looking down the tunnel of trees that rose up on either side of it like hands clasped in prayer. He looked small there, arms hanging loosely at his sides. He did not turn around as she approached, and for a moment she thought he might be seeing them again—Itty or Sunil or Akhil or whoever else might show up late on a Saturday afternoon, wanting to take a tour of the house. She reached for his dangling hand, surprised by the strength with which he grasped her back, the surety. He pulled her to him, his fingers entwining around her own until it hurt.

CHAPTER 4

"Hello, handsome. How are you doing?"

Thomas smiled at the dark-haired nurse who parted the curtains. "Maryann!"

"I tried to get out of working today when they told me you were coming." She smiled, her full Hopi cheeks growing fuller, and kissed Thomas on the cheek before taking a look at the IV. "So what's on the menu today? You started with Decadron?"

"Yup."

"And how'd it go?"

"Fine. Slight head rush in the first thirty seconds or so, but I normalized."

One week later, and at Thomas's insistence, they were starting chemo. A few experimental case studies at MD Anderson had left him convinced that it might work, and although Anyan George had been insistent about the low probability of that, he'd ultimately given in.

The nurse looked at Amina. "Dad's a real favorite around here, you know."

Amina knew. In the two hours since they'd checked in, at least half a dozen nurses and a handful of doctors had already stopped by with enthusiastic smiles and far too many questions about the presumably safe subject of Amina's life.

Maryann wrote something on her clipboard. "How is that arm feeling?"

"Good."

"Cold?"

Thomas hesitated, then nodded.

She patted Thomas's leg affectionately, sad under her smile in a way that made Amina both trust and fear her more than the others. "I'm going to get you a thermal pack. You nauseated yet?"

"It's my first day, you goose."

"Just testing." She slipped back out of the curtain with a wink.

"She's one of the good ones," Thomas said.

Amina nodded. He had said this about every nurse who stopped by.

Outside, the sharp incline of Central showed Albuquerque in strata: parking lots, billboards, apartment buildings, mountains.

"Is it weird being back here?" Amina asked. "At the hospital?"

"No. Not really. I thought it might be, but it's nice actually."

"Familiar?"

He smiled sadly. "It's funny, you do something your whole life . . . and then just the other day I thought, *What if I've touched my last brain?* You get so used to it, you know, using your hands in a certain way." He looked down at his own hands and flexed them, as if testing to see if they were really his. "How about you? How is work?"

"Oh, you know." Amina shrugged. She hadn't brought herself to tell either of her parents about Jane, though whether it was out of guilt or nervousness, she didn't quite know. "It's fine. Glad I'm finding work out here."

"When is your next event?"

"Saturday. The Luceros' son is getting married."

"My God, that's right. Am I supposed to go?"

"Only if you're feeling up to it."

Thomas nodded, looking down at the IV in his arm. He rubbed his shoulder and winced a little.

"Numbness," he said before she could ask. "It's normal. I'll probably lose some sensation in my arms and legs."

Amina stood up and walked to the window so he wouldn't see her face. It was getting harder not to spiral these days, to hear one thing and think of the next and the next, until all that was left was a closet of her father's sweaters and shoes.

"Are you in pain?" she asked.

"Not really. I've been lucky that way."

"Right." Small, furious tears sprang into the corners of her eyes.

"Come sit down, *koche*."

She turned from the window and walked back to the bed. What was it about hospital beds that made everyone look like puppet versions of themselves? She knew her father wasn't actually smaller than he'd been before the diagnosis, yet in the bed his diminishing felt palpable, like a sun setting without the beauty or relief. He put a hand on her arm. His fingers felt like ice.

"You doing okay?" he asked.

She nodded quickly.

"It can be hard, you know. The worrying."

"Dad, please."

"I'm just saying—"

"Can we talk about something else?" She sounded like a child and she knew it. Next to them, the drip beeped a few times.

Thomas took a breath. "How do you know when to take a picture?"

"What?"

"I always wonder. My pictures are terrible."

Amina smiled. He was right. His pictures were the worst, full of missing limbs, double chins, and grimaces.

"It's just practice."

"No, not true. I spent one whole month practicing, and they got worse, not better."

"What were you taking pictures of?"

"Your mother."

"Well, that's your problem. No one can get a good shot of Mom. She's a pretty woman who makes ugly faces."

"My God." Thomas looked both dumbstruck and relieved. "You're absolutely right."

Amina rubbed his cold hands with her own. His palms were peeling.

"Do you ever think about moving back here?" he asked.

"Yeah, sure," she said.

Thomas nodded, looking away so quickly that it took her a minute to understand that this had moved him, his mouth twitching as if he might cry.

"Okay, honey, let's get this on you," Maryann said, coming back through the curtain with the thermal pack and an extra blanket. Amina stood up, listening to the nurse coo at and cajole her father, expert at soothing the body's indignities.

"Your father is too sick to come," Kamala said the following Saturday. She stood by the doorway in Amina's room looking a little sick herself, her hands smoothing and resmoothing the crimson-and-purple sari she had put on for the Lucero wedding.

"Is he throwing up again?" Amina asked.

"Nothing to throw up! He won't eat!"

"That's normal." Amina had read the flyer the nurses had sent them home with so many times, she felt sure she could quote paragraphs at random. "He might not have an appetite for a week or so."

"He'll starve to death!"

"What about chicken broth?"

"Do you know how many chapatis your father can eat in one sitting?" Kamala looked around the room, as if daring the furniture to guess before announcing, "Eight!"

Amina counted rolls of film, packing them into her backpack. These midday weddings would kill her with their too bright, too flat light. Kamala took a step into the room.

"And now he's yelling at me to go. Telling me all the hovering is making him nervous. What else should I do? *Not* check on him? *Not* bring him food when he hasn't eaten for one whole day?"

"Maybe the smell of it is making him sicker."

"The everything is making him sicker! What are we supposed to do about it? Should have just stuck to the radiation!"

Amina took a deep breath. "Give it time."

"What is all this?" Kamala was looking at the things from the garden, which were still lined up on the desk and looking dustier by the day.

Amina sighed. "Yeah, I've been meaning to tell you. I found them in the garden. Near where the jacket had been. They were buried in the same bed. I dug it all up."

Kamala moved forward slowly, leaning down to look at the jar of mango pickle, then the album. She touched the shoes briefly before picking up the bunch of keys. "He told me he'd lost those."

Amina shrugged. "He probably thought he had."

She flinched as her mother dropped the keys and cried out as if she had been cut, understanding too late that it was too much, and that some measure of refuge had been sought out and not found in Amina's company. She moved hastily toward Kamala, hugging her rigid shoulders until she was gently rebuffed.

"You go," Kamala said. "I'll stay here with him."

"No, Ma, come. He wants you to. And I have to. And it's just down the road."

"But someone should stay."

"Prince Philip will stay."

Her mother shook her head at this but smiled a little.

"It's just for a few hours," Amina said, suddenly feeling hopeful, like getting out of the house would somehow change what was going on inside it. "And he can call us if he needs us, right? Let's just go."

"Fine," Kamala sighed, as if this was a war they had been waging for weeks instead of minutes. "Let's go."

The next morning Amina woke to a note.

Your father needs to eat.

It was written in her mother's tiny, curly script and taped to the upstairs bathroom mirror with no further instruction. Amina went downstairs. Her parents' room was empty, blinds raised, bed made.

"Dad?" she called. "Prince Philip?"

The kitchen was also empty, as was the living room. Amina poured herself a large glass of water and gulped it down, walking back to the laundry room. She found her father and the dog on a cot on the porch. Thomas lay like a plank, and over his lower legs, Prince Philip was trying valiantly to curl himself into a neat ball, his paws sliding over the edges. Sunlight streamed in, bleaching the walls and the tools and the piles of newspaper. The dog wagged its tail as Amina approached.

"Dad?"

Thomas's eyes rolled slowly in his sockets, resting on her. He hadn't been asleep.

"Hey." She turned a chair around to face the cot, sat in it. "What's up?"

He shrugged.

"You just wake up?" she asked.

Thomas shifted, prompting Prince Philip to rise and wobble off the cot.

"You want breakfast?" she asked.

Her father rolled onto one side, facing the wall opposite her. Prince Philip turned his head slightly, looking from father to daughter with canine nervousness. Poor dogs. All that intuition and no recourse.

"Dad?"

Thomas shook his head, muttering something. She leaned in closer. "What?"

"I did not ask you to come."

"I know that. Mom left me a note."

Thomas threw an arm over his head, blocking his ears. Prince Philip leaned in to sniff his armpit, and Thomas sprang up, grabbing his muzzle and shoving him away hard.

"Dad, stop! What are you—"

"I DON'T WANT YOU HERE!" Thomas shouted, rising up with his teeth bared, and Amina shot out of her chair, backing away fast. But Thomas was not looking at her. He was looking at the coatrack.

"Dad?"

"GET OUT."

"Who are you talking to?"

Thomas stared furiously at the coats, dragging his eyes from them to Amina as if they were conspiring together.

"Dad? Daddy?"

Thomas flinched. Dropped his head in his hands. Rocked back and forth with his arms wound tight around him. When Amina touched his shoulder, he shuddered.

"What can I do?" Amina asked, trying to hold his rounded shoulders, his flinching spine. "What helps?"

Her father shook his head.

Two nights later, lured by the scent of coriander and ginger, Thomas walked into the kitchen looking slightly puffy but determined. Curls matted around his head in tufts, and his raggy blue robe exposed two knees that looked only slightly larger than another man's Adam's apple.

"Kam—" he began, and his wife set a plate of chicken curry in front of him before he could finish. Two chapatis, one nice drumstick, and a little bit of curds later, he motioned for seconds.

"You going to eat?" he asked Amina between bites.

"Not yet."

It was only six-thirty. She watched her father gnaw the flesh from the bone, the recent loss of weight making him look more like an animal. Human bones devouring chicken bones. Meat eating meat.

Kamala set down a plate in front of her. She had another plate for herself and a foreboding look on her face, as if the only thing standing between Thomas and starvation was everybody eating chicken curry at once. Amina picked up a chapati without a word, and for the first time since the diagnosis, the Eapens enjoyed a regular dinner alone together, parsing the meat and the bread into smaller and smaller portions until they were sweeping their fingers over clean porcelain.

"Maybe I'll take a shower," Thomas said, but he made no move to leave the kitchen. He looked around with the heady gaze of a man stumbling home from a walkabout. "So what's been going on? Any news?"

You've been sick. You thought the coatrack was a person. Amina shrugged. "Not much."

"The Luceros' son got married," Kamala offered.

"Ah, yes, how was it?"

"Awful. Food was terrible. Bride was fat."

"Ma!"

"What? It's true."

"She was pregnant!"

"Well, she was fat, too," Kamala said, licking the pads of her fingers clean like a cat, and Thomas looked amused.

"What else?" he asked.

"I'm having a show," Amina said, and watched as the surprise prismed both her parents' faces. "Or, well, Dimple is. Dimple's gallery is showing my work."

"Wow!" Thomas smiled weakly. "Will people see it?"

"That's the idea."

"When?" Kamala asked.

"It's in September. I'll probably head back for the weekend or something."

"Good for you. Excellent, excellent." Thomas squinted at her like he was seeing her in the future, when she'd finally become the person he always knew she'd be. "What photos? Any we've seen?"

"Not really, no. Some newer stuff. Mostly weird moments at weddings."

"Jane must be so proud."

Amina nodded. *Sure. Why not?*

Thomas stood up, uncurling his spine slowly, and picked up his plate.

"I've got it." Kamala reached for it. "You go take that shower. I put a stool inside in case you need it."

"Pshht! I'm not an invalid, woman."

"I know that. It's only for just in cases." She smiled shyly at him, sweetly, Amina thought, filled with an eagerness to reassure him that there was no frailty she couldn't forget, no action she couldn't rewrite,

and it occurred to Amina that there was never going to be a good time
to talk about what was going on.

"I found a bunch of your things in the garden," she said.

"You want rasmalai for dessert?" Kamala asked, shooting her a
look.

"What things?" Thomas asked.

Amina told him, feeling bad about the way his eyes dropped to the
brick floor, the way he reached for the counter, looking newly nauseated. He sat back down heavily.

"You don't remember putting them there?" Amina asked.

"No."

"Doesn't matter," Kamala said. "Nobody cares anyway."

"None of it?"

He looked at her uneasily. "Not really."

"I thought you had maybe left the shoes for Itty."

"Don't be an idiot!" Kamala huffed. She snatched Amina's plate
away, taking it back to the sink. Thomas looked at her carefully.

"That's who you were seeing the other, day, right?" Amina asked.

Her father's brow knotted, as if he was trying to locate his own
memory. After a long moment, he nodded.

"And the trophy was for Ammachy?"

"Amina," Kamala called over her shoulder. "Leave it."

"I just, I don't want you to feel like you can't talk about it," Amina
said. "You're seeing things. You can't help it. I don't know why we have
to be so weird about it."

"No one is being weird! Who is being weird?"

"You are, Ma."

With surprising force, Kamala lifted a plate above her head and
threw it. It shattered in the sink, releasing a live, buzzing silence.
Amina watched her mother's small body hunch over, hands clutching
the edges of the sink like she would lift the whole thing and slam it
down if she could.

"Itty asked, so I gave them," Thomas said.

Amina nodded calmly, trying to keep her face from registering
any hint of worry, but something in her chest bunched up on itself,
like a cat being cornered. From her periphery, she saw Kamala bend

into the sink and begin picking up the pieces, which scritched against one another like beetle shells.

"Did Ammachy ask for the trophy?"

"No," Thomas said, looking uncomfortable. "I just thought she would like it."

"And the album?"

"That was for Sunil when he . . ." Thomas looked helplessly at the counter.

"He what?"

"He wanted to hear it."

It wasn't stupid to think that talking would make things better. Weren't there entire schools of psychology dedicated to that premise? Wasn't the television talk show confessional born from it? Still, as Thomas leaned in and told Amina about his last few months (haltingly at first, but then faster and more freely, as if each word were water carving out a bigger channel from brain to mouth), as he spoke about not only a brief encounter with Derrick Hanson, but whole weeks of Itty, Sunil, Ammachy, and even Divya ("My God, was she always such a hand wringer?"), she found herself feeling distinctly worse.

Everyone was exactly as they had been before, her father said, no kinder, no better, no more enlightened. They only came to him one at a time. They mostly wanted to see things, like the house or the tools or the supermarket. They looked like they had on the best day of their life.

"Like the best they've ever looked?"

"No. Exactly how they looked on their favorite day. Same age. Same clothes."

But how could there be one favorite day in a whole lifetime? Amina did not ask, but her father shrugged anyway, as if to say, *Who knows how these things work?* And for a minute she felt the pull of that logic as keenly as a hand.

"Enough," Kamala said from the back of the kitchen, her face striped with tears.

"Ma."

"Don't you 'Ma' me. You stop this talk right now."

"I just think we should—"

"You'll bring the devil into this home!"

"We're just talking about what's happening. There's nothing wrong with that."

"Yes, yes, of course, Miss Psychology Degree! Miss Freudian Lips! Because you know what's best, right? Yes, let's dig it all up, get it out in the opening!"

"Okay," Thomas said quietly. "It's fine. Let's just—"

"Idiots! You don't meddle with these things! You don't *bring them in the house.* You don't think they wait for tumors and cancers and whatever else? Of course they do! Weak minds are always the target!"

Amina glared at her mother. "Like yours?"

"Hey!" Thomas barked, but it was too late. Kamala covered her mouth with her hand and then turned and left the kitchen. A few seconds later the master bedroom door slammed, sending a quiver through the house.

Amina looked back at her father, who had slumped over the counter. "She didn't mean that, Dad. She's just—"

"Don't you *ever* talk to your mother that way."

Her face flared hotly. "I was just trying to—"

"This is hard on her."

"It's hard on everyone!"

"She's *your mother.*"

Amina looked down at the counter, sullen and flustered. She never knew what would trigger Thomas's loyalty toward Kamala, but whenever it happened, it was unshakeable, as if all his mishandlings could be vindicated in one act of allegiance.

"Fine," she said.

Her father's shoulders dropped a little. He looked unhappily at the kitchen counter.

"What about the jacket?" Amina asked.

Thomas did not say anything. The lines in his face deepened into shadows.

"Did Akhil want it?"

"No."

"Did you just give it to him?"

"I haven't seen him."

Amina idled into silence, surprised by the answer and the sudden blow of disappointment that came with it. "But then why did you—"

"I have no idea."

"But it was in the garden with the rest!"

"I know."

"Then why—"

"Amina, *I don't know.*" He was angry—angry about the way she'd spoken to Kamala, but now also about this, as if Amina had betrayed him by even thinking any of it meant anything. And hadn't she? Amina watched her father across the white countertop, pained by her own transparency, her need for the fog that was closing in around them to mean something.

Thomas laid his head down on the counter, his pate shining through a corona of curls. He breathed slowly and deeply, and Amina reached out, pressing her fingers to the stubbly spot where the hair from his biopsy was growing back in. How far were they from the tumor? She'd always had a healthy skepticism about shamans and the like, but lately, the conviction that she might somehow will the cancer away with the right amount of desire and supplication was hard to shake.

"They're going, anyway," her father said, his voice soft, begrudging.

"What?"

"The visions. With the chemo. I see them less."

"Really?"

He nodded, his head bobbing under her hand, and Amina said nothing, afraid of her own hope, of leaning too hard on any hint that he might be getting better. Instead she laid her head next to his on the counter, sliding forward until they were skull to skull.

CHAPTER 5

That night Jamie and Amina sipped wine at a new place in the Northeast Heights. Dark and cavernous, it boasted stools that looked like slabs of ice, an impressively large wine list, and an inversely diminutive bartender ("Let me know if I can help," she'd offered, with a face that said she couldn't possibly). On either side of them, Albuquerque's moneyed set watched one another's jewelry catch the light. The bar menus, rich cream card stock embossed with a font so modern it looked like a digital sneeze, suggested things like "rice paper crab" and "foam of duck."

"What are we doing here again?" Amina asked, trying and failing to sit comfortably.

"Risking everything to save innocent lives." Jamie handed her an errant flyer—a lone misstep of cheap pink Kinko's paper. *Come see us for happy hour!* it read. *Watch the sun set in a symphony of color!* "I don't know, I thought maybe we should mix it up with people our age."

"These people are our age?"

"Does that make you feel old?"

"It makes me feel poor."

The bartender came by again, a smile taped to her face. "Any questions?"

"What's a symphony of color?" Jamie asked. He held up the flyer.

She didn't even look at it. "We have a really nice sunset."

"Ah, thanks. Do you also have Budweiser?"

"We only have Sierra Nevada on tap."

"We'll take two," Amina said.

An hour and two beers apiece later, they were grinning. They were also talking too loudly. Amina knew this from the way the bartender was pointedly avoiding them. But who cared? She was on a date with Jamie Anderson. He smelled like something she wanted to eat.

"So I went to Mesa Prep today," Amina said.

"Oh yeah? What for?"

"I don't know. I wanted to take pictures of it. Anyway, I couldn't get in."

"What do you mean?"

"I mean they literally wouldn't let me in. The guard outside."

"Guard? Wait, that little booth at the gate is actually *manned* by someone?"

"Yeah!"

"No way!" Jamie said. "I've passed it a couple of times. I just thought it was for, I don't know, show or something. They have real guards?"

"*Ninjas.*" Amina spat out the word.

Jamie laughed and took a long tug of beer.

"No, really. That's what they're called. Ninja Security. That's what the guy's pocket said. There are, like, twenty-five of them on campus. Apparently they will stop anyone who doesn't have an appointment or a press pass."

Jamie choked a little. "Wait, he asked if you had a *press pass*?"

"Yes. Because I had my camera."

"But you were a student!"

"That's what I said!"

"That's bullshit! It's not like you're some . . . some"— Jamie's hand gestured furiously in the air—*"delinquent!"*

"Sha!"

"I mean, you *paid* to go to *school* there for, like, *years*! And they treat you like a *criminal*?"

"Insulting." Amina nodded. "Criminal."

"So did you complain to someone?"

"I couldn't get in to complain to anyone!"

"Fascists!" He hit the bar with a force. The bartender made a face at another one of the patrons. "I mean, what, so now it's some kind of dictatorship? *Ninjas?*"

"Ninjas," Amina said.

"Fuck them." He set his beer down on the bar. "We're going in."

"Totally."

Jamie waved to the bartender. "Hey, can we settle up?"

"Wait, now? You want to drive all the way to Mesa now?"

"We can hop that fence in, like, two seconds. And then we'll pretty much be on the mesa in the dark until we get to the buildings."

Amina imagined them storming across the marble-floored admissions office and threw her head back, laughing. The bartender smacked down their bill.

"I'm fucking serious!" Jamie glanced at it and set two twenties down. "We're going to take our school back."

Amina did not move.

"What, you're scared of the ninjas?"

She nodded. She was totally scared of the ninjas, whom she had imagined as short and quick and Japanese despite Albuquerque's notably small Asian population.

"Come on, that campus is huge! Forty acres, and most of it just barren mesa! How many of them can there be?"

"Twenty-five."

"So we cut in through a random section of the fence across from that Chinese place—what's it called?—the Great Wall. Yeah. And we stay away from the booth entirely. Then we're golden."

"Jamie." She put a hand on his arm.

"Amina." He pulled it to his chest.

"This isn't a good idea."

"It's *the best* idea."

"What if we get caught?"

"Then we explain to them that we used to go there and decided to take a harmless walk and I *guaran-fucking-tee* you they will not want to press charges against their own alumni, no matter how they deal with people at the gate. I mean, c'mon. I'm a UNM professor. They want to mess with that?"

"Oooh," Amina laughed despite her misgivings. "Are you going to bring the full wrath of your department down on them?"

"I might." Jamie dropped his voice a notch. "Or I could just bring the wrath of my department down on you."

"What does that even mean?"

"No idea. Finish your beer already."

She didn't have to go. She knew this. But there was something really lovely about the smell of hops rising in the air, about Jamie's wincing smile and yellow T-shirt, about how close her hand was to his heart.

She took a last gulp and slid off the bar stool. "Let's go."

Twenty minutes later they sat in Jamie's car, under the yellow glow of the Great Wall.

"Okay," he whispered, like they were already inside the Mesa Prep gates. He pointed to the far north section of the fence. "So I'm thinking we head to the north corner, hop over that big brick thing, and run through the mesa until we hit the parking lots."

"Run through all that mesa? In the dark?"

"Thing is, we've got to avoid the security house and the spot where traffic slows, so I think the only way to do this is take the natural route."

"Cactus," Amina reminded him. "Rattlesnakes."

Jamie leaned over her, opening the glove box with a smile. "Flashlight," he said, handing her the cold metal. "I've got two. And I've got a first-aid kit in the car."

"You've got to be fucking kidding me."

"What?"

"The amount of stuff you keep in your car! It's got to mean something. Savior complex? Abandonment issues?"

"Quit stalling."

Amina opened her door, popping out into the night. Jamie followed. They looked across the street. The wall seemed a little sturdier without the remove of the windshield, a little meaner. It was a combination of iron railing and thick brick posts, the kind of thing well suited to military schools and southern graveyards. Amina started doing jumping jacks.

"What are you doing?"

"Warming up."

"Oh. Right." Jamie followed her lead. They did twenty together and stopped, breathing hard.

Jamie leaned into a lunge. "Remember to stretch your hams and quads."

Amina nodded, lunging. "And we should do our shoulders after this."

Thirty seconds later Jamie was chicken winging his arms with vigor, while Amina pulled her elbows across her chest.

"You ready?" Jamie asked.

Amina looked across the road to the darkened mesa surrounding the school. "Absolutely."

Ten minutes later they panted outside the gate, hands and forearms and shins surprisingly banged up for what was supposed to be an easy hurdle. Amina spat to the side while Jamie paced and coughed.

"Okay," Jamie said, frowning down at his scratched palms. "Okay, so maybe not? Maybe we just quit while we're ahead?"

Amina shook her head. No, they would not be giver-uppers in the face of Mesa Preparatory. Now she wanted this.

"I mean, it's bigger than we thought, right?" he said, motioning to the gate. "Definitely bigger than what you see from the road. So there's that."

MIRA JACOB

"You are simply capable of more," she told Jamie, putting a foot at the base of the ironwork. "Here, give me a boost."

Jamie held his hand out.

"No, dummy, like . . ." Amina wove her fingers together, hunched down.

"What am I, a mind reader?" Jamie leaned down.

"I mean, it's a boost. People know how to give a boost." Amina shoved up and over, holding on unsteadily to the iron railing. And then suddenly she was falling, the spade points receding. She landed on her ass with a thud.

Jamie smiled at her through the fence. "Nice."

"At least I got over."

"Hold on." He followed her lead, looking decidedly nervous as his groin skimmed the iron points. He lowered himself with shaking biceps and grinned at her.

"We're in."

Amina looked at the blank expanse of mesa in front of them, the wooly darkness tinged brown by the edges of sagebrush catching light from the road.

"Don't worry. If there are any snakes here, they've heard us and they're moving out," Jamie assured her.

"You're not going to lay any bullshit on me about them being more scared of us than we are of them, are you? Because I know for a fact that I'm the scaredest animal out here."

Jamie squeezed her hand and they walked forward. On their right, the campus was clearly visible, rows of lights blazing down the cement walkways and bricked arches. On their left lay the football field, ringed by the track and bordered on one side by a small mound of built-in stadium stands.

"Where are we going?"

"Stadium." Jamie pointed.

"What about the ninjas?"

"I mean, it's a football field. What is anyone really going to do to it? Besides, the lights aren't on, so it's not like we'd be so easy to see."

They walked forward for what seemed like fifteen minutes, though of course it could not have been. She followed Jamie, trying to avoid the darkest shadows, until he stopped suddenly, grabbing her arm.

"Shh!"

"What?"

Amina froze, listening. Far away, a car honked at another. Beside her Jamie slowly squatted, holding his finger over his lips. She followed, her heart pounding.

"I thought I heard someone," Jamie whispered after a moment.

"A ninja?" Amina looked around, eyes wide.

"I don't know. What do ninjas sound like?"

"Padded footsteps. Chinese stars."

"It was totally a ninja."

She laughed silently, terrified of the ninjas and of pissing herself. Jamie waited a few moments, then rose slowly to standing and put out his hand, pulling her up. They looked across the road to the stadium, which rose into the black night like a temple, the empty metal benches watching nothing.

"Beautiful," Jamie said.

They split a joint on the grass, staring up at the place the stars would have been if there wasn't a weird, brownish haze clouding the night. The grass was itchier than Amina would have liked, and she needed to pee, but other than that, the campus was bizarrely peaceful, full of the hypnotic symmetry found on campuses everywhere—trees and lampposts and benches evenly spaced. She exhaled a tiny cloud, and it seemed to float right up into the pollution, where it would join gaseous and particle pollutants and come back down as acid rain in some northwestern lake, if that's how that worked. Was that how that worked?

"Who did you have for chemistry?" She handed the joint back.

"Brazier. Who did you have?"

"Wills."

"Huh." Jamie took a long pull. "Why?"

Amina shrugged, not quite sure what she had asked, much less why. She looked over at Jamie, trying to gauge if it was important, but there was a little black seed of something caught in his teeth. She wanted to tell him, but it felt like too much work.

"Remember that night at the dance?" he asked. "You looked so hot."

Amina smiled in the dark, deeply pleased in a way that made it seem like feminism had never existed. "Yeah, right."

"I was dying to do this with you."

"Get me high?"

"No, dummy. Get you next to me."

"Bullshit. You barely looked at me."

"That was just part of my moves, man. Play it cool." Jamie sucked his teeth. "I went to that stupid dance looking for you."

"You did?" Amina sat up, steadying herself. She peered down at him, trying to see if he was fucking with her. "Are you fucking with me?"

"You think I wanted to be there?"

"Aw, Jamie," she said, more touched than she knew what to do with. She rubbed his forehead, the little patch between the edge of his eyebrow and hairline that she'd grown especially fond of, and his hand slid under her shirt.

"Hold on a sec." She stood up and waited for the world to recalibrate so she could walk properly.

"Where are you going?"

"Behind the bleachers to pee."

Jamie raised his head, assessing the dark hill that held the built-in bleachers. "All the way over there? Just squat here."

"I'm not peeing in front of you."

"It's not a huge deal or something."

"Yes it is. It's a commitment."

"What?" Jamie laughed. "What are you talking about?"

"You've been *married*."

"What does that have to do with it?"

She did not know, really, but she knew it had something to do with peeing while talking, and showering with the door open, and being optimistic in a way she had never been. Maybe someday his easiness would rub off on her. Maybe someday she'd even become the kind of woman who could hunker down in front of him, but today was not that day. "Be right back."

She walked across the grass and then the track and then to a little side path that led to the dirt parking lot behind the bleachers. As she rounded the corner and the field disappeared behind her, her skin tingled. It was all patches of light and dark back there. A shaggy ring of piñon trees mostly sheltered her from the bright lights of the parking lot, but the occasional patch of ground glowed eerily, like sun dappling the bottom of a lake. Amina stopped, dropped her pants, and squatted.

Hank Franken. Every time she pissed in the open air, she thought about the boy's weird, freckled face, teeth that seemed to always be gnashing. Senior year, Hank Franken had sat on a cactus trying to take a shit at a mesa kegger. They had heard his screams from far away, and then the cries with each step as he finally emerged into the ring of taillights, pants mid-thigh, dick cupped in his hand, begging someone to pull the needles out. Had someone pulled the needles out? Amina stood up, pulled up her pants.

Someone was smoking a cigarette. It took a moment for Amina to realize this, and another to realize that that was a scary thing, the hair on her arms and neck rising all at once. Whoever it was, was close. Amina's eyes zigzagged through the dark, straining. Was it a ninja? Was he watching her? She heard a small click behind her and turned around slowly, her heart seizing as an orange ember moved through the air a few feet back. Her throat went dry. Just as she felt herself tipping into a quiet, annihilating panic, the smoker took a drag of the cigarette, and the orange halo of light revealed a face so familiar that the night itself seemed to suck in sharply around her, every bit of oxygen rushing toward the flame.

He looked the same. The exact same, his cheekbones stretched into the wide arcs that had risen after the Big Sleep. The glow from the cigarette faded, leaving a light-green smudge against the night.

He was walking toward her. Amina understood this in some paralyzed corner of her brain, the same part that had watched countless glasses slip through her hands, plates shatter on the floor, car crashes occur in neighboring lanes, and just as she had held still in all of those instances, convinced that the damage was too obvious to actually happen, she held still now. Patches of light caught his jeans, his T-shirt, and then he was walking past her, toward the trees.

Amina turned around, hot and chattering. *Wait.*

She could not speak. He did not wait. Akhil parted the branches and walked toward the bright lights of the main campus.

CHAPTER 6

They were running fast across the mesa, sand flooding into their shoes, sagebrush and ditchweed tearing at their calves and ankles.

"Hold on!" Jamie yelled after her.

Amina felt his hand grasping for her shoulder and jerked away. He hadn't said a word as she'd come bolting back from the bleachers. By the time she'd hit the main road out of the campus, he was sprinting alongside her, his long strides keeping pace with her frantic ones.

"Amina, hold the fuck on!" He grabbed her hard this time, yanking her to a stop. "We're safe. No one's following us, I swear."

Amina wriggled away from him. Up in the distance, the spaded tips of the iron fence had just come into view, and she juddered toward it, loosely aware that something was not right with her ankle. She was shaking.

"Hey." Jamie touched her shoulder again lightly. "Hey, are you okay?"

She was not okay. Her ankle felt like it had a pencil lodged in it. Amina stopped.

"What happened? Was it a ninja?" Jamie asked.

Amina shook her head, her brother's face rushing to her like wind through an open door. She covered her face with her hands. A rasping noise came from her throat, and Jamie circled her in his arms, scrunching down to mitigate his height. He was smoothing her hair back in small repetitive movements, the kind designed to soothe cats and babies.

"What happened?"

She shook her head. She wiped her face on her arm, embarrassed and desperately in need of a tissue. "Let's just go."

The drive home was silent. Jamie had insisted on driving her there, on helping her get her car the next day, but now, as the quiet stretched out between them, Amina regretted letting him. To be fair, he had tried to start several conversations, even trying to joke, but her inability to offer back a single word had sapped him, and they sat next to each other in the car like stones thrown together at the bottom of a pond. The car plummeted from the mesa into the valley, city blocks disappearing into the dark, smooth acreage of farmland. Soon they were winding down Corrales Road, signs for horse riders and cattle crossings flashing past them.

"Here," she said, and Jamie turned off of the main road onto a shorter road. She directed him over the ditch, to the dirt road.

"Can you drive to the end?" she asked.

"What?"

"Of this road. Please drive to the end."

They cruised past the entrance to her driveway, the road lit yellow and dusty in front of them. Jamie rolled to a stop at the dead end. He switched off the engine but kept the lights on, and they watched grasshoppers comet in and out of the dark. His shoulders had hitched up high around his ears like he was bracing against a blow.

"I'm sorry," she said.

"Are you okay?"

She nodded but her eyes burned.

"What happened?"

"I think I just got too high."

The wall of ditchweed wavered in front of them, a dark curtain of fronds and bugs that led to the water.

"Sure," he said, sounding unconvinced. She reached for him. She surprised him and his head reared back slightly as her fingers moved to the corner of his mouth, the meat of his lip.

"Listen," he started, in the gentle voice of easy letdowns, and she leaned forward, feeling his mouth warm and still against hers. She kissed his top lip, and then, when he did not respond, his lower lip, sucking it gently. Jamie did not kiss her back, but he did not stop her either, and Amina leaned in a little more, a flash of pain slicing in her ankle as she tasted the beer and salt on him. He pulled away.

She kissed his jaw. Her fingers found the back of his neck, and she pressed it toward her, scared that he would stop her. She did not want to be stopped. Her hand ran along his thigh, his crotch, the warm Braille of his inseam, and she was surprised by how suddenly he moved then, one hand clamping against her neck, the other finding her nipple with a sureness that pulled the air from her lungs. He shifted, coming at her now, his back rising up. Amina reached for the door handle behind her. She stepped out into the swampy air, her legs jittering as she walked to the back of the car and opened the hatch-back.

"Come on."

He did not move.

"Please," she said.

His door opened and she slid into the car, kicking off her shoes in the dark. He slid in next to her, and the car bounced lightly with his weight. She scooted down, lifting his shirt to kiss the hairless patch of skin above his hip bone. She pulled the edge of his boxers and inhaled the root-deep smell of him.

"Wait."

She did not want to wait. His cock was a lovely weight, warm and solid and as reassuring in the dark as a flashlight.

"Amina, wait."

She put it in her mouth.

"Fuck." His hands were in her hair, cradling her skull, pushing her down farther as his hips rocked forward. He tasted like the beach, like relief.

She rolled over to pull her shirt off, wriggling out of her shorts and underwear in the dark. She could feel his eyes on her as she straddled him, ignoring the burst of pain in her knees. His eyes were glassy slits as she rose in the dark and sank down again. One of his hands grabbed her collarbone; the other moved between her legs. She leaned into him until she could not breathe.

"Come," he said, and she did, easy like that, like she was a bomb waiting to go off.

Afterward, she lay her head against the tight pillow of his biceps, the little beats of aftershock pulsing through her.

"You scared me," Jamie finally said with a soft laugh. Her forehead pressed against his throat so that his words hummed through her brain. "You came running out of there so fast, I thought, *Someone is trying to fucking kill her.* Like I was going to have to fight."

He rolled over a little bit, and Amina's ear flattened against his shoulder. For a minute she imagined telling him that she'd seen Akhil behind the bleachers, that he looked like he did after the Big Sleep, but Jamie's hand found her cheek, rubbing it lightly in a way that felt both proprietary and absent, and she realized that what had started as an effort to reclaim him, to bring the night back snug around the two of them and huddle under it like a blanket, was not working.

She did not feel closer to Jamie now. She did not feel the slaking she had come to associate with having sex with him, that full-body release. Instead, she felt like a traitor. The car's windows pressed in around them like eyes, and Amina had the distinct feeling of being watched as she lay there, of being judged. The Akhil sighting (which, as her high wore off, was starting to feel less like a visit from the supernatural and more like a kick from her own subconscious) had thrown a door open, allowing for a world in which she could be found disloyal by some version of her brother that had stayed stuck at Mesa Preparatory for all eternity, while the rest of them—Paige, Jamie, Amina—sauntered off into a bright, mortal future.

"I don't know if I can see Paige yet," Amina said.

Jamie stayed silent for so long, she would have thought he hadn't heard her if his breathing had not suddenly grown shallow.

"So don't," he finally said.

"I mean, what am I even supposed to say to her?"

"Jesus, Amina." Her head slid to the scratchy carpet as he sat up. "Can we not talk about my sister right now?"

"I thought you wanted to talk," she said, embarrassed by the feminine needle in her voice. She looked at the upholstered ceiling, while he shoved his legs back into his boxers.

"I'm sorry," she said. "I just thought it was important, maybe, to tell you."

"Where are my shorts?"

"Here." She lifted her leg, dug them out from under her.

"Thanks." He put them on awkwardly, rolling on one ass cheek, then the other. Amina sat up. "I can walk home from here, if you want."

"That's not what I want." He looked around, finding his sneakers and shoving his feet into them. "You always do this. You get quiet and then pick a fight with me and then try to leave."

"Always?" Her face prickled with heat. "Define *always*."

"I mean, what is this shit? Is it so hard to just tell people what's going on? 'Jamie, I'm sad.' 'Jamie, going to Mesa was the worst idea ever.' 'Jamie, the Paige and Akhil thing is still weird for me.' Is that so hard?"

"Jamie, you're being a dick."

His face tightened into a scowl.

Amina watched him carefully, her heart rabbiting around. "It isn't weird for you?"

"Honestly, I don't think about it that much anymore. All of that stuff happened a really long time ago. They were just kids."

Amina nodded, his words turning over in her head like foreign currency, valuable someplace else. *Just kids.* Akhil was only ever a kid, she wanted to say; he would never be anything *but* a kid, but the grief behind this felt too obvious to let out, too tidal and self-indulgent.

"What happened to you back there?" Jamie asked, not unkindly.

Amina's face burned. "I don't know."

He took her hand, placing it in the damp patch of hair between his ribs, the one that reminded her of dogs and loyalty and protection, and she understood suddenly that she was falling in love with him. He was good, that seemed obvious enough, but there was more there, too, the way in which he felt uniquely *hers,* cut rough from some long-ago place and brought to her, something that she hadn't allowed herself to miss until it had come back. And now what? Now what was she supposed to do with it? She felt his heart tapping lightly against the back of her hand and shut her eyes until that tiny pulse filled the space between them.

CHAPTER 7

Something was wrong with her ankle. The next morning, as Kamala unceremoniously banged open her bedroom door, raised the blinds, and pulled down the blanket, Amina let out a fractured gasp.

"No," she groaned.

"Yes." Kamala opened the dresser and threw a clean pair of underwear at her head. "And hurry up. Your father thinks something is wrong. He's getting a scan this morning."

Amina sat up gingerly, staring at the bulbous knob attached to her foot. "What?"

"He wants us to meet him at Anyan's."

Ten minutes and some hobbling later they sped down Corrales Road, the air conditioner blasting dust motes down their tracheas. Amina sat forward, smothered by a film of beer and sex and weed. She cracked a window, leaning toward it like a dog.

"Air conditioner is on," Kamala snapped.

"I feel funny."

"Oh, so now you're sick?"

"Not exactly."

Her mother looked at her disapprovingly. "I would have woken you at seven, but your father wouldn't let me."

"Thank God."

"No thanking! Here this poor fellow is up all night tossing in bed, and now he has to go to the hospital alone!"

"Ma," she said in a warning tone, and her mother fell silent, grinding the truck into a lower gear as they approached an intersection.

Amina shifted and the pain shifted with her, moving from her ankle to a small flare of guilt between her ribs. "What do you mean, he thinks something is wrong?"

"He thinks something is wrong! Plain English! He's getting a scan!"

"Is he feeling something new?"

"How should I know? You think I am sitting there like some Diane Sawyers as he gets ready and goes? No! I am handing him one egg sandwich!" Her mother glanced sidelong at her but then turned, her whole face suddenly looking her up and down.

"What." Amina glared back.

"Nothing." On the corner, a few kids waved banners for a car wash, pointing excited sponges their way. "You were out with a boy? This friend from before?"

"Yes."

Kamala's gold bracelets clinked against one another as the light turned green, as they motored by the kids. "So bring him to dinner."

"What?"

"To dinner. At the house."

Amina looked out the window to the parched west mesa hills. Her feelings from the night before felt like something borrowed from a dream; they might vanish if exposed to scrutiny. "I don't know."

"Why not?"

Amina shook her head. "I'm not sure if he's quite there yet," she lied.

"Oh, *koche,* you know," her mother said soothingly, but stopped.

"What?"

"No, no, nothing."

"No, what were you going to say?"

Her mother looked at her, seeming to see right through her skin to the uncertainty inside. She tucked a strand of hair behind Amina's ear.

"There's a brush in my purse," she said.

Dr. George's waiting room rang with laughter. The receptionist's face was in her hands, an older couple clutched each other's forearms, and a young woman with a buzz cut wiped tears from her eyes, snorting. In the middle of them all, Thomas stood with a frozen expression of surprise on his face.

It was the one-way-street story. Amina had heard it a thousand times before, her father recounting how on his first month in America he had turned down a road where all the cars were coming at him. "In my country, there are no one-ways!" he liked to say, "Only every-which-ways!" It was a favorite he liked to drag out for American strangers, putting them at ease with his accent, his charm, his inability to navigate spaces they had created.

"Amazing country you have here!" Thomas said now, looking comically perplexed, and a new round of laughter pealed forth. He held out an arm and Amina limped into it.

"What's wrong with your foot?" her father asked.

"Twisted it a little. It's fine."

"You must be the daughter," the woman half of the older couple said, smiling at her too familiarly.

"Yeah."

"We've heard a lot about you."

"You got the scan?" Kamala asked.

"Amina is a photographer!" Thomas said with a flourish, like she was a rabbit he'd pulled from a hat.

"How wonderful," the woman said.

"Anyan is running late?" Kamala tried again.

"Dr. George should be here in about five minutes," the receptionist said, and the room seemed to deflate a little, punctured by the reality of why they were there.

"She's having a show of her work in Seattle," Thomas pressed on, but the others just smiled wanly at Amina. The male half of the older couple stroked his wife's hand.

"Dr. Eapen." Anyan George swung through the waiting room door, looking harried. "Hello, sir. Sorry to be late. I have your slides. You ready to come back?"

"Sure, sure." Thomas winked to the others with the bravado of a mischievous kid slipping into the principal's office. "Let's do it."

Anyan George would not sit down. This would have been unremark-able had he not directed the Eapens into their seats and then sat down himself, only to spring back up seconds later, shoving his chair in. Now he stood at the light board, clutching the envelope in his hands with a strange look. The family watched him for half a minute. Finally Thomas asked, "Everything okay?"

"Yes." He did not elaborate.

"The scans?" Amina prompted.

"Yes." He flipped the switch for the light board and began mount-ing them. Thomas stood up, moved closer. Together, they looked at the scans. Or rather, Thomas looked at the scans, and Dr. George looked at Thomas, a strange, unreadable expression on his face. Her father moved closer to the scan, then farther. He pulled the slide from the light board and read along its edge.

"What." Amina's fingers dug into the chair.

"It's yours," Dr. George said. "I checked."

"My God," Thomas said.

"What's wrong?" Amina asked.

"I was late because I called Wilker in for a second opinion," Dr. George said.

"And he said?"

"Yes. By as much as thirty percent."

"What?" Kamala asked.

No one answered for a long moment. Amina stared at the scan, trying to see whatever they were talking about last time, but it looked the same—the seahorses, the egg, the swirls of cortex.

"Did Lowry take a look?" Thomas asked Dr. George.

"He agreed, though obviously he's concerned that we might not have gotten the angle right, so the reduction might not be quite so significant."

"Reduction. Meaning it's smaller?" Amina asked.

"Yes," Dr. George confirmed.

"It's getting smaller?" Her voice rose.

"It looks that way," Thomas said.

"Ha!" Kamala shouted, jumping to her feet like a tiny, sari-clad swordsman. "Ha, ha, ha!"

Amina looked from her father's perplexed face to Anyan's. Her ankle throbbed dangerously. "That's good, right?"

"It's unusual." Thomas looked at Anyan. "Did you talk to MD Anderson?"

"We're sending the scans to Dr. Salki today."

"Have they seen regression of this sort before?"

"No."

"Is that bad?" Amina asked, hating how her lack of medical understanding left her with a five-year-old's sense of nuance: good/bad, light/dark, nice/scary.

"No, not at all," Dr. George said. "Just unusual. We haven't seen a regression of this sort before, so we're cautious about putting too much faith in it until we know more about what could have caused—"

"A miracle," Kamala cut in. "It's a miracle, isn't it?"

Dr. George looked flustered. "I'm hesitant to call it anything at this point. I think it's important that we temper our hope with—"

"Of course you are!" Kamala scoffed. "You doctors are always hesitant, isn't it? Experts at poking around in the body but unable to accept real healing when it comes from God himself?"

"It came from the chemo, Ma," Amina pointed out, but her father shook his head.

"That's unlikely. I've only gone through one full course. It would be highly unusual for that to have any effect, much less a sizeable one."

"What about your symptoms? Have you noticed any change?" Dr. George asked.

"Yes, actually. The hallucinations have lessened significantly."

"In intensity or frequency?"

"Both. I don't see them as much. I don't hear them talking. Although lately . . ." Thomas shook his head. "I don't know."

"What?"

"I've been smelling something burning for the past few days. At first it was faint enough that I thought it was just one of our neighbors clearing brush a few houses away, but—"

"That's all in his mind," Kamala said to Dr. George, as though this needed explaining. "No one in the village is dumb enough to start fires in June."

"Seizing," Dr. George said.

Thomas nodded. "I thought it might be."

"What?" Amina asked, looking from Thomas to Kamala. "You thought you were having a seizure last night?"

"That's why I wanted a scan," Thomas said.

"The good news is that it appears you weren't," Dr. George said in a calming voice that seemed to trigger his bedside manner. He looked from Kamala to Amina to Thomas, reassurance settling over his features, and took a seat, motioning for Thomas to do the same. "Thomas and I are trained to be skeptical of a sudden shift like this, especially when it has no predecessor, but it is obviously a welcome development. The best option now is to proceed with the exact same treatment over the next month and see how things go."

"Yes," Thomas said, nodding along. "Yes."

"So what," Kamala said. "We do more of everything? Chemo, radiation, everything?"

"Yes. Stick to the course. We'll need to keep an eye out for symptoms, erratic behavior, anything new or unusual. Amina, you'll be in town?"

"Yes. Mostly. I mean, I might travel for a day or so, or a weekend, but yes."

"Amina's having a show!" Thomas burst out, glad to finally have somewhere to put his hopefulness.

Dr. George wrote down something on a prescription pad, handing it to Thomas.

"Very high, prestigious show of work." Kamala nodded, nudging Amina. "An honor of her artsmanship by the authorities of Seattle."

"It's a favor for a friend," Amina corrected, glaring at her mother, but Dr. George seemed to take no notice either way, standing up abruptly.

"So then, barring any changes, I'll see you all back here next week?"

He ushered them out of his office brusquely, his eyes guarded, as if the hope of living was somehow harder to deliver than the threat of death.

Outside, in the bright slam of midmorning light, the Eapens stood stunned on the sidewalk. Amina shifted her weight carefully, but even her ankle felt deceivingly better, and she stood on it gingerly. Nobody knew quite what to say, though there was a palpable relief between them, a collective cord that seemed to have slackened, leaving them both more independent and more connected than they had been entering the office.

"Well," Kamala said, and Amina turned to find her mother's face frozen in a pained, happy grimace, as though her cheeks were trying to detach from the worry that had taken it over for the last months. Thomas saw it, too, and put out his hand, wiggling his fingers like you would for a child until she took it. He squeezed her hand, blinking the wet out of his own eyes.

"Well," he repeated.

BOOK 11

A STATE OF HOPE

ALBUQUERQUE, AUGUST 1998

CHAPTER 1

That night Thomas and Kamala fought each other from one side of the house to the other. Teeth bared, eyes flashing, they tore into each other with carnivorous gusto, laying bare all the injustices they had suffered at each other's hands over the last decades, the slights, the missteps, the heartbreaks. It was as if, released from the burden of having to care for each other, they'd found themselves in a pain deficit and were working hard to restore the equilibrium.

They were doing a good job of it, Amina thought from the safety of her bedroom. While the cause of the fight was unknown to her, the accusations of selfishness, martyrdom, ineptitude, and snobbery were staples from her childhood, none too surprising, though all tripped the same old fears, resurrecting a years-old sadness that her parents, at their core, were absolutely wrong for each other. In the midst of everything, she'd forgotten about that. She called Dimple.

"They're going at it."

Downstairs, the yelling had switched abruptly into Malayalam. It rumbled up the stairs like an oncoming thunderstorm.

"Sounds like fun."

"Pretty much. Anyway, how are you?"

"Good! Good. Really good, actually."

"Yeah?"

"Yeah. I, um . . ." Amina heard the opening of the gallery door. "Hold on a sec." A crinkly paper noise, and when Dimple next spoke, it was through chewing gum. "I'm engaged."

"What?"

"Sajeev and I are getting married."

"*What?*"

"We're—"

"Since when?"

"Last week. I wanted to tell you, but I didn't want to, you know, interrupt."

"Interrupt what? I'm not doing anything out here."

"You're dealing with your dad."

"You're getting married to *Sajeev*?"

"Well, you don't have to say it like that."

"No, I just mean . . . was this a, uh. I mean, did you . . ." Amina swallowed, entirely unsure of what she was trying to ask. "Okay, so wow."

"You sound freaked out."

"No! I'm just a little surprised. You just started seeing each other, you know?"

"We've known each other our whole lives."

"Yeah, but not like, *known* each other."

"I know plenty," Dimple said with a telling laugh.

"Right," Amina said, falling silent until she realized that Dimple was waiting for more, that this was one of those moments they weren't going to get back. She swallowed and threw her voice an entire octave higher. "Congratulations!"

"Don't be a dick."

"No, I'm not! I'm happy for you! I mean, surprised, obviously, but happy!" She was aware that talking in exclamation points was undermining her message but could not stop once she had started. "He seems like a great guy!"

"Well, he is," Dimple said suspiciously. "And we have more in common than you think. He knows a lot about photography."

"I know—that day at the Hilltop. He was talking about it nonstop, remember?"

Dimple's voice changed abruptly, the giddiness returning. "Really?"

"Yes," Amina said, relieved to finally find her footing in the conversation. "Remember? He had all that stuff to say about Charles White, and it was good, really. And then he knew about my stuff, which, you know—"

"Clearly means he's well versed," Dimple finished.

"Exactly." Amina smiled. "So what happened? Did he do the whole knee thing?"

"Well, no, because we were in bed."

"Please tell me you didn't tell your parents that part."

"I haven't told them anything yet. I'm thinking of not telling them at all."

"Oh, c'mon."

"No, really. We were thinking of eloping the weekend after the show. You know, like, Vegas-style or city hall or something."

"You can't do that! What about the family?"

"Oh my God, two months back home and they've brainwashed you."

"No! Well, maybe. I mean, why start things like that? You've got your whole lives to disappoint everyone. Weddings are important."

"Says the woman who captures their most compromising moments."

"Not fair. And you know what I mean."

"Yeah, I know." Dimple was quiet for a long moment, and in that moment Amina realized her parents had stopped yelling. She limped down the hall to Akhil's room and looked down into the driveway. Both cars were still there.

"I feel like my parents won," Dimple said.

"Won what?"

"That's the funny part. I mean, what did they win, really? So I'm going to end up with a Suriani guy. Sajeev, of all people. So what. I just . . . I don't want to deal with my mom gloating."

"She won't gloat."

"Amina."

"Okay, fine, but it's not like you did it *so* she would gloat. That would be worse."

"Do you really think I don't know him well enough?"

"No, it's not that. I guess I just didn't see it coming," Amina said carefully, knowing she wasn't quite telling the truth. She paused, thinking about how sometimes a surprise was just the acknowledgment of something you had tried hard to ignore. Of course Dimple was going to marry Sajeev. Amina said, "I guess it makes sense, in a way."

"I just keep thinking, you know, our parents did it. And they didn't know each other. And Americans get divorced all the time for, like, *no reason*. Someone cheats. Someone spends too much money. Someone tells someone they aren't the person they married, like that's so fucking unusual. So if you need to just close your eyes and jump . . ."

"You might as well do it with an Indian."

"Exactly."

Amina limped over to her desk, where the items found in the garden were now in the active dust-collecting stage. She ran her finger along the edge of the trophy.

"I think I'm falling for Jamie Anderson," she said.

"AMINA!" The bedroom door flew open with a loud smack.

"JESUS!" Amina screamed.

Thomas stood in the door frame, his forehead dotted with sweat from the exertion of fending off Kamala.

"What?" Dimple yelled. "What happened?"

He walked into the room, fists clutched around a dinner roll and a bag of ice.

Amina swallowed. "I've got to go."

"What just happened? Are you okay?"

"I'm fine. My dad's just here."

"Did you just say you were—"

"*Later,*" Amina said as her father glared at her feet.

"Okay, but call me back!"

It was not, in fact, a dinner roll, Amina saw as her father uncurled his fist. It was an Ace bandage. Thomas jerked his hand in the direction of the bed. "Sit."

Amina limped over and sat. Her father pulled up a chair and raised her leg to rest her foot on his knee. His fingers went straight for the spot that hurt the most, pressing it. She gasped.

"How did this happen?" he growled.

"Accident."

"What kind of accident?"

"I was running in the dark."

He placed one hand on her heel and the other on her toes, rotating her foot forward too far. She jerked it away.

"That hurts?"

"Yes."

He pressed his fingers beneath her anklebone. She gritted her teeth and nodded.

"You've sprained it. I'm going to wrap it, and then you should keep it elevated and iced."

"How long will it be sprained?"

"Probably a week or two." He began to unroll the bandage over her foot, wrapping it around. "Why were you running in the dark?"

"I was robbing a bank."

The corner of Thomas's lip twitched, though he was still too wound up to actually crack a smile. Below them, Kamala banged pots and pans. Thomas wrapped the bandage quickly and evenly, putting a nice layer of pressure between Amina and the pain. When he was done he lifted the whole thing and gently helped her swing it onto the bed. He put two pillows under it and then laid the ice over it.

"You've taken Advil for the swelling?"

"No."

He nodded and left, returning shortly with a glass of water, two pills, and two more pillows taken from Akhil's bed, which he put behind her.

"How's that?" He backed up, knocking his head against the canopy.

"Much better, thanks."

"You should take it easy for a few days." He walked to the window, hands in pockets, shoulders rounded, entirely too large for the room. "So your mother tells me you're dating a boy from here."

"Yeah. Jamie Anderson." She paused a moment for the recognition and, getting none, added, "We went to high school together."

"Mesa?"

Amina nodded. Where else? "He's a professor at the university. Anthropology."

"Interesting. Well, tell him I look forward to meeting him next week."

"Yeah. Wait, what are you talking about?"

"Your mother said he's coming to dinner."

"What? No! Jesus! I haven't even asked him yet. I haven't even *decided* to ask him yet. Not that I won't. I just, you know. Never mind. It's fine."

Thomas raised his eyebrows at her.

"It's fine," Amina repeated, embarrassed by her outburst. "I should probably just be thankful that she's over the Anyan George thing."

"I wouldn't go that far. You know your mother."

Amina shook her head. It was amazing, really, how much knowing Kamala didn't actually help.

"Invite the boy to dinner," her father suggested. "It will force her to give up."

This was a lie, the kind Thomas had told Amina often in her teen years, when saying "Nothing can make your mother give up" would have been as unkind as it was true. And Amina nodded, not because she believed him but because she appreciated the sentiment behind the lie, which was simply that her father wanted to help. She grabbed his hand, squeezed it.

"How are you doing?" she asked.

"I'm nervous," he said, and then looked as startled as she felt that he'd said it out loud. He walked a few paces from the bed, stopping short at the sight of things on the desk. "I always tell my patients, it's unwise to believe you'll be the anomaly. Part of a small percentage for whom certain treatments work, maybe, but the anomaly? Not likely."

"Yeah, but it's not like you just *think* you're getting better. Dr. George said—"

"The tests could be wrong," he snapped, and she understood suddenly that the look on Anyan George's face that morning had been fear masquerading as impatience, much as it was on Thomas's now. "Anyway, I should get going. Monica is waiting."

"Now?"

"Yes."

"That was fast," Amina said, with a twinge of sympathy for her mother.

"Getting the business back up to speed will take a while."

"Uh-huh."

"It's not like the money makes itself in this house!"

"I didn't say anything. Did I say anything?"

Thomas opened his mouth as if to say something but then checked himself. "I'll be back in an hour."

"Okay."

He nodded once, dismissing himself, and walked toward the bedroom door.

"I thought I saw Akhil last night."

She had not known that she was going to tell him until she had told him. Thomas stopped at the door, his back squared toward her for several long seconds. He turned around to face her, cheeks pale.

"You what?"

She cleared her throat. "I mean, I didn't, obviously. I just, you know . . . I guess I just wanted to tell you that I get it. Why it was hard for you."

"You saw him here?"

"No. I mean, I thought I did, but—"

"In our yard?"

"No. At Mesa."

"Which mesa?"

"No, Dad, my old school. Mesa Prep."

Her father nodded at this, his features held tightly in place, and Amina knew then how wrong she had been to think they'd had something in common, much less felt the same way about it. Thomas did not look like a man reconciling with hallucinations. He looked like someone hearing a phone ring in the next room and willing himself to stay put.

"Did he say anything to you?" her father asked.

Amina stared at him. "He wasn't real, Dad."

He nodded, looking away.

"Oh God, I'm sorry, I shouldn't have told you. It's not the same thing. I just thought—"

But he was already squeezing her shoulder, walking toward her bedroom door.

"Don't worry about it," he said, and let himself out.

CHAPTER 2

They fell into a state of hope. As the last long weeks of summer sighed out across the mesas, as the mornings grew slightly cooler with the promise of September, good and then better news came to the Eapens. The follow-up scan confirmed what the first had hinted: The tumor was indeed shrinking. Thomas took the news with a bowed head and little emotion, but it was obvious in the days that followed that he had turned a corner, suddenly filled with a frantic, zealous energy. He was going to go back to work. To retrieve his patients from the competition. To show them all what was possible. Even as the second round of chemo took its toll, lining his mouth with cold sores that made it impossible to eat and leaving him eight pounds lighter in five days, he rose to meet with Monica, who clutched Amina like a long-lost relative, whispering "It's a miracle" with such grateful intensity that it seemed she'd gone the way of Kamala.

As for Kamala, she was also getting back to normal, handling her newly free time by pickling a deluge of cucumbers, making Chowpatty corn on the cob, and demanding, along with Mort Hinley, whose radio harangues once again blasted through the kitchen, the fiery repentance of all sinners. Two weeks in, she took the additional step of announcing that she would be perfectly happy to stay home if the rest of the family wanted to take over the chemo rounds. She did all of this so quickly and efficiently that it felt like a wardrobe change in a theater production, and would have been completely believable had Amina not seen the occasional longing look on her mother's face when she glanced out to the porch.

Was it fair to leave Thomas to himself and his work so quickly? To somehow feel slighted in the wake of his recovery? As much as Amina saw the folly in this, she could not deny that as the weeks went on, the feeling of their being unnecessary to her father's recovery was both relieving and damning. Monica was there now, sitting through more and more evenings with him, and the hospital staff was everywhere else, flocking around him from the minute Amina walked him into the hospital until they walked back out the doors.

Gone was the tight, needy family unity, the lulls and spaces in which their best conversations grew, supplanted by an optimism so vigorous that it seemed to scrub away all traces of the last months. Other than a few nights in which Thomas had staggered around the fields, insisting that there was a fire closing in around the house despite their protests, his grip on reality seemed strong enough to not need reinforcement.

And that was how Amina found herself sleeping over at Jamie's house every night. It was a temporary situation, belied by the ticket she booked back to Seattle at the end of September for the show, and yet somehow they fell quickly into a routine that felt—if not permanent—then at least stable. Amina would show up every late afternoon, cut up some vegetables and meat according to Jamie's specifications, and then head out the back door with her camera, wandering around Hidden Park in the cooling dusk as the lights of the houses popped on around her one by one. And though at first she had been lured by the familiar thrill of capturing unaware occupants, she soon found that what she craved most was finding a recently inhabited but empty room, a kitchen with a mug steaming on the counter, a television blaring away at a vacant armchair. Once, she turned the lens on

Jamie's kitchen, fixated by the way the vegetables waited on the chop-
ping board, and was shocked when his shoulder cut into the frame,
filling the space completely.

Their lives had become routine suddenly, the future just another
thing that would unfold as it needed to. And while they had never
talked again about what happened at Mesa, Amina found solace in the
idea that some things could just fade gently away instead of being ana-
lyzed and rationalized and validated. Sometimes, things could just get
better. So she was surprised one afternoon to hear Jamie answer the
phone in the living room and then come and find her, his face dented
with concern.

"It's your aunt," he said, and she wiped her hands on her jeans,
grabbing the receiver.

"You have to come now!" Sanji shouted, and Amina heard yelling
in the background.

"What? What's happened?"

"Thomas has gone!"

"What do you mean? Is he okay?"

"He's *missing*."

"What?"

"Just come!"

She found him easily. Not that Sanji and Anyan George and the nurses
who had been called into the hospital-wide hunt hadn't tried hard
enough, but for Amina, the circuitous path to the ICU lit up before her
like a plane runway, the only obvious way forward, and when she
stepped into that cool, dark room, one raised eyebrow from the
familiar-looking nurse on duty told her she was right. Amina headed
back to the bed that her father stood at, so still he could have been an
IV pole.

"Dad."

Her father looked over, a small smile spreading across his face.
"What are you doing here?"

"Everyone's looking for you."

"I'm right here."

"Yeah, apparently."

The man in the bed was a sandy blond, the kind that made Amina think of California and beach campfires and athletic ability. Something had mangled his legs, leaving one wrapped in a cast and a bandage and the other missing below the knee.

"Jesus," she said.

Her father confirmed this with a nod. "Doesn't look good."

"You knew him?"

"No." Thomas took a short breath, like he was going to explain something, but they were interrupted by the approaching nurse.

"Hey, Doc," she said when she reached them. "Just talked to Maggie in chemo. She said they could hold your spot for another twenty minutes if you want to run down."

"Thanks, Shirley."

"Sure thing." She shot Amina a look as she walked away.

Thomas watched her go. "They're a funny breed."

"We should get going."

"Different than other nurses, in some ways. Very anal, very focused. Very loyal to their patients. Detail-oriented. Sometimes they miss the big picture."

"Huh." Amina turned to leave the ICU. Thomas didn't.

"I'm stopping chemo," he said.

"What?"

"Just for a little while." He nodded as he said this, as if agreeing with someone beside himself.

"What do you mean? What's wrong?" Amina tried to catch his eye, but his focus was wholly on the man on the bed. "Are you feeling too sick today? They said that would happen, remember? Especially this round, they said you might feel especially depleted."

"It's not that."

"Then what?"

"I just think I should hold off for a while."

"A while? How long is that?"

"I don't know. Maybe just a few days, weeks."

"*Weeks?* You can't! I mean, you—Dr. George said—we agreed

you'd stay the course, right? We should just keep doing what we've been doing, right?"

Thomas shrugged, like these were shruggable questions.

"Do you think the tumor is already gone? Are you feeling what you felt before?"

"No."

"Then what?"

He was staring at the patient's hand, the fingers that twitched spasmodically.

"Dad!"

"Shh! Not so loud!"

"Why are you stopping the chemo?" Amina hissed.

Thomas blinked a few times, finally looking over at her. "I saw Akhil in the yard a few nights ago."

The information fractured through Amina's brain, offering several fleeting images—Akhil on the Stoop, Akhil in the driveway, Akhil behind the bleachers at Mesa.

"He was in the garden," Thomas said.

"Dad." Amina looked at him steadily. "He's not real."

"But you saw him, too."

"No I didn't."

"You said!"

"No. I had a weird tired moment that was stupid and that I shouldn't have told you about. It's not the same thing."

"How do you know?"

"Because I know."

"Well, I don't." He looked at her defiantly, daring her to contradict him.

"Okay," she said. "Fine. But why do you have to stop the treatment?"

"Because the chemo will keep him from coming."

Amina shook her head, her words evaporating.

"It's true. I told you before, I don't see them as much with the chemo."

"Dad."

"I want to see my son."

He said it like this was something not only possible but reasonable. *I want to eat something. I want to take a quick shower.* It made sense. It made sense. It did not make sense.

Thomas scratched the back of his hand, studying the loose skin and veins before saying, "Itty asked about you, by the way. That horrible nickname he had for you. What was it? *Mittack!* He was a funny kid, wasn't he?"

No, Amina wanted to say, no, he really wasn't funny at all, but she felt swimmy suddenly, her limbs untethered from gravity.

"And Sunil told me he should have been a dancer," Thomas said.

She blinked. "What?"

"He said it was the one thing that made him really happy. That if I had come back to India like I was supposed to, if he wouldn't have been left to take care of everything on his own, he would have been a dancer."

A cold weight pressed into Amina's chest. The memory of Sunil waltzing in the Salem living room fluttered into her mind, clear and sharp behind the gauzy curtain of time.

"Can you imagine what all might have changed with that one silly thing? Maybe they would all still be here. Maybe your mother would be happy. Maybe Akhil . . ." A grimace surfaced on Thomas's face, and he fought it back. "And you know the funny thing? It was a relief to hear him say that it was my fault. A *relief.* All these years, imagining how he must have hated me, cursed me, and now finally it's done, over, kaput. Now I move on, right?" Thomas smiled at her, but he did not look relieved. He looked exhausted.

"Dad, let's go home."

He looked at her warily.

"You're just tired. It's fine. We'll skip it today."

Thomas turned back to the man on the bed. "I'm tired every day."

"I know." She slid her hand down his arm, reaching for the fingers that clutched the guardrail of the patient's bed, loosening them slowly.

He walked with her down the rows and rows of patients, saluting Shirley on his way out.

"Good to see you, Doc."

Thomas winked. "I'll be back."

"So what did your mom say?" Jamie asked when she got back. He was doing something violent to the tomatoes in the saucepot. Steam fanned up and around his head in a garlicky cloud.

"Didn't tell her yet."

"No?" He glanced over his shoulder, surprised.

"I just wanted to come back here for a second. You know, catch my breath."

Jamie reached for the bag of spaghetti, cracking the noodles in half and throwing them into boiling water. He stirred them slightly with a fork, put it down, and walked over to her. He tucked a strand of hair behind her ear. "Set the table."

There were people who couldn't eat in the face of their stress. They picked at their food distractedly, too worried to do anything but worry. Amina indulged the opposite instinct. The mere whiff of things being unstable had made her ravenous, and that evening she plowed through an entire mop of spaghetti as if trying to prepare her body for a long and brutal winter. It was a good five minutes before she even noticed that Jamie was no longer eating but watching her, his fork suspended midair. She dabbed at her face.

"What's wrong?"

"I've never seen you eat like that."

"Like a hungry person?"

"Like a refugee."

Out the window behind him, the park tripped into dusky blue. Amina sighed. "I don't want to do this right now. Talk to his doctor. Talk to my mother. Talk to the family."

"So don't. Sleep on it."

"I wish." She stood up and took her plate to the sink. "Dr. George is calling tomorrow morning to discuss our options. I need to tell my mom before that."

"Damn. So I guess I'll see you guys tomorrow night."

She looked at him blankly.

"I'm coming to your house for dinner?"

"Oh, shit. I forgot."

Jamie raised his eyebrows. "Wow, you're a regular charm school tonight."

"I'm sorry. It's great. Totally great." Amina nodded enthusiastically. "It will be fun."

"And now you're scaring me."

Amina walked back to the table, bent down, and kissed his cheek. "We're going to eat you alive."

She had to tell Kamala immediately. Amina realized this somewhere between the interstate and the descent into the valley, worry settling in. Hopefully Thomas hadn't broken the news already. It would be worse, somehow, coming from him. Amina felt sure of this, though she was unsure exactly how. Would it be back to the old charge of *devilry*? On to something new? Would she yell? Stop speaking? Move to another room in the house? Anything seemed possible.

Anxious, Amina sped up. There was, of course, the extremely rare possibility that her mother might have already fixed things. Maybe, if Thomas really had been dumb enough to say something, she had already beat him back into chemo. Amina barely noticed the odd glow at the end of the driveway until she rolled right into it.

The house was ablaze with light. Amina stared at it for a good few seconds before opening her door and standing up, the brightness heating her cheeks like actual sunlight. Every single light, inside and out, was on. Lights she had never even known about were on. Porch lights, lamplights, closet lights, lights in the china cabinet. All three sets of hallway lights. Amina walked by a pair of lanterns huddled together on the living room floor, while above them, a muted television threw color into the air. An extension cord snaked out the living room window and into the courtyard, where a halogen lamp made quick and smokey work of curious moths. On the kitchen stove, a lone pot of chicken curry hissed its last liquid into the desert air, the masala brackish. A cooking spoon lay on the floor.

"Mom?" Amina's chest tightened.

Prince Philip whined from the laundry room, nose pressed to the screen. How long had he been sitting there? His tail thumped as she approached, and he darted onto the porch as she opened the door. Every light in the shop was on as well, even those that had not been on in so long that they were bearded with spiderwebs. Twinkling pools of Christmas lights lay around the empty porch chairs. The door to the backyard was open. Prince Philip raced through it, and she followed.

It was their shadows she found first, conjoined and stretching out across the lawn like an impossibly thin giant. They were sitting in lawn chairs. No. Amina blinked. They were sitting in one lawn chair. Kamala perched on the edge of Thomas's knees, staring intently into the yard.

"Mom?"

Her father was holding on to her mother's braid tightly. It was hard to make this out from far away, but as Amina walked closer, she saw the dark coil wrapped around her father's hand like a leash, Kamala leaning forward like a cat tethered from chasing prey.

"What are you guys doing?"

Her parents turned to look at her, and Amina's breath caught in her throat. They were luminous. Pieces of moon fallen from the sky, still reflecting every bit of light from the known universe. Smiling at her across the yard in a way she hadn't seen in years, may have never seen. Amina walked forward, the ground uneven beneath her feet. Her mother waited until she was right next to them, and then found her hand, held it.

"He's here," she said. "He's come back."

Amina shook her head. *No.*

"Yes," her mother said, smiling into the fields. "Yes."

CHAPTER 3

"Where?" Amina asked.

"The garden," her father said.

Amina turned to walk to the garden.

"No, don't!" Kamala said.

"Why not?"

"He'll come when he's ready," Thomas explained. "We just need to wait."

"We don't want to scare him off," Kamala added.

Amina looked at her parents, at their upturned faces, bright and sweet and solemn.

"I couldn't scare Akhil if I wanted to," she said.

Kamala squawked after her, but neither of her parents actually tried to stop her, which was a relief. Unlike the last time she'd wandered out to the garden in the middle of the night with a bobbling flashlight and someone else's hunch, the path was well lit now, the determination her own. Still, as Amina neared the gates, she felt herself standing at the edge of a longing so old and deep and clear that she could barely keep her steps steady. She opened the garden gate and walked in.

It was cooler inside, heavy with dark green shadows. Amina looked out over the dark rows of vegetables, the peppers hanging in waxy clumps, the cucumbers huddled together on the ground. In the back, the bean trellis stood like a soft and furry giant. She walked slowly forward, past the tomato plants, the eggplants, the place where the pumpkins would rise up in the fall. She walked all the way back to the mound that Thomas had buried everything in.

"Akhil?" she whispered. She closed her eyes and felt a light breeze coming off the ditch, bringing her the smell of carp and algae and wet stones but not her brother. She opened her eyes and did a slow 360 just to be sure and then felt the embarrassment of doing a 360 in her mother's vegetable garden in the dark. She walked back to the house.

"I need to talk to you," she said to Kamala, not looking at Thomas and not stopping. She went to the porch and waited.

Kamala banged through the screen door less than a minute later, hastily arranging her sari. "What is it?"

"What are you doing?"

"What do you mean?"

"Do you see him?"

"Of course not!"

"Then why are you pretending?"

"I'm not pretending."

Amina stared at her mother.

"He's come back to see *your father*," Kamala explained. "This is Thomas's miracle."

Amina's brain shook a little with this new piece of information, a train car rattling down a track with too many thoughts inside, but one kept jostling up above the others. Chemo. They had to get him back to chemo. They had to be on the same side if they were going to get him back to chemo. "Bad spirits," she said. "Evil."

Her mother shrugged. "I was wrong."

"But you said—"

"No," Kamala said firmly, even though Amina had not actually asked her anything. "No, no, no."

"But we're running out of time!"

Kamala's eyes snapped shut. They stayed shut as her mouth trembled and then stopped, as she found her hands and clasped them tightly in front of her. When she finally looked at Amina a few moments later, her eyes were shining with a sharp edge of belief that Amina had never been able to bend.

"I'm going back outside to your father," Kamala said, and then turned and did exactly that.

The next morning Amina called Jamie, told him what had happened, and canceled dinner.

"Holy shit."

"I know. It's uh . . . anyway, just give me a few days. I'll get things straightened out and we'll have you over, I promise."

"I wasn't really worried about dinner."

"Three days," Amina said. "Or, like, four."

But over the next four days, the house got worse, not better. Hallways became a collection of light and dust. Never mind that after she'd hung up with Jamie, she'd scrubbed the entire bottom floor from one end to the other and returned all the lamps to their previous spots in the house—by that very evening a moist line of garden soil ran from the porch to the master bedroom, and by night the lamps were back, buzzing like locusts and covering everything with thick, electric light.

Things began to move. The first few days they were little enough—an odd pack of lightbulbs lying abandoned in the courtyard, two pillows from her parents' bed stuffed into the lawn chairs, but on the third night, as Amina dreamt about a ship cratering against an iceberg, Kamala and Thomas somehow found a way to slide the living room couch down the hall, and in the morning, when Amina rose, it was floating in the middle of the field, her parents atop it like two stray penguins.

"What the hell are you doing?" Amina called down from her open bedroom window, and her parents looked in five other directions before turning their gaze upward.

"Oh, hey," Kamala said with a wave. "Sitting! Come down."

"Dad shouldn't be moving furniture!"

"I'm fine!" Thomas yelled.

"No you're not!" Amina yelled back.

And he wasn't. This was verified readily by Anyan George, and then Monica, and Chacko, who called from the hospital the fourth day because it was his turn to sit through the chemo and there was no Thomas to sit with.

"He's not thinking rationally right now," Chacko explained to Amina, as though it needed explaining. "You're just going to have to bring him in."

"I'm working on it. I think in a few days—"

"Few days is too long!"

"What am I supposed to do? Bind and gag him?"

Chacko was silent, and for a moment Amina feared he'd taken her seriously.

"But what about your mother?" he asked. "Surely she can make him go?"

Amina looked out the kitchen window, to where Kamala was busy attaching a surge protector to a cable cord. Her tennis shoes and sari hem were brown with garden soil. Thomas squatted next to her, attaching one headlamp to another.

Amina sighed. She had to tell Chacko, of course, tell all the family how Kamala had risen to this occasion as she always did in the face of disaster, standing staunchly beside Thomas and even helping him do all the things he insisted would put Akhil more at ease (although she had drawn the line at leaving cooked food in the garden). But it seemed cruel somehow, exposing this new collaboration between her parents to scrutiny. She watched through the window as Thomas said something to Kamala, and then quickly, fiercely kissed her cheek, making her mother laugh like a girl.

"What are you guys doing tonight?" Amina asked, and then before Chacko could answer, said, "Because I think you should get the others and come down."

———

They arrived all at once, rolling up in the early-evening light, smashed into the Ramakrishnas' Camry like circus clowns. Sanji, Raj, and Chacko burst out immediately, looking formal and uncomfortable in their American work clothes, while Bala, relatively subdued in an orange-and-gold sari, struggled with a pot of potatoes in the back of the car. Amina led them into the house and back to the porch, ignoring the horrified looks they exchanged as they made their way through the house.

"Where's the couch?" Bala asked. "Are those *clocks*?"

"Where?"

Her aunt pointed to an armchair, to where every clock in the house sat in a pile, cords bundled tightly over their faces.

"Oh." Amina blinked. "Yeah, I guess they are. Huh."

She shuffled toward the kitchen, Sanji hot on her heels.

"Ami baby, what on earth—he did this? Thomas did all this in just a few days? And what is *that*?" Sanji stared into the courtyard, where the halogen lamp had been mummified in Christmas lights.

"A light with lights on it."

"Good gods!" Sanji cried, and the others filed silently into the kitchen. Amina looked from uncle to aunt to uncle to aunt, their familiar faces riddled with concern, discomfort, love. Good God, the love. It was hard to have that much love looking at you in the face at one time and not feel like an asshole.

"My parents are outside," she started to say, but just then the door to the back porch clicked open and their faces panned away from her, toward the laundry room. A few seconds later, Kamala walked out of it, still in the same sari but her hair now unbraided, hanging down in loose waves. She stopped short, a beautiful, dirty apparition.

"What's all this?" She frowned. Amina chewed her lip, unable to answer. Her mother squinted as though she had, and crossed her arms. "And did you tell them?"

"No."

Kamala nodded again, then reached abruptly for Sanji's arm.

"Come," she said, motioning for Bala and Chacko and Raj to follow. "Come see."

And what did they see? The couch, pilled with puffs of cotton dander from the shedding trees, the cushions streaked with mud; Prince
Philip, in the dog heaven of no longer being on the wrong side of every
door; Thomas staring into the garden with binoculars. Amina watched
from the porch as the family made their way to the couch, calling to
Thomas until he put the binoculars down. He turned his head, smiling
when he saw them. He said something Amina couldn't quite hear.

"What?" she heard Sanji ask loudly, and both Eapens began speaking at once, gesticulating toward the empty garden. Amina walked
back to the kitchen.

"Hey," she said when Jamie answered the phone. "Sorry I haven't
called."

"Are you okay? Is your dad okay?"

"Not really. The family is here now."

"I'll come down tomorrow," Jamie said. Behind him she could
hear the faint noise of the Violent Femmes rattling like gravel in a box.
"I've got the day free."

"No! No, I mean, don't worry about it. We're fine. You should go
have a good time."

"What?"

"Go out somewhere or something. Do something fun."

"Amina, what the hell is going on? You sound weird."

"I'm sorry," she said.

"That's not what I mean."

"I love you." Her head pounded in the sharp silence that followed
this, *Eight, eight, I forgot what eight was for,* filling up the phone line
while her face got hot. Someone was running back toward the house,
footsteps heavy on the ground. "Anyway, I should get going."

"Wait a sec—"

"Call you later."

She hung up just in time to see Sanji burst in from the porch like a
wild boar, scuttling into the kitchen and bouncing roundly off the edge
of a counter. She grabbed Amina's arm and shouted, *"What the shit?"*

"Hey," Amina said.

"Gods!" Sanji was breathing hard, flushed. "Bloody hell!"

Amina smiled nervously. "I know," she said. "It's weird."

"Weird? WEIRD? Weird is French foods! Weird is making some contraption that throws bad tomatoes at Chacko for the fun of it! This is really happening? They think he's *living* in the *garden*? That all the damn lights will make him stay?"

"Not living."

"What?"

"Well, not technically. I mean, they don't think he's not dead. They just think Dad can see him."

"In the bloody garden!"

"Right."

Sanji turned, looked at her sharply. "Amina Eapen, please tell me you don't believe this, too."

Amina chose her words carefully. "I believe they believe it."

"Unbelievable!" Sanji resumed pacing, drunk on her own dismay. "Just nuts! All of these years they can't agree on one single thing, and now they are practically singing a duet? And what happened to all Kamala's big talk of bad spirits and weak souls and doing *His righteous work*? All that is just gone now?"

"No. She just thinks His righteous work sent us Akhil."

"Oh, Akhil!" Sanji said, and saying his name aloud seemed to break her a little. She leaned forward against the counter, pinching the bridge of her nose. She looked old.

Amina put a hand on her shoulder, and Sanji turned around and fell into her with such force that it felt like catching a ham more than a human. Her aunt didn't say anything for a long moment, the small gasps of her trying to steady her breathing the only sound in the kitchen. Her bosom shuddered gelatinously. She whispered something.

"What?" Amina asked.

"It's like it's happening all over again," Sanji repeated.

And there it was, the thing Amina had not been able to find her way toward but felt was unmistakably true. She said nothing, her loosely floating fears suddenly converging around that point like water over a drain. That was it, wasn't it? In the midst of all of the rest of it, all the tests and the treatments and the fights, they were rushing back to that dark place.

Sanji sighed a heavy, oniony breath. "All these years and they can barely talk about him. Some days, I will remember and I can hardly bear it myself. He was our first, nah? Our baby. That sweet little boy who ran around putting his chubby hands into everything, stealing our shoes when you and Dimple were still drooling? Ach!"

Because really, it didn't matter whether he was the by-product of Thomas's tumor or some filament of time slipped through a chink in the universe; it didn't matter that Kamala and the others could not, would not, would never see him. The very idea that Akhil could be in the garden had brought back his loss, pushing it into every corner until the house bled with it. If she shut her eyes, Amina could feel exactly how gone her brother was, her ability to weigh his absence extra keen, dialed up like a blind person's ability to hear. Cool air rushed against her cheeks and chest and she realized Sanji was holding her at arm's length.

"I've upset you. Oh, baby, I'm sorry. I don't know why I keep yelling at you all the time about every new thing." She kneaded Amina's forearms. "It's not your fault."

"It's okay."

"No it isn't."

"Okay, it's not."

They held each other for a bit longer, and after that, there didn't seem to be much more to say, so they put water on to boil and filled the teapot with Red Label.

Bala was the next to come back, chattering loudly all the way in through the porch and then quieting abruptly as she saw Sanji and Amina. She looked over her shoulder, whispering loudly, "It's the pain of losing a child."

"No shit," Amina said, and Sanji smacked her hand lightly, but Bala appeared not to hear.

"They say it's unlike anything else. A grief so profound it can bring people closer to the *dying* than the *living*. I saw it on the Ricki Lakes once, a whole family that believed their youngest was still in the garage where she—"

"Oh, shut it," Sanji snapped.

"No, really! And one of my sisters herself had a stillbirth! She was never okay after that."

"Ranjana was never okay before," Chacko announced, walking in from the living room, three lanterns in hand. He held them up for Amina. "These are a fire hazard."

Amina took them. "Thanks."

Her uncle looked at her somberly. "Okay, *koche*. So now we know. Next, we need to take action."

"Yes, but what?" Sanji looked anxiously toward the porch. "You heard them. They're not doing the chemo until the whole thing is over."

"Wait, what?" Amina asked. "They haven't told me this. What's over?"

"The *visit* has to *end*," Bala said, pinching the air for emphasis. "He's only come for a short time, apparently. Thomas said all of the others that have come have gone on their own after a few days, you know, like aliens beamed back into the light, and—"

"He said that? *Beamed back into the light?*"

"No." Sanji glared at Bala. "He did not. He said that he'll start treatment when Akhil is gone, and that Akhil will go when he's ready."

"But he hasn't even talked to him yet!" Bala said. "That was the other thing, no? That Akhil must talk to him, and he hasn't yet? So he's waiting for that."

"Too late," Chacko declared, rocking from his heels to the balls of his feet and back. "We don't have any more time to waste. We need to separate them, incapacitate Thomas, and take him in."

Incapacitate? Amina held the counter as her stomach plummeted.

"Chacko Kurian, have you lost your damn mind?" Sanji exploded. "This isn't an episode of *Laws & Orders*! We can't just take him in like he's a criminal!"

Chacko frowned. "He will thank us later."

"Really? Like Dimple has thanked you?" Sanji snorted and Bala gasped. "What? You know it's true! Fifteen years since you sent her away, and still this girl doesn't come home if she can help it, and now you people think we should try it on Thomas!"

"Well, someone has to do what needs to be done," Chacko said, stung. "And anyway, I don't see you making a better suggestion."

"How about we talk to him like one human? Nah, Ami? Isn't that better?"

They both looked at Amina expectantly, but she was still stuck on *incapacitate him,* her mind racing with horrible images: Thomas felled like a Serengeti lion, reduced to a mass of sleeping fur, while nimble hands checked tags and teeth; Thomas back in the hospital, prisoner to a staff he once directed.

"Yes," Amina said. "Let's talk to him."

Raj was the last to come in, clearly shaken, cotton stars smashed across the back of his pants where he'd taken a seat on the couch. Unlike the others, he had little to offer in the way of advice and began simply making chapatis to eat Bala's aloo with, the puffs of flour rising across his face and mapping the occasional tear that streaked down as he rolled the dough into flat rounds. Half an hour later, the Eapens were corraled to the dining room, despite real grumbling from Thomas.

"So can you see Akhil, too?" Bala asked Kamala, passing her the potatoes.

"Bala!" Sanji scolded.

"What? I'm just asking!"

"Nope," Kamala said. "But did Thomas tell you what he's wearing?"

"Yes," Raj said hurriedly, just as Bala said "No" and Sanji looked like she might kill somebody.

"His jeans are *short* and he has paint on his *hands!*"

Sanji looked at Amina, alarmed.

"Everyone comes back looking like they did on their best day,"

Amina found herself explaining, hoping that it somehow sounded less crazy coming from her, though from the look on Sanji's face, it definitely did not.

"And have you ever seen him, Ami?" Bala asked.

Amina felt the heat rise to her face and avoided looking at her father. She shook her head.

Kamala shrugged. "He hasn't come for us."

"Thomas, what can I get you?" Raj asked. "You're not eating. How about just plain rice and curds?"

"Actually, I should probably just get back outside." Thomas pulled his napkin from his lap. "It's getting late."

"But we just sat!"

"You stay and finish. I'll just be outside."

"No, wait!" Sanji looked flustered. There was a short silence, a flurry of eye contact between the others. "It's just we thought we should all talk about, the, uh—"

"YOU HAVE TO GO BACK TO TREAMENT!" Chacko boomed. Amina looked over to find her uncle standing tensely at the end of the table, fists clenched.

Thomas's eyebrows rose in surprise. He blinked at Chacko a few times before saying, "Of course I will. I told you that."

"Right now." Chacko rapped his knuckles on the table. "Tonight."

Thomas laughed a little. "That seems unlikely."

"This isn't a joke, Thomas."

"I'm aware of that."

"Then quit this now."

Thomas cocked his head, like a dog hearing a frequency unavailable to human ears, and Amina tensed.

"I've already called Presbyterian," Chacko continued. "They have a bed ready for you in Admitting. Dr. George says you can restart your treatments first thing in the morning."

Thomas said nothing for a moment, but Amina could feel him taking in all of them through his periphery. She saw the slight tic behind his eyes as he recalibrated.

"It's not time," he told Chacko.

"You don't have more time!"

"We don't know that."

"I most certainly do."

"No," Thomas said gently. "You don't. My reaction to the treatment has been anomalous."

A high, furious blush rose in Chacko's cheeks, as if he had been slapped. "You know as well as I do that that doesn't mean a damn—"

"The thing is," Sanji intervened smoothly, looking at Raj for backup, "it's not as if recovery is an indefinitely open window, is it? Your health can weaken to the point where it's irreversible, and then no treatment will help, isn't it?"

"It's a calculated risk."

Chacko snorted. "And what about your family? What are they supposed to do with this nonsense?"

Kamala looked up from her plate in surprise. "Who, me?"

"You're willing to risk their future too?"

"I'm not risking their—"

"Of course you are!"

"*Me?*" Kamala repeated.

"They have no problem with this."

"*Eda!* What are you talking? You think they don't—"

"Wait just one minute, Mr. Big Horses!" Kamala yelled at Chacko. "Don't you sit there yak-yakking for me!"

"And Amina?" Chacko pressed on, ignoring her. "After everything, you're going to put her through this?"

At last then, something to penetrate the glimmering sea of Thomas's cheeriness. Amina saw the words sink in, the sharp tug of doubt suddenly creasing an otherwise smooth brow. She could feel her father not looking at her.

"She'll be fine," he said, but his voice no longer held the conviction it had before.

"No she won't! How could she be? A father who would rather die than stay with her?"

A chapati, hurled with significant force, slapped Chacko full across the face. No sooner had it dropped than another replaced it, flung from the surprisingly accurate throwing arm of Kamala.

"Kam! Stop it!" Sanji cried.

Amina watched as her mother took another and chucked it at Chacko for good measure. It smacked into his chest.

"KAMALA," Thomas said loudly, and her mother looked at him, furious, wild-eyed, shaking with adrenaline. He waited for her to lower her arm before saying softly, "Enough."

Her parents looked at each other, the air between them twitching with something so raw and intimate that the others had to look away.

"Go," Kamala said. "I will come soon."

Thomas turned from the table without another word and left.

They sat back down and waited in silence, staring down at the tablecloth grease stains and stray bits of potato until the porch door clicked shut. Then they waited some more.

"Kam," Sanji finally said. "Please."

Kamala leaned back in her chair and crossed her arms, scowling at them.

"Ma."

"What?"

"You're the only one he'll listen to."

"Ha! Your father? Ha *ha*!"

"It's true. You know it is. He'll pretend like he's ignoring you, but in the end, he'll do whatever you say."

Kamala snorted.

"So then what?" Sanji asked, frustration raking her voice. "Just sit back and let him die? Is that what you want?"

Kamala stared at her for so long that the air in the room seemed to harden. "You think that is the worst thing that can happen?"

Sanji looked confused.

"*Fools.*" Kamala hissed the word across the table like a dart, leaned into the silence that followed it. "*Idiots. Know-nothings.* Coming here with your dry potatoes and idiot demands that he get up tomorrow and tomorrow and tomorrow, and for what? So you can say you did everything you could?"

"Ma, stop. They came because I wanted them."

"And what about your father? Did you ask what he wants?"

"He doesn't know what—"

"*He wants to see Akhil.*"

"A hallucination!" Chacko countered. "A side effect!"

"A *miracle.*"

"What does it even matter?" Raj cried, his voice high and wavery. "Kamala, don't you see? He's losing weight! He's stopped sleeping! His bones are poking through his clothes!"

"You think I'm blind? That I don't see?"

"We need to—"

"You think that I don't know this man I have spent some thirty-five years with? I know him better than anyone—any of you! And you are wrong, Miss Amina Knows Everything, he does not listen to me! He has never listened to me! You think *I* don't know what happens next?"

Silence fell over the table, heavy as a net, and in its descent, Amina's head filled with the high electric keening of the lights, all of the lights, their background noise suddenly amplified. It felt like an invisible audience taking a step forward. It felt personal.

"You think he wants to stay with us more than he wants to go to Akhil?" her mother asked, voice tiny behind all the buzzing, and the truth felt like something small and sharp lodged into Amina's heart.

The rest of the family was coming apart, Amina could feel it. At one end of the table, Raj had covered his face with his hands, and at the other, Chacko shook his head from side to side, like a dog trying to shake loose a collar. Bala and Sanji sat between them with wide, pooling eyes, Sanji already whispering, "I'm sorry, I'm sorry," like she had caused what was to come.

"Then what . . . ?" Chacko barked, his mouth trembling.

A spasm of compassion flickered across Kamala's face before it smoothed again.

"Go home," she said.

CHAPTER 4

"I'm coming down," Dimple said the next day.

Amina shut her eyes. This seemed to be everyone's solution, as if it would make a difference. Monica had come just that morning, begging Thomas to change his mind and then weeping bitterly in the driveway when he wouldn't. *Son of a bitch*, she'd said, and smoked two cigarettes right then and there.

"You can't," Amina said.

"Why not?"

It wasn't that she didn't want to see Dimple. She just didn't want to see Dimple seeing what everyone else had. Amina sighed and rolled onto her back, coming face-to-face with the brassy smiles of the Greats.

"The show. It's in three weeks. You don't have time."

"Don't worry about that. It's practically done already, and I can do most of the press from there. They want to talk to Jane more than me anyway, at this point."

"Oh, great."

"It's not what you think. She's saying she likes it."

"She likes it?"

"No, duh, she fucking hates it. But she's giving it good press because it's the smart thing to do. She's also saying you still work there even though she told me that if either of us set foot in Wiley Studios again, she will shank us."

"She said shank us?"

"She said kill us."

"Oh." Amina tried not to feel upset by this. What did she think was going to happen?

Outside, Prince Philip was barking a low, constant complaint. Amina got up from the bed and ambled over to the window. Her parents were weeding in the garden, despite the afternoon heat.

"What?" Dimple asked.

"What?"

"You just said 'nuts.'"

Amina moved away from the window. "My parents. It's weird. They go everywhere together now. The garden, the porch, probably the bathroom for all I know. It's like they're dating or something."

"That's sweet."

"No it's not. It's like having the sun set on the wrong fucking side of the sky."

Dimple was quiet for a moment. "How are you doing?"

Why did everyone always ask that? "I'm fine."

"My mom said last night was awful."

"When are you telling her about Sajeev?"

"What?" Dimple's voice bowed up in surprise. "I don't know. I mean, that's the last thing we need to think about right now, isn't it?"

"Isn't it just better to tell everyone and be done with it?"

"God, Ami. Compared to everything else going on? It's practically a nonissue."

"I mean, especially if you're still planning on eloping after the show." Amina paced around the room. "Because a wedding might be nice, you know. For everyone to think about."

"What, like a distraction?"

"No," Amina said, even though that was exactly what she meant.

Was it really so bad to want something to look forward to? She opened up Akhil's armoire and saw a grimy version of her own tired face staring back at her. "When do you get in?"

"Midnight tonight. We'll come over in the morning. Who is that?"

"What?"

"Ami, seriously? Have your ears melted? Your doorbell just rang."

It rang again. Prince Philip began barking like his back was on fire.

"Shit." Amina looked down. She wasn't wearing a bra, and her damp armpits smelled mildly like coffee. She looked around the floor for her bedroom slippers.

"Do you want me to call back?"

"No, I'll just see you tomorrow." She dropped the phone in the cradle and hurried down the stairs just as the ringing switched to knocking.

"Coming!" she shouted as she approached the door, and this unleashed a torrent of disapproval from Prince Philip, who seemed to be auditioning for the role of ferocious guard dog on the other side of it.

"Thank God," Jamie said when she opened it, eyes looking back at the bared teeth. "Your dog is about to go Cujo on me."

"Oh!" Amina crossed her arms over her chest. "Hey!"

"Can you help me out here?"

"SHUT IT, PRINCE!" Amina shouted, and the dog looked immediately sheepish, tail wagging. He sniffed Jamie's pants.

"Prince like the singer?" Jamie watched him nervously.

"Like Prince Philip of England."

"Ah."

The dog wandered away, and Jamie looked at her expectantly.

"You look great," Amina said.

Actually, he looked like a banker on a business-casual day—chinos, checked shirt, and good leather shoes, face the kind of clean-shaven that felt rubbery—but still.

"Yeah? Cool. I wanted to look nice to meet your parents."

"Ha!" Amina tried to tamp down the flare of panic between her ribs. "Of course. Yes. And they want to meet you, too! We all do. I mean, not me, but you know, have you meet them. The thing is, though, it's just not really a good time."

"Yeah, I figured," Jamie said. He took a step back, glancing at his car as if he were going to get back in it, and for a moment Amina thought it would be that easy. Then he shrugged. "I mean, I get it. I really do. Which is why yesterday when we got off the phone I just thought, *You know what? It might never be a good time. So I might as well just go over.*"

She was nodding like one of those nodding dolls, the ones that go from cute to stupid in about a second. She stopped. "Weird."

Jamie frowned.

She shook her head, tried again. "We are weird right now. And the house. It's . . ." She looked down at the good leather shoes. The good leather shoes were not going to like what was passing for normalcy behind the front door. Amina sighed. "It's fucked."

"Amina."

It seemed like a bad idea, looking right at him. It seemed like the inevitable first step toward some tedious, emotional conversation about how bad things were getting, how shakily she'd handled them, how long it had been since she'd showered. But when she looked up, there was something sympathetic and a little amused in his eyes, and she found herself backing up. Jamie walked inside. He looked around slowly, lingering on the windowsills, the furniture, the chair with the clocks. Overnight, Christmas lights had been laid on the floor on either side of the hallway so that it lit up like a merry runway.

Amina pushed her hair behind her ear. "It doesn't always look like this."

"Okay."

"Do you want some tea or something?"

"Sure."

It was funny to have him walking behind her, his height out of context in her house. She felt like she needed to point out lighting fixtures, doorways, to push the walls a little farther apart. They went into the kitchen, where Thomas had crammed the countertop with candles of all shapes and sizes that morning, despite Kamala's vocal disapproval. Amina turned the kettle on and retrieved a paper bag, opening it with an efficient snap. She began dropping the candles into it.

"Pretty house," Jamie said.

Amina gave him a look.

"No, really. It's obviously not, you know, in its best state right now, but it's still nice. The trees are huge." He looked into the courtyard. "Is that . . . ?"

"A halogen lamp wrapped in Christmas lights. Yes. It's funny how that's the one that gets people. What kind of tea do you want?"

"Anything. Actually, decaf if you have it."

She finished with the candles and rolled the paper bag tight, setting it down on the floor. At the back of the cabinet, she found an old herbal sampler and pulled out a bag of chamomile for him and a Red Label for herself. She turned on the kettle. "You hungry?"

"Nope."

She walked a few paces toward and away from the stove. She could feel him watching her.

"I'm fine," she said preemptively. "I mean, I haven't showered in a while. Or slept, really. And I keep worrying about my parents doing something crazier than they already have, but that's just, you know. Fine."

"Crazier?"

"You know, like pushing the fridge into the garden. Or burning the house down." She laughed self-consciously, and sat. There was something sticky on the countertop, and she scraped her nail against it, aware that Jamie was still watching but unable to stop.

"So how is he?"

She shrugged. "I don't know. Maybe fine? Maybe metastasizing?"

"I'm sorry."

"So am I," she said, and felt a little pop in her chest when he reached across the counter and held her hand. The water heated with a quiet roar. "Was it like this with your mom?"

"Not really."

"Just the part where she covered the whole house in lights?"

Jamie squeezed her hand.

When the teakettle screamed, Amina poured water into both cups, thinking of all the other things she had assumed would kill Thomas one day. The smoking. The scotch. Some kind of extremely rare blood-borne disease that he'd get but save the rest of the hospital from with a final heroic act.

"I guess I just didn't think it would be like this," she said out loud.

"Yeah."

"No, I mean . . . it's not like I never thought about how we would die. When I was a kid that's *all* I thought about for a while—when it would happen and who would be next and how it would feel. I was sure one of them would disintegrate just from having to get up every day and take a shower. That part is the worst. But we made it past that, you know? I just thought we were in the clear."

She heard Jamie get up and come around the counter, and jumped a little as his hands settled on her shoulders. She did not want to cry, so she didn't, she just kept her chin tucked to her neck and let Jamie pull her into a backward hug, his long arms folding around her, his newly smooth chin pressing into her neck.

"And half the time, I don't even know what's real anymore," she said, quieter now because it felt like the kind of secret you keep. "All these days start feeling like one really long day, like there's no difference between being awake and asleep, and nothing will ever make it end, except that it's ending, and I know that, and I don't know what the fuck I'm supposed to do about it."

"I love you," Jamie said.

"Your face feels like a girl's."

His hands folded around either side of her rib cage, holding it in place, and a bolt of relief moved through Amina, leaving her acutely aware of how fragile and strange and necessary breathing was. She leaned back into him.

"I was just caught off guard yesterday," he said. "Over the phone. I'm bad on the phone."

"Yeah. Why is that?"

"I don't know. I think it's because I grew up thinking the government might be listening in. It makes me paranoid now."

"Because the government doesn't want you to love me?"

"Something like that."

The front door opened, the jangling of Kamala's bangles sending them apart.

"Hello?" Amina called out, straightening her shirt. "Ma?"

"It's me," her mother said. "Someone came?"

"It's my friend Jamie."

The soft thud of Kamala's feet hurried down the hall, and then suddenly she popped through the kitchen doorway, all sari and tennis shoes and braid and scrutiny.

"Hi." Jamie stuck out his hand. "Jamie Anderson."

Kamala looked at his hand but didn't take it. "What are you doing?"

"Ma!"

"What? I'm just asking if he wants to stay for dinner!"

"No, no," Amina said quickly. "He just dropped by."

"Dinner sounds great," Jamie said.

"What?" Amina turned around.

He squeezed her arm gently, saying to her mother, "I'd love to have dinner, Mrs. Eapen, as long as I don't put you out."

"Not out! *In*. I'm cooking." She turned to Amina. "He likes fish or chicken?"

"I like both," Jamie said. "And actually, I love to cook, if you don't mind having me in the kitchen."

Kamala wrinkled her nose, squinting from his shoes to his shoulders. "We'll see."

CHAPTER 5

They made a feast. Or rather, Kamala made a feast, instructing Jamie on how exactly to cut each vegetable before she threw it into one of many pots, and answering "some" every time he had a question about how much spice she was adding. How they'd managed to make so much in just over two hours was inconceivable, even with Jamie helping, but there it was, sprawled along the dining table like edible treasure, two kinds of curry (chicken and fish), four sides of vegetables (cabbage, carrots, beets, and cauliflower), pooris, lime rice, regular rice, salad, raita, and an entire array of glossy chutneys.

Thomas insisted on not leaving sight of the garden, so he and Amina made a hasty table from plywood planks and sawhorses, and half an hour later all four of them floated in the darkening green grass between the house and the tomato plants.

"So tell me," Jamie asked, letting Kamala serve him thirds of everything, "why is it that South Indian food is so much better than North? Is it the spices? The rice-based thing?"

Kamala leaned in to expound on her favorite subject, and Amina sat back. At first, it had been strange to see everyone sitting at the same table—like watching a play where she knew too much about all the actors to believe anything they said. But as the day melted around them, as the early-evening sun poured gold into the fields and Jamie kept asking the kind of questions her parents enjoyed answering, she felt herself enjoying the meal, or at least not worrying through every second of it. It helped that they had put the table in the middle of the field, giving Thomas a clear view of the garden. He seemed calm and focused, albeit with two pairs of binoculars (regular and night-vision) on the table beside him.

"And we live better, too," Kamala said, finishing up a small diatribe that pinpointed reasons as varied as better cows (for finer paneers and ghees) and better genetic makeup ("far superior" Dravidian taste buds). "What laughing? No jokes! Thomas, tell him! Everything is better when you're not constantly worried about the cold and the dust and the crazy Mughals slaughtering everyone!"

"Kamala has always been an excellent cook," Thomas said, adeptly sidestepping the historical assertions. "First time she cooked for me, I thought I had died and gone to heaven."

"And when was that?"

"Nineteen sixty-four. We were just married, staying at my mother's house for one month before we got our own flat." Thomas scraped his plate with the pads of his fingers. "You remember, Kam? How Amma had to bribe Mary-the-Cook to leave the kitchen to you?"

"What leaving? She stood there huffing and puffing over everything I did, telling me I am cutting onions wrong and too much of cloves and the biryani will be too wet!"

"It was perfect," Thomas said, shutting his eyes like he could still taste it. "Best I've ever had."

"And what year did you come here?" Jamie took a sip of beer.

"Nineteen sixty-eight. JFK to St. Louis airport to here," Kamala said, plotting the points across her plate with her middle finger. "I was just pregnant with Amina. We went back to get Akhil a few months later."

"Wow. Albuquerque must have been so small back then."

"You don't know! One tiny speck of city in so much of brown!"

Thomas's eyes snapped open. He squinted at the garden. Sat up a little.

"Had you always wanted to be a brain surgeon?" Jamie asked him. Thomas did not answer. Amina prodded him with her foot.

"No," Thomas said, dragging his eyes from the garden to Jamie with some effort. "When I was young, I wanted to be a pilot."

"What about you?" Kamala said, spooning a little more rice onto Jamie's plate. "You always wanted to go into teaching?"

"Not at all. I just really enjoyed the field studies I was doing, and this is one way to keep doing them."

"Amina said you're in archeology?" Thomas asked.

"Anthropology."

"Anthropology," Thomas repeated. "So do you just teach all day, or—"

"No, actually, my tenure-track status is pursuant to a study I'm conducting, so I spend a portion of my week out in the field. Or, well, at casinos."

"Like the Sandia Casino?" Kamala asked.

"Actually, that's the one I'm looking at right now."

"*Chi!*" she shook her head. "Horrible place! So dark inside! And not one thing to eat at the all-you-can-eat!"

"Not even the chicken fingers?"

Kamala looked aghast. "Who eats chicken's fingers?"

"So Amina must have told you about all that terrible business with her picture," Thomas said. "The Puyallup Indians and all that."

"Uh, no, actually," Amina said. "Can someone pass me the beets?"

"What picture?" Jamie asked.

"Nothing." Amina shook her head dismissively. "Another time."

"The Indian man jumping from a bridge!" Kamala said excitedly. "Not Indian our Indian, Indian feathers on the head. It's famous! She didn't tell you?"

"Wait, not the one from a couple of years ago. In Seattle? The chief?"

"Community leader," Amina corrected with a wince.

"You took *that* picture?"

"You know it?" Kamala nudged Thomas, who was back to looking at the garden, jittery. "He knows it."

"You took that?" Jamie looked impressed.

"Yes! And after, she became a wedding photographer," Kamala said, nodding. "And now she might be starting her own highly successful events-photography business out here."

"*Ma.*"

"What? You might! Did she at least tell you there will be one show of her work in a Seattle gallery in a few weeks?"

"Yes, that I know."

"Be right back," Thomas said, rising from his chair and making a beeline for the garden.

"Mrs. Eapen, would you mind if I had one more poori?"

"Have, have!" Kamala handed Jamie two more, and they fell into a discussion on pooris and why (in Kamala's opinion) they were superior to fry bread and why hers (just ask anyone) were better than most. Amina turned around and watched as her father walked rigidly out to the garden, stopping at the gate. He leaned over it. Said something. Waited. Said it again. Then he turned around to come back, his face drum tight.

"Oh, hey, Dimple's coming tomorrow," Amina said, suddenly remembering. "Well, today, actually, but she'll come over here tomorrow morning."

Kamala frowned. "Why?"

"She wants to see Dad."

"Pish. She should be so concerned about her own parents. Bala worries for her all the time only."

Thomas returned to the table, sitting heavily.

Amina leaned forward, trying to catch his eye. "So, I was just telling Mom that Dimple is coming to see you tomorrow. Sometime in the morning."

"Dimple is Amina's old friend from school," Kamala explained to Jamie. "Not much in common anymore, but what can you do?"

"Yeah, I remember her from school."

"Oh!" Kamala's face lit up. "You went to Mesa Preparatory? I didn't realize! No one said!"

"It's not some huge deal, Ma."

"But then he will know everyone you know! All the kids and everyone who is out here. You're in touch? Lots of socializing?"

"Uh, kind of."

Amina looked away, distracted by Thomas. His eyes pinged from side to side, like he was trying to remember where he'd put something important. Amina nudged him with her foot again.

Kamala chewed her food a little, swallowing before asking, "So you knew Akhil, too?"

"Yes. Actually, he dated my sister, Paige."

Kamala blinked rapidly, mouth moving slightly, as if she was finishing the rest of the sentence without sound, and Thomas's gaze snapped from the garden to Jamie. "You're Paige's brother?"

"Yes."

He leaned forward. "From high school? That girl he dated?"

"Paige Anderson."

"Paige *Anderson,*" Kamala repeated softly, like a lyric to a song she'd been trying to remember.

"The girl." Thomas looked at Amina for confirmation. "The one."

"She came here once, I think," Kamala said, and Jamie nodded.

"Unbelievable!" Thomas howled, and slapped the table.

"Yeah," Jamie started. "Kind of a strange coincidence, I guess."

Thomas laughed loudly, and Jamie smiled despite the strangeness of the situation, because who could resist Thomas's sudden burst of joy, his smile growing by the second like he'd won some sort of cosmic lottery?

"Did you hear that?" Thomas called out to the garden. "Paige Anderson's brother is *here!*"

Amina shot Kamala an alarmed look.

"*Here!*" her father shouted, a little louder. He pointed at Jamie. "Right here!"

"Pa," Kamala said, touching his arm softly, but he shooed her away, fumbling for his binoculars.

"Hold on, I want to see his face."

Kamala bent her head to his ear, slipping into a heated whisper of Malayalam that Thomas did not even pretend to listen to.

"He's ignoring me. Pretending he can't hear me again."

Amina tugged Jamie's arm, but he was riveted, his mouth slightly open, like he was watching a movie.

"YOU HEAR ME?" Thomas yelled, a thread of frustration in his voice making them jump. He was growing agitated, one hand holding the binoculars while the other clenched and unclenched. His arm shook as he motioned to the garden. "See how he does that? Acts like he's not listening but he's listening? I used to do the same thing. Drove my mother nuts."

Amina looked helplessly at the garden, the blue evening spreading out around it like water.

"Me too," Jamie said.

Thomas turned to him.

"My mother hated it," Jamie continued, a flush rising to his cheeks. "Told me I'd regret it someday."

Thomas looked at him for several long seconds before sitting back down slowly. "And did you?"

"Yeah. I did, actually."

"And are you close now?"

"She died a few years ago. Breast cancer."

"And were you with her when she died?"

"Yes."

"In the room? Right there?"

"Dad!" Amina said, but Jamie was already nodding, a sad, surprised smile on his face, like he'd just caught an unexpected glimpse of a place he missed, and this seemed to mean something to Thomas, who leaned back in his chair, shutting his eyes.

"You have nothing to regret," he said.

After dinner, she led Jamie up to her room and went down the hall to take a shower. When she came back, he was lying awkwardly across her bed, entirely too large for it, staring at the canopy.

"So this is what girls like?" He motioned upward, the lines in his face carved deep with thought. "Looking up at tiny flowers all day and night?"

"When they're, like, seven." She sat down.

"Can we talk about Air Supply?"

"Nope."

"Damn." He wiped a drop of water from her shoulder. "I knew you'd say that."

He looked exhausted, bags the color of bruises under his eyes. Amina bent over and kissed his cheek, then his forehead. "We wore you out."

"I sleep better with you in the bed."

Amina smiled, her eyes moving from his mouth to his neck to the button she most wanted to undo on his shirt. She leaned over him, letting the towel unfold.

"Whoa. Wait, no." Jamie sat up, pushing it closed with both hands. "Not happening. Not in here."

"Seriously? They won't even know."

"Yes they will. Your father will know. And then he will come up here and he will kill me with his freakishly large thumbs."

"Jamie."

"And there's no way I'm getting turned on in this bed. And frankly, you should question the moral fiber of any guy who does."

Amina looked at the bedroom door, perplexed. "My dad has large thumbs?"

"How do you not know that?"

She lay back on the bed. "So you survived dinner."

He grunted.

"I'm sorry about that whole thing. Your mom."

"It's fine," he said, and when she looked at him, he looked fine, the plates in his face shifted to seal off whatever had pierced through when he was talking to Thomas. "Anyway, they're way nicer than you said."

"Last month my mother wouldn't have even talked to you."

"Yes she would have."

"You don't know my mother!"

"Okay, fine. She would have thrown chutneys at my head. So what, now she's too worried about your dad to bother?"

"No, she's in love," Amina said, understanding it was true as she said it. She thought of her mother's face that night at the table, waiting to laugh at some story Thomas had told a thousand times, and her chest tightened like she'd swallowed a pocket of wind.

"Love is good," Jamie muttered, his eyelids heavy.

Amina watched his breathing, the little flickering pulse at the base of his neck. Just when she thought he had fallen asleep, he said, "So that picture. That was the one, huh?"

"Yeah."

His eyes fluttered open. "Do you like it?"

"It's horrific."

"That's not what I asked."

It was a funny question because no one had ever asked her before, and because she wasn't sure she knew the answer until she felt herself nodding, and then she knew it absolutely. Jamie's eyes slid shut.

"I'd like to see it," he said.

"Really?"

"Yeah, of course."

Amina chewed at her cuticle, watching him. "You want to fly out with me for the opening?"

"Drive."

"What?"

"Let's drive."

"That's a long way to drive," she said, but he was already drifting away, the knot between his eyebrows smoothing.

Amina rolled onto her back, staring up at the canopy. She reached out, pinching a corner of his T-shirt between two fingers, feeling it rise and fall with his breaths. She imagined them driving north and west, the aspen, the Tetons, the ragged coast of Oregon. Jamie's profile against a blur of landscape. They slept.

CHAPTER 6

How had she forgotten about Dimple's beauty? And could it have actually increased in her absence? The next morning Amina stared, trying not to be thrown by the surreality of her cousin's overlarge cheekbones and liquid eyes, the way her skin glowed like a baby's butt in a diaper commercial.

"He's so skinny," Dimple said, watching Kamala and Thomas garden through the screen door on the porch. She had come over before the others, claiming she'd wanted some time alone with Thomas, but now that she was there, she seemed stuck somehow, unable to actually go into the yard.

"The meds kill his appetite," Amina explained.

"Isn't there something you can do about that? Like a permanent IV or something?"

"Not really."

"Or, like, fatty foods? Can he just eat really fatty things?"

"He can't keep them down."

"Fuck." Dimple's chin trembled and she quickly rubbed it.

"You want me to go out with you?" Amina asked.

Dimple shook her head, her face shadowed with nervousness. She watched Thomas bend down, biting her cuticle.

"Do you want to go have a smoke on the Stoop?"

"Yes. I mean, no." She took a sharp breath. "I just . . . I think some part of me really believed that it was an exaggeration. Like maybe he was doing better than everyone thought, or maybe everyone had been here too long to see things clearly." She swept a fingertip under her left eye, quickly ridding it of the tear that threatened to spill over. "The fucking height of narcissism, right?"

Amina shrugged. "It's hard to get it unless you see it."

Outside, Thomas rose slowly, his legs shaking until Kamala rose too, wedging herself under his arm. Dimple turned away, her eyelashes shivering over the shop, the piles of lights, the parched mound of what had been Akhil's jacket. "So is there anything I should know? Anything I shouldn't, you know, talk about?"

"Oh, you know. Treatment. Tumors, medications, prognoses. Eating, sleeping. Akhil, but I guess that was always the case, although now if you talk about him, you'll hear all sorts of stuff."

"Like everyone comes back looking like they did on their best day?"

"Like clocks make it harder to see them."

"Wow."

They watched Thomas and Kamala walk away from the tomato plants, toward the back of the garden.

"You know what I don't get?" Dimple said. "How do you know what your best day is? I mean, aren't some of them tied?"

Amina smiled, nudging her cousin gently. "So are you going to do this or what?"

Dimple nodded but didn't move.

"He's the same person," Amina lied, unsure if it was cruel to do so, but distinctly thankful as Dimple finally pushed the screen door open, stepping into the sunlight. Thomas looked over as it banged shut, his dark face lightening into a blur of teeth.

"Dimpledimpledimple!" he called, and held his arms open as she ran to him.

"Lunacy!" Chacko shouted an hour later, finger jammed into the air. "Idiocy!"

"Who is asking him?" Thomas shouted back. "Did anyone ask him?"

That afternoon, while the rest of the family cringed and Kamala shelled peas like she was being timed for an Olympic event, Thomas and Chacko went at it in the living room with renewed gusto, as if they'd been doing nothing but storing up counterarguments for the last five days.

"Even a *child* knows this, Thomas! My own *daughter* has come home to beg you to just—"

"Do I come in his house and yell at him over his decisions? No, I do not! Why? Because it's HIS HOUSE."

"Ho!" Sanji flapped around them like an anxious parrot. "Hey! Indoor voices! Let's be discussing this like adults, no?"

"Well, if I was acting like you, I'd hope you'd be MAN ENOUGH to come to my house and face me!"

"Sit," Raj pleaded. "Let's all just—"

"Oh no, let him keep going, please! Perhaps Chacko can kill me himself with his superiority complex!"

"Please!" Bala cried. "The girls!"

It took a moment, but this appeared to be the right tactic as the two men backed away from each other, hunch-shouldered, razor-eyed. Thomas lowered himself shakily into one of the few remaining chairs, and Chacko backed himself into an actual corner, his shoulders squeezed in by the walls. Sanji, Bala, and Raj hovered over the spot of carpet where the couch used to be. Kamala shelled peas.

"Christ." Dimple's voice shook. "Is this how you guys have been the whole time? No wonder everyone looks like shit."

"No Christ, no shit!" Kamala snapped, not looking up.

"You haven't been here," Chacko sulked. "You don't know."

"Know what? That yelling at Thomas Uncle isn't going to change his mind? Yeah, Dad, I'm pretty clear on that one. And if you guys can't talk about something else, then maybe you should just go home and not see each other for a while."

"Okay, okay." Sanji waggled her head. "No need to go for extremes."

"No, this girl is right!" Chacko said. "If we're not here to be honest, then why be here at all? What else is there to talk about?"

"Chackoji," Raj said, the *please* inherent in his voice. "Let's just settle down for a moment."

No one said anything for a long time. Raj looked at Sanji, Bala looked at Dimple, and Amina dropped her eyes to the floor, both irritated and amazed by the steady *plink! plink!* of the peas hitting the metal bowl. So this was it? Thirty years of no one getting a word in edgewise, and they'd run out of things to say?

"I'm getting married," Dimple said.

Amina's mouth dropped open.

"What?" Chacko's face fell.

"To Sajeev."

"What?" Bala whispered, like saying anything louder might trigger a bomb that would detonate the entire future.

"Sajeev and I are getting married."

Kamala made a strangling noise from the floor, her hands frozen in midair.

"OH MY GOD!" Sanji jumped up, her arms swinging through the air until they pinioned Dimple, swung her from side to side. "You see? You see? All this time I've been telling you to be patient and you will find the right one and have your babies before your uterus dries up like one Turkish apricot, and look! It's happened!"

"Sajeev *Roy*?" Bala asked, trembling.

"Yes, Mom. God, what other Sajeev do we know?"

"He knows?" Kamala frowned. "He is wanting this?"

"Ma." Amina rolled her eyes. "He *asked* her."

"SAJEEV ROY?" Bala screamed, and then began jumping up and down, bangles and sari and face a blur of green and gold, and everyone went nuts. Thomas bellowed. Kamala muttered. Raj and Sanji hugged each other and the girls, while Chacko blinked with the stunned disorientation of a man who'd gone to sleep in one country and woken up in another.

"Come here, you little rat!" Thomas shouted, and Dimple went to him, bending down so he could hug her.

"All this time!" Sanji scolded the rest of them. "All this time you people are worried about how will Dimple ever find someone you like and here this girl picks Sajeev Roy himself!"

"You're getting married?" Chacko asked.

"Oh, Dimple, he's going to cry," Thomas said, nudging her toward him. "Look what you've done to your poor father's heart!"

"We will have to go to Mumbai to get the proper lehenga and jewelry!" Bala yelled at nobody in particular. "Three outfits at least!"

"No, wait, Mom, we're not—"

"What time of year? Winter? Summer? Then only we'll know the right gown, nah? Someone call the Roys!"

"Not yet! Sajeev should tell them first, okay? But listen, we're not—"

"They will want to do the engagement party in Wyoming, nah? Fine with me, right, Chacko? Party at the groom's, wedding at the bride's?"

"No!" Dimple yelled. "Stop!"

Bala frowned. "Wedding in Seattle?"

"No wedding! We're eloping."

Bala blinked, bludgeoned with confusion.

"We've already planned it," Dimple explained. "We're going to the courthouse in Seattle in three weeks, just the two of us. You know, keep it simple."

The family catapulted into silence. They did not know. Bala especially did not know, her eyes pinging around the room feverishly like there was a punch line to be found somewhere.

"But not even us?" Sanji's face was rigid with dismay.

"We already planned it," Dimple repeated, looking to Amina for help. "It's really not that big of a deal. People do it all the time."

"Who?" Sanji demanded. "Americans? Orphans?"

"It will just be so much simpler. And cheap! Cheap, Dad. Don't pretend you're not excited about that."

"No wedding?" Chacko asked sadly. And then, even more sadly, "No father-daughter dance?"

"You want a father-daughter *dance*?"

"Of course he wants!" Thomas huffed. "What's wrong with you?"

"Mad," Sanji said, wagging a finger. "Absolutely bonkers nutso. Fine-fine not coming home and all, busy girl with a busy life, but a *wedding*? Without *family*? Might as well have a zoo without animals!"

Dimple gave Amina a pleading look as Bala's crying filled the room, soft and pervasive as humidity.

"What about a simple court ceremony and a small-small reception of only one hundred?" Raj waggled his head from side to side like this was *really* no different from eloping.

"No," Dimple sighed. "That's going to take too much planning. We just want to do this and—"

"I can plan!" Bala said, seizing on this like a lifesaver thrown into an ocean. "All the details only, okay? Flowers and dresses and guest list and food and cake—nothing will be left to you, nah?"

"No, that's not—listen, Mom, it's a nice offer, but I don't want to."

"But a dress!" Bala whimpered. "Surely you want something beautiful? We don't even have to go ourselves, I can have my sister order one simple neemzari lehenga and it can be here in just six weeks and—"

"NO. It's not happening, okay? I'm not waiting six goddamn weeks and inviting a hundred people to sit around and squeeze me! And I'm definitely not wearing some hoochie ghagra choli stomach-baring atrocity!"

Sanji squinted hard at her. "You're pregnant."

"Oh my God," Amina said, finally moving to jump in. "Seriously, you guys, it's not like it's some huge surprise, is it? This is Dimple. And anyway, she's still marrying Sajeev, so it's still a great thing, right?"

"I'm pregnant," Dimple said.

"Ho!" Kamala shouted as Chacko's face paled to gray. "Ho, ho, ho! Now we see!"

"See *what*?" Dimple glared.

"*Choo!*" Sanji stared at the floor, looking awfully surprised for having been so prescient just moments before. She thumped her palms against her sides, as if resurrecting circulation. "So there it is. So now we know."

"*Pregnant?*" Amina asked.

"I'm sorry." Dimple looked at her, wide-eyed. "I wanted to tell you first. I should have told you first. I tried, on the porch this morning. I just couldn't."

"Do the Roys know?" Kamala asked.

"*Ma.*"

"What? Just asking!"

"Oh my God," Bala moaned, clutching her bangles as if to protect them. "It's a *scandal.* We will be *scandalized.*"

"Oh, come on." Dimple rolled her eyes. "Do you even know what a scandal is? I'm in love and I'm having a kid and we're getting married. Big deal."

"But everyone will know when the baby comes! What will the Roys think of us? Ach!"

"Who cares what they think!" Chacko snarled, finally recovering. "What do *we* think? What kind of a family does this? I'm going to have a talk with this boy! Set him straight!"

"Dad, *stop.* This isn't the 1950s."

But wasn't it always the 1950s for Chacko? And not even the American 1950s, but the Indian 1950s, in which a pregnant unmarried daughter in her thirties was as inconceivable as a unicorn in heat? His face sweltered with the indignity of it.

"Hey," Thomas said, trying to catch Chacko's eye. "She's right, you know. It's not so bad."

"What do you know about it?" Chacko glared.

"So then, let's just do it as soon as possible," Sanji said, as though coming to the end of a conversation with herself. "Right, Dimple? That's why you wanted it alone, nah? Not because you don't want us there, but to get it done fast?"

"I don't . . . I mean, mostly, yes."

"So how about this weekend?"

"What?"

"In four days' time! You are staying until Sunday anyway. That is enough for us to make the party. Wedding is just a party, nah? We make parties all the time."

"Yes!" Raj clapped. "It's a good idea, actually. So simple for us to pull something together, right, Bala?"

Dimple looked nervously around the room. "We don't need to do that. I mean, Thomas Uncle has plenty to deal with right now, we don't need to—"

"Judge Montano is an old patient; he can perform the ceremony! And the backyard is so nice at this time of year, no?" Thomas said. "And if you do it here, I won't have to travel, which would be so wonderful. And the Roys can come down easily from Wyoming, and Kamala can cook!"

"I can?"

"We'll both cook," Raj said, nodding eagerly.

"What do you think?" Amina asked Dimple quietly, as though the others weren't listening, and her cousin instinctively patted her pockets, looking for the assurance of a cigarette pack before remembering why it was gone.

She chewed her nail. "I mean, Sajeev would have to agree, obviously."

"So call him already!" Sanji said. "What else do you need?"

What else did she need? Dimple turned to Chacko, her face disconcertingly blank, a vault holding in three decades of disappointment. From her periphery, Amina could see Bala nodding, willing him to concede, to not make the breach between them any more permanent than it already was.

"Hey," Thomas said softly, and this time Chacko looked at him. "You will see your daughter married. You will know her children. Isn't that enough?"

His question hung in the air, a gentle missive. And then what was it that Chacko said, what did he do to bring the soft collapse of relief to the room? Amina did not know because she was no longer looking at her uncle but at the empty spot of floor where the couch used to be, the full weight of the future she was losing with Thomas falling through her like a rock. The air current shifted, the family swishing and dipping and spooling toward one another, Dimple heading to the phone while the rest started making the kinds of plans they loved to make, where everyone had something to deliver. Amina held her breath, rigid, waiting for the worst to pass. She, Kamala, and Raj would handle the food. Bala would take care of decorations. Sanji would keep a running list of everything that needed to get done and make all the trips to the store. Thomas's hand clasped the back of Amina's neck, warm and dry. She looked over, surprised to find him standing, to have him so close. How much strength had it cost him to shuffle over? He pulled her to him, and she pressed her hot face into his shoulder, relieved to have a place to hide it.

CHAPTER 7

"Tell me again," Jamie puffed, hoisting an enormous chandelier made of at least twenty round white paper lanterns into the sturdy branches of a cottonwood, "why this is a good idea?"

"Because if we put these up, we can get rid of most of the other lights and the house will stop looking like a Broadway show mental ward."

"So there's a light quota?"

"Apparently, yes."

He grunted and dug his heels into the foldout linoleum dance floor Thomas had dug up from some corner of the porch. Poor Jamie. They had really put him to work once they realized the advantage of his size, making him Thomas's proxy. So far he had repositioned the couch in the field, added another length to the dining table, handed Kamala every single dish from the top shelves of her cabinets, and emptied the truck of bags of sod (not a wedding duty per se, but something Kamala and Thomas had been so excited about, he couldn't really say no). Amina zoomed in on his hands on the rope, then lowered the camera, looking at the instant replica of him in the viewfinder.

"Is that high enough?" he asked, panting.

She looked up. "Maybe like a foot more?"

"You're insane."

"I mean, can you believe this?" She turned the camera toward him, showing him the tiny picture of his own hands.

The digital camera was a present from Sajeev, who had arrived the day before to a flurry of cheek pinchings from the women and handshakes from the men (with the exception of Chacko, who nodded stiffly at him and then left to walk the perimeter of the yard, as though checking for intruders). Amina had promised to familiarize herself with the new camera before the wedding though Dimple was adamant that she not use it.

"Oh my God!" her cousin said now, coming around the side of the house with two potted plants. "Is that the light thing? That one we're standing under?"

"You like it?" Jamie asked, his arms shaking. They hadn't exactly been fast friends, Jamie and Dimple, sniffing around each other with a fair amount of suspicion, but they were making an effort, more enthusiastic with each other than they'd ever been alone with Amina.

"It's amazing! How did you get it to do that? All those clusters?"

"Don't ask," he grunted, tying the end of the rope to the stake. "Or not unless you want to hear Amina's dad talk about it for a really, really long time."

"Speaking of," Dimple said, looking over her shoulder. "Someone should really get him out of the kitchen before Raj and your mother kill him. And then someone should get Raj out, too."

"That bad?" Amina pulled the lens tight on her cousin's face, liking how the marigolds threw ochre at her cheeks and chin. She showed Dimple the result.

"Ugh! Stop with that. It's so annoying."

"It's instant gratification!"

"Gratification should be delayed."

"Whatever, single mom."

"Shht!" Dimple glanced over her shoulder for the Roys, who had flown in that morning, befuddled but well mannered as ever, and who, the family had decided, did not actually need to know about Dimple's pregnancy until the wedding was over and everyone was safely back in their separate states. ("And even then," Bala had said over dinner the night before, "babies come early all the time, no? Who's to say this one didn't?")

"I thought your mom had the Roys working on the flower garlands," Amina said.

"She did. And like most normal people, Sajeev's dad decided he'd rather shoot himself. Last I saw him, he was looking at some weird sign in the back with a cat on it."

"Raccoon," Amina said. "It's the Raccooner."

"Okay," Jamie said, wiping his hands across his shirt and checking the raw marks on them. "Should we try it out?"

Amina began backing into the field, camera pressed to her face. "Go."

He bent over, head down, and suddenly the lanterns blazed above him, circles upon circles of light bouncing off one another. Jamie and Dimple stood under it, heads turned up. They looked like a fairy tale, a giant, an imp, and a bubbling moon hovering over them.

"Come here. You've got to see this."

"Who?" Dimple asked.

"Both of you," Amina said, and they came, picking their way across the grass, turning around to look back.

It was not the most beautiful wedding she had ever photographed. For one, the potted marigolds didn't hold quite the same amount of romance as other, traditional bouquets, say, calla lilies or white roses. For another, the mismatched tablecloths, folding dining chairs, and rainbow of napkins made the dinner setup look like a deranged child's tea party. But that evening, as Dimple and Sajeev said their vows under Thomas's constellation, as Sanji fanned her face hard enough to keep her dry-eyed, and all the other adults (save Kamala) gave in to a quiet weep, Amina understood that these pictures would be the ones she would never tire of looking at.

Dimple, standing in Amina's bedroom in a towel, bony-shouldered and frazzled with excitement. Bala running down the driveway with flowers so that the Roys would not enter the property without something of beauty to welcome them. Thomas and Chacko, heads bent over the fuse box, trying to figure out what had tripped the outage in the back half of the house. Kamala sprinkling more chili powder into Raj's sambar while he looked in the fridge. Sanji, sneaking a cigarette out on the Stoop because "What are you girls, if not my very own heart growing up once and for all?"

Later, there would be the arrival of the Roys, Sajeev shaking hands with Chacko at last, the fumbling of rings, the dinner. Prince Philip would make off with a leg of tandoori, Chacko and Dimple would have the pined-for father-daughter dance, and Amina and Thomas would join in at the end, at the beckoning of the others.

At nine o'clock, just when it looked like the Roys were getting ready to announce their departure for their hotel, Amina put on "At Last" and waited for it to work its magic. It did not disappoint. Couple by couple went to the dance floor until all five were dancing. Sanji and Raj clung to each other, exhausted, while the Roys floated by. Dimple and Sajeev swayed, her head tucked firmly under his chin. Bala kept talking to everyone, no matter which way Chacko turned her. Kamala and Thomas barely moved, foreheads pressed together, hands clasped around each other's waist. Amina stepped onto a dining chair to get a shot of everyone, while Jamie steadied her hips.

The talking started sometime after midnight. Amina knew because it didn't seem like that long since she'd fallen asleep, and then suddenly there was Thomas's voice in the dark, as sonorous and insistent as a ringing phone, dragging her back from her dreams. She sat up in bed. Made her way to the window.

The wedding lanterns were still on, casting a faint golden glow into the fields and defining the back ridge of the sofa and the light smudge of Thomas's head, so that when the breeze parted the grass he looked like a rafter awash in a green-black sea. His words floated up in patches. Amina leaned forward. What was he saying? Nothing she could make sense of so far away. She went downstairs.

The kitchen was dark, drying china spread out on every countertop like the bones of some prehistoric animal. She walked carefully past them, through the laundry room and onto the dark back porch. She pressed her face to the screen door.

"The bow and arrow," Thomas said. "For concentration."

Next to him in the grass, Prince Philip's tail thumped in reply.

"Hey, Dad—" Amina yelped as a hand slammed over her mouth.

"No!" Kamala hissed, dragging her backward and down. "No talking!"

"Mmph!" Amina tried to stand straight, but Kamala clung to her, eyes gleaming like a feral monkey's until Amina forced herself to take a deep breath and nod at her mother to signify she understood. *Yes. Fine. No talking.* Kamala slowly loosened her grip. Outside, Thomas rocked back and forth in his seat, excited about something.

"You're right," he said. "You're absolutely right."

"Is it—?" Amina started, but she didn't need to finish. There was really no one else it could be.

It was an outpouring, a monsoon. The entire night and into the dawn, Thomas sat on the couch, a deluge falling from his lips. While much of what he said to Akhil was spoken too softly to be understood from their spot on the porch, the tiny bits that Amina could make sense of—how a shunt works, why cricket games could last so long and still be exciting, what it was like to bring Akhil home from the hospital as a baby—seemed to be equally unrelated and urgent, as if there was a list of subjects he'd sworn to cover before the day was over.

By midmorning he showed no signs of slowing down, and Kamala made tea and toast, stepping around a disapproving Amina to deliver it to him.

"I thought you said no talking."

"What talking, dummy? This is *eating.*"

Amina followed her mother out to the couch, where her father greeted both of them with a preemptively raised hand, as though he was on a phone call.

"Tea!" Kamala announced. "Toast!"

"But he won the Oscar," Thomas said, motioning for her to leave the tray. "And the Padma Shri! You think the Indian government goes around giving honors to people who insult the integrity of the country?"

"Ben Kingsley?" Amina couldn't help asking, and her father nodded irritably, shooing her away.

By the late afternoon they were back, taking turns sitting on the couch with him. Kamala darned socks for the better part of an hour, while Amina shot three rolls of close-ups. It wasn't that she needed to know what he was saying, Amina told herself, taking a picture of Thomas's much thinned profile, but rather that the rambling was renewing in some way, the *rat-tat-tat-tat* of a soft summer rain on a tin roof, washing off the heat and misery they had endured.

Her father was finally happy. It was not hard to see this. Joy blossomed across his face, filling his cheeks and eyes with an intensity not seen since he had performed his last surgery. His hands flew around as if reaping the air for sentences. He laughed on occasion. Once, he even turned and winked at her, making her feel like she was in on an elaborate, goofy conspiracy.

"Maybe it's healing him?" Raj asked when he arrived the next morning to retrieve his dishes, and the hope in his voice nipped at Amina's heart even before he went to sit on the couch himself, listening and nodding along.

That afternoon, the family came in shifts, first Sanji, then Bala, and at last Chacko, who surprised everyone by showing remarkable endurance for the natter, sitting for an eight-hour stretch before dismissing himself to go home and sleep.

"Still?" Jamie asked that night.

"Still," Amina confirmed. She held the phone close to her bedroom window, where Thomas's voice droned in like a swarm of bees. "You hear that?"

"Nope."

"Oh. Well, he's still there."

It wasn't until the fourth day, when Thomas stopped eating, that she began to really worry. Sanji, Kamala, and Amina sat in the kitchen, staring at the rejected bowl of chicken and rice like it was a bowl of snakes.

"Nothing for breakfast either?" Sanji asked, and Amina pointed to the toast she'd left on the counter hopefully, as though he might come look for it.

"Probably just queasy or something," Sanji said, but called Chacko at the office anyway.

"*Eda*," Chacko said that evening, kneeling in front of Thomas so he'd be forced to make eye contact, to stop talking. "You have to eat."

"Later," Thomas said.

Chacko patted his leg. "You need your strength. You're getting depleted."

"Later," he repeated, ignoring further entreaties from everyone, including Raj, who brought down a box of every single one of Thomas's favorite foods by dinnertime. That night the family sat in the kitchen, the uneasy silence between them emphasized by Thomas's increasingly frenetic chatter. Contrary to what Chacko had warned, he was growing more animated than ever, jumping breathlessly from subject to subject like a man auctioning off entire areas of thought.

"The exodus is subsiding," he said.

"You mother didn't think so."

"Slingshots!"

On the sixth morning, he skipped his tea and juice.

"You have to drink," Amina said, bringing him a plain glass of water, just in case that was the problem.

"But some narcolepsy responds to norepinephrine reuptake inhibitors," Thomas said, and a tendril of panic curled around her lungs.

"Dad, you're getting dehydrated."

Thomas looked up. His pupils dilated and retracted, finding her for the first time in days.

"I'm coming to your show," he said.

"What?"

"I don't know why we didn't think of it earlier." His breath was sweet and rotten, like bread fermenting in a bag. "Your mother will love it."

She found Kamala in the laundry room washing bedsheets.

"Yes," her mother said after she'd been dragged to the porch to look at him. "I see."

"So what now?" Amina clenched and unclenched her hands, wiping them on her jeans. How would they get him all the way out to the car? They needed to get him into the car. Chacko and Raj would both have to come down to help—there was no other way to manage.

"What do you mean?"

"We've got to get him to the hospital," Amina repeated, annoyed. Had Kamala gone soft, too? Taken tranquilizers? Her mother's eyelashes beat slowly in consideration, butterfly wings testing the wind.

"Not yet," she said.

But when? That day, as Thomas's voice went from hoarse to ragged, as his lips dried into twin strips of beef jerky and the sun dawdled across the sky, Amina paced the field, unable to sit next to her father or to let him out of her sight. He was still talking, or at least trying to talk, his voice a low, droning motor. It looked painful now, his tongue dry and dark in his mouth, the corners of his lips crusted with white. He grimaced as he shifted, and Amina realized that he must have been skipping his pain medication, too.

"Please," she said, sitting down next to him with the pills, and when he didn't even acknowledge her, a voice that must have been hers screamed, "PLEASE! PLEASE! PLEASE!"

"Amina?" Kamala came running from the house. "What is it? What happened?"

"He's not drinking!" Amina said, her voice breaking, and her mother sat next to her on the couch, taking the pills and water from her hand.

"Go," she told Amina. "Sleep."

That night, Thomas's words crawled like insects into Amina's dreams, filling them with a low, humming buzz that kept her tossing and did not fade as she woke up. It was the seventh day. Her brain hurt. If Thomas were Creation, he'd be making Man by now. Amina got up and looked out the window. He was still on the couch.

Kamala was plucking coriander leaves from the stems when she entered the kitchen.

"Did he drink anything?" Amina asked, and when her mother shook her head, it came to her finally, something so obvious and unimaginable that it clattered through her body, rearranging her bones to make space for a grief so large it felt like a new organ. She clutched the counter, panting.

Kamala was standing in front of her, saying her name, pushing her hair behind her ear. *Koche,* she was saying. *Baby. My girl.* She kissed Amina's hands, one by one, and then each cheek, her eyes blazing. "You're going to be okay," she said.

But could this be Kamala? Could this be the same mother that Amina had grown up with, the unwilling immigrant, the dubious participant, the damned and damning loner? That afternoon, as Monica's big blue sedan rolled into the driveway, Amina watched her mother hug the woman she'd barely talked to over the last twenty years, then take her by the hand and lead her into the house and down the hall.

"Thanks for calling me," Monica said as Kamala opened the porch door.

"He'll be so glad to see you," Kamala said.

Whether Thomas registered Monica at all was debatable, his voice reduced to an occasional grunt, but Amina watched through the window as her father's physician's assistant wept, holding on to his hand, kissing his forehead as she stood up. Outside in the driveway, she handed Amina a vial of morphine.

"If he needs it," she said, and barreled into her car and down the driveway before Amina could think of what to say.

The next to come was Anyan George, who didn't stay long or sit at all but said some very nice things nonetheless, his hands tugging at his shirt cuffs, his eyes focused on the space above Thomas's head.

At the end of the day Kamala led the family out to him. Bala knelt and touched his feet. Sanji kissed his cheeks and forehead. Raj whispered something sweet and rushed into his ear before fleeing back to the car. Chacko held his face between his hands like he was trying to carve it into his own memory, and Thomas looked at him, blinking. He grunted.

"What?" Chacko asked, leaning in. "What is it?"

"*Later,*" Thomas whispered.

Jamie hated flying. Not that he was copping to it, or even hinting at it, but it was obvious from the way he fidgeted in his seat as the plane taxied down the runway, flipping open the flight safety cards and the long-defunct ashtrays like they might contain an escape hatch.

"You want to leave?" Amina asked. "Should we just call it quits right now so you can get out while you can?"

"Yes." Jamie closed and opened the window shade with a wince in either direction. "You know me so well."

He lifted her hand to his face, inhaling her wrist like it was a calming agent, and Amina turned to look out the window to the shimmering runway, the barren stretch of mesa spreading out behind it for miles. It seemed ridiculous to be leaving so soon after the funeral.

"What ridiculous?" Sanji had asked when she'd said as much the night before, both of them watching Kamala scrub the courtyard bricks from the kitchen window. "You can't miss your own show, dummy. And you'll be back in a few days. The grief will still be here;

your mother will still be here. The mess might even still be here if that bloody woman doesn't quit driving us fifty kinds of crazy!"

Why Thomas's departure had unleashed a cleaning frenzy in Kamala was anyone's guess, but in the days since, she had been terrorizing every room in the house and the family right along with them. So far Raj and Chacko had beaten twenty-odd rugs while Sanji cleaned the pantry and Bala took on the fridge. And while all of them complained to Amina about being "forced into slave labor" (Sanji's words), they also seemed to be strangely happy doing it, their hands and heads fully occupied with the work. Kamala, for her part, stalked from room to room, zealous and tyrannical. At night she slept on Thomas's side of the bed, clutching a couch cushion like it was a flotation device.

"This is it, right?" Jamie said as the plane gathered speed. "It's happening now?"

"Jesus, have you ever been on a plane?" Amina wrapped her hand over his clenched one.

Outside, the mesa blurred into a line of beige and the air pressed hard against them, slamming them into their seats as the plane ascended. Jamie looked pale and a little sick, his eyes shut tight as the plane banked north.

They were turning now, panning past the Sandias, the deep black-green crags and rocky faces, the ribbon of road leading to the white crest. Amina looked down on Albuquerque, the light bouncing off the sprawling tile of houses and pools, the cars running along the highways like busy insects. She imagined all of it gone, undone, erased back to 1968, when the city was nothing but eighty miles of hope huddling in a dust storm. She imagined Kamala on the tarmac, walking toward a life in the desert, her body pulled forward by faith and dirty wind.

ACKNOWLEDGMENTS

When it takes you ten years to write a book, you have many people to thank. My immense gratitude goes to:

My husband, Jed Rothstein, for telling me when a scene wasn't working, no matter how awkward it made dinner; my agent, Michelle Tessler, for believing in this book when it was just a handful of scenes; my best friend and partner in crime, Alison Hart, whose countless comments over the years made this smarter and sharper with every pass.

My mother, for instilling my early love of books, politics, and food; my brother, for instilling my early love of heavy metal. Also, thanks to both of you in advance for not smacking anyone who makes the regrettable mistake of thinking either of you are Kamala or Akhil. (And sorry about that.)

My family around the world, the Seattle Jacobs, the Rothsteins, the Cheriyans, the Abrahams, and the formidably charming Eliamma Thomas. My "family in this country, anyway"—the Koshy/Avasthi/Kulasinghe/Weissman/Mangalik/Kurians—most especially Anita Koshy, who provided invaluable medical expertise, and Koshy Uncle, who chased after obscure facts with the diligence of a bloodhound.

Sean Mills, who gave me a space to write and a series of great conversations when I needed them most; Jacob Chacko, who read this book and then answered more questions than any person should have to without getting a cash prize afterward.

My fantastic readers throughout the many stages of this book: Amanda McBaine, Chelsea Bacon, Joanna Yas, Alice Bradley, Karla Murthy, Sara Voorhees, Emily Voorhees, Monica Bielanko, Deborah Copaken Kogan, Noa Meyer, Garrett Carey, and Abigail Walch. Mentors Dani Shapiro, Abigail Thomas, Honor Moore, Sylvia Watanabe, Diane Vruels, and Robert Polito. David Dunbar and his City Term classes.

My editor, Kendra Harpster, for her sharp eye and enthusiasm; Susan Kamil, Karen Fink, Kaela Myers, and the entire team at Random House for their incredible efforts; Diya Kar Hazra and Helen Garnons-Williams of Bloomsbury for their thoughtfulness and input.

John D'Agata, for his essay "Collage History of Art by Henry Darger."

Everyone at Building on Bond who kept me fed and caffeinated while I wrote, especially Norman Lynn Vineyard.

Andy McDowell, Dave Thrasher, all the fine folks at Pete's Candy Store, and every single reader who ever graced our stage.

My son, for turning it up to eleven.

My father, Philip Jacob. I still see you everywhere.

AUTHOR'S NOTE

As is often true in novels, historical events in this novel have been distorted, embellished, and reimagined. While the $162 million settlement for the Puyallup Tribe of Tacoma Indians was a real event, Bobby McCloud is an invented character, and his tragedy and the resulting quotes from tribe members are wholly fictional imaginings; any other resemblance to actual events, locales, or persons, living or dead, is entirely coincidental. I do not intend to speak for the tribe or their feelings about the settlement—my interest was with the intersection of the "Indian" narratives, and what it means, as an immigrant, to make a life in a stolen country.